Book Two in the Elemental Series
By
Shauna Granger

This is a work of fiction. Names, characters, places and incidents either are the product of the author's imagination or are used fictitiously and any resemblance to actual persons, living or dead, business establishments, events or locales is entirely coincidental.

All rights reserved. No part of this publication may be reproduced, stored in a retrieval system, or transmitted, in any form or by any means, electronic, mechanical, photocopying, recording, or otherwise, without prior written permission from the author.

Published by Shauna Granger
Copyright © 2011 by Shauna Granger
Cover art designed by Stephanie Mooney - www.stephaniemooney.blogspot.com

For you,
because you deserve magic in your life.

Chapter 1

Magic is real. It is in the air you breathe, the ground you walk on; it's even in the emotions you experience day to day. We are born with an innate ability to use magic; we are just told at a very early age that there is no such thing. We unlearn how to see it, feel it, use it. I am an Earth Elemental, I am an Empath. In another time you would have called me a Witch.

Sometimes it strikes me as strange that I am still in high school. Luckily it's nearly summer break and, believe me, I need the break. Last October my two best friends and I battled a demon that had been summoned from the Underworld and saved the lives of a friend of ours and a boy that I liked. Sadly, it was his twin brother who had done the summoning. Ian was now finishing out his high school career at a boy's correctional facility and when he turns eighteen in a few months he'll be transferred to a real prison, where he'll serve his ten to fifteen year sentence. I still think the sentence was too light, but "first time offense" and "being a minor" still carries some weight in the judicial system apparently. If he had successfully killed Tracy or his brother, Jensen, he would have been facing life behind bars.

I glanced at the clock and saw that it was only minutes away from the end of the day; soon I would hear the beautiful shrilling noise of the bell that would release us for the weekend. Then it was only one last week before summer break. Now that finals were over, the last week of school almost seemed pointless. Steven, the fire elemental to my earth and one of my best friends, had volunteered us to help set up for the seniors' graduation so next week would be even shorter for us, pulling us out of classes for rehearsals and decoration detail. Although I wasn't too pleased to find out the part of decoration detail we would be helping with was the Daisy Chain. Which basically meant we would be dressing up in white dresses (for me and Jodi at least) and in two rows carry a length of green plastic swag decorated with white flowers for the graduates to walk through on their way to their seats. I think they stole the idea from a college, but no one has explained it to us yet.

"So are we all meeting up for dinner before the movie?" Jodi, the air elemental in our little trio, whispered to me under the cover of our History teacher's lecture. Finals were over but she was still sticking to her schedule.

"Yeah, Steven says he has a date too, so it'll be five of us. I've just got to go see Deb beforehand so I will meet you guys there." After everything settled down last fall, I was left with a lot more power and ability than I'd ever had in my life and was taking lessons from a friend of mine who ran the local metaphysical shop in town.

"Who's your date?" Jodi asked a little louder, leaning across me to get Steven's attention, tucking her short blonde hair behind one ear as it fell forward.

"Anthony," Steven said with a Cheshire cat smile.

"Niiice," Jodi said with her own smile, leaning away from me and settling back in her chair. Anthony was a freshman in junior college who Steven had met in an art class they had both signed up for on Tuesday and Thursday nights. Steven was a very gifted artist; I hadn't heard of one media that Steven couldn't create something amazing with. It was times like when he was creating a masterpiece that I wondered how he wasn't a water elemental, but it isn't something you choose, it chooses you. "So, how are things going with Deb?" Jodi asked, returning her attention to me. "Good, slow, but good," I said with a shrug, keeping my eyes forward just in case the teacher looked back.

"What do you mean slow?"

"Eh, it probably isn't slow, it just feels like it. I mean all that power came rushing to me last autumn and it was so easy and now we're working at a normal pace to keep it under control rather than learning how to really use it, so it feels slow." I scribbled on my paper, pretending to make a note of something the teacher said. "It probably isn't slow."

"Dude, I wouldn't care if it were slow, I'd kill to have what you have," Jodi said quickly, staring firmly ahead. I cringed at her choice of words and shook my head.

"I wouldn't say things like that so easily if I were you," I whispered as I touched her wrist with my hand and sent her a mental image of Ian's twisted, demonic smile with a sinister looking blade caught in his fist, raised back ready to strike. I felt Jodi tremble under my hand and I broke the picture off. "Like I said, I wouldn't say things like that." It was a harsh reminder, but we had all agreed to try and keep our feelings of teenage jealousy and hate under better control after what we saw Ian attempt to do.

Just then the bell rang long and loud and everyone jumped to their feet quickly, scrambling to gather their items and get out of class. I caught Jodi wiping a tear away from her cheek before she composed herself and blinked a half-hearted smile at me. I gave her a reassuring smile back and I saw some of the pain of the jealousy she tended to carry around ease away from her blue eyes. I imagine it is hard being the youngest of three girls, always feeling inadequate in their wake.

"So," I turned to Jodi and Steven who were side by side now, looking every bit the opposite of each other; Jodi was shy of five foot four, Steven was shy of six foot, she was fair and blonde and he was tan and dark. Yet, some how, they went together. "Meet you guys at six?" I asked.

"Yep," Steven said with a smile. He leaned over and kissed my cheek and took Jodi's hand and pulled her with him, leading the way out of the classroom. I went straight out to the student parking lot.

It was a beautiful June day, waves of heat shimmered above the asphalt and the sky was a perfect clear blue. Now, as a rule, I'm a winter girl; I like my crisp breezes and gray and white skies. But after last autumn, with the artic winds and freezing rain called to life from the evil Ian unleashed in our world, I have a better appreciation of sunny skies and warm air. There is one benefit that hot weather affords that I truly love; I got to wear flip-flops. They are the next best thing to being barefoot. As a girl, I love shoes – all fifty pair that are in my closet now – but as an earth elemental I hate them. They bind my feet and cut me off from my main source of power and energy.

As I came around another aisle of cars, I saw Jensen's sporty little coupe parked next to mine. I stopped and stared at it for a moment, not realizing Jensen was standing by my car. He turned at the sound of my approach. I was struck again by his dramatic features – the sharp cheek bones, the full mouth, even his eye brows looked manicured. But it would always be his eyes, the storm over an ocean blue, that would get me. I recovered quickly before he caught me staring and continued towards my car. I am a little embarrassed to say I checked my reflection in the car windows I passed as I approached. It had been so hot I had gone with basic jeans, flip flops and a tank top and tied my long auburn hair up in a high ponytail. I didn't look bad, but next to Jensen it was hard to tell. At least I had let Steven do my make up at lunch, knowing we were going out tonight and I would forget to do it later, so I felt a little more confident that my green eyes were sparkling and my lips glossy thanks to his expert hands.

"Hey," he said, trying for casual. I still liked him a lot but I still had a hard time trusting him. Our potential relationship had been strained ever since I found out he had originally been helping his brother with his black magic spells. Intellectually, I knew Jensen tried to stop Ian but emotionally it was hard to get past the betrayal I had felt.

"Hey," I replied, reaching past him to unlock my door and throw in my books, keeping my bag on my shoulder.

"Going to the store to see Deb?" he asked.

"Yep," I nudged his hip to get him to move away from my door so I could open it fully.

"Want a ride?"

"I've already got one," I said, jingling my keys at him.

"I thought it was hard to drive after a session with her."

"Sometimes it is," I agreed.

"Well I could drive you so you don't have to drive after." He was trying so hard, but half of me always felt like running away from him. When I hesitated he said, "You know, you're not giving us a fair chance. Haven't we had some good dates?" He had me there.

We had been on a handful of dates in the last few months after I got over my initial anger. It was nice going out with a guy who I could be myself around. Jodi and Steven didn't have empathetic or psychic abilities like I did so their magic didn't cramp their social life like mine did. But with Jensen, he knew about my powers and although they scared him, I didn't have to totally hide them from him. Our dates were surprisingly easy; we could talk for hours, we hardly ever argued about what movie to go see or where to eat. Twice over the last couple of months, when his house was empty, we'd slept together. It wasn't either of our first times but, I had to admit, it had been amazing. I didn't have to hold back when I was with Jensen, trying to control my magic while my emotional shields were down. I could just enjoy being with a boy who liked me and wanted to be with me. Still, I couldn't help but hate myself just a little bit; Jensen wanted a girlfriend but I did not want a boyfriend. After each night I felt as though I had taken advantage of him. Jensen cleared his throat, bringing me out of my thoughts and back to the hot parking lot.

"Yeah, we have had some good dates," I agreed with a sigh, glancing at his car. It had A/C too, a luxury my beautiful black Camaro didn't have. It was hot today. I sighed again and motioned to the car, "Yeah, alright."

"Not exactly a rousing agreement, but I'll take it," he joked, hitting the button on his key chain to unlock the doors.

Jensen opened my door for me and took my bag from my shoulder before I could fall into my seat. He shut the door behind me; cutting off the breeze from outside and making the car feel like an industrial sized oven. I heard the trunk close after Jensen tossed our things inside and he was next to me in another moment. As soon as he turned the engine on I punched the window control button, rolling my window down and not waiting for the air conditioner to catch up. I fanned myself and took deep lungfuls of air.

"Sorry, forgot the sun shade," Jensen said, messing with the A/C controls and vents.

"No worries, I just have a hard time with warm air," I said, pulling my head back into the car, not wanting to look like a dog on a summer drive. He put the car in reverse and eased out of the parking space and into the long line of cars angling for the exit. Although Jensen drove a sporty little car he never felt the need to break the speed limit just to get somewhere a few minutes faster. I liked that about him. "Now, you're sure you don't mind waiting outside while I'm in with Deb?"

"You know I don't." He had us out of the jammed parking lot much faster than I ever managed to. I had a feeling part of the reason why Jensen wanted to take me to The Oak, Ash and Thorn was so that he could pursue the book section.

In the extreme stress caused by Ian, Jensen had manifested some prophetic abilities that showed him when people he cared for were in danger. It came to him in visions similar to my power of prophetic dreams, but not nearly as strong. He had tried to keep me away from his brother because of these visions, but it hadn't worked. I knew this power scared him, but it wasn't just going to go away on his own so he had been trying to read anything he could get his hands on that would explain the ability to him so he could control it. Although part of me wondered if he was just trying to figure out how to shut it down.

His most valuable ability was his ability to shield his mind from unwanted or dangerous entities. He was so good at shielding that he could keep my own empathetic abilities away from him. In the first few weeks that we had known each other I could never feel his emotions. When I *felt* for him all I would get was a void, a sense of nothingness. Of course, he also thought I was some kind of psychic vampire that fed off of people's emotions and was only trying to protect himself. He knew better now, not that he was any more comfortable with it.

I had lost myself in my thoughts and hadn't noticed we'd made it all the way across town and were parked in front of the store until I heard Jensen shut his door and walk around to get mine. Jensen's mother had taken a lot of care to make sure her sons were gentlemen, whether it was for their girlfriends or helping a little old lady out to her car with groceries. It had surprised me at first when he always seemed to get to a door faster than me but I didn't let a little chivalry bug my sense of women's lib. He could open the doors for me if he wanted to.

I was shaking my head to clear my mind when he pulled my door open and held out his hand for mine. "You okay?" Jensen asked, leaning over to see why I had hesitated in taking his hand.

"Oh yeah, sorry, spaced out I guess," I took his hand and let him lead me out of the car and to the front door, which of course he pulled open for me. Because it was Friday afternoon and schools were out, there were already more young customers inside than there were all week long. I tried to not let their presence bother me, knowing the store needed customers to stay open, but knew that they didn't really belong here. There were the usual girls grouped together around the aromatic oils and love charms that had as much power to them as your average bottle of Chanel No. 5. I walked past them and made my way to the back. Jensen stepped away into the small, cluttered reading area.

I tapped on the door to the private room they kept in back for card and psychic readings and waited patiently until Deb unlocked the door and opened it wide enough for me to step in. I took one last glance at Jensen, appreciating the play of muscles the thin t-shirt he was wearing afforded me to see. Jensen wasn't into any sports, thank goodness, but he did still care about what he looked like, thank goodness again. His shoulders were firm and round, pulling away from his full chest without being overly muscled.

"A-hem?" Deb cleared her throat loudly just next to my ear and I jumped on the spot, gasping a little less than would have been embarrassing. "Enjoying the view?" she asked with a good-humored tease in her voice.

"As a matter of fact I was," I said and stuck my tongue out at her before slipping in behind her through the door and away from the eyes of the other teenage girls that had been just within ear-shot, who were now giggling. I sat down in the plush armchair that was off in a corner and sunk down into its cushions, my legs stretched out in front of me with my ankles crossed.

Deb was still chuckling to herself as she shut and locked the door and sat in an identical chair just a few feet away from me. Deb reached for a cup of tea she had prepared for herself before I got there, stirring it quietly, letting it cool. She didn't offer me a cup. After seven months of me declining, she just didn't bother anymore. I used to say yes to a cup, but I got tired of being desperate to run to the bathroom before we were finished.

"All right, my dear, now if I remember correctly, we left off last week discussing how to send your power out to search for people, entities, whatever it is you need to look for," Deb said over the top of her steaming mug.

"Yes," I said with a sigh, slumping a little farther down into my chair.

"What's wrong?"

"I know how to do that, Deb." I realized my voice sounded a little petulant, even to me, so I sat up a little straighter and tried to tone down my impatience.

"You don't know how to do it *well*," she started and caught the look on my face, which I'm sure must have resembled the look you make when you taste something too sour. "Oh you can send out your power easily enough and even identify something when you find it, but tell me, Shayna, can whatever it is you've looked for sense you once your power has touched it?" She looked at me, calm as a Hindu cow, already knowing the answer to her own question. I sighed and nodded in answer. "Well then, how useful can it be in a defensive situation?"

"Okay, I see your point," I conceded. I sat up, pulling my feet under me so I couldn't slouch again and turned my full attention on her. Finally, at least, we were going to learn something I didn't already think I knew.

"Good. Now the problem you have with this particular talent is how you perceive your power." She set her cup back down on the table, rested her hands on the arms of the chair and shook her long dark hair back away from her face, visibly relaxing into her environment. In that moment she looked like a wise elfin mage, her skin fair and glowing features ageless and sharp. Even the delicate tattoos peeking past her clothing spoke to something magical about her. When she opened her brown eyes they glowed like warm honey. "You see it as opening a channel and because of that it really is a channel, like a telephone line. What you need to do is send out power without making it a channel. Think of it as using a homing device or radar, you can see them, find them, but they can't trace it back to you."

"Okay…" I said, uncertainty clear in my voice. I really didn't know how radar and homing devices worked, so how exactly I was going to use that visual I had no idea. Deb seemed to sense my unease because just then she smiled, let out a deep breath, and closed her eyes. I watched her for a few moments as I felt the air in the room grow thicker with each passing second. I could taste Deb's power on my tongue like spicy cloves in winter; it flicked through the room and danced across my skin like something alive and electric. Faster than I thought was possible the air suddenly thinned and the hairs on my arm settled back into place. Deb came back to herself with a deep breath.

"Now, remember how that felt..." she trailed off, not finishing the comment, closing her eyes again, exhaling audibly. Nothing in the air changed to give any hint that she was doing anything; I felt my brow furrow as I studied her face, trying to feel anything. There was a tiny chill on the back of my neck, but just for a moment and as soon as I felt it, it was gone. Deb came back to herself, her eyes fluttering open again and looked at me, expectantly.

"What?" I asked.

"Did you feel anything that time?" She asked, reaching for her tea again to take a sip.

"Um, not like the first time. The first time I could even taste your signature, but that second time it was just a little tingling on the back of my neck. As soon as I recognized it, it was gone." I said all this, trying to think of anything else I noticed the second time, but nothing came to me.

"Wonderful," Deb was pleased and that always made me happy with myself. A teacher's pet to the very end, that was me. "Now, the fact that you could even pick up that little bit that second time tells me how powerful you really are; you shouldn't have picked up anything from me. Of course, you were probably trying to feel something and that could explain why you did." I nodded. That made sense to me; if I hadn't know she was trying to do something I wouldn't have given that tiny tingle a second thought. "Now, I want you to try."

An hour later and I wasn't much better at it than I had been when we started. I came back to myself after my fifth try totally exhausted. I slumped to the side, catching myself on the arm of my chair and tried to catch my breath. "You're getting much better, honey," Deb said, trying to reassure me. I caught a glance of my reflection in a mirror on the counter and startled myself. My fair skin looked sallow and there were dark circles under my eyes. Even the green of my eyes looked murky.

"Oh please, I can still practically hear your thoughts when I search for you. It's still a channel," I complained, my voice a little breathy with exhaustion. I was going to make a pig of myself at dinner, I just knew it.

"Well, this is your first day trying this in a new way, so really it's an entirely new skill. Don't be so hard on yourself." She leaned over and patted my knee. It was easy enough for her to say that, but I was always hard on myself. I had to be good at everything I tried, otherwise I was totally embarrassed. I know, not very enlightened of me, but I'm still a teenage girl after all. "You really are getting better, though. No, really," she insisted when she saw the look on my face. "The first two times I could taste flowers and dirt in my mouth and now I can't, so that's a real improvement."

"Yeah, I guess so," I sighed again and pushed myself back upright and settled back into the chair.

"When you're ready, we'll try again."

I groaned and let my shoulders slump again. I didn't want to take too much time though because the longer I waited to call up the power the harder it became. Just like when you're tired; as long as you keep moving you can ignore it, but once you let yourself sit down, it's all over with.

I pulled myself upright and settled my shoulders back against the chair, tilted my head up and closed my eyes. I relaxed my body into the cushions and opened my mind's eye to see my aura. It was spiking and jumping away from my body and erratic colors were racing through it with my exhaustion. I concentrated very carefully on the palm of my right hand only and watched the light of my aura swirl in the center of it, gathering upon itself until it was brighter than the rest of my body.

Carefully, I began to peel away the layers of my personal signature from it, folding them back into the rest of my aura until all that was left in my hand was the faintest whisper of energy, like spun gold waiting to be threaded out. I extended it slowly away from my hand, forming a thin line of glowing energy reaching out away from me, searching for something for it to recognize as important. I felt the automatic draw of Deb's aura just feet away from me like a magnetic pull of the tendril of energy. I let it answer that call and sent it forward, careful not give it too much of a push, afraid my signature would reattach itself to the thread.

I felt it slide against Deb's shields, dancing around it, looking for the tiniest of cracks to get through. There, just behind her right ear, it found an opening and slid in, disappearing from my view into the waves of her brunette hair. Cloves filled my mouth suddenly and

I pulled gently on the thread, bringing it back to me, careful not to let it snap back at me.

"Well now! That was wonderful!" I heard Deb praise me wholeheartedly before I opened my eyes to the light of the room. I took a deep and shuddering breath, holding it in until it nearly burned my lungs when I finally exhaled. I laughed before I knew it was coming. It was one of those shaky, brushes with death kind of laughs that comes instead of tears. Deb reached over and patted my knee again; a proud, motherly smile lit her face. "Now, have some water, it'll help with the nerves." She handed me a bottle of water that she had ready next to her teacup. I took a few small sips, concentrating on the feeling of the cool water coursing through my body and the sound of my breath in my head.

"Better," I said with a smile, my voice still a little breathy. Deb nodded, still waiting for me to recover. "Why do I feel so… so… shaken?" I asked, paying more attention to screwing the cap back on the water bottle than should have been necessary.

"Like I said, it's really a new power for you, so you don't really know how to gauge the amount of energy it needs yet," Deb said simply. "Now, if you're ready, I'd like you to try once more, but farther out, just to make sure you've got the knack of it before we leave off for the day."

"Farther out? What do you mean?"

"Jensen is just outside. I'd like you to try and reach out and find him." Deb was still holding her teacup casually in her hand as if we were at afternoon tea, smiling serenely at me.

"Jensen doesn't like me to read him without his permission," I said quietly. This was one of the issues Jensen and I argued over. It was instinctive for me to read and help those closest to me, but it unnerved him and he felt it was an invasion of privacy. Of course, that made me feel rejected. But he argued that I had an unfair advantage. He worried I would try to replace his feelings with the ones I thought he should be experiencing. That wasn't what I did at all, but he was so reluctant to let me show him I hadn't been able to convince him otherwise. It was something of a sore subject between us.

"You aren't reading him, honey, you're finding him, it's different," Deb explained.

"If he feels it, I don't think he'd agree with you." I shook my head and sighed, picking at the piping on the arm of the chair.

"Well, you know Tony well enough, find him," Deb offered quickly, knowing I didn't want therapy today for my relationship with Jensen.

"Yeah, okay," I agreed with a shrug. I closed my eyes again and found that swirling energy in my palm much quicker this time than before, as if it was waiting for me to call it back. I didn't even have to peel away my signature from it this time. Tony was one of the part-time clerks that worked the cash register. He had some intuition abilities and was very good at imbibing good vibes into power tools – crystals, pentagrams and the like – but other than that he was simply Tony. Tall, lanky with sandy blonde hair that sprung sudden and bright white highlights when summer came. He had warm, comforting brown eyes, but there was nothing else extraordinary about him. I held that image in my mind, reaching out, sending that tendril of energy through the locked door and out into the store beyond.

My power skirted around the milling bodies of the thinning after-school crowd, ignoring their signatures as flotsam in a riverbed until it hit a wall just at the counter I knew Tony was standing behind. I pressed harder and it wouldn't yield. I slid to the side looking for a crack, just like I had with Deb's shields, but failed to find one. I pulled back a little and reached forward again, this time sliding down the wall towards the floor, finally finding the tiniest of weak spots, but it wasn't a crack, not yet anyway. I pushed with my power and felt the give in the shield, but it didn't break. I hesitated, like taking a breath before you throw the punch, and I shoved my energy into the shield until I felt the crack give way and slid inside.

A man was standing in front of the counter, surrounded by the shield that stretched over him until it reached Tony and encased him, like two peas in one pod. I reached my energy out to Tony and felt the overwhelming iciness of fear and pleading that shocked me and nearly broke my concentration. I steadied myself and turned my energy back to the man in front of him and reached out for him and felt fear, anger, and impatience. I prodded at him with the energy until I felt the alien sensation of metal and death – he had a gun in his pocket. With more control than I knew I had, I drew my energy back into myself without snapping it back and risking shock.

I opened my eyes and turned to Deb. "There's a man out there! He's got Tony at gun point!" I said in a rush, already out of my seat and rushing for the door. Deb was next to me with a hand on my wrist before I even knew she was out of her chair.

"Wait just a moment," she said calmly, pulling me away from the door before I could get it open.

"What? Deb, did you hear me? Come on!" I heard my voice rising in panic, but Deb was calm and stepping to a panel that blended almost seamlessly into the wall opposite the door.

"And what do you expect to do against a gun, sweetie?" Deb opened the panel and pushed a large white button inside; it looked like a breaker panel for the electrical system in the store. Deb closed the panel and came back to me. "I've just triggered the silent alarm in case Tony didn't hit the one at the counter. Now we're going to be calm and rational and go out there, okay?" I nodded at her, my breathing still a little too rapid and shallow to let me trust my voice. Deb opened the door and stepped out like nothing was wrong and walked straight towards the counter. I wanted to reach out for her and pull her away from the armed man and hide her behind me, but I trusted Deb not to do anything stupid.

"Look man, I'm sorry, that's all I got, okay?" I heard Tony pleading with the man in a whisper. I had a moment to wonder why I could hear Tony whispering this far away before the robber realized Deb and I were approaching and turned his attention to us.

"That's close enough," he said calmly, one hand inside his jacket pocket, pointing it at Deb. A jacket in eighty degree weather, what did Tony think the guy was doing?

"That's fine, but I'm the manager, perhaps I can help you better than Tony can?" Deb's voice was level and calm, as if she was talking to an everyday customer.

"Oh, yeah, but don't try anything, no one needs to get hurt here." He waved her behind the counter and I started moving with her. "No, you stay where you are," he pointed his jacket at me and I froze where I was, still more than three feet away. I didn't understand why none of the customers seemed to care that Deb and Tony were being robbed.

"Sir, if you could just keep that pointed at me? That would be fine," Deb said with a smile. She looked down into the open cash register and then back up at the armed man. "It looks like Tony has already helped you all that we can. Was there something else?" I noticed the shopping bag on the counter and assumed the cash register was already empty.

"Yeah, you can open the safe under the counter and give me that as well." His voice was arrogant but still threaded with the desperate fear I'd felt earlier. I could smell his sweat mixing with stale cigarette smoke and old coffee.

"No, I'm afraid I can't do that," Deb said simply. "It's a key lock and only the Armored Truck men have a key to open it. See, we put the money in a slot that rotates down and drops the money inside. We can't open it."

"That's bullshit!" The man leaned over the counter, putting his face closer to Deb's but keeping his voice at a strained whisper. Again I wanted to grab Deb and pull her away from him, but I stayed still, watching.

"Sir, I'm sorry, I don't know what you want me to do about it," Deb said, and I noticed that Tony was inching farther away from her.

"Oh, you bitch!" The man yelled and I suddenly heard the distant wail of sirens growing as the police finally started to arrive. Everyone in the store turned at the sound of his yell. I felt Jensen walking towards me but I sent a wall of energy up in front of him, stopping him in his tracks to keep him back. I heard screams and shrieks of the girls closest to the man and turned to see that he had pulled his gun out of his pocket and had it in clear view of those around him. "You stupid bitch!" he yelled again and started to raise his arm up.

I screamed and time slowed to an unimaginable crawl. I could see every detail in front of me, from the slow blink of Deb's large brown eyes to the tears welling in Tony's, who was now frozen in place. The man was raising the gun up while his empty hand was reaching for the bag of money on the counter. I saw the tension in his body slowly grip him and knew I only had seconds to act. I grabbed hold of the ever-present swirling earth energy that pulsed in the middle of my body and forced all of my energy down in a violent, spinning vortex into the ground below the floor, wood, and cement foundation of the building. The Earth rocked back just as violently and I heard more screams as the familiar rumbling thunder of an earthquake flooded my ears and the glass shelves behind the man shook and tipped back until it was one falling mass of jewelry and crystals and glass.

    The earthquake knocked the man down in its ferocity, causing his arm to arc up towards the ceiling. He had already begun to squeeze the trigger when he was knocked over. The gunshot reverberated over the sounds of shattering glass and his screams of pain as he landed in the mess of shattered glass. The bullet struck home in the ceiling, missing Deb entirely, and I fell to my knees as the power slammed back into me, trying to balance it again. I was completely spent as the police came running in against the tide of girls trying to get out. Jensen was at my side, free of the shield that I could no longer hold in place and was propping me up in his arms gently.

    Distantly I could hear the raised voices of the officers intermingled with the screams of the robber under the jagged shards of glass, calling for an ambulance. His clothing was torn in some places, but his face wasn't much more than a mass of ribbons, glittering with crystals and clear glass. I felt the earth rumble again, settling back into its natural shifting rotation and releasing me. Jensen was whispering to me but I couldn't hear him over the screams of the robber and the rush of my blood in my ears. I watched his mouth make the shape of comforting words before the world became black.

Chapter 2

"That's it. Come on, honey, wake up." Deb's voice floated back to me in the abyss, a lifeline drawing me to the surface of the black water surrounding me. "Honey, if you don't wake up the EMTs are gonna want to take you to the hospital." That did it. My body at an awkward angle, my legs on a hard surface and my back and shoulders cradled against another body. I concentrated on opening my eyes, blinking against the glare of overhead lights in the store.

"There she is," a familiar male voice said very close to my ear, warm breath coming through the curtain of hair hanging on the side of my face. My vision was still blurred as if I had gone to sleep and hadn't gotten enough hours before being woken. "Shay? Can you hear me?" It took longer than it should have for me to realize it was Jensen talking to me and holding me against him. I could feel his heart beating against my back, finding an off-rhythm to the beat of my own.

"Yeah," I said in a rough whisper, thicker than my normal voice. "What happened?"

"Later, later." I felt his arms tighten around me, hugging me closer to him, and he pressed a kiss to my hair before resting his cheek there.

"Okay, she's awake, just fainted, no problem!" Deb said cheerfully as she stood up and turned to face the waiting EMTs behind her.

"We should really check and make sure there's no trauma to her head," one of the men said, starting to step around Deb. I watched as Deb reached a hand out to the man, touching his bare forearm, and felt the prickling of her magic dance on my skin and could taste the cloves in my mouth.

"I'm sure she's fine," Deb's usual lovely voice sounded even softer, melodic, almost hypnotic. The man's eyes glazed over just for a moment as Deb's Jedi mind trick convinced him I wasn't the droid he was looking for.

"Yeah, she looks fine to me," he responded in a monotone before he blinked his vision clear and took back the step he had made towards me. "Alright, little lady," I cringed, "you just be careful and if you start to get a headache or anything out of the ordinary, be sure to come down to the hospital." I gave him a smile that I knew didn't reach my eyes and tried to sit up straighter in Jensen's arms without really pulling away from him. Deb walked out with the men, careful of all of the glittering shambles of glass and crystals all over the floor.

"How did she do that?" Jensen whispered to me, and, for the first time, his voice didn't cause shivers to run down my spine.

"If you don't like my powers, you don't want to know," I said, I heard how sullen my voice sounded and pulled away from him to sit up on my own. Jensen released me a little reluctantly but helped me, putting his hands on my shoulders until I was steady. We were standing by the time Deb came back.

"You okay, Shayna?" she asked, reaching a hand out for mine. I took her hand willingly, stepping closer to her and away from Jensen. We both closed our eyes and automatically opened the channel between us, my senses overwhelmed with damp earth, moss and clovers mingling together. I felt the wooziness draining away from me and my legs becoming steadier. Deb eased away from me, drawing away the scent of cloves until I came back to myself and felt stronger than I had just moments ago.

"Better now," I said, smiling at her. "What happened?" I asked, looking between her and Jensen, the store now empty of anyone else.

"You over did it a bit and it drained you, honey," Deb said simply, walking around us and over to the storage closet where she got a broom and dustpan.

"You're not seriously going to try and clean this up yourself, are you?" Jensen said, stepping in front of her as if he meant to bar her way.

"No, no," she laughed, lighting up her entire face. "I'm just going to clear a path for us. Nancy is on her way, she'll call people to come clean it professionally." Nancy was the owner of the store and oddly was one of the least magically gifted people who knew about metaphysics that I'd ever met.

"What do you mean I over did it?" I asked, bringing their attention back to me.

"Well, do you remember last fall when you caused that boy to break his collarbone?" Deb asked, casual as could be, sweeping a narrow path in the glittering mass. I felt Jensen shift uncomfortably next to me.

"Yes," I said. My friend Tracy had been dating a physically and sexually abusive football player in the beginning of the school year. One night I had come upon them in his over-compensating pick-up truck and heard her cries of pain. Once I had gotten Tracy out of his clutches he had tried to lunge for us. In my anger and panic, I had caused a small earthquake to open a large crack at his feet in the sidewalk. Nick had twisted his ankle and fell hard on the cement, cracking his collarbone, keeping him from playing football the rest of the year and ruining any chance of a football scholarship he might've landed that season. Karma's a bitch and so am I.

"Well, it looked very similar to what you described to me from that night. He fell on top of the shelves as they shattered. He's on his way to the emergency room now." Deb finished her explanation just as she made it to the front door and set the broom aside. "When you use that much raw power, you drain yourself because you're not controlling what you're doing."

"I didn't mean to do it, but I could see that he was about to pull the trigger and I don't really know what happened then." I shook my head, bringing my hand up to my forehead, confused.

"No, he wasn't about to pull the trigger, he did pull it," Jensen said pointing up to the ceiling where I saw the dime sized hole staring back at me. I felt my stomach flip and held out a hand to Jensen to steady myself.

"Yes," Deb said, making her way back to me and pulled me into a hug. Her long, dark hair scented with vanilla and jasmine tickled my face. "Thank you, love, he would've found his mark had you not been here." I knew I was crying so I held on tighter to her until I could control myself. Deb didn't mind, she held on like a mother would.

"Oh my god!" I heard Nancy's raised and terrified voice from the front of the store. I pulled away from Deb so she could go to her and start explaining. I listened as she told Nancy the same story I assumed she told the police to explain the mess: *The man had heard the sirens of the police cruisers and instinctively turned towards the door and in his momentum he slipped on a fallen crystal no one had noticed before. He stumbled backwards and caught himself on the shelves behind him but they gave under his weight, causing him to discharge the gun and hit the ceiling.*

I watched the emotions war over Nancy's face while she listened, knowing that she was getting a very edited version of the truth, but couldn't say so without accusing Deb of lying to her, and that was something you just didn't do.

"Listen, Deb, now that Nancy's here to help, I think we should go," I said, happy to hear how steady and normal my voice sounded. I reached a hand back for Jensen and led the way to the front of the store. I stopped and hugged Deb tightly again before turning to Nancy. "Listen, Nancy, if you need any help, call me. Jodi, Steven and I'll be down in a heartbeat, okay?" I touched her forearm and leaned in and pressed my cheek to hers and kissed at the air. She mimicked me.

"Thanks, honey, and thanks for staying with Deb until I got here," Nancy said, her eyes glittering like the broken glass on the floor behind unshed tears. I did not want to be around to hear the call to the insurance company.

Twenty minutes later we got to the restaurant only ten minutes late for dinner with everyone. What I thought had taken hours had all happened in less than forty minutes. Time and magic are a strange couple that I never expect to truly understand. Jensen and I recounted the events to everyone. Poor Anthony seemed at a loss as to why it was so devastating to us that this little store had been violated. Although Jay, Jodi's boyfriend, was practically a magically null person, he knew how much we loved that store and the people inside.

Of course I had to be very careful about how we told the story, taking a cue from Deb's version for Nancy and the cops for the benefit of Jay and especially Anthony, whom we knew precious little about. I was next to Jodi and slid my hand to hers under the table to open the channel between us so I could mindspeak to her, an ability we had developed over the years of working so closely together. Unfortunately Steven was separated from Jodi by Jay and we couldn't invite him in. *I'll tell you what really happened later, when there aren't prying ears around us.*

What do you mean 'what really happened?' Jodi answered me with her yellow tinted words.

Remember Nick and his collarbone? I thought at her.

Seriously? You did that again? Her thoughts were a brighter yellow, like a noonday sun.

Worse, there was lots of glass around this time. I thought solemnly.

Oh God, Terra-

Later, I thought at her more forcefully. Jodi had used my elemental name and I knew it was just the beginning of her determined pressing for details. The three of us had private names for each other that embodied our elemental powers. I was Terra, for mother and Earth; Jodi was Fae for Air, shortened from Faeries, an element of Air; Steven was Drake for Fire, from Dragons, an element of Fire. Jodi accepted my warning and we broke the connection, bringing our hands back out on the table. I caught Steven's eye and the look on his face told me he knew he'd missed something and didn't like it. I shrugged at him, what could I do? They'd chosen the seating arrangement before I'd gotten there.

We changed the subject, to my great relief, and focused on having dinner and a good time, which of course for Jodi and me consisted of a good and thorough grilling of Anthony. If he was going to date our favorite guy, we had to approve, girl rule number seven. Anthony was a freshman in junior college, getting his General Ed classes out of the way so he could focus on his Art major once he enrolled in a university. He was currently working days as a manager at Macy's in the mall, which paid surprisingly well. So far – he had goals, wasn't a deadbeat, and answered all of our questions without complaint – we liked him. For now, anyway.

"Dude that is so cool," Steven said an hour later, huddled in the backseat of Jensen's car. There was no way I could drive after power had knocked me on my ass, so I had invited Jensen to dinner with us.

"It is not cool, Drake," Jodi admonished from the passenger seat next to me. Jensen was outside the car talking with Anthony and Jay to keep them company while we had a little family meeting inside the car so I could tell Jodi and Steven the real details about what had happened at the store.

"What's not cool about it? I mean she said the guy was already pulling the trigger! If Terra hadn't done what she did, then he would've shot Deb. Maybe she would've been okay, but maybe not. I mean that's a really close range shot, its not like he was gonna miss. You should know better than any of us, Fae." Steven looked at Jodi with a tilt of his head. Jodi's father was a Deputy Sheriff and had taught Jodi how to handle a gun, sparing no details about what a gunshot wound could do. I had spent weeks helping soothe her nerves after that little lesson.

"I agree that it is great that Terra was able to save Deb, but don't you see why she's worried?"

"No."

"Fae," I stopped Jodi from explaining with a hand on her wrist. She had opened her mouth to speak but closed it without argument. "Drake," I turned my attention to Steven. "I didn't consciously do it. That's the second time I didn't consciously decide to cause an earthquake and hurt someone. That's scary."

"But both times you did that it was to save a friend. Are you saying you don't want that power?" Steven asked me.

"No, I do, but it's not the kind of power I want to have and not have any control over. It's not like muscle memory in a fight where you've trained your body to know just what to do when a situation presents itself. It's not even instinct; it's like my emotions take over and let the power control me. That's not safe. What if the shelves hadn't landed on the floor? There were customers in the store, you know." That caused Steven to pale and stop arguing with me while he considered the alternatives. Finally, after swallowing loud enough for me to hear, he nodded.

"So, what are we gonna do about it?" Jodi asked.

"Nothing, I'm just gonna keep working with Deb to harness and control this. I just wanted you guys to know what really happened. And," I hesitated, looking down, not meeting either of their eyes.

"What?" Jodi asked, her voice almost in a whisper.

"Just, help keep an eye on me," I finished, a knot in my stomach pulled heavily on me.

"What do you mean?" Steven asked, leaning forward to rest his chin on my shoulder.

"I don't know. This time I used up so much energy, I passed out for like twenty minutes. It's just kinda scary and the fact that I'm doing these things when my emotions get the better of me... Just watch me. Maybe you can be my anchors if it happens again? Help control it?" I could hear my voice shaking as I spoke. One of my biggest fears is not being in control of myself; it was one of the main reasons I had always been straightedge.

"Yeah, sure, of course we will," Jodi said, reaching her hand out for mine, squeezing it gently. Steven snaked his arms around the back of the seat, hugging me against it. I smiled and opened the channel between the three of us and let their warmth, concern, and love fill the cold hallow that had formed somewhere inside me after leaving the store.

"Listen, if you want, we can skip the movie tonight," Steven offered with another squeeze to my shoulders.

"No, no, you guys really want to go," I said quickly, looking from one face to the other.

"Yeah, but you've had a rough night," Jodi said.

"Yeah, but if I just go home all I'll do is dwell on it. I have plenty of reasons not to get to sleep at night without adding another to the list," I said, trying to make light of it.

"Only if you're sure," Steven said, releasing me from his grip.

"Yeah, let's go before your dates wonder what we're doing in here," I said opening my door to get out. Jodi and Steven followed suit on the other side so they could join their respective dates and I could walk around to the passenger side door of Jensen's car.

"Everyone ready?" Jensen's voice carried easily, his voice was casual and bright.

"Ready Freddy!" Steven called back at him, waggling his eyebrows at me mischievously. I chuckled with a shake of my head and fell into the passenger seat. We drove across town to the movie theater in a caravan. Steven was constantly trying to get Jensen to race down the freeway with him, but thankfully Jensen wasn't interested in plowing us into the guardrail. Eventually we lost sight of both Steven and Jay's cars as they finally took up a race between each other, dashing in and out of the lanes of the freeway. I covered my eyes and said a silent prayer to any guardian angels that might be listening to keep those two idiots – and anyone else on the freeway – safe.

The movie was your classic shoot 'em up, no real plot to speak of, feel good, and over in less than two hour blockbuster. We'd let Jay pick the movie. I wasn't fond of movie theaters as a rule. Usually there were just too many bodies around me to block out all of their emotions and pulsating energies, but we'd picked a row of seats to the side. I was able to put just enough distance between the larger crowd and myself to help keep everything at bay. I was sandwiched between Jensen and Jodi and that helped, too (and the fact that I was shielding as hard as I could after my little display in the store).

It was after ten when we walked out of the theater and a cool breeze had picked up, easing the heavy night air, still warm from today's high temperatures. I stood with my chin tilted up, lifting my face to the breeze and let it swirl through my hair. Jensen came up behind me, having trailed back to throw our trash away, and slipped his hand through mine, interlacing our fingers.

"Shall we?" he asked, voice soft as if he didn't want to shatter my quiet moment with the breeze.

"Yeah, they're waiting for us," I said. I gently pulled my hand free of his and we started across the parking lot to the coffee shop. We were all going to have some coffee and listen to the live band that was playing tonight. The shop had changed hands at least three times in the last ten years but it always stayed a coffee shop, as if each owner could make it a better success than the last guy. The music grew louder as we got closer since the doors had been thrown open against the earlier heat of the day and the bodies inside. When we finally stepped inside the music died down in the last echoes of the song and we got in line to order our coffees. The others had already ordered theirs and were sitting at a table too tiny for six people, but were trying to make it work anyway.

"Okay, well it's after ten, so that makes it after hours time, people!" a twenty-something brunette said way too loudly into the microphone as the musicians climbed off the small bandstand for their break. "So now we're opening the mic up to anyone for the next hour!" She was just a little too excited for amateurs' night.

"Maybe we should put you up there so you can read some of your poetry…" Jensen teased. I paled at that but recovered quickly to punch him in the arm.

"I'd like to see you try," I said and Jensen raised his eyebrows at that with a sly smile and turned away from me towards the stage and started forward. I reached quickly and grabbed the collar of his shirt and tugged him backwards toward me. "Don't you dare!" I hissed at him but he just laughed in the way that made his blue, blue eyes dance in the light and tighten my stomach with butterflies. We got to the counter and Jensen ordered us two coffees. I didn't even worry about the caffeine anymore because how much or little I had usually had no effect on how much or little sleep I got. We weaved our way through the tables and chairs and people until we reached ours and squeezed into two chairs they'd stolen from another table for us.

"Oh no…" I heard Steven moan quietly as he covered his eyes with one hand and leaned his forehead on Anthony's shoulder.

"What?" Jay asked, setting his cup on the table.

"Jeremy," Jodi answered for him. Just the name and we all three knew exactly what that meant. Jeremy McCormack was a kid in our same year at our school; Jay and Anthony didn't recognize him because they didn't go to our high school.

Jeremy was a sad boy and took great pains to live up to that image every day. He was very pale, as if just walking out into the sun would cause him to burst into flames or melt dead away, with dark greasy hair that I swore hadn't seen the right side of a shower in weeks. He was a little too thin with a pinched look in his face and I always wondered if he'd become one of those creepy teenage anorexic boys and wore all black to match his hair. I'd never seen him with friends in or out of school. He was always angry and had many a fight with teachers just because he didn't want to talk. Hell, he probably still hadn't had his first kiss yet. And to top it all off, he wrote dark, angry poetry and had started carrying around a journal very similar to mine, which brought on a wave of jeers at my expense that maybe we should start a club together.

Of course, my journal wasn't primarily for writing poems in. It was my Grimoire, my Book of Shadows, my spell book and I had a feeling that Jeremy's didn't have too many spells or power thoughts in the pages of his. But the reason why three of us bemoaned seeing

Jeremy take the stage was because we had once heard one of Jeremy's poems recited in English class entitled "Die Sunny-faced Girl, Die. An Ode to Charlotte Bronte." Pretty profound, right?

"What's up?" Anthony asked, looking just as confused as Jay with Jodi's clipped answer.

"You'll see," I said and shook my head, watching Jeremy raise the microphone up to his height and open his journal.

"I can hear the rain, tapping on my windowpane," Jeremy's wavering voice cut through the near silence in the coffee house.

"Oh God, he's rhyming…" I whispered before I could stop myself. Steven snickered behind his coffee cup, trying very hard not to spit latte all over the table.

"And my throat clenches as the water drenches," Jeremy paused for dramatic effect, "the ground outside and my mind falters like the coming tide."

"This is it, this is how I'm going to die," Jodi said, eyes wide in horror as she stared at the black and white boy on stage. Conversations had already started to pick back up as the other patrons decided they'd heard enough, their voices rumbling through the quiet.

"When will my thoughts cease, to give me just a moment's peace?" Jeremy's voice broke, magnified by the microphone and people laughed. Jeremy flushed in embarrassment and I watched as anger ate away at his color, his eyes narrowing in his usual scowl.

"Dude, get off the stage!" someone yelled. We turned to look for the face of the familiar voice that called out over the laughter and saw Jimmy, Jeremy's older brother, who was just a week away from graduation. People clapped and echoed Jimmy's demand, starting up a chant to chase Jeremy off the stage. Jeremy began to tremble in rage, his face completely devoid of anything but pure, unadulterated hate, all of it directed at Jimmy.

"Get off the stage, queerboy!" Jimmy yelled again at the approval of the crowd. He crumpled up an empty to-go cup and threw it at Jeremy, hitting him square in the chest. Of course, being star pitcher of our baseball team guaranteed he'd hit his mark. Jimmy was everything Jeremy was not; Jimmy was muscular and tan, popular with his classic California boy good looks and dating an equally popular and beautiful girl.

Jeremy slammed his book closed and held it clutched to his chest that was heaving in his struggle to breathe normally. I half expected him to scream at Jimmy, but this wasn't the first time we'd seen the older brother pick on him in public and Jeremy never stood up for himself. A red flush was creeping back up into Jeremy's face, coloring the edges of his eyes, and I felt a trickling of energy run up my arms. I sat up straighter, watching, waiting. The breeze from outside swirled into the shop, fluttering skirts and scattering napkins. A waitress rushed over to pull the door closed, but that still didn't stop the swirling breeze. It was like a tiny whirlwind trapped inside now. I could hear the thrumming of a thousand tiny wings and turned to look for the source. I saw out of the corner of my eye that Jodi was looking around too, confusion plain on her face.

"Okay, thank you, um…." The brunette from before was back on stage and trying to step in-between Jeremy and the mic, but had forgotten his name. "Um… okay! So who's next?" she asked a little too brightly, her voice higher than it should have been. Jeremy let out the breath he'd been holding and stalked off the stage and right out the side door. When it fell closed behind him, the air settled instantly. I turned to look around to see if anyone else had noticed and saw that Jimmy was waving a little frantically at the air around his head, as if a fly were zooming around him.

Did you hear the faeries? Jodi's yellow thoughts startled me; I hadn't even felt her place a hand on my leg to open the channel between us.

What? I asked her, confused by the question.

Before Jeremy got off the stage, did you hear the faeries? she asked again and, as if summoned by her question, the memory of the thrumming of a thousand tiny wings echoed in my mind.

Chapter 3

Jodi and I excused ourselves quickly and were out the door, behind Jeremy before anyone else at the table could say anything to stop us. The cool breeze that toyed with our hair from earlier had died while we were in the coffee shop. Cars still crowded the large parking lot, groups of people were mingling in front of the movie theater, talking animatedly with each other, and the smokers from the coffee shop lounged on the outside seating, gray swirling clouds hanging over their heads.

"I don't see him," Jodi said, leaning towards me to whisper.

"Neither do I," I sighed heavily, looking back and forth from one end of the parking lot to the other. I bit my lower lip and thought of earlier that afternoon, sitting with Deb and learning how to search in a wider scope. "Okay, come on!" I urged Jodi, grabbing her wrist and pulling her with me to round the corner of the building to be out of sight.

"What're we doing?" Jodi asked when we stopped.

"I'm gonna try to find Jeremy, you're gonna keep a look out in case someone comes by while I'm doing it." Jodi just nodded, no arguments. After the constant explanations I seemed to be giving Jensen about our abilities, it was refreshing. I spread my feet hip width apart, let my arms rest at my sides with my hands open and palms turned out. I closed my eyes, grounded and centered myself, tilting my chin up to raise my face to the night sky. Instantly I felt the white tingling tendril of power curled in my palm. Now that I knew what it should feel like, it was easy to access it. I willed it to uncurl and sent it out from my body, searching around the building we were standing by.

I concentrated on the memory of the sound of the thrumming wings that I now knew were faerie wings, giving my power something to look for, like a bloodhound with a sent. It swirled around the building, to stretch out through the parking lot, reaching for the loitering people. They all had a light in them, a signature, but none were familiar, none matched the scent my power was looking for.

The twisting, drifting tendril of power caressed over faces, swirling through fingers, ever searching, but nothing called to it. My mouth watered with anticipation as I called up energy from the ground, fed it to the tendril and urged it further on, out of the parking lot to the road beyond. It grew thinner and taut, no longer drifting easily until suddenly, a block away from where we stood, I felt it pull, an urgency in the line of power flared to life that wasn't there before. The near deafening beat of a thousand wings echoed back to me along the cord of power.

Jeremy was running down the street away from the coffee shop, presumably on his way home. I drew the tendril back, carefully but faster than I normally would have, despite my fear of it lashing back into me. I needed to come out of the trance and get Jodi and me moving before we lost him again. I felt the cord grow thicker, the tautness from being stretched so far folding back on itself. Finally, after what felt like too long, it curled tiny and content in my palm, heating my arm up to my shoulder. I opened my eyes, blinking against the darkness where we stood, drawing in any light my eyes could find to focus my sight.

"Well?" Jodi asked a little frantic. I grabbed her wrist again and took off at a dead run. Jodi stumbled at first but recovered quickly and was running beside me, our feet striking against the sidewalk loudly in the deserted street, leaving the noise of people and businesses behind us. "Where are we going?" Jodi asked, panting heavily.

"I saw him running this way," I said, my words halting. "If we don't hurry, we'll lose him again and I can't risk searching for him like that again."

"Why," Jodi coughed, drawing in a ragged breath, "why are we chasing him, why is this so important?"

"Well," I said before swallowing, "he was so upset he summoned that energy without thinking about it. What if," now I coughed and breathed painfully, "what if he unleashes it?"

"It was just faeries, Shay," Jodi coughed again and I knew if we didn't catch him soon we weren't going to be able to keep up this pace. If you're not being chased for your life, it's hard to keep running past your breaking point.

"No, Jodi, it wasn't just faeries, it was hundreds of faeries, hundreds, Jodi," I panted, rounding the corner of a block instinctively. "Who can call hundreds so easily? You can't, I can't! We've only done it once and that was combining our powers and with quite a bit of effort."

"Okay, but why are we so worried about this?" Faeries are Jodi's favorite Air Elementals. She often called them to her when we were working, but we had a select few that we trusted to help us when needed. I had always had a relationship with faeries as a child. Earth being my element to call, I was often spending days in forests and fields where faeries dwelled and, once they recognized me as a kindred spirit, they took a liking to me. But faeries, like any elemental being, are unpredictable and just as individual people are smarter than a crowd of people, so goes the same with faeries, imps, gnomes, and goblins.

"Because, what could he have done or promised them to get so many of them to answer to his call?" I saw a figure of a man up ahead of us, a block and a half away, clearly running in the same direction we were, huddled upon himself. "You know how volatile faeries can be, and heaven forbid we're wrong, it could be something else, something worse, posing as faeries to gain his trust." I could feel my side splitting open like a wound, battery acid churning in my veins, my feet growing heavier.

"Okay, look, I can't take this," Jodi said and she stopped so abruptly that she nearly stumbled forward.

"What're you doing?" I forced myself to stop, shocks running up my shins, and I knew I would be paying for that mistake later.

"Jeremy!" Jodi screamed out, her voice cutting through the silence of the deserted street like a siren. I actually flinched and tried to cover my ears from the shock of it. I turned and looked down the street towards Jeremy and saw him stop so quickly that he too nearly fell. "Jeremy, wait!" Jodi called out again, waving one hand up in the air frantically. "Go!" Jodi said with a shove to my shoulder and we were running again.

Jeremy hesitated, clearly confused, and we were able to get within thirty feet of him before he could start off again. "No, no, no! Jeremy wait, we just want to talk to you for a second," I yelled after him and, with one last burst of speed, I darted forward and grabbed the sleeve of his jacket, pulling him backwards into me as I stopped.

"Get off me!" Jeremy yelled frantically, waving his arms around and batting at me like a frightened child. "Let go!" Jeremy's voice cut through me, making me cringe, and that same breeze that had swirled through the coffee shop earlier came up with such a force, swirling around the two of us, I felt caught up in a vortex. I heard the thrumming of the wings and felt them beat at my face and tangle in my hair. These were not my faeries, nor were they Jodi's. I couldn't recognize their magic. I flung a tendril of energy out to Jodi, anchoring on to her magic and opened the channel between us.

I felt the building of our air magic surrounding the vortex Jeremy and I were caught in, pushing it down and away from us, like soothing an angry cat. It began to fade and my hearing came back in stages as the wings began to dissipate and Jeremy stopped struggling against me. He turned wide and frightened eyes to me. "What're you doing?" he asked, his voice hardly more than a whisper, but as soon as the fight went out of him so did the energy of the vortex.

It fell away from us just as suddenly as it had come, leaving Jeremy and I standing free on the sidewalk in the middle of a mundane neighborhood. Jodi reached out physically for me, taking hold of my hand and pulling me back towards her, but more importantly away from Jeremy. She stood slightly behind me but to the side so the line of her body touched mine completely. I could feel the tension singing through her body like the strumming of a violin. *Something's not right. I don't trust him. If he uses those things again, I want us together. It'll make it easier to call my magic.* Jodi's yellow thoughts were as tight as the muscles in her body.

Those things? You didn't recognize them as faeries either, did you? I asked her, keeping my eyes on Jeremy.

No, I'm not sure what they were.

"How did you do that?" Jeremy's strangled whisper was hard to hear.

"We actually wanted to ask you the same thing." I said carefully, suddenly thinking of a trapped rabbit in the woods, not wanting to make any sudden movements to scare it away.

"Did what?" he asked.

"Oh, come on!" Jodi said impatiently. I reached back and took her hand in mine and gave it a squeeze.

Don't, he'll run. I thought at her. "Jeremy," I said to bring his attention back to me. "Jeremy, were you trying to do anything back there, in the coffee shop when your brother upset you?" I was trying to be careful with my choice of words; I could still feel the stinging anger and humiliation coming off of him in hot waves. I very much wanted to call up a soothing breeze through my connection with Jodi, but I was afraid Jeremy would know what we were doing.

"I was trying to read a poem," he said, sounding very much like a petulant child.

"No, I know that," I said patiently, "I mean after you stopped, when you got upset."

"I'm always upset," he said, but he'd said it so quietly I think he was talking more to himself just then. "Look, I don't know what you're talking about and I don't care, but you're not going to do that weird shit to me again." The strength came back into his voice and he nearly spit the last word at me like a curse before he turned on his heel and started to go.

"Wait, okay, um…" Jodi had started to speak, letting go of my hand and reaching towards him. I could feel the electric pulse of her energy start to bite against my skin, she was calling her magic, maybe to reach out to the first kindred spirit she'd found since I helped bring her into her magic, but I didn't trust Jeremy just yet.

"Don't," I whispered to her, grabbing her upper arm and keeping her against me. I opened my channel to her and started flooding her electric magic with my own grounding earth magic.

"What are you doing?" Jeremy asked again and when we turned to look at him he was running his hands up and down his arms like he was cold, but in the warm summer night he was already wearing a jacket. Jodi's electricity had touched him too and he was trying to chase away the goose bumps that had risen on his skin. But before either of us could say anything, Jeremy suddenly shook his head, fear and confusion plain on his face. He turned and ran. This time we didn't try to stop him.

We walked quickly back to the coffee shop, huddled close together as if it were a cold winter night. We were arm in arm, more for safety than anything else, but also for comfort. I could feel the tension in Jodi's body almost vibrating against mine. "Okay, so what the hell? We ran like a mile to catch him and then you just let him go? Nothing, no questions answered, no explanation!" Jodi said furiously.

"I know, I know, but you saw him, he was completely freaked. First his brother humiliates him for the millionth time in public, then the... well... whatever the hell those things were, come on him and we chase him down, he gets caught up in a vortex of those *things* and then we put on a magic show for him." I paused to swallow and lick my suddenly dry lips. The parking lot was only a block away now so I stopped, pulling on Jodi's arm to stop her with me. "I think if we'd've forced him to stay there and talk to us, he would've shut down and not only not told us anything, but probably would've thought we were trying to trick him or something."

"Yeah, maybe. So you don't think those were faeries?" Jodi asked, looking a little confused.

"I think they sounded like faeries, yeah, but have you ever seen faeries behave that way? It was crazy!" I shuddered at the memory of so many tiny elemental beings swirling around me.

"Well, if you endanger one of their own or invade their home, yeah, they get really, really pissed off. When faeries are mad, it's not a good thing to be around," she said with a shrug. I knew she was right, we'd seen it happen before, but they became mischievous, irksome, not some swirling vortex of anger.

"Yeah... I've just never seen anything like this before." I looked off in the distance, not really seeing the street around me.

"There is always the possibility that he's found a new or different kind of faerie, one we haven't come across out here yet," Jodi offered. I considered that. It had possibilities. I had no idea how many species of faerie existed. Maybe he had called faeries from the land of his heritage? It was worth looking into.

"Well then, I guess I know how I'm spending my weekend," I said with a sigh, having looked forward to a calm, mundane weekend. That was out the window now.

"If the store is trashed, you can't go there," Jodi said.

"Yeah, but I can still go to the regular bookstore. They'll have plenty of books on folklore and the occult section has books on faeries," I said.

"None as good as what Deb's got in the library."

"True, but it's a start."

We started walking again and let the discussion lie, not wanting to be overheard. The bright lights of the coffee shop cut through the dim light of the parking lot long before we reached it. All the boys were waiting for us outside. Jensen, Jay and Steven all looking more than a little annoyed with us. We'd have some explaining to do later when Anthony wasn't around. I knew Jodi could handle Jay on her own, so we didn't worry about concocting a story between us before we closed the distance between us and our waiting men.

"What was that about?" Jay asked belligerently as soon as we hit the sidewalk where they were waiting.

"What?" Jodi asked and I could hear the defensive tone creeping into her voice immediately.

"You guys just take off in the middle of the night, by yourselves, down the street? You don't say where you're going or if you'll be back?" Jay's voice rose a little and he was swiveling his head back and forth between the two of us. Jay and I had been best friends in elementary school until I had met Jodi, but I still thought of him as my little brother, even though at times, like this, he would behave like an older, over-protective brother.

"And what of it?" Jodi countered. I stayed quiet. I would let them have the boyfriend, girlfriend argument first, unless Jay forced me to join in.

"What if something had happened to you? We didn't know where you were going!" Now Jay wasn't even worried about the level of his voice.

"What, because we can't take care of ourselves, is that it?" Jodi asked. She had cocked one hip to the side, her hand resting on it. I felt more than saw the three other men start to edge away from Jay, as if they didn't want to be associated with his tactic.

"Dude, that is not what I said!"

"Then what did you say, Jay?"

"I just mean that you should've told me where you were going, or brought us along or something." Jay's voice was a few octaves higher pitched than normal now.

"Because we can't take care of ourselves," Jodi said matter-of-factly.

"Ugh! You are a girl!" Jay said in a frustrated growl.

"Nice of you to notice," Jodi said sarcastically.

"You two go running off in the middle of the night, you don't think some guy just might try to attack you? Are you stupid or something?" I watched as Jay's face paled as soon as the words left his mouth. I knew if it had been physically possible, he would have snatched the words out of the air and shoved them back down his throat before we could hear them.

"Excuse me?" I said, very carefully. I felt my eyes narrow and knew I had instinctively adopted the same angry girl pose that Jodi was standing in.

"You did not just call us stupid," Jodi said, her voice dropping dangerously low. I knew the three other men had finally stepped completely away, not wanting to be in the line of fire or even associated with him.

"Um… no… that's not what…" Jay stammered, putting his hands up in front of him as if to ward us off.

"Don't say that's not what you said again, Jay," I said, leaning towards him menacingly. "Look, we're not stupid, if you didn't realize that. There was something we needed to do, it's none of your damn business whether we tell you or not. You're no one's keeper, Jay. Do you understand me?"

"Yes," Jay said a little lamely.

"Next time, you may just try something like, 'Hey, you had me worried. Please don't run off like that again,'" Jodi said, condescension dripping from her words like venom.

"We're big girls who can take care of ourselves. You'll do well to remember that it's your ass we've saved more than once, Jay," I said, wanting to remind Jay that we had more than once in the last couple of years had to go get him out of parties that he didn't belong at before the cops showed up to raid them. That was the one bad thing about going to a different school; he was making different friends, friends we didn't like. But we didn't try to act like his mothers and tell him whom he could and could not hang out with; we just didn't go with him when we didn't like the company he was keeping.

"Sorry, I wasn't trying to piss you guys off."

"Well, good job," Jodi snapped at him. "You know what?" she asked, turning to look at Steven and Anthony. "I think I'd like someone else to give me a ride home. Do you gentlemen mind?"

"Yeah, sure, hon," Steven said quickly, almost tripping over the words in his haste to answer, and to get out of here if I wasn't mistaken.

"Oh, babe, come on!" Jay said, his hands reaching out again towards her, pleading with her.

"No, Jay, I don't think I need to be around you just now." Jodi shook her head stubbornly and crossed her arms over her chest before walking to stand next to Steven.

"Shay, help me out here," Jay turned his pleading eyes to me and I couldn't help but smirk at him. Cold, I know.

"Seriously? You scold us like you're our father, Jodi wants some space from you so she doesn't do or say anything one or both of you may regret in the morning, and you expect me to come to your rescue? Really, Jay, really?" I was still standing in a very defensive pose and leaning towards him, invading his personal space. He didn't argue with me, but he did turn to Jodi, who just turned from him quickly, marching off into the parking lot towards Steven's car. Jay hurried after her like a lost puppy and we all watched as they drifted out of earshot but we could still read their body language. He was still begging for forgiveness and for her to go home with him, but she was resolutely saying no.

"Okay, well, this has been fun," Steven said in an overly cheery voice. Anthony laughed uncomfortably, looking between me, Steven, and Jensen.

"Have fun with your headache," I said with a smile and walked over to give Steven a hug good-bye. *If Jodi doesn't tell you, I will tomorrow,* I thought at him before breaking the connection to say good-bye to Anthony and walk with Jensen to his car. We walked past Jodi and Jay on our way to Jensen's car. Jay was still trying his hardest to apologize but Jodi was plainly ignoring him. Most days they make a good couple, but on those days that they didn't, well, you took cover. Jay wasn't the brightest out of our group and he didn't always think about what he was going to say and Jodi was pretty high-maintenance when it came to being a girlfriend. Hell, she was a little high-maintenance when it came to just being a friend. But Jay needed a strong, opinionated girlfriend because he could be such a pushover.

Jay was always so worried about everyone else liking him that he almost always got himself into trouble when he didn't have someone around to take care of him, which is why he very quickly became like a little brother to me in elementary school. He thought the best way to keep from being beaten up by the bullies was to entertain them and do their bidding. I caught him getting ready to pull the fire alarm one day and stopped him. I convinced the other boys that a teacher was on their way down the hall and they ran off, leaving Jay behind to take any punishment for being out of class without a hall pass. There was no teacher, but from that day on Jay was my shadow.

But even though Jay needed a strong, opinionated girlfriend and they had been dating for about three years now, he still hadn't learned when to shut up and that was the cause of most of their arguments. He was that guy who answered his girlfriend honestly if she asked if a pair of pants made her look fat. Enough said.

Jensen opened my car door for me and I slid into the passenger seat and snuggled down into it, just now realizing how exhausted I really was. It had been a long, emotionally draining day and that mile run hadn't helped. Jensen got in and started up the car. The engine was amazingly quiet compared to the roaring beast that was my Chevy Camaro.

"So," Jensen said carefully as he pulled out of the parking space. "Are you gonna tell me what happened or are you gonna pick a fight with me like Jodi?" That caught my attention. I turned and looked at him, slack jawed and wide eyed.

"Excuse me?"

"You gotta admit she did kinda over react," he said with a laugh.

"No, I don't gotta do nothing. You don't know Jay like we do. For him to imply that we can't take care of ourselves, or at the very least need a big, strong man to protect us and to argue about it is stupid. Jodi and I have pulled his ass out of the fire more times than I care to count." I felt my temper like the first stirrings of water just about to boil. If he pressed this, we were going to have our own fight.

"Okay, I'm sorry, that's not what I was going for. I guess I thought your behavior was a little rude, how about that?"

"What do you mean?"

"Well, you did just take off without telling us where you were going and you were gone for like a half hour. If I did that, you'd be furious with me." He had me there and if I argued, I'd be lying and he'd know it. Damn it.

"I'll give you that much. I'm sorry for ditching you, okay?"

"Okay, but can I still know what happened?" He softened his voice to a low rumbling sound. I sighed heavily, thinking about how to explain. Jensen's reluctance to accept how much magic was a factor in my life always made talking to him about it difficult. He was fine with the concept of it, but the psychic abilities that came with it made him uncomfortable. I knew that which made us the most uncomfortable in others was what they reflected in you.

"Well, you remember when Jeremy was reading that poem?" I asked, starting out slowly.

"Yes," Jensen nodded, waiting for me to continue.

"Okay, well, when he got upset with his brother, Jodi and I could hear something in the air." I really didn't know how Jensen was going to feel about faeries, belief in magic or not. Mythical creatures were always harder for people to accept as real.

"Oh yeah, I remember the air felt thicker, heavier," Jensen said, surprising me. I turned wide eyes to him and saw that he was rubbing his arms like Jeremy had when we faced him on the sidewalk.

"Did you hear anything?" I asked.

"No, but I remember that odd feeling like something was about to happen, but then he ran off and it was like my ears popped and that feeling was gone."

I was shaking my head slowly, not really aware of the motion. "Anyway, it was a flock of faeries, a big flock of faeries. At least, we thought they were faeries." I waited for him to laugh or scoff at me, but he simply looked confused.

"Faeries, you mean like Tinkerbell?" And there was the light sarcasm so many people get when you talk about the Fae Folk.

"No, not like Tinkerbell." My voice dripped with my own sarcasm and I rolled my eyes. "Faeries, gnomes, pixies, they're all real and don't sprinkle faerie dust and grant wishes. They can be helpful, don't get me wrong, but mostly they can be mischievous and playful."

"Okay, but why did you seem so upset?" Jensen asked as he eased to a stop in the school parking lot by my car, putting the car in park.

"Well, they're helpful when they want to be, mischievous and playful when they're bored, but when you piss them off..." I shivered and closed my eyes. "When you anger them, well, things can go real bad and that many together... I've never seen that many together outside of a faerie ring."

"A faerie ring?" Jensen asked and the sarcasm had left his voice.

"Um, yeah, it's a Celtic folk tale. Have you ever seen a ring of toadstools?"

"No. I mean, I know what you're talking about, but I've never actually seen one, not a complete circle," he said, shaking his head.

"Yeah, they're not as common as they used to be. Too many people break them up before they can form the whole ring. But when they do, that's a faerie ring. It's like a doorway to the land of faerie," I explained and, right on cue, Jensen laughed, just like everyone does when I gave this explanation. "Yes, yes, laugh it up." I could hear the impatience in my voice and I was happy for it. I didn't like being laughed at. I had proven over and over to Jensen that magic was real and I knew how to use it and here he was laughing about faeries when he himself felt them in the air.

"I'm sorry, it just sounds so corny, like a fairytale." He was still chuckling and I wanted nothing more than to wipe that stupid grin off his face.

"You sat there and told me that you felt the air change when Jeremy got upset, but now you laugh when I tell you what it was. You know, I'm getting pretty sick and tired of constantly explaining myself to you." I reached for the door handle and started to get out but just as I turned my body, Jensen laid his hand carefully on my other wrist.

"Wait, I'm sorry, you're right." He sighed heavily and, when I turned to look at him, his eyes were closed and his head had dropped. I pulled the door closed again and turned towards him. "It's just after what I saw my brother do with magic last year, it's really hard for me to act like all of this is normal and… okay," he finished with a shrug. I felt a knot form in the bottom of my stomach and knew I had been equally insensitive about this whole thing.

"That's the first time you've said anything like that." My voice was quiet and embarrassed.

"I know. I'm sorry." He opened his eyes to look at me. "I'm trying, I really am." He looked so wounded it hurt my heart to see him like this. I reached a hand out and cupped his cheek, pulling him into me. His breath was hot against my face and his skin smelled of a heady, musky fragrance that I could never pinpoint all of the flavors of. I felt my mouth water and laid my lips against his, which were hot and rough against mine. I slid my hand up, slipping my fingers into the soft thickness of his hair, twining them and scratching my nails along his scalp. I felt him shiver against my mouth and he was suddenly kissing me roughly enough to pull a sound from my throat. He slid his arms around my waist, pulling me against his chest over the center console.

The emergency brake dug into my knee and I didn't care. I felt like we would crawl inside each other's mouths or tear each other apart. It was such a sudden change in behavior from just a moment ago it stole any breath I had left in me. I broke away from him with a gasp and laughed, stunned a little. I blinked my vision back to normal and he eased his arms from around my waist, letting me slide back into my seat. "Sorry," he whispered, his voice a little breathy.

"No worries," I giggled, to my mortification, but if you can't giggle on a date, then when can you?

"I guess I just needed to admit what my problem was and it was like a weight was lifted and it felt so good and then you kissed me…" I reached out and put my fingertips on his lips to stop him, still feeling the heat of my kiss lingering there.

"Don't explain, I understand. I'll try to be more patient with you, okay? Just as long as you try to be more open-minded." He smiled under my touch and kissed my fingertips before taking my hand in his.

"Sounds good."

"I take it you'll be at the bookstore tomorrow?" Jensen asked as I reached down to grab my purse before opening the door.

"Yeah, I didn't really recognize what those things were and I need to find out."

"I thought you said they were faeries?"

"Well, they probably were, but they didn't feel like anything Jodi and I have ever dealt with before, so better safe than sorry." Jensen nodded, accepting what I said without argument, which was a nice change. He walked me to the car door, kissing me one last time before I unlocked the door and slid inside. He waved at me through the window and I drove off.

Chapter 4

The house was full dark save for the hallway light my dad always left on for me. They didn't wait up for me anymore to see if I'd made it in by curfew. I had spent the first two years of having a curfew so terrified of being even a few minutes late that I had actually earned their trust that I would be in by the time I was supposed to be and if not, I'd call. I just knew it was better to abide by the rules and have my privileges rather than test the limits and push the envelope just to get grounded over an extra half hour in the middle of the night.

I was still a little weak in the knees from Jensen's voracious kiss but I pushed away from the door, making sure it was locked, and stepped into the pool of light at the entrance to the hallway. My room was at the end of the hall where the second switch for the hallway was. I had a light switch system for our house; I could get to my room and to either end of the house without ever being in the dark. I'd get to my room, open the door, and turn on the light before I turned off the hallway light at that end. I have never been afraid of the dark; just what I knew was hiding in it. I knew those things were still there in the light of day, but I also knew they were cowards and feared the light.

I had shields on my house, believe me, but my belief in monsters gave them life and access inside the house. Intellectually, I knew this. I knew all I had to do was stop giving them energy by not thinking about them and I could make them go away, but when you feel their breath in your hair, their eyes on the small of your back, and can hear the whisper of claws on the walls it's hard not to think about them. It's hard not to run down the hall for your room and want nothing more than to dive for the bed and pull the covers over your head and hide. I chose not to lose my childlike faith in the pretty mythical creatures; therefore I couldn't lose faith in the ugly, scary, and mean things out there either.

I opened my bedroom door and reached into the darkness beyond with as little of my hand as I could until I felt the slick cool touch of plastic and flipped the switch. The light flooded inside the room and my hand felt lighter. I passed the threshold into the bedroom, dropping my purse at the foot of the bed, and grabbed hold of the doorframe with my right hand and leaned out, straining against my own fingers until I could reach the hall light switch and pulled myself in like a drowning victim out of the rushing sea before the dark could cut into the pool of light from my bedroom. I stepped to the side and shut the door tight, leaning against it with a deep, shuttering breath.

"Get a grip, girl," I whispered to myself, trying to stop my hands from shaking and more than a little aware of the cold sweat that had broken out on my skin. I caught my breath and shook my head, trying to clear it. "What the hell?" I looked around my room, as if the answer to my disquieted nerves was hidden somewhere among my bookshelves and nick knacks. Sure the dark put me on edge, but this was extreme even for me. I pushed away from the door, feeling the darkness behind the wood pressing against me like a hand trying to open the door. Maybe it was my imagination, but I wanted away from it. I turned and faced it, raising my right hand up and laying the first two fingertips against it and drew banishing and protection symbols over it, whispering a prayer to my guardian angel.

Relief washed over me like a splash of cold water in the morning. A tightness in my chest that I hadn't realized was there loosened. "Damn pixies..." I muttered to myself, shaking my head again and immediately kicked off my shoes, stripped my socks, and walked to the middle of my room where an area rug covered the hardwood floor. Underneath the rug I had a pentagram of casting and protection drawn in acrylic crayon on the floor so that I could use it whenever the spirit moved me. I had originally tried chalk, but found that eventually the lines would smudge and break. With the acrylic crayon I didn't have to re-draw the circle over and over again, reciting the prayers and casting the spells it took for fear my parents might walk in on me in the middle of it. I may have inherited my powers from my mother's side of the family, but that didn't change the fact that it made her uncomfortable.

My mother had some psychic abilities; her strongest skill was in reading tarot and medicine cards. She used to read all the time, until one day she was reading a layout for a friend and saw the death of that friend's brother. Sadly, the horrible event came to pass and my mother's friend never spoke to her again. My mother had wrapped her cards up and packed them away. She couldn't throw them away, but she would never read them again just the same. So the decks sit, waiting for me to claim them when I want them. Card reading has never been my strong suit. Since that happened my mother has been increasingly uncomfortable with the supernatural so as the years went by I just stopped talking to her about it. But I have so many more powers than she ever did that I can't just tuck them neatly away and ignore them. My father on the other hand was raised in a Christian home and my mother never spoke to him about her family's abilities so I've just taken my cue from her.

    I found the center without looking. It was just part of me now, like breathing. I fell into a half-lotus, hands opens, head back, eyes closed, and found my center, grounding into the earth. I fell into the meditative trance I needed, feeling the give and take of energy from my body to the earth keeping me anchored to the here and now and stepped away from my physical body.

    I turned and looked at myself, shimmering in the golden and silver power running in and through my body from the earth beneath the floor and the circle I sat in. Last year, when I had first done this, I had discovered large, black and sliver angel wings hung from my back just like any great and terrible angel I had ever seen. One tip always seemed to be dripping blood into the ground, but where that blood came from I could never tell. I remembered that angels were once, and if allowed, still are the warriors of Heaven. But although I was in awe of the vision of the wings on my back, I still didn't understand why they were there.

    Carefully, as if I could break the edges of the circle, I walked around myself until I could see my back, but the wings obscured my view. Stepping around them was more awkward than it should have been, but I still wasn't used to moving like this. I knelt between the wings and there I saw, in the small of my back, a cloying green smear. I shook my head, the room wavering before me, and sighed. *A spell. How the hell did I not feel that? Damn pixies!*

    I reached out a hand and found the green mass sticky and warm, but I grabbed a hold of it and peeled it painfully away from my body. I could feel it tearing against my back, nearly breaking my concentration and forcing me back into my body, but I held firm, determined to win out. It came away from my physical body in a rush, almost knocking me on my back and out of the circle. I stumbled and regained my balance, gripping the green mass in my hand. I heard an angry whispering and the stomp of a foot that made me jump, looking around the room. There, just inside my bedroom door was a tiny man with a mane of hair like a bushel of broken twigs, narrow hips, and a squashed nose. He wasn't more than six inches tall and he was pointing sharp, skinny fingers at me, gnashing terribly ugly teeth and cursing in a language I didn't know.

"Hobyah!" I hissed the name of the evil little faerie at him, anger at my foolishness flooding through me. He stopped his temper tantrum and grinned up at me, flourishing his hand in the air and bowing low to the ground. That same creeping, clammy feeling began to grow at the small of my back. "Oh no, you don't, you little trickster!" I whispered angrily at him. I closed my eyes, knowing he wouldn't come near enough to touch me for fear I'd snatch him, and visualized Jensen's smiling face, letting the beauty of his endless blue eyes and sharp cheekbones fill my vision. I sighed, appreciating the view and let my mind wander to earlier with Jensen's arms wrapped around my waist and the heat of his kiss filling me. I smiled and heard one last tiny curse and then silence filled my room again. I opened my eyes and saw the Hobyah was gone. One good happy thought and he was no more. Tinker bell philosophy at its best. I shook my head and looked at the green mass still coating my hand, beginning to seep down my arm. "And now to get rid of you."

I visualized a small but powerful vortex swirling around my hand, encasing the foreign substance, and opening a channel back to the source of all things. With the force of my will, I sent it back, casting it into the source to be absorbed rather than sending it out to the world to grow into something more sinister and harmful. I closed the channel and found my way carefully back into my body, settling into it like a comfortable chair.

I came back to myself in a rush of air, rocking back a few inches and settling forward. Instinctively, I reached behind me and felt the small of my back. It still tingled from the magic, but the remnants of the spell were gone. It was tender to the touch so I would probably have a bruise or a welt by the morning.

I knew I had angered Jeremy's faeries by accidentally frightening him, but to lay a spell of fear and reluctance on me without really knowing my intentions seemed rash, even for faeries or pixies. Scare me away from Jeremy, sure, but cast against me, now that was out of character.

The next morning I was sitting in my room, hunched over my desk with the few books I owned about faeries spread out around me, a cup of coffee steaming in one hand and my cell phone in the other.

"A Hobyah? You have got to be kidding," Jodi said and I could hear surprise in her voice, giving me an image of her eyebrows arching high on her forehead.

"No, an honest to Nicnivin Hobyah," I said, shaking my head before taking a sip of my coffee.

"Nicnivin… queen of the faeries, right?" Jodi asked.

"Of the bad ones, yeah." I nodded even though she couldn't see me and set my cup down, pulling an open book closer to me.

"I thought there weren't any good or bad faeries, they just are."

"Yeah, yeah, yeah. Just like there is no good or bad magic, just the practitioner doing the work." I flipped the page to the illustration of the Hobyah the artist had rendered, a spitting image of the angry little gray man in my room. "Look, if all you do all day long is help with housework or tend the flowers in the garden, then I'd say you're a good faerie. If all you do all day long is try to scare the hell out of someone or steal things away just because they're there to grab, I'd say you're a bad faerie."

"They don't like to be categorized," Jodi said, her voice falling a little.

"I know that, babe, believe me, I know it just as well as you do, but you've never been visited by a Hobyah and now I have. Trust me, he's not a good faerie. And the fact that I was able to make him go away with a happy thought… well, you make your own conclusions." I closed the book on the picture of the Hobyah so roughly I nearly sloshed my coffee out of the cup.

"Huh, you've got a point there," Jodi conceded. "What I want to know is how he got in? I mean you've got the best shields on your house that I've ever seen."

"Yeah, but good or bad, faeries aren't really evil so they can get through the shields. He may have meant to scare me, but he didn't mean to harm me. Faerie logic at its best," I said with a sigh.

"I guess so. They may be my element but I don't think I'll ever really understand them," Jodi said and I could hear the sadness in her voice.

"Honey, that's because not all faeries are Air elementals. You can't expect to understand the Earth faeries or the Fire ones and certainly not the Water ones." I tried to sound reassuring but she was still silent on the other end of the phone. "Fae?" I asked tentatively..

"Yeah…" she paused and I waited, not wanting to press her. "Yeah, you're right, I mean its not like you understand everything either. Hell, neither does Deb! I need to stop being so hard on myself."

"Wow, that's probably the most mature thing I've ever heard you say!" I laughed.

"Bitch!" she said, but I heard her fighting the laughter in her voice.

"Love you too!" We both laughed. It was refreshing and therapeutic, something we both needed. As the laughter died away and the breathing slowed, I wiped a tear away from my eye.

"Okay, so have you figured out what those things were from last night with Jeremy yet?" Jodi asked, hiccupping her last giggle.

"No, not yet. I'm really only well-versed in Celtic Faeries and there are faeries all over the world. For all I know, he's got some Indonesian faeries helping him," I said, leaning back in my chair and away from the clutter on my desk.

"Well, his last name is McCormack. Isn't than Scottish or something?"

"Actually, I think it's Irish."

"Well, you're Irish. That shouldn't be a problem for you," Jodi said and I could see her shrugging her shoulder as if it was all so easy.

"That's only if he's attracting faeries based on his heritage. He could've just as easily found a faerie mound out here and has attracted faeries indigenous to America and there's just not as much information on those." I chewed on my lip. "You know, if we could just talk to him…"

"Is this a big deal though?" Jodi asked.

"What do you mean?"

"Well, is it such a big deal that he has faeries looking after him? Do we really need to worry about this?" I could hear rustling over the phone and knew that she'd finally crawled out of bed.

"Well, I don't know. I guess not…"

"Do we always have to come to the rescue? I mean, school's almost over for the year, we've had a really rough one, don't we deserve a break? So what if the sad little boy can talk to faeries? At least he has some friends," Jodi said and her voice was clearer now than it had been for the entire conversation.

"Well, yeah, but what if he's not just talking to them? What if they're not benevolent faeries? I mean, you saw how they caught us up in a vortex when we tried to talk to him and then that Hobyah just randomly shows up after that? I mean, that's a really odd coincidence, don't you think?" I was glad to hear my voice so calm, that Hobyah had really freaked me out.

"Okay, I'll give you that, but I just mean, do we have to make this into a big thing? Why not just keep an eye on him and if nothing out of the ordinary happens, then fine. If something does, then we can worry about it," Jodi said, sounding so damn rational.

"All right, lets say we just sit back and keep an eye on him and then something does happen, something bad, and we didn't take the time to find out what we're dealing with and don't know how to fix it," I said.

"Fine, I'll give you that. We can figure out what those things are and if they're not technically *evil*," I could hear the air quotes over the word "evil" when she said it, "then we'll leave the poor kid alone."

"Okay, I can live with that," I said.

"Good."

"But if it does turn out that he is up to something, or he's attracted the attention of the less than *good* faeries, you'll help me figure out what to do." I was careful to keep my voice level. One of my abilities as an empath was the ability to affect people with my voice, whether to soothe them of some anxiety or to help them see my way about something. I wanted Jodi to make the decision on her own, without force of will from me.

"Of course, you know that," Jodi said lightly, as if it were stupid to think otherwise. We hung up then, me back to my research, she back to bed.

I gripped the edge of my desk, staring at the open books laid out before me and sighed, not knowing where to start. I had re-read the description of the Hobyah just to be sure I was right about what kind of faerie I had seen last night, but the Hobyah didn't have wings, nor were known to be shape shifters, so it still didn't explain what it was that had followed Jeremy out of the coffee house and surrounded us on the street. I laid my head down against the cool wood surface of my desk and closed my bleary eyes, trying to clear my mind. I had actually woken Jodi up when I called her to tell her about the Hobyah so when she told Steven about the faeries from last night she could tell him about that too. It was still very early in the morning.

Dawn was still a little ways off, the sky inked in grays and the air still cool from the night, not yet hinting at the promise of another hot June day. I heard the tinkling, water-like sound of the wind chimes that hung outside my window, making me look up, more than a little confused. I had a special knack of knowing what the weather was going to be like. I could even tell you when it was going to rain days before the meteorologists could, and I hadn't anticipated any winds this weekend. I thought of it more as intuition rather than magic, so it wasn't a perfect science, but I was still surprised to hear the chimes.

I stood up and moved to the side of my desk to get at the window and slid it open to look outside. The chimes sang again, swaying and dancing, the thin copper tubes colliding gently into one another. I watched them, almost mesmerized, and had to blink and shake my head to break away from the trance I was falling into. When I opened my eyes again, I was careful not to look at the wind chimes. I looked farther into the backyard, to the tree with my tree house that my dad built for me as a child still stood. The limbs and leaves were completely still, not so much as a rustle or a stir. I looked back up at the chimes and they were still dancing in a wind of their own. I took a deep breath and closed my eyes again.

"In this early morning light, I open my eyes with second sight," I whispered the spell and felt the tingling sensation on my cheeks and opened my eyes to the laughing and upside-down brown and pink faerie, hanging amongst the copper chimes. "Good morning," I said to it with a smile, but the faerie just laughed again and sprung from the chimes, its iridescent wings pulling it into the air with the speed and skill of a hummingbird. "Wait," I said, reaching my hand out, but was stopped by the netting of the window screen.

    It drifted backwards, inching farther away from me, and lifted its slender arm towards me and motioned with tiny fingers for me to follow. I turned from the window and pulled on flip-flops over my bare feet and crept out of my bedroom as quietly as I could to keep from waking my parents. I made it to the back door and outside without incident and pulled the door closed behind me. The faerie had drifted from the air to land on the ground, sitting on a fresh toadstool, chewing absentmindedly on a stalk of grass. "Um," I started to say, but as soon as I opened my mouth to speak, it shot up into the air and hovered eyelevel with me and motioned again for me to follow.

    It soared higher into the air and over the back fence that led into an orchard behind our house. In that moment, I suddenly remembered that orchards were a favorite place in the mortal realm for faeries to dwell. It is said in folklore that orchards hold an abundance of magic; it was earth that we nurtured year round to give birth to nutrition and life, careful not to exhaust the soil. I was suddenly excited to see all the faeries that must be hiding therein.

    I ran to the fence and looked over the top of it and found the faerie waiting patiently for me just ten feet away, but it was alone. I knew it would be too easy just to look and see a crowd of faeries waiting for me. I turned to the tree that my tree house was in and climbed up the ladder on the trunk and stepped from a top rung to the top of the fence, balancing carefully. This side of the fence was the traditional backyard fence made up of thin strips of wood, but along the other side, tracing the edges of the orchard, was a chain link fence so I'd have a much easier time getting back over when I came back. I dropped to the ground and stumbled a little, kicking up a cloud of dirt around me.

    I heard the faerie laugh delightedly at my clumsiness and felt the heat of a blush creep up my face before I could help it, which of course just entertained it all the more. "Yes, it's all very amusing," I said sarcastically, only to send my faerie guide into a summersault of laughter in the air. The laughter was almost intoxicating, like a warm drink on a freezing winter's night. It was so beautiful and melodic that it made me smile in spite of my momentary embarrassment.

I started walking forward towards it and it composed itself as much as a faerie will when it's enjoying itself and started drifting through the orange trees. Foolishly, I started following it everywhere it went until I realized that it was flying in circles and backtracking only to dart forward again in and around the trees. I stopped, realizing it was playing with me and it was far too early in the morning for games.

"Okay, very funny, you got me. First the Hobyah and now you. Well done." I was embarrassed again, but it was an embarrassment borne of anger so my words were strong and clear. I turned around and started walking back towards my house but the little faerie flew in front of my face and stopped, just two inches in front of me.

"I'm sorry," he, for its voice was very masculine for its tiny body, said, resigned. "I meant no harm, it was just games." He had interlaced his tiny fingers in front of him and held his hands out towards me, pleading, his eyes gone round with worry. The light around him had dimmed with his mood so I didn't have to squint to look at him. His skin was a soft brown, like leaves turning in Autumn, his hair was a mess of auburn springs bursting from his head and his face was dominated by his large, green eyes.

"Well, I'm not in the mood for faerie games. If you have something to show me, then you better get to it, otherwise I'll treat you like that Hobyah," I said, not letting my voice soften at all.

"A Hobyah? There are no Hobyahs here." He put one hand on his narrow hip and tilted his head to the side, studying my face. "You know better than to lie to the Fae Folk."

"Yes, I do." I nodded and took a step back; he was too close to focus on and not get a headache. "But there was a Hobyah in my house last night who played his tricks on me."

"My, my, my… then milady was right to come," he pursed his full brown and pink lips together as he studied my face.

"What lady?" I asked.

"You will see if you follow me." He grinned.

"Oh no, no rhyming, it's much too early for rhymes." I shook my head.

He spun dramatically in the air, the rays of sunlight cutting through his own light before he settled at eyelevel in the air and started leading me again. Finally we were walking in straight lines, moving through the orchard with an obvious direction and the dizziness I had started to feel earlier was wearing off.

"Um," I said, clearing my throat to get the faerie's attention. He hesitated as I took a few steps closer. "Do you have a name?"

"I do," he answered simply, not giving me anything more.

"Can you tell me?"

"Tell you what?" I exhaled loudly, annoyed with myself for walking right into the word games again.

"Can you," I stopped myself, seeing the next trap I was setting for myself and tried again. "What is your name?"

"Well done, I am Tegan," he bowed to me.

"Well met, Tegan, I am Shayna." I nodded my head in a small bow.

"You know better than to lie to the faerie folk." He looked up at me; one eye brow rose in an arch and struck out a finger towards me, waving it back and forth.

"I didn't lie…" I said, confused.

"We know your name and it is not Shayna." He sounded so sure of himself and I was nothing but confused. "You are an Earth mother, and worthy of the proper name. Now tell me your proper name." I felt my jaw drop and my eyes go wide, shocked that he knew the private, magical name that I saved for just Jodi and Steven for when we invoked our magics. I blinked and closed my mouth, regaining my composure visibly.

"I am Terra," I felt the reverberating air as if I had just spoken the clear sounds of a powerful spell. The leaves of the orange trees stirred, shivering in the now heavy air. Clouds swirled overhead, racing against the blue sky, streaked in pinks, purples, and golds. I could hear the chiming of a hundred faerie laughs and goose bumps rose on my skin as magic drifted through the air, over and around me.

"Well met, Terra, Earth mother." He bowed again and suddenly I didn't know what do to with my hands. "Now, follow me, Iris, the Faerie Queen awaits you."

Chapter 5

I followed Tegan through the trees deeper into the orchard in a straight and determined line. Now that we had made the proper introductions and I had passed the test of word games, Tegan no longer flitted in and out of the trees trying to get me to chase him and wander through the maze of leaves and fallen fruit. My stomach was in knots as I kept my eyes on his tiny brown and pink body, bright white light emanating from his wings that beat so furiously it was impossible to see them clearly. I was about to meet a faerie queen, something I had never been privy to.

When Jodi and I were kids and had just met, we had a knack of finding faeries, pixies, brownies, and house hobs. At the time, we didn't know not everyone could see and hear them. We knew they were special but we didn't know we were. Not until one day in elementary school when we were sitting out in the school field among faeries and pixies and a group of kids came up behind us. They heard us talking to the invisible creatures. Then we knew we were different.

We endured months of teasing and torment from our classmates. The faeries and pixies at school came to our aide more than once, the pixies especially. The larger boys who tormented us to no end would stand up from their desks and fall face down, their shoelaces mysteriously tied together.

Luckily, because Jodi was an Air elemental she helped me see the Air faeries as easily as I could find the Earth faeries and I did the same for her. Once I knew how to see them as clearly as the birds in the trees or a house cat, I met our house hob, Boone. He lived in a cupboard under the oven that was set high in the wall.

He had a knack for baking and could always find a way to warn my mom just before something was going to burn. I often heard my mom comment, "If I had let it go just a minute more…" and I knew Boone had stuck his nose in the air. The only time that Boone didn't seem to help was when she baked cornbread. I had asked him once why and he explained that it was because my mom liked to bake her cornbread in a cast-iron skillet and iron bothered him. But in these last few years I had felt my connection to the faerie folk slipping as I delved deeper into my elemental magic. With a pang of guilt, I realized it had been almost a year since I had seen a faerie, or even thought about one.

But even when faeries were almost a part of my every day life, I had never even hoped to meet a king or queen of the faeries, and here I was being brought before one. Tegan slowed, hovering in the air just a few trees away from me and waited, turning in the air to look at me. I stopped, not sure what to do.

"She is just beyond these trees. Do not be nervous, she is not the High Queen. She is Iris of the Shattered Light and she brings hope to you." Tegan smiled reassuringly at me. I wasn't sure what the Shattered Light meant, but I didn't want to appear ignorant so I just swallowed and nodded. Stepping forward slowly, I felt like I was walking through sand.

I came forward finally. Tegan flew backwards a few more feet but pointed to his right so I wouldn't turn down another aisle of trees. I took a deep breath and held it, letting it burn my lungs, desperate to escape, before I turned. It took my eyes a moment to adjust to what I was seeing; the sky overhead was still churning in black, gray, and white, but what was before me sparkled like the face of the sun, moon, and all the stars in between. As my vision cleared, I saw one of the most beautiful women I had ever seen in my life.

She was, in fact, taller than me in human form. Her skin was palest blue, nearly purple. She had dark curly hair that tumbled past her shoulders and was tangled with the most breathtaking purple irises. The irises were the largest that I had ever seen and they sat on her head like a crown. She was nude, but I was only vaguely aware of that; her complete lack of modesty and human embarrassment made me forget that fact. Huge, feathery wings erupted from her back and spread out behind her, breaking the skyline above her. She was as majestic as any angel I had ever seen. Had Tegan not told me she was a faerie queen, I would have assumed she was some grand, medieval angel. I was used to seeing faeries with butterfly wings, moth wings, some with almost gauzy wings made of light like Tegan's, but I had never seen a faerie with angel wings.

I had to blink and force myself to look away from her to see all the tiny winged faeries dancing in the air around her and the gnomes sitting at her feet and under the orange trees, propped up on the narrow trunks. I saw toads and faeries that, at first glance, looked like owls and then realized the toads were frog faeries, hiding themselves with glamour, but because I had invoked second sight I could see them for what they were. Beautiful creatures, male and female, that could have been the queen's siblings, except for the lack of wings and the borrowed legs and feet of striped toads. These were some of my familiars and I couldn't help but smile at them.

    I exhaled finally in a rush of breath and all the faeries laughed, a sound so amazing I was brought to tears. I looked back at Iris, the queen, and felt my heart skip a beat. Not knowing what to do, I fell to my knees in front of her, bowing my head.

    "Oh no, no, no, child, none of that." Her voice was like wind chimes caught in a breeze. I felt her coming closer to me and I looked up to watch her move, suddenly realizing what Queen of the Shattered Light meant. As she moved and her wings drifted lazily behind her, the very air around her shimmered and I watched as prisms appeared around her. Her wings, when they moved, seemed to have rainbows trapped in the feathers themselves. She reached a hand out to me and I took it, slowly, realizing my own hand was shaking. She lifted me off of the ground to stand back up. "I am not the High Queen and you recognize us all for what we are. You need not bow to us."

    "Um, okay, I didn't…" I trailed off, not really knowing what to say and suddenly I was very much missing being that ten-year-old girl who knew exactly how to act and behave around so many faerie folk.

    "Calmly now," Iris said gently, pulling me a little closer to her. She kept my hand in hers and I could feel a warmth that not even blood could create coming from her. She reached with her other hand and brushed it through my auburn locks, pushing them away from my face. She gazed into my eyes and I couldn't decide if she looked at me like a lover would or a proud mother; there was simply some happy appreciation in her face when she looked at me. I tried to be uncomfortable, as is the natural reaction for a human, but under her soothing touch I just couldn't be. "I have come to warn you, child."

"Against what?" I asked and was mortified to hear my voice come out in a breathy whisper but knew there was no dignified way to clear my throat.

"You are already searching for answers, and it is well that you continue the search, but you must tread carefully." She let her hand fall free of my hair and I saw as the strands dropped away from her fingers the bright red and copper highlights gleamed as if struck by sunlight but the storm clouds still raced overhead. I shook my head to clear my mind, trying to focus on what she was saying; I didn't want to become bespelled accidentally.

"You're talking about Jeremy," I said and didn't make it a question; there was nothing else she could have been referring to. She didn't nod but kept staring at me, as if she would memorize the very pattern of the iris' of my eyes. "Does he mean me harm?"

"Perhaps, perhaps not." Faerie word games. Not one of the things I was best at; I lacked the patience required to play those games. "He does, however, mean others harm, although I doubt he means as much harm as he will cause. And because he means others harm, you will not stand idly by and allow it to happen and then he may mean you harm." She was talking about my natural instinct to rail against those who would use magic for what I, and most, would consider evil.

"Who does he mean to harm?" I asked, a cold clammy feeling in my stomach. But she just smiled at me and raised her hand once more to caress my cheek and just as my skin began to tingle under her touch, she began to fade. I didn't realize she and all her entourage were fading; my eyes were still watching the display of prisms and rainbows glittering and shimmering over her skin, in her hair and feathers. The sun broke through the clouds overhead, blinding me momentarily and finally making me blink to clear my vision. I was standing alone in the orange trees. I looked up and watched as the gray and black rolling clouds faded to white and soft blue as the sky peeked out where they began to break apart and drift over the crest of the mountains. A bright rainbow arced across the sky in deep red, soft pink, orange, yellow, green, and that ever-elusive blue that a rainbow never seems to manage.

Not one fairy stayed behind to see me home through the orchard or explain the cryptic messages Iris had given me. "Tegan?" I called out, not really expecting to get a response. I spun around on the spot, looking between the rows of trees and fallen oranges, but he was nowhere to be found. "Tegan," I called out again, "Tegan, if you answer me, I have sweet cream at my home!" I raised my voice as if I expected him to be flying out over the tops of the trees.

"Sweet cream, the earth mother says?" I heard the tinkling voice answer me, just a few feet away.

"Yes, and I'll bring you a whole bowl full…" I let my voice take on a tempting quality.

"Well now, is the only part of my bargain to simply come home with you?" I watched as Tegan slowly began to take shape again, fluttering in the air before me, a Cheshire cat smile on his pink and brown face. His wings beat slowly enough that I could finally make out a shape to them; they looked like fall leaves, tarnished orange and deep earthy brown, rough edges whistling through the air.

"Your wings…" I said, my voice gone soft as my eyes had gone wide. "You're an earth faerie, aren't you?"

"Of course. Why do you think they sent me to speak to you?" He tsked at me as if I should have picked up on these facts immediately.

"I guess it's been too long since I've spoken to the fae folk," I said, hearing my voice sound sad and guilty.

"It is never too late to right a wrong, Terra," Tegan said in a comforting voice, drifting closer to my face, his sneaky smile melting at the edges to look more consoling. "Now, about our bargain?"

"I will give you sweet cream to come home with me, and if you answer my questions," I said.

"Hmmm, but your questions could be ones I do not have the answers to, so if I cannot answer them you can refuse to uphold your end of the bargain," Tegan said, tilting his head to the side.

"I will promise that if you answer any questions that you know the answers to, and do so truthfully, I will not punish you for not answering the questions that you don't know the answers to." I was careful to word my request just right. Had I not added that he must be truthful, he could have danced around answers he may not want to give me. Tegan studied my face for a few moments before he finally nodded

"Alright Terra, we have an accord."

We made our way back through the orchard, Tegan being of little help getting me through the maze by playing in my hair, flitting in and out of the trees, and singing his tiny little lungs out. I tried very hard not to lose my patience, but it was times like these when I hated being as short at I was. Five foot four inches is not conducive to seeing over the tops of row after row of trees to figure out where my backyard fence was. I couldn't even see my tree house.

"Okay look, I'm lost, and since you were the one to lead me out here and got me all confused with your games when we first came out here, I think it would only be gentlemanly of you to show me the way back." I had balled up my fists, digging my nails into my palms to distract myself enough to keep my voice even.

"As my lady commands," Tegan said with a smile and bowed in the air in front of me. "All you had to do was ask," he added with a laugh and took off like a shot in the opposite direction I had been going. I followed him with a groan. Ten minutes later I was climbing over my fence and dropping down into my backyard.

"Thank you," I said a little less than graciously as I dusted my hands off on my pajama bottoms. I looked around and realized that dawn was just breaking over the horizon in the East, the entire adventure had lasted less than a half hour. "I will never get used to that," I whispered to myself, shaking my head and making my way to the back door. Faeries had the ability to alter time to their convenience. If they needed a little extra time, it was like they could slow the very rotation of the Earth. "Tegan?" I looked around and didn't see my little faerie guide anywhere.

"I will await you in your room," I heard his melodic voice and turned towards it; he was hovering by my window, alighting on the ledge and nodded towards me. I smiled and couldn't help myself; it had been far too long since I spoke to the fae folk. I made it to the back door and opened it slowly and as quietly as possible and stepped inside. Luckily my parents weren't up yet, which was surprising in and of itself. Both my parents tended to be early risers.

I darted into the kitchen and grabbed a shallow bowl out of the cabinet and filled it with cream that we used in coffee and hurried back to my room, careful not to spill any of the liquid. I shut my door quietly behind me and walked over to my desk where I saw Tegan, glowing by his own light in the dimness of my room, playing with my paperclips and pens. He fluttered over to my computer keyboard and started dancing over the keys, tapping to his heart's content. I heard an echo of chimes when he laughed and looked out my window to see my wind chimes caught in a light breeze.

"Here you go," I said, setting the bowl down, away from the keyboard in case, in his exuberance, he spilled any of the cream. Tegan stopped laughing abruptly and darted over to the bowl. I had a moment to realize the wind chimes outside stopped as well before he dove head first into the bowl. I laughed, sudden and loudly, startling myself before I covered my mouth with my hand and cringed, waiting to hear my parents come down the hall. After a few tense, but silent moments I moved my hand from my mouth and breathed again. Tegan dipped his face into the cream and took long, grateful gulps.

"Lovely, just lovely," Tegan breathed heavily, falling back from the bowl to land with a bump on the desktop. He reclined on his back; his stomach full and swollen and the air around him glowed in a warm amber color. "All right… all right," he said slowly, rolling himself on to his side and propping himself up on one elbow. "I will answer your questions, Terra, ask away."

"I'm not really sure where to start," I said finally, walking away from the desk and back over to my bed. I was finally aware how chilly the morning had been and wanted my covers. I crawled back under the covers and snuggled against my pillows. Tegan watched my every move.

"Well," he said, staying where he was, "start with an easy question and maybe the rest will follow."

"Okay, well, I guess I was a little surprised by the kind of wings that Iris had," I said and, as soon as I said it, I realized it wasn't a question. I suddenly felt like a contestant on Jeopardy. "So I guess my question is, why did she have angel wings?"

"Why do you assume they were angel wings?" he countered with his own question.

"I don't know…" I said, feeling my brow wrinkle as I thought about that. "I guess it's just that she looked human, like angels do, and then her wings looked a lot like the angel wings I've seen." I shrugged against my pillows.

"Did you notice all of the creatures that joined her in the orchard?" Tegan asked.

"Yes, I did," I tried to remember all of the creatures, but there had been too many to take in all of them. "Well, a lot of them at any rate."

"What did you see?" he asked.

"Um, well, I saw the frog faeries, and some that looked a lot like you and some gnomes." I stopped, realizing there were probably quite a few more that I had missed once Iris had started speaking.

"I did not mean what kinds of fae folk you saw. I meant the creatures, animals with her," Tegan said, sitting up and swinging his legs over the edge, letting his feet dangle in the air. I gave him a confused look for a moment but he didn't elaborate. I looked away from him and tried to think back to the grove and the beautiful Iris. I searched my memory and looked around her rather that at her in my mind and I saw the toads that were in fact frog faeries and the gnomes sitting in and around the trees and the winged faeries drifting in and out of the branches. Birds were in the trees; owls, blue jays, sparrows, and a few others hidden in the shadow of the leaves.

"Birds…" I whispered, opening my eyes and looking at Tegan who was nodding at me. "Her wings are like bird wings?"

"We often reflect that which we relate to," Tegan explained.

"But her name was Iris. That's a flower and she casts rainbows, that's water and light. I don't get it?"

"She also communes with the elements of air, therefore…" he left the sentence hanging for me to finish.

"Birds," I said softly.

"Did you know that people used to confuse us with your angels?" Tegan asked, reaching for a paperclip to play with. "Yes, because so many of us enjoy the company of humans and have the wings of birds and you find us beautiful your people think us angels."

"I can see that," I sat up in my bed, propping pillows up behind me to recline on.

"We don't actually need wings to fly," Tegan fluttered his wings behind him for emphasis. "We just enjoy them. We actually have the ability to fly just because we know we can."

"Another faerie riddle," I said with a sigh.

"No, that is the truth. We can fly because we know how. We do it with thought." His voice was earnest, as if he were desperate for me to believe.

"Maybe I don't get it because I don't know how to fly?" I offered and watched as his whole body relaxed. He thought about my comment and he smiled with a nod.

"Well put, Terra."

"So you just have wings because you like them?" I asked, looking past his face to the wings he was showing off.

"Yes." He smiled and twirled where he was, showing them off even more. "We really like bird wings so many use those, but others, like me who are of the earth, prefer other kinds. I have used leaves because I have always enjoyed watching them fall to earth in autumn and how they glide on the breezes. Most of my element enjoy butterfly, moth, and dragonfly wings." He folded his wings down carefully against his back, settling them into place. "Now, that is not what you really wanted to ask me. Please, ask your question."

"Okay, well then, I guess my real question is, why did Iris come to warn me?" I asked, pulling my bottom lip in to chew on.

"Because you needed to be warned about what you endeavor to do," Tegan said, his light and airy voice growing serious and more mature.

"I understand that, but why her? Why Iris the Queen of Shattered Light?" I asked, realizing my stomach had clenched tight once Tegan's voice had changed.

"One of the things that Iris can do, as you saw this morning, is to bring beauty in the face of fear and darkness," Tegan said, his voice keeping that serious tone.

"The rainbow," I said, not embarrassed to state the obvious because he nodded encouragingly at me.

"Iris reminds us that, even in the darkest times, there is hope and beauty," Tegan said softly. He rose off of my desk with the furious beat of his leaf-like wings and flew to me, alighting on the pillow by my hand. "And she can do it in a way that no lesser fae can do. You work to keep the balance and deserved the audience."

"Jeremy's gotten himself into something bad, hasn't he?" I whispered the question, afraid of the answer.

"No, he did not cause his predicament," Tegan said, cryptic again.

"What does that mean?" I asked.

"Sometimes, it is not our fault when we find ourselves at the mercy of our emotions."

"Are you being elusive on purpose?"

"I answer you in the only way I know how," Tegan said with a shrug.

"Okay, well, whether or not it's Jeremy's fault that he's where he's at now, he really is into something bad, isn't he?" I asked, trying to word it just right.

"Not yet he's not, but we do fear that will soon change."

"Why does it have to be me?" I asked the question out loud, but it was more for myself than for an answer from anyone.

"You know that answer, Terra." Tegan's voice invaded my mind and I opened my eyes to see that he hovered just above my face. Though his eyes were small, they held the depths of any ocean. "You are not alone, but sometimes the burden falls on us and we cannot wait for someone else to carry it for us."

Chapter 6

I allowed myself to go back to sleep for a few more hours since it was Saturday and dawn had just broken through the morning fog. Tegan promised to stay with me in case I had more questions on the stipulation that I had more sweet cream and perhaps some nuts or candy hidden away. When Tegan curled up on one of my pillows, I told him I was a little nervous about rolling over and crushing him, but he just laughed that melodic wind-chime laugh of his and dared me to take him in my hand and squeeze him with all my strength. It took a little convincing on his part for me to finally try it, but when I did I was shocked to feel how strong he was. The tiny, delicate bones I expected to feel under his forest-floor tinged skin felt like steel bars under my grip.

When I woke I saw that it was just before nine o'clock. I got dressed and pulled my hair up into a loose ponytail. Tegan fluttered up to my head and settled himself around the base of the ponytail, laying his wings flat and imitating a decorative hair-tie. In case, by some chance, one of my parents could see him. I was on my way to the Oak, Ash and Thorn to see how things were going and if I could do anything to help with the clean up since I felt like it was mostly my fault that they had sustained so much damage. I would have brought the store down, brick by brick, to save Deb from that bullet, though.

Tegan had spent the entire car ride perched on the driver's side view mirror because being inside the "metal cage" was intolerable to him. My good humor was washed away in a rush when I saw the inside of the store. Even from the parking lot I could see Deb and Nancy worrying over the mess inside. Apparently Nancy hadn't gotten anyone out to start the clean up yet.

I got out of the car and went inside with Tegan clinging to my hair, hiding his face from the other women. "It's going to be okay, Nancy. We really haven't lost very much inventory," I heard Deb saying, one hand patting Nancy on the shoulder.

"Yes, but the cost to clean this up… that alone…" Nancy's usually brisk voice sounded far away, like she couldn't let herself finish any thoughts.

"We will find a way. Spirit moves around us, don't forget that." Deb's voice was rich with magic. I heard the familiar tone that I often used when comforting a friend. I had always suspected Deb of being an empath as well, but she always insisted that it was just love that she used when comforting others. I saw Nancy's shoulders shake and knew she was crying.

"There, there, we are never given more than what we can handle," Deb whispered to her, petting her hair and smoothing it over her back. Deb looked up and saw me standing there, offering me a sad smile.

"What are you doing here, love?" Deb asked.

"I thought I'd see if I could help clean up. After all, I caused this mess," I said with a hand gesture to the room at large.

"None of that," Nancy said, regaining her usual voice. "This is nothing to take blame for. You saved Deb's life. I wouldn't care if you had rocked the store to it's foundation to do it," I smiled shyly, a little unnerved by her choice of words, so close to the very thoughts I had just had.

"Thank you," Deb said, looking at Nancy behind a glitter of unshed tears. "But really, hon, you don't need to help. This isn't all that safe and I'd hate for something to happen to you."

"Yes, that's a good point," Nancy said with a nod. I opened my mouth to argue, but just then Tegan chose to rise from my ponytail and hover just over my shoulder. I heard Deb gasp and watched as her eyes grew round for a moment.

"He's beautiful," Deb whispered behind her hand that she'd slapped to her mouth.

"Who is?" Nancy asked and I realized she didn't have second sight like Deb and me. Deb gave me a knowing look and I nodded. I turned my head trying to look at Tegan, but the angle was awkward. He flew forward to look me in the eye.

"We can help, you know," Tegan said, his voice high with excitement.

"Help with what?" I asked.

"What?" Nancy looked at me, confusion etched in every wrinkle on her face.

"With the mess of course," he said with a laugh, as if it was the most obvious thing in the world. "That is, if you would have our help."

"Of course we would, but it's so much…" Deb interjected, looking down at the floor again.

"Not for us," Tegan said with a shake of his head and with that he darted back towards the front door and outside.

"Who are you two talking to?" Nancy asked, her voice edging close to hysteria.

"Shay, can you help her?" Deb asked me, gesturing towards Nancy.

"Maybe," I said and stepped closer to Nancy and raised my hand towards her face. "Nancy, could you close your eyes?"

"What are you doing?" she asked, skepticism clear in her voice, leaning back from me.

"You can't see what we're talking to. If you'll let me, I'll try to fix that," I explained, my hand hovering closer to her face.

"Okay…" she said, not too confidently and righting herself, but I could feel her reluctance thick on my tongue and it irked me.

"Don't worry," I said and she closed her eyes and I laid my hand over them. Centering myself and taking a cleansing breath, I said, "In this the late morning light, I give the gift of second sight." The air between my palm and Nancy's eyes grew warm before I let my hand drop away. Nancy opened her eyes and looked around, letting her brow wrinkle in confusion.

"Um… nothing's different," she said.

"Oh yeah, well, he left. I think he's coming back though," I explained, but the look on Nancy's face clearly stated she didn't believe me. Luckily I didn't have to defend myself because just then she gasped and her eyes flew wide as she looked past me to the front door. I turned to see what had startled her and saw Tegan flying through the open door, followed by a cloud of butterflies, moths, and fall leaves. I closed my eyes and shook my head, opening my eyes again to see the faeries as they really were, just with wings of the creatures they mimicked so well. Along the floor, I watched as a small group of brownies marched in underneath the cloud of winged faeries, all of them coming right towards us. I held out a hand for

Tegan to land on, surprised again at the strength of his legs in my hand.

"If you'll allow us?" he asked with a bow of his head towards his people.

"Um, sure," I said, my voice a little breathy, not really knowing what they were doing.

"Where did they all come from?" This came from Deb, who looked like Tegan had just arrived with Christmas morning come months early.

"From your garden, of course. They are ever grateful for the honeysuckle and blackberry bush you've planted out there," Tegan said with a smile.

"Oh…" Deb said, comprehension easing the confused creases from her face.

"Garden?" I asked.

"I, uh, planted flowers in the boxes around the shopping center and there's a patch of dirt out back where I planted a few that only grow in dark and dank," Deb managed to explain. I turned and watched as the winged faeries swooped up and down from the floor, deftly picking out the crystals, jewels, and other inventory that were still intact that had been buried under the debris and lifting them to shelves.

Nancy's face remained confused and a little frightened as she watched the miracle working in front of us. I had a moment of pure anger flood through me as I watched her face and wanted to slap that look off of it. Tegan nudged one of my fingers with his foot to draw my attention towards him. I looked at him and saw in his face the unspoken understanding. Nancy wasn't reacting this way on purpose; she was just being very human, not believing what she was seeing. I guess I could understand that. Just moments ago she was crying over the thought of the cost and expense it would be for her to have this professionally done and now, thanks to the magic her store promoted, she was saved. It was a little too good to be true.

In what felt like a very short amount of time, I watched the faeries fly out with the glittering shards of glass and broken crystals. The brownies stepped forward, brown and wrinkled like creatures burst from the very earth of the garden, making my heart swell to see them. I felt power tingle and jump over the skin on my arms as they held out their hands, raising the hairs on my arms and sending chills down my back. The tiniest but most sinister looking slivers of glass fought their way free of the carpet and hung in the air. There were so many tiny pieces of glass hidden in the carpet that it looked like a shattered pane of glass hanging in the air, inches above the floor. Another pulse of magic went through the air and the glass disappeared. They turned silently and walked out of the store.

Nancy let out a sound that was half a sob and half laughter. I turned to look at her and saw Deb already going to her to hug her tightly. Nancy's shoulders shook against Deb's embrace.

"Why are you crying?" I asked, completely confused.

"I just can't believe it," Nancy said with a sniff, pulling away from Deb so she could speak and wipe her face. "I mean, do you have any idea how much that would've cost to have professionals come in? I just can't believe it…" I watched as she stared at the now clean carpet, shaking her head in complete disbelief.

"You own a store devoted to magic and the Craft and you can't believe you had faeries living in your garden that would help if you'd only ask?" I said and, try as I might to keep my voice even, a little anger peeked out. It had always bothered me that Nancy had final say in her store because she was almost a magical and psychic null. Oftentimes when she'd come into the store she'd have no idea what half the conversations taking place were about. Doesn't really give the store a lot of credit.

"Well… I mean…" she stuttered under my stare and suddenly looked decades younger than her age when she looked to Deb for rescue. Deb looked at me and we shared a moment where we knew that people like Nancy can be unreachable. When Nancy had opened the store years before I was born, she had done so because she knew there was a market in the county for it and no one else had tapped that market. I didn't blame her for her entrepreneurship, but I did blame her for not knowing more about the products she sold and promoted. It would be like someone running a comic book shop just for the money, but thought the comics themselves were pointless and lame; your customers won't appreciate that attitude. I had always promised myself that when Nancy finally decided to retire and sell the place, if Deb didn't want to buy, I would try to.

"It's fine, Nancy," I said with a wave, trying to make her stop looking at me so desperately. "At least it's done. Deb, I wouldn't let it go unanswered," I said as I started to turn for the door.

"Don't worry, hon, it won't." Deb said from behind me.

"Wait, Shayna, there's no reason to go away mad. What did I do?" Nancy called to me and I could tell by her voice that she had started towards me, but I didn't want to look at Nancy's uncomprehending face again.

"Nancy, just leave it for now," I heard Deb's soothing voice, but more than that, I felt it. I would have to question her abilities that she may have neglected to tell me about.

"Just a tip," I said from the door, looking over my shoulder, "Tegan, the winged faerie I came in with?"

"Yes," Deb said.

"He's partial to sweet cream, so I'd imagine his brethren would be too." Deb nodded at me and I hesitated. "Nancy, the spell will be broken when I leave, so don't expect to be able to see them after the door closes." With that I walked out the door, letting it fall closed behind me.

Once I was back in my car, I realized Tegan wasn't with me. I looked around frantically for a few moments before I called out his name, but there was no answer. Sadness came over me in a wave, heavier than I would have expected for so short a time, but he was the first faerie to come back to me in years. I turned the key in the ignition and, as the engine roared to life, I said a little prayer that he wasn't gone for good.

I had wanted to stay and talk with Deb about the warning I had gotten earlier that morning about the harm Jeremy was going to cause someone, somewhere, sometime, but I had upset Nancy and that was a big enough headache for her to deal with right now. Besides, I had others that I could go to for help. I drove right over to Jodi's house, knowing Steven would be there with her. Ever since the incident in the forest last fall our connection had grown exponentially. On that night we had been able to speak mind to mind without touching each other, but that had faded by morning. Fortunately, some of the side effects from all the magic we had called stayed with us. Now we could find each other no matter how far apart we were just by thinking about each other.

"You know, I love you, but seriously, do you always have to come to the rescue?" Steven asked from Jodi's bed after I had arrived and explained to them what the faerie queen had told me. "I mean, we're not the Three Musketeers!"

"Yeah, but if we can do something about it and might be the only ones who can, then why not us?" Jodi said from the floor where she was bunched up awkwardly, painting her toenails.

"Thank you!" I said a little exasperatedly, giving a dirty look to Steven. "Are you that guy that ignores the screams of a woman or a child in someone's house just because it's not someone you know?"

"Oh my god! Of course not!" Steven nearly yelled.

"Well, it's the same thing! If you know something bad is happening to someone, you don't ignore it just because it doesn't affect you directly," I snapped back at him. "It's that attitude that makes self-defense instructors tell women to yell 'fire!' instead of 'help!' now because so few people will respond to that." I tsked at him shaking my head.

"Good God, Steven, I thought better of you," Jodi said, her voice a little muffled from her position.

"Ugh! You know that's not me!" Steven said, his voice sullen and embarrassed. He sat up on the bed, grabbing a pillow and clutching it to his chest, looking for the entire world like a pouting five-year-old.

"Well then, don't ask stupid questions like that."

"Dude, what does it say about you that when Shay tells you a freaking faerie queen came to her with a message the first thing you ask about is your precious butt," Jodi said, straightening out her leg and wiggling her toes. "I mean, come on! Can we focus for one minute?"

"Oh, yeah…" Steven said, looking embarrassed as a flush crept over his cheeks. "Sorry, it's just something incredible like that happens to Shay and it almost sounds… I don't know, normal I guess."

"A faerie queen comes to see me with all her entourage in an orchard and you think that's normal?" I asked through a laugh.

"I know what you mean," Jodi said with a knowing look thrown my way.

"This is not normal!" I said, my voice rising a little before I could catch myself. "I mean… it's amazing."

"Well, yeah we know that, but we're not surprised it happened to you, that's all," Steven said. "If it had been me, that would've been surprising. Even Jodi, although she'd get a visit like that before I would, but we'd still be a little surprised. But not for you, babe." He finished with his own shrug.

"Look, don't get us wrong, we're in awe of it, but we're almost always in awe of you," Jodi said, her voice softening as if worried I'd start yelling again.

"But you two have abilities, amazing, wondrous abilities. You act like you're nothing compared to me," I heard my voice take on a pleading tone.

"Yeah, but you're our teacher, you know that. You should be better than us," Jodi said.

"I'm not *better* than you two," I said, shaking my head in disagreement.

"Ha!" Steven said so loudly it made me jump. "Of course you are, but that's okay. If you weren't better than us, then we'd've never learned what we have so far."

"Well said," Jodi nodded at him.

"No, no," Steven said to me, raising his hand up to stop me from arguing. "Just stop arguing. If you want to be modest, fine, but Jodi and I both know that you live and breathe magic like a fish in water, while Jodi and I are always learning how to swim. Every day we get better, but we'd never challenge you in a race to the end of the pool because you'd beat us every time." I couldn't argue with him on that. Although my magic laid primarily in the Earth element, all four elements came to me much easier than to most. Oftentimes when Steven or Jodi wanted to learn a new skill in their elements, I would have to learn it first in order to teach it to them.

"Fine," I said, rubbing my eyes with my fingertips, pressing against them until lights burst behind my closed eyelids. "Fine, no more arguing, but we can all agree that this is important, more so than we can know just yet if a queen is going to deliver the message rather than just any faerie."

"Very true," Jodi said, waving a hand in front of her toes, urging the paint to dry. "What do you want to do about it? Whatever 'it' is."

"Well, I guess we need to keep an eye on Jeremy. What else can we do?" I said, trying to find a place to sit down. Jodi's room was always a mess; clothing, shoes, books, make-up and even toys always cluttered her floor, bed, and tabletops. "Dude, how you do this?"

"Do what?" Jodi asked.

"Live like this!" I said, waving both hands. "I can't even sit down!"

"Oh poo," Jodi said, sticking her tongue out at me. Jodi was as much of a control-freak as I was; it was one of the reasons we got along so well, as well as the main reason we argued as much as we did. But it wasn't until you got into her room that you remembered she really was the embodiment of the air element. Air elementals could be flighty and erratic, even more so than fire, if left to their own devices.

"Here, come over here," Steven said pushing aside a pile of clothes and shoes from the bed until we could see the covers. I crawled up on the bed and leaned my back against the wall it was pushed up against.

"Anyway, I guess we just need to keep an eye on him," I said again.

"Don't you think we need to do more than that? I mean, we don't see him enough to know what he's doing all the time," Steven asked.

"You mean like follow the guy around all day and night?" Jodi asked skeptically.

"Well... I mean, yeah," Steven said sounding defensive.

"No, he might be right," I said, forestalling Jodi's retort. "I mean, if you're going to do something to cause someone harm, you're probably not going to be obvious about it."

"Yeah, true. Not really how I want to spend my last week at school," Jodi said and we all agreed with that sentiment. "Hey, do you think he's responsible for that Hobyah?"

"Yeah, I do," I said, nodding.

"Well, if you really think so, why don't we confront him with that?" Jodi asked.

"Oooh, that's not a bad idea," Steven said, sitting up a little straighter.

"Well, you saw how he reacted when we tried to talk to him about the faeries that followed him out of the coffee shop," I said.

"Yeah, but he was pretty upset then. Maybe if we find him when he's not freaking out over his brother humiliating him in front of a bunch of people he'll be more open to discussion," Jodi said.

"Oh yeah, I can see him reacting real calm to that. 'Listen, Jeremy, set any angry little faeries on anyone lately?'" Steven said sarcastically, but I still laughed. "Yeah, that'll be great!"

"I only meant…" Jodi started to say, but I stopped her.

"I know what you meant and you might have something there," I said with a shrug. "I'd say it couldn't hurt to ask, but after how strong that little Hobyah was, it just *may* hurt to ask."

"Good point," Steven said darkly.

"Well, we can just go spy on him," Jodi offered.

"Whatever we do, I think we should get going," I said, sliding off the bed, setting my feet carefully on the floor, trying not to crush anything hidden in the mess. "Come on," I said, picking my way to the door. Jodi slid her feet into a pair of flip-flops, careful of the still soft polish on her toes, and followed Steven and me out the door.

We had seen Jeremy haunting our favorite bookstore often enough to use that as our starting point to find Jeremy. If he wasn't there, I really had no other idea where to find him. We knew where he lived because everyone knew his brother. He was popular enough that every party he threw town half the school turned up for them. But we had no reason to go knocking on his door unless we meant to confront him openly and, as much as I knew he was responsible for that Hobyah in my house, I really didn't want to ask him directly.

As I got in the car and pulled away from the curb, a sudden overwhelming urgency took over. I didn't know why, but it was suddenly very important to find Jeremy and soon. I peeled down the street in a scream of rubber on asphalt and whispered a prayer that we would find him in time. But in time for what, I had no idea.

Chapter 7

We pulled into the parking lot in front of the bookstore in a squeal of tires. I had explained to Steven and Jodi that something was urging me to get here as fast as I could, but I had no idea why. Thankfully, after years of my intuition proving correct, they didn't question me further. I was tempted to park against the curb in front of the store despite the red paint denoting it a fire lane, but I had that tiny voice in my head reminding me I wasn't infallible and that maybe, just maybe, there wouldn't be anything wrong when I got inside. So, I pulled into the first parking space I could find. We climbed out of the car and it took all of my self-control not to take off at a dead run for the door.

I walked stiff legged and straight-backed down the aisle clutching my purse in my hands until the blood vessels ran red against my pale skin. "Dude, are you okay?" Jodi asked almost in a whisper as she walked next to me.

"I don't know, but I don't want to go running in there like a maniac and find out nothing happened, you know?" I was surprised to hear how calm and level my voice was because my stomach was a riot of butterflies.

"What do you think's going on in there?" Steven asked from my other side.

"No clue, I just know we needed to get here fast." We were finally at the front doors; Steven reached over my head and pulled it open, holding it for Jodi and me. We stepped inside the first set of doors and I pulled open the interior door before Steven could reach for it and rushed inside, looking around.

"Everything seems fine…" Jodi said, looking in all directions with me.

"Yeah, it does…" I sounded almost disappointed. "Guess it's a good thing I didn't come running in here like an idiot." I shrugged, trying to make light of the situation.

"Right, so, coffee?" Steven asked, visibly relaxing. He didn't wait for us to answer, just started off towards the coffee counter by the magazine section. Jodi stood with me, waiting to see what I would do.

"I just don't get it. I mean… I really thought something was going to happen," I said, shaking my head.

"Don't worry about it. I mean, it's good that nothing's wrong, right?" Jodi asked, watching my face carefully.

"Well yeah, obviously," I said but even to me I didn't sound convincing. I let Jodi take me by the arm and lead me to a table off in a corner, grabbing a third chair on her way for Steven. She pushed me into one of the chairs and set her purse down in another.

"Ice tea with lemonade?" Jodi asked me and I nodded. "Passion or Black?"

"Passion," I said and she turned and walked to join Steven in line to order our drinks before Steven could pick for us. Knowing him, he'd come back with some fat-free, sugar-free, taste-free concoction no one in their right mind would spend money on. I settled back into the chair and dropped my purse to the floor, scooting it under the table with my foot. The bookstore was one of my favorite places to go. I knew the inventory of the three sections that I usually haunted better than any of the employees. It was two stories tall with the second floor open to the first all the way around like a large balcony. Up on that second floor was the Fantasy and Fiction section that I practically lived in when I was here. Just off to the left of that was the Occult section that I had searched through many times when I had exhausted Deb and Nancy's books.

From where I was sitting I could see up through to the second floor and to the Fantasy section, though the Occult section was obstructed by the turn of the railing. I remembered that I was all out of new books and, now that school was nearly out for the year, our English teacher hadn't bothered with any more assigned reading. I decided before we left I'd go up and pick out a new book for the start of summer. Just that thought made me feel a little better. It was times like these that I realized just how much of a nerd I was at seventeen, but at the same time, I just didn't care.

"Dude you are terrible!" Jodi was saying as she came back to our table, two large plastic cups in her hands, handing one to me.

"What? He was cute!" Steven replied defensively.

"What about Anthony?" she asked.

"What about Anthony?" Steven asked back, shrugging his shoulders.

"What! He's adorable and we like him!" Jodi pointed between the two of us as she took the seat next to me, leaving the one across from me for Steven.

"I like him too. What does it matter if you two like him?"

"What! You know we have to approve anyone you date!" Jodi said.

"Since when?"

"Since you had three boyfriends in a row last year that neither one of us liked even a little bit and each of them screwed you over royally," Jodi said, smacking the table for emphasis.

"Oh come on, not all of them were bad. Ryan was nice," Steven said, but the volume of his voice began to drop.

"Ryan was nice? Ryan was nice!?" Jodi's voice rose higher in pitch. "Are you getting this?" she asked me.

"I'm hearing it, but not getting it. Ryan was not nice, Steven," I said, looking at him as if he'd sprouted a second head.

"What was wrong with Ryan?" he asked.

"Well, he stole all your shoes and pawned them to buy body jewelry for one thing," I said.

"Oh big deal…"

"And then he stole my horn and tried to pawn that," Jodi said. Jodi was in our high school marching band.

"And the only thing that stopped the pawn shop guy from taking it was seeing Jodi's name on the case and recognizing it because of her father," I said. Her father was a County Sheriff and well-known in town.

"So he didn't pawn it then. See, not all bad," Steven said.

"Okay, how about the time that you drove him to San Diego for that concert and he left you for dead after slipping you that mickey and taking off with your mother's car?" Jodi said frantically.

"You woke up a mile on the wrong side of the border in your underwear! We nearly didn't get you back from the *Federales*," I said, my voice rising to match Jodi's.

"Okay, okay, okay! Shut up!" Steven said, putting his hands in surrender.

"Okay, so what's this about? Steven flirting again? What's the big deal?" I asked looking back and forth between them.

"Yes, there was some blonde haired cliché in line and he was flirting like a little girl!" Jodi said.

"So what?" he asked defensively.

"An-thon-y!" Jodi said, over-pronouncing every syllable.

"It's not like we're going steady," he said.

"Going steady?" I said with a smirk. "You mean he hasn't given you his pin yet?"

"Shut up," Steven said, sticking his tongue out at me. "I don't see you settling down with Jensen. Why should I be any different?"

"Okay, you two battle it out, I'm going to go get a book," I said, laughing as I pushed away from the small table to stand up.

"Ooh, me too!" Jodi said, her voice changing completely. We left Steven to hold the table and made our way past the other tiny cluttered tables until we broke free of the coffee shop area and got to the escalators.

"Ugh! Doesn't waste any time, does he?" I turned to look where Jodi was staring as we glided up the stairs and saw the blonde haired cliché she had spoken of already sitting in Jodi's seat, smiling broadly at Steven.

"Oh well, what are you gonna do?" I said, stepping off of the moving stairs as we reached the top, Jodi right behind me.

"Nothing, I guess…" She followed me around the border of the second floor to the Fiction section. I turned into the first row of the fantasy books and started browsing slowly, Jodi started on the opposite side of the same row. I had started to reach for a book when I heard a voice that froze me.

"It's not a work of fiction! It shouldn't be in this section!" Jeremy's cold, angry voice whined over the rows of books and struck me like a blow in the center of my back. I spun around and grabbed at Jodi, who had also clearly heard him and stopped dead in her tracks as well.

"I'm sorry, I don't make those decisions. You wanted to know where it was, this is where it is…" I heard the familiar voice of a sales clerk that had helped me many times in the past, though now his voice sounded clipped and a little confused.

"That's crap! You people always do this! Don't look at me like that!" Jeremy was yelling now and I grabbed Jodi's arm and started pulling her with me to hurry to find him.

"There's no reason to raise your voice. If you can't control yourself, I'll have to ask you to leave," the clerk said.

"I'd like to see you try!" Jeremy's voice cracked as he nearly screamed at the poor man. I rounded the end of the aisle and nearly ran right into Jeremy's back. I could see the clerk's confused face just past his shoulder. His eyes darted to me for a second before going back to Jeremy, as if afraid to look away from him for too long.

"You don't have to leave, but you do have to lower your voice." He had put his hands up in front of him, like a man trying to talk another off of the ledge of a building.

"I don't have to do anything! You people think you know everything! You mock people like me, but you don't know!" Jeremy continued to scream and other customers had come closer to get a look at the scene he was causing, milling around the edges of both ends of the aisle.

The Manager is coming, Jodi thought at me, reminding me I still had a hold of her arm; if I had let go she would have had to touch me to open the channel between us to speak mind to mind.

*Not just the Manager I hope...*I thought back at her.

No, the escalator is full of all of the male employees.

I don't know if that's good or bad... I stepped forward, reaching out a hand to Jeremy. I could feel the rage rolling off of him in waves, nearly searing my skin. His raw emotions were churning my stomach and undoing my shields that I held in place naturally when out in public. It spoke volumes of how out of control he was. I thought about just pushing his emotions back and under a wave of calm and understanding, but his were so strong I knew I needed to be touching him for it to have a chance of working. He was like a feral cat that had never known the comfort of being a human's pet.

Carefully... Jodi's thoughts, always yellow to me, were bright and shining like a noonday sun in her anxiety. Suddenly I remembered an exercise Deb had taught me years ago when honing my empathy. I leaned forward a few inches until I could feel the edges of Jeremy's aura on the skin of my face; it was thick and sluggish, unhealthy, like cancer in the lungs. My breath caught in my throat, but I pushed past it and the heat of Jeremy's anger, and thought of cool, still waters, holding the image in my mind as I drew in a deep breath and blew it softly against his bare neck. I saw his skin tinge blue under the cool air and his whole body shivered and, just for a heartbeat. The rage pulled back, creating an opening for me.

I reached out quickly and grabbed his shoulder and spun him around to face me. His face was slack with ease, but in a flash confusion chased across his face, followed quickly by anger and recognition when he focused on my face. I gripped Jodi's wrist tighter with my other hand and she stepped forward to slide her free hand up to the small of my back, sliding her fingers under the edge of my shirt until she met with bare skin. She was acting as my anchor. If things got out of control, she could help pull me out of the magic and back to reality. I opened a channel between Jeremy and myself and pushed at his rage with a gentle, but firm hand of compassion and calm understanding. I watched him waver under my power, emotions running over his face in a confused jumble.

*Wings… oh God, wings…*Jodi's voice sounded farther away, but I knew that's because I was focused on Jeremy's energy and my mind was farther away. I heard them then, like a thousand birds coming in every direction. A wind came up and swirled around the three of us, teasing our hair up and away from our faces, I heard a few gasps in the crowd and knew that there were a few psychically sensitive people around us sensing the faeries he was summoning with his rage.

"You, it's always you…" Jeremy hissed at me between his clenched teeth. "You need to learn to mind your own damn business," he said, his eyes narrowing into a glare. I felt Jodi's fingers dig into my skin painfully. I held onto that pain, knowing it was real.

"Jeremy, we just want to talk to you, help you. That's all," I spoke in soothing tones, letting my voice carry the power of my abilities, trying to get past the wall of his rage. I felt his resolve waver again and saw fear in his eyes, but he wasn't afraid of me. It was the fear of being lied to again, rejected again. "Jeremy," I whispered so only he and Jodi could hear me. "We're not like everyone else, we don't lie…" His eyes started to shimmer in the over-head lights. "Jeremy," I whispered again and gave another rush of emotions, compassion and hope. I felt the press of bodies around us now. The men from the escalators were here now, but I was afraid of losing him again and reached out to them emotionally, urging them to wait and see if I could talk Jeremy down. They waited.

"Lies…" Jeremy whispered, shaking his head. I started to open my mouth to argue and I felt wings battering at my face suddenly, causing me to blink and break my eye contact with Jeremy. "Lies…" he said again, his voice stronger, and I felt him begin to turn his body out of my hand. I tried to grip tighter.

"No, Jeremy, we don't lie…" I said, wanting desperately to free one of my hands to bat at the invisible things swirling around me. Then it hit me. They were invisible to me. I had invoked second sight this morning, but I still couldn't see them. In the time it took to realize that, I had distracted myself and broken the connection I had started to form with Jeremy.

"Lies!" he screamed suddenly and rushed me, grabbing my shoulders and running full out into me, forcing me to stumble backwards in his momentum. Jodi screamed as he knocked her over to the ground, forcing her to let go of me. I heard the people around us yelling and screaming and felt hands reaching out to help me, but the swirling mass of faeries made them just miss me and helped Jeremy run faster. I knew the railing could only be a few more feet behind us so I tried to turn out of his grip, but whatever his little helpers were, they were strong. I felt my body lift subtly off of the floor so it felt like Jeremy was carrying me through the air. I struggled in his hands and watched the rage contort his face into some unrecognizable mask.

"No!" I heard Jodi scream loud, wrenching through the air and saw a flash of bright white light strike just next to Jeremy. It was so sudden that it stopped him momentarily, but not long enough for me to take advantage of the situation. The sound of wings became deafening and I watched as Jeremy nodded, answering something only he could hear. His body tensed and, in the next second, he shoved me with all his strength, letting me go.

Pain shot through my body as I collided with the wood railing and it splintered under the force of the impact. I flipped over it, twisting backwards and sideways. I could hear screaming and saw a mass of bodies rush towards me and the world turned upside down as I flipped over. I could see the people gathered on the first floor and the gleam of the marble of the floor like some menacing promise of pain and darkness. My head snapped backwards when a hand caught my ankle, suddenly stopping my fall. Instinctively I tightened my stomach muscles, pulling myself up just enough to keep from slapping my head against the edge of the balcony. The crowd let out a collective breath.

"Stop him!" someone in the crowd screamed. I turned to look and watched as the stranger pulled me carefully back over the railing as Jeremy darted out the doors on the second floor that led to the large balcony outside. People seemed frozen, like a movie on pause, and when they finally got their wits about them and started rushing for the doors, Jeremy jumped from the balcony to the parking lot below. Another woman screamed before she fainted and the men that had rushed upstairs to help turned as one and ran for the escalators to get outside.

"He'll break his legs!" someone yelled in disbelief.

"Or crack his head open!" someone else answered.

"Terra, Terra, are you okay?" Jodi asked, suddenly in front of me, holding my face in her hands, searching my eyes for something. I nodded, not trusting my voice yet; my heart was hammering against my ribs like a bird caught in a cage. I was vaguely aware of a dull pain somewhere in my body, promising worse for later.

"Oh my god!" I heard someone yell from the balcony, the doors left open under the press of so many bodies. I grabbed Jodi's arm and hurried to the doors to see what had become of Jeremy. We got outside where I was overcome with the rush of so many people and their emotions of shock and fear. I nearly fell to my knees.

"Terra?" Jodi asked, grabbing my arm, trying to support my weight.

"Sorry… my shields…" I was choking on so many people's emotions. Jeremy, or the things with him, or the combination of both, had stripped my defenses and I wasn't holding out anyone's emotions. They ran over me like angry, wild dogs tearing at me with teeth and claws. Fear is worse than any anger you can imagine. I was crying without even realizing when I had started. Jodi eased me to the floor and the cold of the cement balcony shocked me enough to give me a moment of peace from the wave of emotions.

"Tell me what to do," Jodi said, her face schooled very carefully. I could tell she was trying desperately to keep all of her emotions back behind her own shields.

"Steven… I need… him… too…" I was gasping. They were suffocating me as more and more people rushed to the edge of the balcony to see what the others were looking at. Jodi let go of me and ran back inside, nearly running head first into Steven, who had tried to run to us but had been held back by the milling crowd. She grabbed him and pulled him outside, almost throwing them both to the ground in front of me. I reached out for both of them with my hands and they took hold. I could feel that they had already grounded and centered themselves; they could do it as easily and deftly as I could now, having practiced diligently after last fall.

I grabbed a hold of their calm centers and pulled myself into their energies. To the naked eye, I just looked like a scared girl, huddled in the corner, holding on to my two best friends while I cried my shock away. I found their connections to me and to each other and pulled it inside of me, finding the cord of love they had for each other and for me and began to feed on it. It silenced the rushing emotions of the strangers and gave me the moment of peace I needed to start building my shields again. I felt Jodi's power of air begin to swirl around me in a shimmering, electric vortex. Once it covered me from head to toe, I felt heat outside of it and knew that Steven was building a wall of flame around Jodi's air. It was a power that was both offensive and defensive; he was giving me a shield that would burn anyone trying to break through my shields. Once I was encased in both of their powers, I was able to pull my natural shields back around me like a well-worn coat.

Every muscle in my body relaxed so suddenly I fell back and nearly pulled Steven and Jodi on top of me. Sound came back to me in a rush, deafening me in a whole new way. I blinked past it and felt the air cooling the tears on my cheeks. I wiped at my cheeks and pushed my hair back away from my face. It took Jodi a few tries for me to hear her clearly. "Shay, are you okay?" she asked again, in a tone that told me that she must've asked me more than once.

"Better, better," I said, nodding. Steven stood up and reached for my hands to help me stand. "What's going on? Is he down there?" I nodded towards the crowd of people still standing there.

"I don't know, hold on," Jodi said, breaking away from us and walking to the railing to look for herself. She turned back and looked at us, shrugging her shoulders and spreading her hands in front of her. She walked over to the crowd of people and started talking to them. We waited, me clutching at Steven's shirt, pressing my face into his chest while he circled his arms around my shoulders. I often forgot how muscled and toned Steven was until I hugged him. He was so much one of the girls I rarely saw him physically as the man that he was. Right now, he was more comforting than anything in the world for me. Jodi came back, awe and disbelief clear on her face as she shook her head.

"What?" Steven asked from above me.

"He's gone," she said, looking from one of us to the other. I finally heard the distant wail of the ambulance sirens somewhere near the freeway.

"They already picked him up?" I asked, wondering why the paramedics hadn't checked me out before they took off.

"No, they haven't even gotten here yet," Jodi said, looking back over her shoulder in the direction of the sirens. "He jumped and ran off…"

"What? How?" Steven asked, his voice loud enough to make me jump.

"I don't know. I guess he landed in front of someone coming into the store and she said he just took off running."

"That's not possible," Steven said, clutching me closer to his body, and I realized he was taking comfort as much as he was giving it, which was totally fine by me. I circled my arms around his waist and held him tighter to me. I was short enough that I could fit into the crook where his arm and chest made a hollow; that place on a man's body that was just made for a woman to fit, it was just too goddamn bad that he was gay.

"Actually, I think it is," I said. "I nearly got out of his grip when he rushed me, but just as I was about to, whatever those things are were suddenly swarming around me and my feet lifted off of the ground just enough so I couldn't stop him." Jodi looked at me, her eyes wide with fear and anger intermingling naturally.

The sirens were loud and close now. I could hear the horn of a fire truck blaring at the traffic light that controlled traffic at the entrance to the parking lot. The ambulance and fire truck pulled into the parking lot and in front of the store, stopping in the exact same place I had thought about parking when we first got here. The paramedics and EMTs came filing out of their vehicles like ants out of a hill and into the store. Men and women were on me in less than a minute. I let them do their tests and worry over me all they wanted, but firmly refused when they tried to get me to agree to go to the hospital. I knew I didn't have a concussion; if I had, I couldn't have put my shields back into place as quickly as I did. Blood in your brain kinda slows you down.

    I finally had to resort to magical coercion on the officer in charge so he would tell the rest to leave me alone. It wasn't something I liked to do and was very vocal about not using your abilities to control others, but this one time I thought it was okay. I flooded the uniformed man with feelings of respect and compassion and he put a stop to the insistences of the others, saying that I was a bright, mature girl who could decide if she needed to go to the hospital or not. I knew my back and side would be bruised, probably as quickly as tonight, but I also knew there were no broken bones and I didn't have the luxury of health insurance and I didn't want to bankrupt my parents with a trip to the ER over so minor an injury.

    Jodi and I both had to give our statements three times before they were satisfied and let us leave. The cops wanted me to press charges and, when I hesitated, they told me they wouldn't be able to pick him up if I didn't. The damage to the store was minimal and they would be sending his parents a fine, but if he was going to be punished, I needed to press charges. Both Steven and Jodi wanted me to, but something told me it was a mistake. I needed to speak to Jeremy. We needed to know what he was up to and if he needed help or if he needed to be stopped. Either way, he wasn't going to talk to me if he wasn't forced to. In the end, I agreed to press charges. The officer told me they would call me when they found him so I could identify him and we'd go from there. They offered Jodi the same chance to press charges since he knocked her over too and they all knew who she was. Jodi didn't hesitate at all.

    "Why didn't you want to press charges?" Jodi asked from behind the wheel of my car. Neither she, nor Steven thought I should be driving. Maybe I didn't have a concussion or broken ribs, but I was shaken up and a car accident wouldn't help anything.

"Because, you remember the Hobyah just after I tried to talk to him? I mean, it's bad enough what just happened in the bookstore. How do you think he's gonna react when he finds out that I've pressed charges?" I shuddered at the thought.

"Oh, I dare him," Jodi started to say.

"Don't finish that," I said, cutting her off. "We're dealing with fae folk now, don't challenge them." I shook my head.

"Well, if he does dare then we'll go after him, give him a little lesson in the rule of three," Steven said, anger clear in his voice. Any one involved in the arts who believed in Karma lived by the rule of three. It was very much like The Golden Rule, except that it stated whatever you put out into the world, for good or ill, will come back to you threefold. If you did good, you would be rewarded threefold. If you did ill, well, you better be prepared for the consequences.

"Don't say something like that lightly, Drake," I said, using his elemental name to remind him of the severity of what he threatened.

"Oh, I'm not, Terra. I mean every word I say," Steven said, looking me in the eye so directly that I thought he could see into my very soul. "Are you going to let him get away with these things?"

"No. No, I'm not." I said, slumping down into the seat. "He's clearly losing his mind or his hold on reality, but more than that, he was able to jump over twenty feet to the ground without so much as scraping his hands… He's borrowing powers that no person should have and we've been told what he plans to do with those powers. We cannot let it lie."

CHAPTER 8

To my horror, the police called my parents. I should have known this was going to happen, especially since Jodi was with me and, once they had my license information, they knew I was still technically a minor. Damn those four months. Jodi's father called my parents personally to let them know what happened. My cell phone rang shrilly in the silence of the car, making all three of us jump before I fumbled with my purse, finally pulling it out.

"Hi, mom," I said automatically, knowing it had to be her.

"Where are you?" she asked, her voice already at that level that she got when I was a child and she knew I had done something wrong and was lying to try to cover it up.

"I'm in the car with Jodi and Steven, near Main St. Why?" I realized my voice was dull and monotone, very close to the sound of someone in shock. I knew I wasn't in shock, but I had to be careful not to let anyone think I was. Once people think something is wrong with you, it's very hard to convince them otherwise.

"Jodi's father just told us what happened in the bookstore!" She sounded frantic. I knew that the truth of what happened to me and what she was told was probably miles apart.

"Mom, I'm fine," I said and automatically reached over to slap Jodi on the shoulder, as if her father calling my mother was her fault.

"Ow! What?" Jodi snapped at me in a whisper, but I had slumped farther in my seat and was covering my eyes with my free hand, ready for the argument with my mom.

"Oh, I'm sure being pushed over the banister on the second floor means you're fine," Ah, there it was.

"Mom, I was not pushed over. If I was, I would have landed on a book display downstairs and would be at the hospital right now."

"He said you refused to go to the hospital, that the paramedics tried everything to get you into the ambulance except putting you into a straightjacket." I could almost hear her foot tapping over the phone. I hit Jodi again, a little harder this time.

"Damnit, what?" She braked hard, having looked away from the road at me and not seen the car in front of us stopping.

"Dude, obviously your dad called her parents," Steven said from the backseat.

"Get your butt home right now, young lady," my mom said. Young lady. I nearly get *killed* and I'm in trouble for not wanting my parents to be saddled with a needless hospital bill.

"How do you know my dad called her parents?" Jodi asked Steven.

"Mom, everything is fine," I pleaded into the phone.

"Because her mom obviously knows what happened and she's hitting you, duh," Steven explained to Jodi.

"I'm not asking you to come home, Shayna. I'm telling you. Now." Her voice held the tone of finality all parents master the moment we come out of the womb. I didn't really see any point in arguing since I didn't know where we were going right now anyway.

"Fine. Fine, just calm down, I'll be home in like ten minutes," I said with a sigh, happy to be able to get off the phone.

"Dude, I did not tell my dad to call your mom," Jodi said defensively.

"I know you didn't, but it's not like I'm going to hit your dad and you are right here in the line of fire," I said and, as nonsensical as we both knew that was, Jodi accepted it, making the left turn that would lead us back to our neighborhood. And, just like I said, in less than ten minutes we were at my house. The amazing thing about our town is that it really is a little big town. It's small enough to get everywhere within fifteen minutes, but the population is big enough that you never have to run into anyone you know when out in town. Strange, but kind of nice.

"Oh, honey, are you okay?" my mom asked, opening the door before I could grab the doorknob. She reached for me and pulled me into a hug that made my side hurt and I knew the bruise must already be blooming there.

"Yes, mom, I told you, I'm fine," I said in the patent teenage monotone.

"We'll see about that." She pulled me inside towards my father and then turned automatically to Jodi and pulled her into a hug too. "And you? I'm sure you're fine too, right?"

"Um... yes?" Jodi looked from my mom to me, uncertainty in her eyes.

"Mom, I'm sure whatever you were told was greatly exaggerated," I said, pulling her off of Jodi.

"Honey," my dad said, putting a hand on my shoulder to turn me towards him, "it's enough that Jodi's father agrees to the two of you pressing charges."

"Yeah, I know, dad. I didn't want to, though," I said, shooting Jodi a look, letting her know I'd hit her again if my parents weren't there.

"Dude, he did try to kill you," Jodi said defensively, almost angrily.

"Hey, she's right," Steven said, stopping me from arguing back, just as I opened my mouth to.

"I wouldn't have died," I said, but even to me my voice sounded resigned.

"Okay, you're going to upset your mother more. Explain what happened," my dad said and from his tone, I knew it wasn't just my mother who was starting to suffer from anxiety.

"Look, this kid we know from school was freaking out in an aisle next to us, yelling at this poor clerk that a book was mis-categorized. So we walked over to see what was wrong and if we could help," I started explaining.

"Whoa, a guy was freaking out and you tried to intervene?" my dad asked.

"We knew the guy, dad," I said, looking to Jodi and Steven for back up and they both nodded. "Anyway, when we got his attention, we tried to calm him down and tell him we'd help him with whatever was wrong and he just flipped out and lunged at me and knocked Jodi over when he did and he shoved me towards the banister. I hit the banister, but some other guy was there to catch me before anything bad happened and then he just ran off out of the store. That's all that happened. That's it." I finished when my dad didn't continue to argue with me. I know I left out a lot of details, but I told them enough that it satisfied them. I didn't think they needed to know about the faeries helping shove me or the fact that I really did almost go over the banister or the fact that Jeremy practically flew off the balcony outside.

"That's it? That's it?" my mom said, her voice rising in pitch. "How can you say 'That's it' like it's no big deal?"

"Because we're okay," I said, letting my frustration be heard.

"Honey, can we see your side?" my dad asked, his voice more gentle than my mom's, surprisingly.

"Um…" I hadn't seen my side yet and until I knew how bad it was, I wasn't sure I wanted them to see.

"Honey, we know you pressed charges. We need to see how badly hurt you are," my dad said, still in that strangely calm voice. My dad was the kind of dad that scared all the little boys when I was young from ever picking on me outside of the usual name-calling. He was the kind of dad that just seeing him once kept my dates in line. My dad staying so rational while hearing a boy tried to hurt me reminded me of the calm before the storm.

I looked to Jodi and Steven for some help in getting out of this, but they both just looked at me like deer caught in headlights, no help at all. I chewed on my bottom lip again and tried to think of some way out of it, but there just wasn't. I gathered the edge of my shirt in my hands and carefully lifted it up, tilting towards my left, making my body arc. I heard Jodi gasp and Steven hiss. From my awkward position, I tried to look down at my side, but the swell of my breast made it almost impossible to see it clearly. I turned and walked down the hallway, with my parents right behind me, to the bathroom and looked in the mirror. I caught my breath just as Jodi had done. Upon seeing the bruise, the pain started, a dull and heavy ache. It was the width of two hands on my stomach, curving to my back and up my ribcage, had blossomed like evil flowers in black, blue, and angry swollen red. I turned my torso so I could watch the progression of the bruise as it rounded to my back. I could understand now why the paramedics thought I had broken ribs, but I couldn't explain to them how I knew I didn't. More than that, I couldn't go to a hospital. Beyond my parents not being able to afford it, if they had taken me to a hospital so soon after my shields had been ripped away from me, I probably would have gone into shock and lost my mind to the emotional turmoil contained therein.

I watched my dad's face in the mirror and saw the flicker in his eye of suppressed rage. Anger was too mild a word. What raced over his face and flashed in his eye was the complete animalistic emotion of one's home or family being threatened. "Dad," I said carefully, drawing his attention back up to my face. "I'm really okay."

"You're pressing charges on this guy," he said, his voice too controlled for the situation at hand.

"That's right she is," my mother said from my other side. Her voice had lost all its earlier worry and now sounded angry enough to match my dad's face.

"Yes, mom." I let go of the hem of my shirt and let it fall back over the bruising, hiding it away. "Both Jodi and I pressed charges and we'll go down-"

"No," my dad said, stopping me mid-sentence. "We spoke to Jodi's father and he said because you're still seventeen, we have to go with you. And we are. You are not going down there by yourself."

"Dad," I started to argue.

"Do not argue with us, Shayna Bridget," my mother said, looking me straight in the eye. Over the last seventeen years, I had grown to hate my middle name. As pretty as I could've thought it was, only ever hearing your middle name when you were in trouble will taint your emotions that are evoked when you hear it.

"Fine, whatever," I said, hearing the years of maturity slip away in my response. I pushed through the crowd of bodies out of the suddenly too small bathroom and made it down the hall and back into the kitchen. I got a glass of water and found the painkillers we kept in a cabinet and took a few. The pain in my side was growing more and more persistent with each passing moment now that I was aware of the damage done. It was going to be much harder to get to talk to Jeremy with my parents looming over my shoulder, if not impossible. I was pouring the rest of my water into the sink when the house phone rang and my mother rushed to answer it.

"Hello?" I heard her say from the living room. Jodi and Steven walked in to stand near me as we waited. "Yes, this is she." A pause. "Yes," another pause. "Yes, we can come down right now." I knew they had found Jeremy. "Okay, we'll be there as quickly as we can," my mother said just before I heard her hang up the phone.

"They found him already?" my dad asked my mom, standing in the perfect spot to see both the kitchen and the living room.

"Yes, they want Shayna and Jodi to come down to fill out some paperwork," my mother said, coming around so that we could see her. She already had her purse in her hand. "Let's go," she said, waving at us to come with her.

"Okay," I said, reaching for my purse and keys that we'd set on the kitchen table when I came in.

"You're riding with us, Shayna," my mom said, her voice more than a little irritated.

"Mom, we're not all going to fit in the backseat and Jodi and Steven don't have a car here," I said slowly, trying to will her to see the logic in my voice. I tried very hard not to influence my parents with my empathetic abilities; my mom always seemed to know when I was doing it and my dad never reacted well when he thought he was being manipulated.

"Honey, it's fine," my dad said, reaching out and touching my mom's arm to get her to follow him out the door. She seemed to be battling her own internal fight to let me out of her sight. Finally, she exhaled loudly and turned to follow my dad out the door without arguing the point further. As we turned away from the door, I stopped suddenly, seeing an approaching officer, his cruiser parked behind my Camaro.

"Shayna?" the officer asked, stopping a few feet away from us, standing in that easy way all cops adapt with his feet hip-width apart and his hands hovering near his utility belt.

"Yes?" I answered.

"We have apprehended a man that matches your description of the suspect that attacked you in the bookstore. We need you and Jodi," he glanced at Jodi then and I realized he knew exactly who she was without asking, "to come with me and we'll do a quick drive by where he's being held and you can confirm if it is, in fact, him."

"A drive by?" My dad asked as he stepped forward.

"Yes. We don't really do 'line ups' any more and, since we believe we've caught the man very close to the scene of the crime, we've detained him there and would like to have your daughter and Jodi identify him there before we bring him in on full charges." Jodi let me take the front seat in the cruiser because of the pain of my bruises. The backseat was molded plastic shaped in a way that, if you were handcuffed behind your back, your arms would fit into the form the seat was in. I appreciated the offer and, for once, took it rather than argued.

In another ten minutes, we were cruising by a neighborhood only a few blocks away from the bookstore and I saw two police cruisers parked against a curb with their caution lights flashing. The officers were standing on the sidewalk, looming over the crouched form of a third man. We slowed almost to a stop as we got close to the three men and there I saw very clearly Jeremy's crouched form, twisted uncomfortably with his hands cuffed behind his back. His face was pink with exertion or rage. I couldn't tell which.

"Yeah, that's Jeremy," I said with a nod, noting how sad my voice sounded.

"Jodi?" The officer asked, glancing into the rearview mirror.

"Yeah, Jeremy McCormack, that's the guy that attacked her," Jodi answered in much more detail than I had given. The officer nodded and sped up to the normal speed limit and continued on to the jail we were going to in order to fill out paperwork for the charges.

I had thought we would be going down to County where the courthouses were, thinking that was where our city precinct was, but the officer turned back towards the direction that the bookstore was in. We turned down Victoria Ave and then down Ralston St until we came to Dowell Ave and I suddenly realized how many times I had driven by the police station and never really paid attention to it. I almost laughed at myself, realizing for the first time that there were three police cruisers to every one civilian car in the parking lot. It's amazing how many things in your own town that will escape your attention if you're not specifically looking for it. If we had continued just a little farther down Ralston St and came around the bend in the road, we would have come up to the side parking lot entrance to the strip mall the bookstore was in. I had a moment while we were parking to wonder if Jeremy had been stupid enough to try to run right by the police station when he fled the scene, especially considering how quickly they found him.

I unfastened my seatbelt before the officer turned off the engine. The irresistible urge to turn around pulled at me so hard I nearly gave myself a crick in the neck when I whirled to the right to look out the rear window and saw Jensen's car parked on the other side of the aisle. He was standing there, waiting for me.

"Tell my parents I'll be right in," I said to Jodi and the officer as I forced my door open and got out to walk across the aisle to meet Jensen. I hesitated for a moment, and then closed the distance between us, wrapping him into a hug. His chest was firm and his arms circled around my shoulders, pressing me into the warmth of his body. He rested his cheek on top of my head, breathing in the perfume of my shampoo. I felt a momentary tension in his body when I first wrapped myself around it, but as his arms nearly crushed me, the tension fled his body with an exhaled breath. I knew it was unfair of me to take the comfort he offered and not be able to be his girlfriend, always keeping him at arm's length when it came to our emotions, but I really needed that hug.

"How'd you find out?" I asked, my voice muffled against him.

"I saw it," he said simply.

"I didn't see you there?" I said, pulling away from him just enough to turn my face up to look at his. He looked down at me. His eyes had grown dark, like the ocean in a violent storm. Promises of angry, foam-capped waves were held in those eyes and I felt the chill of the ocean spray on my face. "You weren't there, were you?" My voice dropped to a whisper as I spoke. He shook his head, his lips pressing together in a tight line. "But you saw it?" He nodded in answer.

"Shayna, if you keep trying to get yourself killed, you're going to give me a heart attack." He tried to make his voice light, but the look in his eyes said enough.

"I wasn't trying to get myself killed. I was afraid he was going to do something violent to that clerk. I couldn't just stand by and let him do that," I said, taking care not to sound defensive.

"I know," he stopped, taking a breath and pulling me closer into his chest again. I didn't fight him to look at his face. "What you do terrifies me, you know?"

"I know," I said softly. "But at least we've gained something from this."

"What? That they've arrested the bastard?" he asked.

"No, I think we've proven one of your abilities is prophesy." I pulled away again to look at him.

"Yes, I think you're right. I saw the whole thing happen, from when you were standing behind him before you got his attention, to when he rushed you, the man catching you just before you went over, and then you rushing out to see where he'd gone. But then you became hard to see; your whole body became blurry like a T.V. screen covered in snow and it hurt to hold on to the vision." He looked at me, a line of worry creasing between his eyes.

"Was it hard to look at anyone else when it happened?" I asked.

"No, I could see Jodi and Steven reaching out to you, clear as a bell. Why is that?"

"Some how Jeremy or those things with him stripped my shields and there were too many raw emotions around me. I felt like I was being pulled apart by my very nerve endings." I realized I was digging my fingernails into my palms. I eased my grip just as something occurred to me. "Hey, could you see the things with Jeremy?"

"No, but when they were around you, it was a little blurry, like you were caught in a tornado or something." I nodded, knowing exactly what he meant and couldn't help but be disappointed. Maybe if he had seen them and could tell me what they looked like, I could have figured out what they were. "So, you pressed charges? I didn't expect you to do that."

"Yeah, well, I didn't want to. Jodi and Steven convinced me. Jodi pressed charges, too, since he knocked her over," I said.

"Still though, you don't let yourself get convinced if it's not something you want to do." He looked at me then, his head tilted to the side, curiosity sifting through his eyes. "What are you up to?"

"What do you mean?"

"Don't be coy. What are you planning?"

"I'm not being coy," I said, stepping back, but he stepped with me. That only worked to put me on edge, wanting to widen the space between us all the more.

"This isn't like you. Why did you want him arrested?" he pressed, his voice holding no room for argument.

"I didn't want him arrested, but…" I sighed, knowing if I wanted Jensen to trust me enough to help him with his abilities I couldn't keep secrets from him. "I want to talk to him and he's obviously not going to let me do that on his own, so…" I let the sentence hang there.

"Shayna, you can't be serious!" Jensen said. "He tried to kill you and you want to have a chat with him?"

"Look, I think whatever he's gotten into is affecting him and making him act in a way that he never would. You're still new, you don't know what Jeremy used to be like. This isn't him," I said, shaking my head, remembering the quiet, almost beaten down boy we'd grown up with.

"So what, you expect them to let you talk to him here?" Jensen asked skeptically.

"Why not?" I asked. "It's secure. I mean, cops are everywhere."

"Because you're his victim. He's the accused. They're not going to let you talk in private," he said.

"It's worth a shot," I said, shrugging my shoulders, knowing he was probably right, now that I stopped to think about it.

"Just don't get your hopes up?" he said. I stepped away to start towards the front doors. I felt Jensen's hand slide down my back to rest on the small of my back, but as his arm grazed my size, I flinched with pain. I stepped out of his reach. "Something wrong?" he asked, looking at me from the side.

"I'll show you later. Not now, okay?" I looked up at him and saw the hesitation in his eyes. I kept walking, forcing him to follow or be left behind.

We pushed open the plate glass doors that looked so much like the doors to the grocery store or a department store in the mall. It was a completely surreal moment when I walked into the midst of so many police officers. My parents were standing in front of a counter talking with Jodi's father, who I wasn't at all surprised to see. Jodi's father was a County Sheriff and therefore did not work at this station, but rather out in the middle of town at our County Courthouse. But he was well-known and liked amongst most of the departments, so I imagine they didn't feel intimidated to see him show up once they knew his daughter had been involved. I looked around and saw that Steven and Jodi were sitting in some hard plastic chairs against the wall, just to the side of the front doors. Jodi waved me over and patted the seat next to her, but before I could even take a step in her direction, my mom caught my eye and motioned me over to them.

"You doin' alright, kiddo?" Jodi's father asked. We were all "kiddo" to him. He made no excuses for never remembering any of our names.

"Yeah, thanks, just want to get out of here," I said.

"We'll try to make this quick," he said as if he was in charge around here, which we both knew he wasn't. "Jodi?" he called, turning to the side just enough to see where his daughter was. Jodi stood and walked over to us at his call. "Okay, you're both going to go into the room and you'll each have to try to identify him, but you'll be going in separately, do you understand?"

"Sure," I said as Jodi said, "Yes, dad."

"Your friends will have to stay out here," he said, motioning to both Jensen and Steven with his chin.

"No problem, sir," Jensen said. He was the first teenage boy I had ever met that managed to call anyone's father 'sir' and not have it sound sarcastic. Jensen walked over to take Jodi's now vacant seat.

"Okay, Jodi, you and I will be going in together and then you and your parents will be going in after," Jodi's father explained, looking at me

"Dad, why are you guys acting like we're kids? We don't need to have our hands held while we do this," Jodi said, careful to keep her voice even so she didn't ruin the speech by sounding insolent.

"You're seventeen," he said, as if that explained everything.

"I'll be eighteen in just a couple of months and Shay will be eighteen in another month after that. If we were here as the accused, you'd be treating us like adults, so why does that change just because we're the victims?" I watched Jodi's whole body language change as she made the very credible argument, but I could tell nothing fazed her old man.

"Because it's the law. Now, that's enough," and he said it like Jodi had said all of that during the midst of a temper tantrum.

"Jodi," I said softly, leaning towards her and placing my hand on her wrist. "It's not that big of a deal, let it go." I felt Jodi tense under my touch and I knew she expected me to ease her feelings of anger and resentment, but I didn't take that liberty this time and, because of that, she relaxed under my touch and nodded slightly.

"Yeah, fine, let's go, dad." Jodi turned and waited for her father to lead the way. Another cop behind the counter led all five of us through a hallway lined with doors, stopping in front of one that didn't look any different to me than all the others. He reached and unlocked the door and held it open for Jodi and her father, stopping my mother from trying to follow.

"Once they're done, we'll let you all in," the officer explained. We waited for almost five minutes before another officer inside the room opened the door and waved us in. The room was small and gray with a rectangular table in the middle with four chairs around it.

"Okay," an officer said from farther inside our room. "Shayna, is it?" he asked, looking up from a paper folder, although I had a feeling he knew my name perfectly well.

"Yeah," I said. I walked over to him.

"Now, we have some pictures here; one of them may or may not be the suspect. If you think you see someone familiar, you just point them out to me, okay?"

"Can I ask a question?" I asked, looking up at the officer who nodded. "I just identified Jeremy in person outside. Why do I have to do this again?"

"It's procedure," the officer said with no facial expression whatsoever. I thought about pressing the redundant issue, but my desire to get out of there was greater than my desire to argue. I remembered having to give my statement so many times at the bookstore, so why would this be any different?

I nodded and waited as they laid out five headshots of men, all of whom had that criminal look to them. If you saw them walking down the street you'd cross to the other side just to keep your distance. But even if they had found five guys that could have passed for Jeremy's twin, there was no mistaking the wild look in his eye that I had finally seen inside the bookstore. "Shayna, do you see anyone who you think is Jeremy?" the officer asked me, keeping his voice low and steady, as if speaking to someone in a hospital bed.

"Yeah," I said after licking my suddenly dry lips. "Yeah, he's number two." I wrapped my arms around myself for comfort before I remembered the angry bruises on my side, causing me wince and hiss in pain.

"What's the matter?" the officer asked, taking half a step towards me.

"Nothing," I said, shaking my head.

"It is not nothing, Shayna Bridget. You show the officer what's wrong," my mother's angry voice came at me from the darkness of the room.

"Damnit, mom, stop middle naming me!" I said, having to control the sudden urge to stamp my foot.

"Shayna, do you have injuries from today's altercation?" Officer Adams asked. I had caught his name badge in the light from the window when he stepped closer to me.

"It's just a little bruising," I said easily.

"It's not little," my mom said, coming closer to us.

"Okay," Officer Adams said, putting his hand up towards my mom to stop the pending argument. "Shayna, big or little, we'll need to see it and take pictures." He walked back over to the wall and pressed a button for an intercom that I hadn't noticed before and spoke into it.

"Honey, you okay?" my mother asked, touching my shoulder, her voice having changed from angry mama-bear to concerned in a heartbeat.

"Yeah, I just want to get this over with." I looked at Officer Adams. "I was wondering if I could talk to Jeremy?"

"I'm sorry?" Officer Adams looked at me, completely confused.

"I just wanted to talk to him, find out what's wrong. I think he's really disturbed about something."

"Oh no, I'm afraid that's impossible. We do not allow victims to speak to the accused unless we trying to get an admittance of guilt out of them. And with over twenty witnesses in the bookstore, we don't need that this time." Officer Adams said with no room for argument.

When I didn't argue, Officer Adams walked to the door on the opposite side of the room as the one we came in through and spoke to someone standing outside of it. A female officer came in. She was petite for a cop, about my height and had yellow blond hair like Jodi's, bound up and away from her face in a French braid. She looked around the room with a sweep of hard cop eyes before she found me. Once her gaze settled on my face she gave me a warm, easy smile. I realized how pretty she must be when out of uniform.

"Shayna, if you'll come with me, we'll get these horrible pictures out of the way so you can get out of here." The female officer held a hand out to me and I walked towards her, feeling my mother following closely at my back. I knew that, because she had to be present during the identifying of Jeremy, she would have to be present during the next uncomfortable part. Officer Brown, as that was the name on her name badge, walked us down the hall until we came to an interrogation room where Jodi and another female cop were waiting for us.

    I found out that Jeremy had shoved Jodi so hard that her arm had struck a bookshelf hard enough that she already had her own bruise blooming over her left tricep. Jodi didn't have to take off her shirt to have her pictures taken, so I was a more than a little annoyed that I had to, especially in front of an audience, even if they were all women. Officer Brown took over a dozen pictures of the bruising from every angle imaginable before she would let me put my shirt back on and leave. Jodi was surprisingly sensitive about the whole thing. Jodi had more body issues that even I had. I always felt I was over-endowed and she always felt she was under-endowed and, every time she was reminded of our differences, she took her bitter anger out on me. But not this time. This time, after I had my shirt back into place, she just gave me a careful hug and walked out with me, arm in arm.

Chapter 9

Jodi's father wanted her to go home and my parents wanted me to come home with them, but neither of us wanted to be separated; we had much to talk about and needed privacy to do so. If we went to my house, with Jensen with us, my parents would make me leave my bedroom door open, completely negating the privacy we were seeking. We could go to Jodi's house, but her room was so small and cluttered it would be more than a little uncomfortable. I made the command decision to take everyone to my house, knowing there was one last place for us to hide out. My tree house in the back yard was completely warded against magical or psychic attacks and full of our magical working supplies.

We were all walking out to the parking lot when we saw Jeremy's parents walking towards a dark SUV. Because of his star athlete older brother, we all knew who the McCormacks were. Mr. McCormack looked like an older version of Jimmy; sandy blonde hair, chiseled features, and lovely hazel eyes that bled from brown to green and back again. He was as tall and broad shouldered as Jimmy was and, unlike most fathers, he hadn't gone soft around the middle in his later years.

Mrs. McCormack, however, was the clear explanation for where Jeremy got his genetics. She was smaller than her husband by almost a hundred pounds and nearly a foot shorter. Her hair was a pretty chestnut brown that I remembered Jeremy's used to be in elementary school before he dyed his hair that awful shoe polish black. The only difference was that Mrs. McCormack's skin wasn't so much pale, like Jeremy's, but fair and almost luminous, the color I suspected Jeremy's could be if he took better care of himself.

"I just can't believe this bullshit," Mr. McCormack's voice came back to us from across the parking lot, which let me know he was yelling just for the sake of yelling. "He is going to earn every penny of that bail money back!"

I turned back towards my parents' car and started walking towards it. When I realized no one else was walking with me, I stopped and looked over my shoulder. Jeremy's father was walking across the parking lot towards us. My stomach knotted up against my spine and my hands tingled with nerves. I closed my eyes and caught my breath so I could reinforce my shields against the anger I felt rolling off of Mr. McCormack in waves of heat that stung my face, even at this distance. I felt a press of fingers in one of my palms and a familiar warmth; I wrapped my hand around Steven's hand, interlacing our fingers. *He's a fire sign, that's why it feels like that,* Steven's red thoughts eased through my mind like a warm fire on a cold winter's night. His own inherent Fire abilities helped me shield tightly against the other man.

"Hello," Mr. McCormack said in a voice roughened by yelling as he held out a hand to my father who took it for a firm handshake between the two large men. "I just wanted to apologize for this whole thing," he said carefully, but I could taste the metallic anger of his voice on my tongue.

"Well, we appreciate that," my father said, releasing the other man's hand first and stepping back half a step to stand next to my mother. Mr. McCormack crossed his arms over a very broad chest and looked back over his shoulder to the jail. If he could have burned a hole through the cement and glass and scorched Jeremy, I knew he would.

"I just don't understand how this happened," Mr. McCormack said, more to himself than to my parents. "I just want you to know there're no hard feelings between me and my wife and you all. We completely agree with the girls pressing charges." He nodded towards Jodi and me behind my parents. "I would've let the boy sit in a cell over night if it wasn't for his mother," he said the last with a shake of his head, "but she wanted to post bail, so here we are. At least the paperwork will take a while and he can cool his heels in the cell until then."

"Well, that's between you and your wife. I appreciate your understanding, but the officers told us not to discuss this further with your family, so if you don't mind." My father held his hand out for another handshake to be polite before breaking off the conversation. I watched Mr. McCormack stare at my father's hand for a moment as if he wouldn't take it, but finally he reached out and the two men grasped hands and said good-bye. I was thankful that the awkward conversation was so short.

Fifteen minutes later, we were pulling up in front of my house and making our way into the backyard. We grabbed some sodas and a few snacks to take with us as we passed the kitchen. My body was growing stiff with pain from my injuries and Jensen had to help me climb up the ladder and through the trap door into the tree house. I was breathing faster than a quick climb up my tree should have warranted. I grabbed one of the large pillows I had up there for seating and laid on it.

Steven was pulling on a rope that was attached to a limb outside the window on one end and to a basket on the ground at the other; it was how we brought up supplies or food without having to carry it up the ladder. Jensen was sitting by my knees with his legs crossed and had pulled my legs into his lap, keeping us close together and giving Jodi and Steven as much room as possible. Although my father had built me a rather large tree house, as tree houses go, now that we were all adult size, once you had more than two of us in here at a time it started to feel a little cramped.

"Okay, so what now?" Jodi asked, settling herself against the opposite wall from me. Steven took the wall between us that connected the two walls, leaving precious little floor space between the four of us.

"I have no idea," I said with an exhale of breath, shaking my head at the ceiling.

"I can't believe they're going to let him out," Steven said, cracking open a soda can and taking a sip.

"Dude, they let wife beaters out if they make bail, why not a teenager?" Jodi said.

"But it's not like he's a minor. He turned eighteen in January, that makes him an adult," Steven said.

"Still made bail though and will be released into the custody of his parents. That's all they care about," she finished with a shrug.

"So he's free to hurt Shayna again," Steven said, anger coloring his words and, though my eyes were closed, I could see an aura of red pulsing in the direction Steven was sitting in. It made me smile. Jensen was rubbing my leg gently under my jeans, massaging the calf muscle. I had a feeling it was as much for my comfort as it was for his own.

"Maybe if she just stays away from him, he won't do anything to her," Jensen said quietly. I opened my eyes and looked down the length of my body to him. He was carefully avoiding looking at my face, watching his own hands.

"You think this is my fault, don't you?" I said, careful to make sure I didn't sound too defensive.

"Well, he only attacks you when you confront him," Jensen said, finally looking up at me. Both Steven and Jodi had gone completely quiet and still, afraid to move and bring my attention to them.

"I don't confront him, Jensen. I've tried to talk to him, tell him that we can help him if he'd let us." I was surprised to hear how calm I was, not jumping into an argument with Jensen. Probably because I knew he was partly right, not that I was going to admit that to him.

"Okay, but he doesn't see it that way. Maybe you just need to leave the poor bastard alone," he said, looking back down at my leg.

"I can't do that, Jensen."

"Why?" he asked, his voice finally sounding as strained as I knew he was feeling. I hesitated to answer him for a moment until I felt both Jodi and Steven's emotional push to just explain it to him. I told him about the visit I'd had with Iris the Faerie Queen and the warning she'd given me. Jensen had stayed quiet through the entire story and remained so now that I was finished. His face betrayed none of the emotions that he might have been feeling. I waited, not wanting to press him before he was ready. Although he knew what I was and what my friends were and what we did, he was still coming to terms with it and his own growing abilities. I tried not to shove the magical side of my life in his face too often, but I couldn't help it this time.

"More faeries?" Jensen finally said, his face finally breaking the mask and showing his skepticism.

"I know, I know, there are no such things, right?" I said, propping myself up on my elbows, watching him.

"Right," Jensen said, as if it was stating the obvious, despite our conversation after our date. I smiled at him and knew it wasn't entirely friendly. He wrinkled his brow at me.

"Tegan?" I called out clearly; suddenly knowing he would just answer my call, even though he had left me after helping with the store earlier.

"Tegan?" Jensen made his name a question, looking all the more bewildered.

"You called?" Tegan's melodic voice rang through the silence of the tree house before he appeared on the window ledge above my head. I tilted my head back, stretching my neck almost painfully to look up at the window and the beautiful little man now with rich, dark fall leaves for wings. Tegan was standing on the window ledge, leaning against the side of the window at complete ease.

"What was that?" Jodi asked, looking from me to the window where I was looking. I saw that the neither of the boys seemed to be able to see what I was looking at either.

"Whoa, you can't see him?" I asked, sitting up too quickly for my bruises, wincing and hissing in pain. As long as we had known each other, we had been able to see the same faeries the other could see, even though sometimes she had to help me see the Air faeries and I her the Earth faeries. And that made me remember; I couldn't see Tegan at first this morning either. "Come here," I motioned her over to me with my hand, propping myself up with my other hand.

"What am I missing?" Jensen asked, even as Jodi crawled over to me. I knew she realized she had heard a faerie's voice, but just couldn't understand it and had come to me unquestioningly.

"In this the late afternoon light, I give the gift of second sight," I whispered to Jodi as I covered her eyes with my hand, pulling it away and watched her eyes open and seek out Tegan immediately. I watched as a smile curled her pale pink lips and a sparkle lit her blue eyes. It warmed my heart to see that smile. It was a smile she had when we were six years old sitting under trees surrounded by the tiny creatures.

"Well met, I am Jodi," she said to Tegan, her voice a little breathy when she said it.

"Ah, and you an Air Spirit, you should know just as well as our Earth Mother not to lie to the fae folk," Tegan said, pushing away from the edge of the window and crossing his arms over his chest, looking down into Jodi's face.

"Did you hear bells?" Steven asked and Jensen shook his head.

"I don't under-," Jodi began, but I stopped her with a hand on her wrist.

"He knows me as Terra," I said quietly to her, realizing for the first time that none of us had revealed our elemental names to Jensen and, here I was, outing us without asking the other two if it was okay. But here we were and Tegan wasn't going to accept our mundane names that our parents had chosen for us. Jodi's mouth formed a perfect 'O' as understanding came over her.

"Fae, I am Fae," she said more clearly when she had returned her attention back to Tegan.

"Well met, Fae. I am Tegan," he said with a bow that was more graceful than anything I could do.

"What is going on?" Steven asked, frustration leaking out of his voice as he looked between the two of us.

"You know, I can't believe we call me Fae and you're the one who made it possible for me to see and understand him," Jodi said, pain clear in her voice. We called Jodi Fae, short for Faerie, because that was the first elemental of her magic that had come to her.

"I couldn't see him, either. I couldn't understand him at first. I just had a gut feeling there was a faerie outside my window and I had to invoke second sight before I could see him too." That made the pain leave her face, replaced by confusion.

"Here, Jodi, try to give Steven the sight. That'll prove you're still Fae," I said, motioning towards Steven with a bob of my head. She reached over to Steven and covered his eyes and whispered the same spell I had just done on her. When Steven blinked his eyes open, I watched them go wide and round and I knew he could see Tegan as clearly as I could. I tried the same spell on Jensen and it didn't work. Jodi tried as well, but it still didn't work. All that happened after I laid my hand on his eyes was that the light that Tegan just seemed to emit from his body became slightly visible to Jensen and he could pick out some words from the sound of bells that he heard when Tegan spoke. But Jensen was a psychic and, although many people think that's part of magic, it just isn't and nothing I could do right now could make him see Tegan like we all could.

Surprisingly, Jensen didn't seem as disappointed as I would have been if someone told me I didn't have enough magic in me to see a faerie. In fact, he almost seemed relieved. I had to remind myself that Jensen saw his abilities as a burden. When they only manifest themselves when something is going terribly wrong, I could almost understand. Almost.

"Well, even though you can't see him clearly, do you believe Shayna now, Jensen?" Steven asked in a tone of voice I seldom heard come out of him. It was both defiant and very deeply masculine.

"Of course I do," Jensen said, almost angrily. I put a hand on his wrist to stop him from rising to Steven's bait.

"Steven," I said carefully, "Jensen's not used to this kind of thing. Most of what is normal to you and me is fantasy to him, more like a faerie tale that your parents tell you when you're a child. You can't hold what he doesn't know against him."

"I can hold it against him if, every time you share something with him, he acts likes you're crazy or making it up." The color in Steven's cheeks was rising and I realized he was trembling a little. I held shields in place against most of the world all day long, but between the three people around me right now, I allowed channels between us to remain opened so I could always find them. I realized his magic was starting to bubble like boiling water beginning to roll in a pot.

"You know, Jensen, he's right." I turned my face back to Jensen, my legs still cradled in his lap and my body stretched out over the large pillow to ease the pain in my side. "I know you're trying, but you could really try harder. I know most of what I tell you sounds impossible, but after last fall, I'd think you'd be more receptive." Jensen kept his face schooled, but I could see and feel the internal desire to squirm under the weight of all three of our gazes.

"I *am* trying," Jensen said.

"I know, I said you were, but we need you to try harder," I said, keeping my voice easy and level, not wanting this to turn into a fight.

"*We* need? Not *you* need? I'm not in a relationship with them." He nodded towards Jodi and Steven and I felt the air crack and tingle with their energies. He'd offended them.

"And we aren't in a relationship, we're just dating. But unfortunately, when you date me, you date all of us. Kinda like a single parent. Same goes for their boyfriends." I shrugged. "I know it's weird, but we're so close and so involved in each others' lives that when we bring someone else into the mix, the other two are affected. I told you that when we started dating. I wasn't kidding, Jensen. It's also a big part of why I don't want us in an exclusive relationship."

"I guess I didn't realize how serious you were."

"Are you okay with it?"

"Do I have a choice?"

"Of course you do, we can end this right now." I didn't mean for it to sound as flippant as it came out, but I was being honest. I had no illusions that this was forever, but for right now I was happy.

"I don't want to end it," he said softly and I realized that the world had narrowed down to the two of us in those few seconds when I wasn't sure what his response was going to be.

"Then you need to try harder to understand me, us, and our world. I know it's hard to undo nearly eighteen years of beliefs, but all we're asking is that you try harder. Don't laugh every time something mystical or magical happens. Don't shut down every time one of your abilities comes to light. We want to help you as much as we can, but if you keep picking at me, at us, then it's going to turn ugly." I reached out and took his hand in both of mine, rubbing a thumb over his knuckles. "Just think about how amazing the world would be if we all knew that magic wasn't only real, but entirely possible for us."

"Okay," he said and nodded, looking from me to Steven to Jodi and finally back to me. "I'll try harder."

"You'll need to remember that seeing isn't always believing, Jensen," Jodi said. "As you can see, you can't see Tegan like we can, but you can't deny that something is there in front of you." She pointed to Tegan, who smiled at all of us.

"You're right," Jensen said. "If you had told me this time last year that my brother would be in jail for the attempted murder of his girlfriend because he was trying to sacrifice her to gain the powers of a demon from Hell…" He took a breath and let it out in a sound that was half a laugh and half something painful, not quite a sob. "I would have thought you were clinically insane."

"I know. I wish it was all happy endings, but as magical as things can be, it's still reality," I squeezed his hand gently and sat up carefully until I could reach for him and pull him into a hug.

"Okay, well, if I'm going to try harder, then I have to stop ignoring things," Jensen said, steeling himself with a deep breath. "When I saw what was happening earlier, I thought I saw lightening strike inside the store. What was that about?" Jensen looked at me, normal confusion on his face. I had a memory of white light flashing nearby when Jodi screamed just as Jeremy had lunged for me.

"I totally forgot about that," I said quickly, looking at Jodi expectantly. "Did you do that?"

"Do what?" Jodi asked surprised.

"Ooooh yeah," Steven said suddenly. "I saw that, but it was too fast for me to realize what it was. I guess it did look like lightening."

"What are you all talking about?" Jodi asked.

"You screamed when Jeremy lunged for me, remember?" I asked and she nodded. "Well, then I saw and heard a crack of, I guess, lightening, right next to me and Jeremy, like it was aimed at him, but missed."

"I didn't, I mean, I don't remember," Jodi stuttered, shaking her head and looking at her hands as if they held some important secret there. "I've never…"

"Ah, my little Air Spirit, you do not know your powers yet," Tegan chimed in with a laugh. It was strange to hear a six-inch man call someone our size "little."

"What do you mean?" I asked.

"What did he say?" Jensen asked.

"He said Jodi doesn't know her powers yet."

"She is an Air Spirit," Tegan said, shrugging his tiny shoulders as if that explained everything.

"You know, when I look at you when I meditate, you look like you're made out of electricity," I said, watching Jodi carefully.

"I remember," she said with a nod. When I had gone on so many spirit walks and into deep meditations last fall, I had learned that Jodi and Steven were the pure embodiments of their elements, as if a promise of what they could be in another life, on another plane.

"And the other day in the store Deb said I was able to do what I did to that robber because I'd lost control of my power. Maybe that's what happened to you? Maybe you lost control."

"Are you saying I can draw down lightening?" Jodi asked with a laugh.

"Why is that funny?" I asked, silencing her laughter. "If I try hard enough, I can cause small earthquakes around me. When I meditate on the ground, I become part of the dirt and grass. You can bring a wind on a perfectly still day. Why can't you do something more spectacular when under extreme stress?" Jodi wasn't really looking at me anymore; her eyes had lost focus, looking more inside herself, rather than out.

"I guess… I've just never done it before. I don't even know how to do it. How could I do something if I don't know how to do it in the first place?" Jodi asked.

"Of course you know how to do it; it is a part of you," Tegan said, pushing off of the floor and fluttering up to be eye-level with Jodi. "Do not question it. It is part of you. You merely have to accept it." Tegan floated ever closer to Jodi's face until he was close enough to lean forward and place a kiss on her nose. Jodi giggled and I had to concentrate on not laughing when she did. Tegan began to grow brighter and brighter until we all had to turn our eyes away or be blinded. In the next moment, the blinding light was gone and the tree house seemed darker than normal. Tegan was gone.

The day had been stolen from us and, with a chill in the air, we realized the sun was sinking below the horizon, casting long shadows through the orchard beyond my window. Jodi and Steven climbed down the tree, deciding to walk home and leave Jensen and me alone. I needed warm comfort that went beyond what friends alone could offer with just platonic affection. I needed heat and to feel grateful to be alive.

As soon as the trapdoor was shut behind them, Jensen reached out and carefully gathered me into his arms and pulled me into his lap. It was awkward for me at first, being cradled in his crossed legs like a child in a parent's lap. Bracing myself on his shoulders, I pulled myself up enough to wrap my legs around his waist and sit in his lap, facing him.

I laid my hands on the swell of his chest and looked into his blue, blue eyes. His fingers massaged the small of my back, careful of the bruise on one side. I breathed in the scent of him, the wonderful combination of musk, cinnamon, and something sweet I could never figure out the name of.

"I know you said dating one of you means dating all of you, but I'm glad I only get to do this with you," Jensen whispered into my hair, breathing against my ear, sending chills up my back, over my arms and out my fingertips, making tiny sparks of light flicker between our bodies. This might not be a committed, full-blown relationship, but we were the only people we were intimate with. And thank goodness, because I don't think I could've shared.

"Jensen, I'm not sure we should," I whispered, pushing on his chest to distance myself from him, if even only a couple of inches.

"Shay, we've talked about this," he said, leaning toward my neck again. "I know we're not boyfriend and girlfriend. You're not taking advantage of me," his breath was hot against my skin, making me shiver again.

He chuckled quietly and lowered his lips to my collarbone, kissing lightly. I tilted my chin up and felt the shift in energy around us; it was suddenly alive and swirling, playing with the locks of my hair, caressing my skin just as he laid feather light kisses on my shoulder and neck. I felt the sap trapped beneath the bark of the tree that broke the line of the walls run faster, in time with my pulse, as if the faster and hotter my blood ran, so did the life in the tree.

I felt a warm summer breeze come to life outside and rush in around us, heavy with the scents of grass, salt, and moist earth. I caught my breath just as Jensen's teeth found the muscle in my neck and bit down, just hard enough, and the wind paused in time with me. When I exhaled, the wind rushed around us again. My skin was alive with nerves and energy waiting to be released. Jensen's fingers pressed harder into my back, as if he would claw into my skin and I would have welcomed it. My back arched, pressing me against him, and I felt him catch his breath, his chest trembling under the pressure of my fingers as I clung to him. My thighs tightened around his waist, bringing a small sound from his parted lips. I felt his body swelling in answer to my body pressing against him.

He turned his face up to mine and I found his lips, pressing them gently into a kiss that grew almost immediately into something fiercer, almost desperate, as if the very air we breathed was locked in the other's mouth. The energy around me built subtly and I felt it press against us. One of his hands slid up my back, tracing a tingling line of power dancing on my skin, until he found the back of my head and twined his fingers into the richness of my hair. He held it tightly against the base of my skull, just this side of painful, causing me to whimper against his mouth.

The energy that was building around us was almost too much for me to ignore as it became like a second pressure on my body, separate from his arms and chest, making it difficult to breathe. I broke from our kiss, gasping in a deep breath. Before I could exhale, I was suddenly moving, Jensen lifting me and turning our bodies until I was pressed into the floor with the weight of him above me. I had a moment to realize that it should have hurt and didn't and that I could see lovely white flowers, huge and in bloom on the branches of the tree outside the window that had never before been there before. He pressed me back into a kiss and his hands found their way to my skin.

The next hour was lost in a blur of skin, raking fingers, and heavy breathing. Not until we were laying back, me curled into Jensen's side, resting my head in the hollow where chest and shoulder meet, did I remember that I wasn't in pain anymore. I was lying on my left side and the bruising had been on my right, but even my breathing was easier. I lifted my head and looked down the line of our bodies, raising my arm up above my head to look at my side. The violently colored bruise was still there, but the pain was gone, like a week old bruise you've forgotten about and only the dark mark on your skin reminded you that it was there.

"What's up?" Jensen asked, his voice gone slow and deep with physical satisfaction.

"It doesn't hurt anymore," I said, rolling away from him enough to touch my side to be sure, but no matter how hard I pressed, it just didn't hurt.

"But it's still bruised?" Jensen asked, reaching out to touch my skin gently.

"I know, but it's like it's healed or *healing*, at least," I said and looked up, remembering the flowers blooming in the tree outside my window. Sure enough, in the fading light of the last few rays of the sunset I saw the large white flowers decorating the tree. I didn't know what kind of flower they were because I had never seen them before, but their perfume was as thick and heady as magnolias. Jensen followed my gaze until he saw the flowers.

"Where did those come from?"

"Us…I think," I said as I sat up, gathering my clothes and putting myself back in order before I went to the window and leaned out to reach for one. The closer to the flower I got, the bigger I realized they were. One flower was the size of both of my hands completely outstretched. Caressing the silky petal, I suddenly didn't have the heart to pluck one from the branches, as if I could feel the tree brace around me, expecting the pain in the same way I would brace for the prick of a needle when getting a shot. I pulled my hand back to me, clutching it to my chest, and turned back to Jensen, who was putting himself back together, getting dressed and running a hand through his hair.

"Well, you are an Earth Elemental and this has been your refuge for how long?" Jensen asked and made me think a lot more of him in that one question.

"Over ten years now," I said quietly, remembering the build and press of energy as we became closer and more intimate. Jensen walked over to me, placing his hands on my upper arms, making me raise my face up to look at him.

"You are at your most amazing when you let your guards down." He leaned in and pressed a kiss to my forehead. "It's one of the reasons why you scare the hell out of me." He smiled when he said it, keeping me from reacting. "Sometimes I'm afraid your energy, or your magic, or power, whatever it is, is going to rip me apart when it gets like that."

"It's never been like that before…"

"Not as obvious, you're right, but remember, just like you can feel wild emotions easier than everyday ones, I can feel magic and energy, kind of like a warning system." He raised a hand up and stroked my cheek with his thumb, leaving a thin line of heat on the skin that he touched. "It almost always feels like that to me, but because it's part of you, it's easier for you not to notice. I'm not sure why this was different."

"Long, stressful weekend. My defenses are low," I said, more to myself than to him.

"Probably," he said and just then the world went silent and the tree rocked with the backlash of a power strike, trembling the leaves and cracking the earth around the roots. Only Jensen's grip on my arms kept me from falling over. "What the hell was that?" Jensen asked, looking around frantically, but my eyes were all for the window behind him and the sound of a thousand tiny wings growing louder in the distance.

Chapter 10

"Jeremy," I whispered angrily, feeling my hands ball up into tight fists until my fingernails dug into the skin of my palms. The sound of furious wings were so close now, I was sure they were just outside of my shields and wards on the tree house.

"Jeremy? He did that?" Jensen asked, his voice a little frantic.

"Either him or those things that seem to be doing his bidding," I said, looking out the window at nothing since I still couldn't see them. "Can you hear it?" I turned and looked at Jensen when I asked, wanting to watch his face.

"I hear something," he said, shaking his head in confusion.

"What does it sound like?"

"Static maybe? I'm not sure, but it's annoying, like the buzzing of a lot of bees."

"Not like wings then?"

"No…" he said, furrowing his brow at me with a small shake of his head.

"Hmmm… well, you couldn't see Tegan or hear him clearly either. I was hoping if you could understand these better, maybe that would rule them out as faeries, but I guess not," I sighed, looking back out the window into the distance. The sound grew louder and then began to drift away and I had the mental image of a thousand tiny birds swirling away only to circle back and make a dive straight for my window. I had the momentary urge to grab Jensen and duck, but I steeled myself and found my center to reach down my line of power into the tree I was standing in and draw the energy of the earth below through the roots and trunk of the tree and into me. I pushed the power out and fed my shields and reinforced the wards and braced myself. Just as I sealed the last little bit of extra power into the outer most shield, another strike hit, rocking us back and making the tree tremble around us, but the shields held and the things were still outside unable to reach us.

"What the hell is happening, Shayna?" Jensen asked from behind me.

"Jeremy must've sent these things to punish me for pressing charges, but I don't think they can get through. So long as my shields hold, we should be safe." I was careful not to turn my attention away from the window, as if if they broke through my shields, I would be able to physically see it happen.

"Why aren't your parents coming out to see what's going on?" Jensen asked, looking out the window and down into my backyard. The backdoor was still shut as if no one could hear the battering ram that was hitting the tree.

"Maybe because it's magic?" I said, scanning the sky. The sound had faded again, but I could still hear it in the not too far distance.

"What does that have to do with anything?"

"Magic is all around us everyday. People learn not to see it, so maybe no one can see or hear what's happening right now. Or maybe it's only happening for us; maybe it's not loud outside my shields..." I stopped then, letting the thought run to completion in my head.

"Shay? What is it?" Jensen asked, leaning in to get a closer look at my face.

"It's not real, it's a glamour," I said, my voice just above a whisper.

"What do you mean it's a glamour? Isn't that for changing your looks?"

"More like other people's perceptions," I said quickly and went to the window, looking down at the ground with my new knowledge and, sure enough, the ground around the tree roots was no longer cracked and crumbling. "It's a glamour, a spell; this isn't real," I said the last a little louder and felt the energy in the air shift, as if hesitating. "They're trying to find a crack in my shields, so they're trying to scare me into thinking they're doing something violent, but they're not!" I yelled the last out into the air and, like the flipping of a switch, the sound stopped and the air stilled. They were gone.

"How did you do that?" Jensen asked from my side.

"I broke the spell," I said simply.

"How though?"

"With glamour magic, once you know it's glamour, the caster can't keep the illusion in place. It depends on who ever you're casting against believing in the spell. I saw it for what it was and didn't believe in it anymore," I explained.

"That seems kinda simple," he said skeptically.

"You're right, that's because it is simple," I said, spreading my hands wide in front of me with a shrug of my shoulders. "I really can't give you a better, more complicated answer. It is what it is." He was still looking at me like I keeping something from him. "Okay, look, you know what I look like right?"

"Right," he said slowly.

"You know my hair is auburn and I have green eyes and fair skin, so say I wanted to change one or all of those so you wouldn't recognize me, but then I said something and you recognized my voice. You'd know it was me right away and then you'd realize I had altered my looks and the spell would break," I explained, shrugging. "So long as you don't realize it's a spell, it holds, but once you know you can't unknow it, get it?"

"I think so. I guess it just seems too easy," Jensen said.

"That's the thing with magic; it *is* easy. It used to be part of our everyday lives, even if all someone did was ward their house or bless their garden. All of it was everyday for people." I turned and looked at him then. "Then all of a sudden, you get different religions wanting to control people and the first thing they do is adopt some of the basic beliefs and High Holy days of the people and eventually you tell them their beliefs and practices are heresy and bad so people stop doing them. Eventually, they forget how to do it and finally it's all fairytales."

"Okay, well, back to the situation at hand," Jensen said. "If this couldn't do anything to you, why do it at all? It seems pointless."

"Not if he thought it would scare me. He may not be able to really do anything powerful enough to actually hurt me, so he tried to scare me instead," I said.

"I don't know," Jensen said looking out the window in the direction the sounds had come from.

"What is it? What are you thinking?" I asked him.

"Well, you said those things were strong enough to pick you up at the store right?"

"Yeah…"

"So they have the power to do something physical and instead of doing anything to you, they throw a glamour? Just doesn't make sense," he finished, shaking his head.

"Maybe he's not trying to hurt me-"

"Shayna, he tried to throw you from a balcony in front of a few dozen people. I don't think he has any hang-ups about hurting you," Jensen said quickly.

"What's your point?"

"My point is he wants to hurt you, otherwise he wouldn't have tried to kill you earlier today. Maybe these things need him around to be able to be at full force?" He nodded then, as if agreeing with himself, and I realized he wasn't so much talking to me as figuring out his hypotheses out loud. "Or maybe he didn't know he couldn't hurt you with those things from a distance?"

"Well, he'll know the answer to that one now," I said.

"Yeah, he will. Maybe he didn't believe you that you could help him, that you knew what you were talking about? So either he'll be more receptive to you or even angrier now."

"Oh that's great, because he was so calm and collected before." I walked back over to the window, bracing my hands on the sill. I leaned out to breathe in the heady perfume of the new flowers.

"You know there is one other possibility," Jensen said carefully. I heard him closer behind me now than he had been a moment ago.

"What's that?" I asked, turning around and leaning against the edge of the sill, crossing my arms over my chest.

"Well, it seems like an awful lot of trouble to go to just to scare you. Maybe he was trying to distract you," he said, taking the half step needed to close the distance between us. He put his hands on my shoulders and leaned down to press our foreheads together.

"Distract me from what?" I asked, automatically lowering my voice because his face was so close to mine.

"I don't know, but it just makes more sense to go through all that trouble if he was trying to keep you from noticing what he was really up to. After all, you said that faerie queen warned you he meant to do someone harm, right?" I nodded, making him nod with me as I thought about what he said. It did make sense.

"If you're right, he's doing something to someone right now," I sighed, my breath coming back at me in a warm whisper. It was near dark now, the shadows grown thicker in the tree house. If Jensen's face hadn't been right up to mine, I might not have been able to see him. "And I have no idea who he could be doing whatever it is to, wherever he is." My voice sounded as defeated as I felt.

"I'm sorry," Jensen whispered, turning his face to press a kiss to my cheek, just under my eye.

"What for?"

"If I had better control over whatever it is I can do, I could probably help you better." He stood up straight and I saw the regret in his face.

"Jensen," I said, reaching a hand up to his face to keep his gaze on my face, "I have a feeling your abilities wouldn't help us now anyway."

"Why not?"

"Because it seems like they only manifest clearly enough for you when someone important to you is involved," I explained.

"How do you know that?" he asked.

"I can't be sure, obviously, but today made me think so. You were really buzzing with power last fall and both me and your twin brother were involved in that. And then today, with me in danger at the bookstore. But the other day in the store, that guy almost shot Deb and you didn't even have an inkling anything was wrong and you were there." He started to open his mouth to say something and I could feel it was going to be defensive. I stopped him by putting a hand up. "You like Deb just fine, but she's not extremely important to you, not like us, you know?"

"Yeah, I think I do," he said, but not like he liked it.

"That could be just for now though. With practice and effort, you could be as good as any clairvoyant." I reached up with my other hand so I was cupping his face between them and pulled him down into a kiss. "Don't feel bad, Jensen. It's actually a really common ability; most mothers develop it. If you can't ever have your powers work for any one but those that mean the most to you, then that's not a bad thing really. Kind of like a guardian angel for your friends."

"Some guardian angel. I can't seem to get to whoever needs me in time." He pulled away from me and took a few steps back. I watched his face close down to hide his emotions. "It's almost like I get the visions just in time to be late. What good is that?"

"That's right now, Jensen. If you start working on it, and I mean working on it for real, not just reading books and trying to figure out what it is or isn't, then I'm sure you'll be able to figure out a way to channel your visions better, sooner." I watched the emotions run across his face; he always seemed to have a harder time hiding his emotions than I did. "But right now, we don't have time for this. We need to find out why Jeremy sent those things after me if they weren't meant to hurt me." Jensen looked up at me and I realized he looked a little embarrassed. "What's wrong?"

"You are so good at focusing on the bigger picture; it makes me feel so childish, so damn selfish." He laughed a little and shook his head, visibly clearing his mind. "What do we do first?"

A half an hour later Jensen, Jodi, Steven and I were sitting in my car, parked on the dimly lit street that Jeremy's family lived on. We had all been to enough of Jimmy McCormack's parties over the last couple of years to know where they lived. Strangely, both their parent's cars and Jimmy's car were parked outside the house. Jimmy had a very steady girlfriend, Cindy Wright, class president and too pretty for high school, and it was Saturday night, they should have been out on a date. There wasn't a third car for Jeremy because he hadn't done anything to make his dad think he deserved one. Jimmy got his truck on his sixteenth birthday, right on schedule for the pretty-boy jock. Who cares if he was barely passing most of his classes?

I expected to see Jeremy's mother's car to be missing from the rest, waiting at the station until the bail paperwork finally went through and they released Jeremy. "I guess his dad bullied his mom enough to stay home until the jail calls to tell them Jeremy's released," Jodi said, echoing my thoughts.

"Yeah, I guess so," I said.

"So, what are we doing here? I mean, what were you expecting?" Steven asked over the back of my seat.

"I dunno, maybe it's nothing here. I guess I kinda expected him to be home already," I answered, looking out the window past Jodi who was sitting up front with me.

"Oh no, ten hours minimum and it's usually twelve hours on average before someone is bailed out," Jodi said with a shake of her head. "Maybe we need to go to the jail then?" she suggested.

"Yeah, maybe," I said but something told me not to leave. Something was wrong here, but from the outside, I just couldn't see what it could be.

"Come on, Shay, let's go down to the jail. If it has anything to do with Jeremy, you know that's where he is," Steven urged, reaching over to touch my shoulder. I finally agreed and drove us the short trip across town until I was pulling into the parking lot of the police station. It was past eight, which meant the station would only be open for less than an hour.

"Now what?" Jensen asked from the back.

"We go inside," I said simply, opening my door and stepping out.

"And do what?" Jensen asked as he followed Jodi out on the other side of the car.

"I have no idea," I replied and started across the parking lot to the visitor's entrance.

"At least we have a plan," Steven said as he followed me and Jodi, with Jensen beside him. I pushed the door open, holding it behind me so it wouldn't fall closed on Jodi, and let go once I knew she was right behind me. We walked straight up to the woman at the counter and asked to see Jeremy McCormack.

"Visiting hours are over," the lady said in a clipped voice.

"I understand that, but I was hoping we could just have five minutes with him?" I fed the smallest amount of sympathy out of me and into her and watched as the suspicious frown lines in her face softened into something prettier, a shadow of the loveliness that she once was twenty or thirty years ago.

"Well, I'm sure I could ask Officer Adams if it would be okay, just this once." She said the last with a conspiratory wink and smile.

"Do we need to involve Office Adams?" I asked quickly before her fingers found the call button she was reaching for.

"Oh yes, dear, you have to be escorted through the station. We can't have four teenagers wandering through here." She shook her head at me and pressed the button and spoke into a speaker I couldn't see, requesting Officer Adams. I felt my stomach knot up immediately and felt the tension flowing off of my three companions like fire ants on my skin.

"Calm down or you all are going to send me screaming out of here," I whispered at them, my voice sounding very closely to a hiss.

"Sorry, babe," Jodi said and I watched her try to collect herself, but the air didn't shift around me to make me more comfortable. As a matter of fact, as soon as we heard the heavy footfalls of the officer coming closer, my skin felt like it was alive with angry little welts and I was forced to put up stronger shields against them and cut them off from me. Jensen made a face as if he could hear something in the distance, but both Jodi and Steven turned stunned and hurt faces towards me.

"I told you guys to calm down," I said quickly and quietly before Officer Adams was in earshot.

"How can I help you guys?" Officer Adams asked as he closed the last few feet between the five of us. "Did you finally go see a doctor and have more injuries to report?"

"Oh no, no, we're fine," I said deciding to take the lead since this was my idea. "We were actually hoping to talk to Jeremy?" I didn't mean for it to sound like a question.

"Shayna, I already told you, that's not going to happen. He attacked you. We can't have you in the same room with him." The one thing I liked about Officer Adams was that he remembered he wasn't that much older than me, so he didn't speak to me like a child or a wounded little girl; his voice was as matter of fact as it would be if he was speaking to anyone.

"What about through the glass on the phone, you know, like during visiting hours?" Jodi asked quickly before I was reduced to pleading with him.

"Visiting hours are over," he said with a shake of his head and I realized I was going to have to break one of my cardinal rules when it came to cops for the second time today. I *reached* out to him until I felt the heat of his aura and tapped into it, creating a channel between us and started projecting at him. I watched his face go slack for a few moments while the feeling of total understanding washed over him. He furrowed his brow at me and then at Jodi. "Well, I don't see why that would hurt anything. Yeah, sure, it's not like there's a ton of people on right now, just me and my partner." He turned without waiting for us and started walking back the way he had come.

Did you just do what I think you did? Jodi's yellow thoughts drifted into my mind like my own thoughts.

Shut up, I thought back at her and had the feeling my thoughts were bright green in her mind. She smirked at me and let her hand fall away from my arm. We followed Officer Adams down a hallway and around a corner to a flight of stairs I would have never known were there that led down instead of up. We went down to the floor below and through another corridor and around more corners until I knew there was no way I would find my way out on my own. Finally the smell hit me; a strange combination of industrial cleanser and something sour, like candy gone wrong. I reinforced my shields as we walked because I could feel the press of fear and anger growing stronger as we neared a door with a small rectangular window. Officer Adam had to unlocked the door before we could step through.

"Okay," Officer Adams said, stopping in front of another door just feet away from the one we'd just come through. "Now, only one of you can go in and talk to him at a time and, since it's after hours, I really can only let one of you talk to him at all."

"That's fine, I'll talk to him," I said, stepping forward and away from my group.

"Are you sure? I mean, you're the one he attacked," he asked, clearly not understanding my decision. I glanced back towards Jodi and Steven and they both gave me a small nod. I turned my attention back to Officer Adams and started feeding him an extra dose of understanding laced with the desire to help me. His face clouded over and for a moment he looked utterly confused, but he just turned around and unlocked the door and held it open for me.

I was sitting on a metal stool in front of a small counter with a Plexiglas window in front of me with a phone to one side of me. The space was smaller than your average stall in a public bathroom. I was concentrating very hard on not freaking out and letting my claustrophobia take over. I don't have bad claustrophobia. I can handle elevators just fine, but this was more than a little creepy. I heard the slam of a door and looked off to the right and watched as Officer Adams led Jeremy to the stool in front of me on the other side of the window. Jeremy looked from me to Officer Adams quickly, completely confused. Officer Adams just shrugged at him and walked away to the door, stopping just to the side of it, not leaving the room.

I picked up the phone on my side and held it to my ear, waiting for Jeremy to do the same. He stared at me for a few tense moments, not moving. He finally picked up his phone and leaned in closer to the window. "I don't get it, what are you doing here?" He asked.

"I told you in the bookstore, I just wanted to talk to you. If you'd let me, I can help you," I said, careful of my tone, but still letting an edge of frustration leak through.

"I shoved you over the balcony. I tried to kill you. Why do you want to help me?"

"Because I think you've gotten yourself into something that you don't know how to control and maybe my friends and I can help you out of it," I said, letting my voice soften.

"You have no idea what I'm into," Jeremy said in a distant voice.

"I think I do," I said, drawing his attention back to me. He gave me a look that clearly said he didn't believe me. "It's all magic, Jeremy, all of it. Whatever those things are that you think are helping you, you flying off of the balcony outside the store, everything, it's just magic." He blinked at me, at my boldness and his jaw went slack, letting his mouth hang open.

"How did you... What are... How?" he stuttered at me.

"See, Jeremy, if you had just let me talk to you, rather than freaking out every time, then maybe we could have avoided this whole ugly thing," I said and again I had to catch myself before my voice betrayed just how annoyed I had been with him. "I understand these things are kinda scary when they're new to you, but you can't let your emotions get away from you like that."

"That's the thing though," Jeremy said suddenly, sitting up and inching closer to the glass and lowering his voice as he spoke into the phone. "I'm not sure that's all me, the freaking out, I mean." He stopped and glanced over his shoulder at the officer, but he was still standing sentinel by the door. "See, I'll get upset, maybe mad, but nothing out of the ordinary and then all of a sudden it's out of control and I'm just furious and then my faeries show up to help me-"

"Your faeries?" I asked, interrupting him.

"Well, yeah, I mean you knew, didn't you?" he asked, his eyes going wide as if afraid he'd over-shared.

"No, no, I knew there was something, but I didn't think they were faeries, that's all," I said quickly, lifting my free hand as if I could pat his arm to reassure him. I watched as he visibly relaxed and collected himself. He leaned towards the window again.

"Oh, okay. Yeah, they tell me they're faeries," he said, shrugging his rounded shoulders. I nodded, urging him to continue, not wanting to say anything else that might upset him again. "I really am sorry about today. I really don't know what was wrong with me. I just kinda lost it and then you were there in front of me and I felt trapped. I don't know why though…" His voice drifted off and I got the impression that he was really talking more to himself than to me.

"And then the faeries showed up," I said and he nodded slowly at me. "And that's how you survived that jump from the balcony." He nodded again. "So, you show a little emotion and these things come flying to your side and whatever emotion you're feeling just gets worse?" He just nodded again, almost in a trance.

"I hate this, I really hate this," he whispered urgently and I saw in the overhead lighting his eyes shimmered behind unshed tears. I had made sure to completely block out his emotions just in case he got out of control again, so the sight of those sad little tears took me by surprise. "My dad's always hated me because I wasn't like Jimmy. Jimmy's always hated me because he does whatever dad does. Mom…" He blinked back the tears and shook his head. "Well, mom's weak. I just…" He took a deep breath and I continued to hold mine, not wanting to say anything to scare him off. "I just wanted to be special, you know? I've always been so average, so normal. Not just not special enough, just not special at all."

"Most people who have normal lives live for moments of wonder, Jeremy," I said. "Me, magic is everywhere in my life, so I live for moments of normality." He just stared at me, blinking, uncomprehending. "Jeremy, no one is entirely happy with their lives, no one. If someone says they are, then they're either lying or are in denial. But whether you're normal or *special* by your father's definition, either way you have problems, it's just a matter of which problems you get. But the more special you are, usually the bigger problems you have. Trust me, I know."

"Yeah, like crazy people trying to kill you in a bookstore," he said with a smirk and, for the first time, I saw what Jeremy could have always looked like had his father and brother not been there his entire life to beat him down. When he smiled, his eyes actually sparkled, making the gray of his irises look like quicksilver. Color flushed his cheeks, making his skin look fair rather than pale. He could have been cute enough, maybe not handsome standing next to someone like Jimmy or Jensen, but he could've held his own just fine. I could see then that if he found even a small measure of happiness, he'd be one of those guys that grows up to look handsome and distinguished in the decades to follow.

"Listen, Jeremy, I'm really sorry I got you arrested. I really was just trying to help you, but there were so many people around that saw what you did-"

"Don't apologize, Shayna. If it had been the other way around, I would have been livid," he said, dismissing what I'd said.

"Okay, if you say so, but listen, I was serious when I said I wanted to help you. If you let me help you, I would be willing to drop the charges," I said, leaning in and lowering my voice as if I could whisper to him through the glass.

"Why are you so determined to help me? I've been nothing but an ass to you," he asked.

"Because you need someone to help you. So many people don't get the help they need when their powers or abilities manifest and they eventually lose control of them. More often than not, those poor people get labeled as crazy. If I can help stop that, then I will." I watched him study my face, as if afraid I was trying to fool him or was looking for the trap I was laying for him.

"You're serious, aren't you?"

"Yes," I said with a nod.

"What about Jodi? Would she drop the charges too?" I could tell he was trying to control his voice, but the doubt was there nonetheless.

"I think I could persuade her to," I said carefully.

"It's tempting to say 'no' so they'd throw me in jail and I could just get away from my dad," he said, lowering his eyes not to look at me.

"Yeah, he seems like a real nice guy," I let the sarcasm drip from my voice.

"You met him? When?"

"Earlier today. He was leaving at the same time we were. He came up to talk to my dad and apologize for everything," I shrugged at the end, trying to make light of the situation.

"I bet he had a lot of nice things to say about me." He shook his head and I saw his shoulders round forward as he drew into himself automatically.

"No, I mean…" I started to say.

"No! Don't lie!" Jeremy snapped at me so suddenly that I jumped in my seat, nearly dropping the receiver. I glanced towards Officer Adams, who had stepped away from the wall as if he'd come over. I gave a firm shake of my head to tell him to stay. I could feel the channel still open between us, though it was thinning, so he stopped mid-step and waited.

"Jeremy, listen…" I said, but he wasn't hearing me now.

"He's always telling people what a screw up I am. He's always letting everyone know he isn't proud to be my father, like people will excuse him from blame for me being the way I am." His voice grew progressively louder as he spoke. I could feel his anger rising as if it was always just under the surface, waiting to be prodded to life. But, unlike other people, his cheeks didn't flush with color when he got angry. All the color in his face that had come with our conversation drained away, leaving a sallow, pinched look behind. "Jimmy! Jimmy's perfect and I'm everything he's not!" He slammed his fist down on the counter, the echo coming back through the corridor.

"Jeremy, calm down, please. I didn't mean to upset you."

"He's always doing this to me! Reminding me how embarrassing it is to have me as a son!" I looked up and saw the officer coming closer again, but I saw hesitation in his face, my earlier suggestions still working on him, but they were obviously starting to wear off.

I quickly peeled back a few layers of my shields and almost immediately felt the heat of Jeremy's anger against my skin, a dry and biting desert wind in the middle of summer. His eyes were wide and wild now and I had the fleeting thought that he wasn't even seeing me now. I *reached* out towards him until I felt his aura, just as I had done earlier with Officer Adams, but rather than feeling the heat of him, I felt something dark and pliable, sticky and slow. I had the sudden thought of cancer and realized his aura was coated in sickness, eating away at him just like his father's harsh words ate away at his self-esteem.

I calmed the churning in my stomach and pushed back the taste of bile in my throat and started to force my way through the black mass that coated his energy, trying to find him. It was too thick. I gave up getting through it and just started projecting sympathy and empathy to him, letting him know someone was here and willing to help. He turned those wild eyes on me and I saw the years of pain and anger burning out of them.

"What are you doing?" he asked me in a voice heavy with distrust.

"Trying to help you Jeremy," I whispered, careful not to break the channel we were forming.

"Lies, all lies, you're just trying to manipulate me too!" he hissed at me and then spat at the window, making me flinch, even though I knew the spit couldn't reach me.

"Don't do this, Jeremy," I pleaded with him, but he only shook his head and gripped the phone receiver so hard that white and red lines traced his knuckles. I heard the cracking and squeaking of the plastic just before the phone crumbled in his hand. I looked up into his eyes and realized Jeremy just wasn't in there anymore, but I still whispered, "Don't do this…" I was aware of Jodi, Jensen, and Steven behind me on the other side of the closed door, their anxiety like a weight on my back, and I saw Officer Adams moving forward towards Jeremy. I knew he was moving faster than I thought he was, but the world had narrowed down to just me, Jeremy in front of me, and the suddenly loud noise of a thousand thrumming wings.

Chapter 11

Three things happened all at once: Jeremy ripped the phone receiver out of the wall and slammed his fist into the Plexiglas window, actually causing it to crack; Officer Adams drew his Taser gun and fired, the sinister pins finding a home in Jeremy's leg, bringing him to the ground in a writhing, twitching dance; and Steven, Jodi and Jensen forced their way into the little booth I was sitting in, grabbing me from behind and pulling me out backwards. I heard the commotion of Adams' partner bursting through the door and rushing at Jeremy on the ground to handcuff him. I struggled to stand up with so many hands trying to lift me and I had a momentary panic attack from so much help.

"Stop," I said as calmly and clearly as I could and all three of them froze in place, hovering over me, not much of an improvement. "Back off, let me up before I panic or suffocate." Jodi was the first to move, grabbing both the boys by an arm and pulling them backwards awkwardly, but quickly, making them both stumble before regaining their balance. As soon as they had taken one step back, the air was lighter and easier for me to breathe. I pushed myself up and carefully got to my feet, assessing myself to make sure they hadn't hurt me in their rush to put some distance between Jeremy and me. I ached a little, I might have some new bruises in the morning, but I was okay.

"Alright, guys," Officer Adams said as he came into our side of the room. "You gotta go. I'm sorry, I didn't think he'd react that way. Kinda weird actually," he finished, shaking his head in confusion. He raised his hands up to usher us through the far door and out of Jeremy's sight. I could still hear him moaning in shock and pain from the fifty thousand volts of electricity and the bite of the silver pins.

"What do you mean 'weird?'" Steven asked as we made our way towards the door.

"Well, he seemed fine for so long and then, all of a sudden," Adams just shook his head again and reached for the door to hold it open for us to troop past him into the anterior room before unlocking the next door to let us out. We were walking up the stairs we had come down earlier before he looked at me and spoke again. "What did you say before he got so angry?"

"Um," I said, blinking at him stupidly, trying to go over the conversation in my mind. "Oh, he said something about his father and I told him we'd run into him in the parking lot earlier and he started going on about what he thought his father said about him and I was trying to tell him that didn't happen and he accused me of lying and then everything went to hell," I finished with a shrug.

"He reacted like a crazy person," he said and I realized he was watching my face out of the corner of his eye, as if waiting for my reaction.

"Isn't that a little politically incorrect?" I asked, making him laugh a sudden loud and brief sound.

"Shayna, I'm a cop. There really aren't any other people more politically incorrect than us besides Rush Limbaugh." And that made me laugh.

"Fine, I suppose you're right," I said, stopping at the last door that led to the parking lot and turning to look at him. "I guess he did react kinda crazy. Is that going to affect his bail?"

"Oh yeah, we're gonna have to call his parents and tell them what happened and keep him here. We may bring in a doctor and have him examined, find out if he's on some meds or drugs he didn't tell us about." He sighed and shook his head, reaching for his keys to unlock the door for us. Steven and Jodi went through first with Jensen following after, but he stopped when he realized I wasn't right behind him. I was torn; wanting to tell Officer Adams that Jeremy wasn't in his right mind, that this wasn't completely his fault, but at a loss for how I could explain that. I started to open my mouth to speak when he raised a hand to stop me. "No, Shayna, I shouldn't have let you talk to him in the first place. I'm not even sure why I did, but there isn't anything else you can do now, so just do me a favor and go home." His voice had gone from that easy candor that reminded us he wasn't much older than we were to that practiced cop voice that left no room for arguments.

"Thanks anyway," I said and stepped past him. We started walking toward the car. It was close to ten o'clock when I started up the engine and drove us out of the parking lot.

"That was insane!" Steven said suddenly from the back seat, almost making me jump and the car swerve. "I mean, he was almost out of there on his dad's dime and he throws it all away like that?"

"I don't think he meant to," I said, twisting my hands back and forth on the steering wheel, a nervous habit I had picked up. It seemed like I always had to drive when things started to go wrong.

"Then why did he summon the faeries?" Jodi asked from next to me.

"He didn't summon them. I think they just show up when they sense him start to feel some volatile emotion so they can feed on it and make it worse," I said.

"What are you talking about?" Jodi asked, turning in her seat so she could look at me.

"You know what a Banshee is, right?" I asked, realizing I had been thinking about this example since Jeremy started explaining himself.

"You mean the Irish tale of the howling woman who screams when someone dies? And her wail could, in fact, kill you?" Jodi asked.

"Yes and no," I said, turning onto the freeway to take the short cut across town to get to Jodi's house. "A banshee actually shows up before someone dies, like a warning to let everyone know what's going to happen. Some think that every family has their own banshee, like a family ghost that lives in an attic."

"Okay, what does that have to do with what happened to Jeremy?" Jensen asked, sitting forward like Steven to listen closely.

"Well, banshees are emotionally connected to people and with death comes strong, volatile emotions. Maybe these things are connected to Jeremy by his emotions and when he starts to feel something, they show up and it gets worse," I twisted my hands again, making the leather of the steering wheel squeak under my hands. "Maybe he has no control over these things."

"So do you think these things are a type of banshee?" Steven asked.

"No, no, not at all, but they're the only ones of the old Faerie Tales that I can remember that seem emotionally connected to a person. I mean it's easy to upset any faerie, but this is so…" I searched for the right words, "out of control."

Half an hour later I was sitting alone in my room over my circle of protection hidden under the area rug with my journal in my lap. I had started to detail the events of the last few days in my journal while sitting at my desk and felt a cold, creeping feeling on my back, making me uneasy, but as soon as I stepped into my circle, the feeling slipped away. It was more difficult than I had thought it would be to record the details about the faeries themselves, considering I only had sound and movement to go off of, not even having a feeling about what they may or may not look like. I was like a blind person, having to depend on my other senses to tell me what they were and what to do.

Just as I decided to meditate on the problem and had set my book aside and was settling into a comfortable position inside the circle, my cell phone vibrated loudly against the wood of my desk. I got up on my knees and reached for it as it danced close to the edge, threatening to jump off. "What's up?" I asked, seeing on the screen that it was Jodi calling.

"Turn on the news, right now, channel three," she said, quickly but calmly. I stood up and walked to my bedside table and grabbed the TV remote, turning on the TV and changing the channel as I walked back inside my circle. That creeping feeling was trying to slide its way up my back as soon as I was outside of it.

"Police are refusing to comment on the incident, but an insider has confirmed that one prisoner has escaped. Who he is and why he was arrested are still unknown," a well dressed field reporter spoke into her microphone with a serious face and almost angry eyes.

"Oh. My. God." I said, punctuating every word.

"I know!" Jodi said in a whispered scream.

"Did they say how they knew about the breakout?"

"There was a freaking explosion!" she said frantically. "There's a hole in the wall and he just walked out."

"But he was cuffed!" I said quickly.

"Dude, he blew a damn hole in a prison wall… do you really think handcuffs mean anything to him?" she asked, her voice dripping with incredulousness.

"And Steven thought what happened earlier was insane…" I said, staring wide-eyed at the TV screen.

"There's something else, Shay," Jodi said slowly, sounding a little afraid to tell me.

"What?"

"They said one of the officers inside was injured and they showed him being wheeled into an ambulance and rushed off." She said it all in a rush, trying to get through it as quickly as possible.

"Did they say who?"

"No, but I saw his face when the camera tried to zoom in and focus on him."

"Adams?"

"Yeah…"

"Damnit!" I swore a little too loudly and waited to see if either of my parents would be knocking at my door. When no one came, I let out the breath I was holding and let my shoulders relax.

"So do we go to the hospital or do we find Jeremy?" Jodi asked, reminding me I was still clutching the phone to my ear.

"I don't think there's any reason to go to the hospital. Even if we can get to Adams, what is he gonna tell us that we don't already know?" I said. I was already pulling on my jeans.

"Good point, but do you have any idea where Jeremy would be now?" she asked.

"No clue," I said, tying my shoelace.

"Great, at least we have a plan."

"That joke is getting old," I said and then hung up the phone, tossing it into my purse and rushing out the door. My parents were usually in bed pretty early by a teenager's standards, but my mom was in the kitchen sneaking a midnight snack when I came to the end of the hall.

"Going somewhere?" she asked with a raised eyebrow when she saw me.

"Yeah, if it's cool?" I said, making a show of checking my purse and trying to look sufficiently annoyed. "Jodi got into a fight with Jay and she just called asking for a ride,", rolling my eyes and shaking my head at the ceiling as if I were a parent praying for strength.

"Another fight? I swear those two get into it almost every other week," my mom said, reaching for something in fridge.

"I know, but you know how she gets. Now she doesn't want him to drive her home, but she has no other way to get home."

"Where is she?" My mom asked into the fridge and I realized I hadn't thought that far ahead. I searched my mind frantically for a plausible location that was far enough away that would put my mom back to sleep before I came home so she wouldn't notice how late I came back.

"State Street," I said quickly, remembering Santa Barbara's main drag, popular on the weekends with restaurants, movie theaters, and dance clubs, was my best bet.

"State Street?" My mom said, sounding shocked enough to knot up my stomach, and then she turned and glanced at the clock over the oven. "At this hour?"

"I guess they went to dinner and a movie and were gonna go dancing, so that's where she's at now," I explained, hitching my purse on my shoulder and reaching for my keys.

"I don't think your father would want you going all the way up to Santa Barbara this late," she said, but I could hear the uncertainty in her voice. She was close to the edge of either agreeing to let me leave or making me stay. How I played it would push her one way or the other.

"Well," I said, blowing out a breath as I jiggled my keys in my hand, carefully not looking at her. "I mean, if you don't want me to go. I don't want to go myself. It's just that Steven doesn't have a car, so he can't go get her and you know how her sisters are."

"What about her parents?"

"She's afraid her parents will get mad and they'll tell her she can't see Jay anymore if she's willing to get this angry with him," I looked up at her again, raising both eyebrows. "And you know all that'll do is make her sneak around with him."

"Yeah," she nodded, sounding tired. "You're right."

"I don't have to go. I can call Steven and see if he can convince his mother to let him borrow the car," I let my voice trail off and started to turn back towards the hallway.

"Ugh, fine," my mother said, defeat clear in her voice. I rushed over to her and gave her a kiss on the cheek before I hurried back to the door. "But try not to be too late, okay?" She said.

"Well, I can't totally promise that. It is Saturday night, traffic will probably suck up there, yanno?" I said carefully as I pulled open the front door and looked at her over my shoulder.

"Okay, just be safe and try to get home as soon as possible," she conceded, but I could tell she still had some argument in her that she was holding back. I waved and walked out the door, hearing her call after me not to speed. This ruse had worked in the past because Jodi and Jay really did argue like cats and dogs and when it reached a certain point, Jodi became the Queen of Silent Treatment and out right refused to let Jay drive her home. Too bad for him that if she drove, she was known to abandon him wherever they may have been. After that happened for a second time, Jay always insisted on driving when they went out as a precautionary measure.

Steven was already waiting outside Jodi's house when I pulled up to the curb. He stood up and climbed into the backseat as Jodi came out the front door. "Why were you waiting outside?"

"I didn't know what Jodi's story was gonna be and didn't want to spoil it by showing up if I wasn't involved in it," Steven explained as he settled into the dark backseat. Jodi was in the passenger seat in short order, pulling the door shut carefully, as if keeping it from slamming on purpose.

"Are you just sneaking out?" I asked, furrowing my brow at her.

"Basically," she said as she pulled the seatbelt over her. "My parents are already down for the night and no one else is home, so if anyone notices I'm gone, I'll just make up some emergency with you guys or something." Jodi shrugged as if it was no big deal. I decided not to argue with her about it, knowing full well after the episode in the bookstore today, her parents wouldn't be too happy with her just sneaking off in the middle of the night.

"Okay, where are we going?" Steven asked, leaning forward and bracing himself between the two front seats.

"I have no idea…" I said as I pulled away from the curb and headed down the road to round the corner and get out of sight of Jodi's house. "I don't think going to the hospital will do any good."

"Should we try his house?" Jodi asked.

"Do you think he'd be there?" I asked.

"Doubtful," Steven said with a shake of his head.

"We're not going to run around town in the middle of the night like crazy people calling Ollie Ollie oxen free!" I said, more than a little annoyed, and gunned the car forward, rounded another corner, and squealed to a stop in a parking lot by a city park that Jodi and I used to play in as children.

"What are you doing?" Jodi called from inside the car, as I was already halfway out and heading to the grass. I didn't answer; they were going to follow me whether or not I answered them. As soon as I stepped onto the thick grass, I felt my energy, my magic, shift through my body as if it was always looking for a place to settle and once I was on pure earth it found its place. I stepped on the heel of my right shoe with my left toe and pulled my foot free of it, doing the same with the left, and bent down to peel off my socks and dropped them to the ground. I was vaguely aware of Jodi and Steven behind me, feeling them as soon as they stepped onto the grass.

The cold night dew sent shivers through my feet and up into my calves, but it was a welcome feeling, bringing me closer to the blades of grass and the damp earth hidden beneath. I felt my magic singing through my body, pushing my blood to run faster and my heart to beat deeper, stronger, in tune with the Earth's heartbeat. Jodi and Steven wisely kept silent as I continued forward until I found the exact spot I was looking for When Jodi and I were children in this park, it was here where we first found our faeries and as we got older, we felt the natural magic we laid into the earth and air in this place. Something close to consecrating the ground, latent magic waiting to be called upon and used. I was going to use it tonight to find Jeremy.

My eyes were closed and my fingers were splayed wide, palms facing outward as I walked, searching for that perfect place. Behind my eyelids I could feel the night get darker, as if something took away the moon and stars. I had found the trees at one end of the park where we had played. In another moment, I felt the world shift and all the ambient noise fell silent. I had found it, stepped right into the middle of our secret place, and it was holding me still, asking me to take it, use it. I pushed through my body, down into the earth, grounded myself and found my center with a few deep breaths. I felt a circle of power tracing around me and knew without looking that Steven and Jodi were working together to create a circle of protection around me. Only years of practice and trust could forge this silent working knowledge between us.

I didn't know how I knew how to do this; it was just something inside me that was guiding me and I was following it unquestioningly. I waited until I felt the circle Jodi and Steven were making close. There is no way to explain how it felt once it was closed, you just suddenly felt more comfortable in your surroundings. When I was young, it reminded me of hiding under the covers when you watched a scary movie. Once under their warm comfort, no monster could penetrate their barrier. As soon as I felt that moment come, I knelt to the ground, digging my fingers and toes into the dirt, lowering my face to the grass and breathing in the fragrance. I stretched out my legs and lowered my body to lie on the damp earth and sank. Giving myself over to the power of the earth, it took me in, my hands sinking in farther and faster than the rest of me.

As my face became lost to sight, sinking below the surface of the grass and then the dirt, my breathing stayed as calm and easy as if I were still breathing air. I knew I wasn't completely lost to sight, but felt like I was wrapped in a cocoon of grass, dirt, and roots. It was then that I sent out my magic, pulsing through the earth, water, roots of trees and bushes, searching for Jeremy's signature. Unless he was flying, I would find him and know how to get to him. I felt like I was gliding through the earth, skimming smoothly like a fish through water, but I wasn't moving anywhere; it was my magic, that part of me that was other. I could feel it searching through the roots of trees, hidden streams of water and snaking to the surface, touching people on the surface with the barest of caresses, moving on when the signature was the wrong one. I felt like I was being pulled in every direction as my magic stretched further and further away from my physical body. I pulled back on some of my magic, reaching out to Jodi and Steven to anchore to them and felt better immediately. I was in more control and aware of both my body and the searching tendrils of my magic.

Just as I was about to give up and believe the impossible that Jeremy just might be flying somewhere, I felt the jolt of electricity shock through me and I knew I had found him. I concentrated all of my other senses on that one spot where I had found him to figure out just where that was. His flavor was harsh and almost metallic, like stagnate water left to sour in the shadows, and the bile rising in my throat was nearly enough to break my concentration. I knew where he was and, what was worse, I could tell that his brother was nearby.

We were racing across town towards Jimmy's girlfriend's house. Cindy Wright's parents often took off on the weekends, leaving the house free of parental supervision, trusting in Cindy's good grades and extra curricular activities to assure them that she never did anything wrong when they weren't around. Good thing for her they never decided to cut any of their weekend escapes short and catch their perfect little girl *en flagrante delicto* with Jimmy or any of the monstrous parties she liked to throw on Saturday nights. Since next weekend Cindy would be graduating, they decided to take off this weekend so they could throw Cindy a graduation party, to which we were all invited, us and half of the city.

Cindy lived in a house in the neighborhood those of us couldn't afford to live in called "The Hill." It was a large sprawling neighborhood set into the mountain range that bordered one side of town. All of the houses seemed to loom over the rest of us, checking on us, making sure we weren't giving them a bad name with our lower and middle-class manners. Her parents had made sure that, despite the odd configuration of property lines, their nearest neighbor was still a good thirty feet away, which was quite a distance in Southern California. The noise of my engine seemed magnified in the silent neighborhood, but I didn't feel so much as a pang of guilt as I tore up and around the hairpin turns until I was in front of Cindy's house.

"Gate's unlocked," Steven said as we were climbing out of the car. "Is that good or bad?" Neither Jodi nor I answered him as we pushed the gate open that towered feet over our heads and started walking up the drive to the front door.

"It's really quiet. You sure something's wrong?" Jodi asked, looking sideways as me as we walked.

"No, but just because you're paranoid doesn't mean someone's not following you, does it?" I said as I started up the steps leading up to the front door. Jodi didn't respond. If I was wrong, great, but if I wasn't and we hadn't acted, then we'd feel horrible in the morning. I balled up my fist and was raising my arm up to knock on the front door when we heard a muffled commotion inside, like a body hitting a wood floor. We all shared a look and I lowered my hand to reach for the doorknob. The cold metal bit into my hand, but it turned easily. It was unlocked. Now *that* wasn't good. I pushed the door open slowly, ready for an ambush on the other side. When nothing reacted to the door opening, I pushed it all the way open until it hit the wall, ensuring no one was behind it, before I let any of us step inside.

It was one of those grand houses that you don't really expect to find in California, with a large, open marble floored foyer that led in four different directions to various rooms through out. We walked into the middle, me facing forward and Jodi and Steven facing out, watching all sides. We waited, listening for another noise to tell us which way to go. My stomach was in knots, curled against my spine, and my energy was singing through my body, fast enough to make my fingertips burn with it, like built up static electricity waiting to shock someone. Off to the right we heard a giggle, distant and almost too quiet to hear, but it was there nonetheless. I turned towards it with Jodi and Steven next to me, staring at the doorway leading to whatever room Cindy was in.

If she's giggling, then nothings wrong... Steven's red thoughts drifted into my mind.

Why was the door unlocked then? Jodi asked us both. I felt both their fingers pressing into the small of my back.

Maybe they just forgot? Steven offered.

Yeah... I guess, I thought back at them and let my thoughts sound as unconvinced as I felt. I took a step forward, careful not to make any noise, and in doing so broke the connection between the three of us. I took a few more steps so I could lean forward and look around the edge of the doorframe. I saw Cindy and Jimmy in a tangle of limbs on an overstuffed couch. I looked around for any sign of Jeremy or anything out of place and nothing struck me as wrong. I leaned back and looked at Jodi and Steven and shook my head, letting them know there wasn't anything wrong. Jodi motioned towards the back of the house and I remembered the large, perfectly manicured backyard and followed her lead towards the three sets of French doors that led out from the dinning room.

"Okay, what do you want to do? Should we wait and see if he shows up?" Jodi asked me once we were outside and the door was shut behind us.

"He's here though. It wasn't that I could tell he was on his way, it was that he was already here," I said, hearing the urgent desperation in my voice for them to believe me.

"Shay, calm down, we believe you," Jodi said, echoing my thoughts. I looked around at the overdone landscaping and realized it was the first time I didn't feel at home outside, like the plants and grass were no more alive out here than the cemented patio and walkways. I had thought about reaching out to find Jeremy again, but knew instantly this earth couldn't help me. Just as I was turning to tell Jodi and Steven that, Jodi grabbed us both. "Do you hear it?" she asked in an urgent whisper.

"Oh my god…" Steven whispered in answer and I took the moment I needed to clear my head and then I heard the wings of Jeremy's creatures. I lunged for the back door and wrenched it open and ran through with Jodi and Steven on my heels. Just as we got through, the three sets of doors shuddered and all three locks turned in place. A moment longer and we would have been locked outside. We marveled at the doors for too long and then we heard Cindy screaming and ran for her. We scrambled into the living room, nearly falling on top of each other as we looked around for whatever was wrong.

"Oh my god!" Cindy screamed and half ran, half crawled to us from her position on the floor. There was a bruise already swelling over her left eye as if someone had back-handed her with a closed fist.

"Cindy!" Jodi yelled, rushing forward to help steady her on her feet. "What happened?" Jodi asked the important question while I looked around for where Jeremy might have run out.

"I don't know! Jeremy just came bursting in here and then before we could do anything, he hit me and I fell to the floor." The words spilled out of her in a rush, making them sound slurred. "I think I must've blacked out for a minute because then they were gone, just gone!" She was crying full out now, clutching Jodi's arms, nearly pulling her into a bow, so upset it hadn't even occurred to her to think it strange that the three of us just showed up out of nowhere in the middle of the night; for that I was grateful. A window out to the front lawn was open. It was a fancy window with no screen; surely flies and spiders wouldn't defile such a beautiful home.

I heard Jodi making soothing noises to Cindy, walking her out of the room and up the stairs, presumably to put her to bed. I hoped Jodi remembered the spell of calm I had taught her a few years ago when she couldn't sleep because of stress over finals, otherwise there'd be no getting Cindy to stay in bed and out of our way. That was the easy task. Finding Jeremy before he did whatever he was planning to do to Jimmy, now that was going to be a bitch.

Chapter 12

I'd like to tell you that we got in the car and raced to Jimmy's rescue. I'd like to tell you that, but life doesn't always work out the way we hope it will. We drove around for hours looking for them; Jodi attempting to invoke her Air magic to locate the faeries, me trying to sense them again by using the Earth. We even called upon Tegan to appear again and try to help us. But as the first few pink and white beams of light burst over the edge of the mountains off to East, we knew we weren't going to find them in time, if ever.

"I just don't understand how he's doing this!" Steven said angrily. He was gripping the back of my seat so tightly that his knuckles were red with the effort.

"Oh, I don't think he's doing it," I said into my dashboard, as I was leaning forward, resting my forehead on the steering wheel. "I think it's those things."

"Why don't you just call them faeries?" Jodi asked.

"Because I just don't think they are faeries. Maybe imps or something, but not faeries," I said, lifting my head and rolling my shoulders, trying to loosen the tension in them.

"Not all faeries are good, Terra. Hell, most of them aren't," Jodi said, giving me a confused look, knowing she shouldn't have to explain this sort of thing to me.

"I know that, Fae," I said her elemental name back at her with an undertone of frustration to let her know I had read her face correctly. "But none of us can see them or hear them properly. They don't behave like any faeries I've ever heard of, so if you don't mind, I'd rather not classify them until I know for sure." I watched as she shrank in on herself a little and I felt a pang of guilt for it, but I let it be anyway.

"Okay, whatever the hell they are, we need to find them. For all we know, they've flown off with Jimmy and Jeremy and dropped them off a cliff and killed them both," Steven said in a tone that sounded more tired that his words.

"Don't make jokes like that! For all we know, it could very well be what they're trying to do," I said, turning the key in the ignition to turn the car back on and head back to Jodi's house before our parents started to wake for the day and realized we were all gone. I dropped Jodi off first and then Steven, both sneaking into their backyards to get into their houses from the back. I pulled up in front of my house and decided to just be dignified and go through the front door. Luckily my parents weren't up yet. Despite how early they usually got up, it was still much too early for even them. I slipped down the hall and shut my door as quietly as possible behind me before I heard the first rustlings from my parents' room.

I tore off my clothes and grabbed the over-sized shirt I slept in and pulled it over my head and dove for the covers, pulling them up to cover half of my face and shut my eyes just as I heard my mom open my door, slowly, and peek in. She used to do this to Jodi and me when we'd have sleepovers as children, making sure we weren't staying up too late. She waited her customary fifteen seconds before being satisfied that I really was under the covers and not some wonderful lifelike pile of pillows and a wig. After she pulled back and shut the door, I felt the tension melt away from my shoulders and sleep pulled at me like a rip tide in the ocean, fighting it only meant it was going to drown you faster.

When I dream, it is difficult for me to realize that I actually am dreaming because they are so vivid and oftentimes I wake with vestiges of things that happened in the dreams. Last fall, I was pursued a number of times by a demon that always managed to almost catch me and in doing so would claw some part of my body and then I would wake with that injury. So when I let sleep drag me under in that early morning, I wasn't surprised to find myself standing on a beach, the sand gray with wetness and dim moonlight. The black and menacing waves were lapping gently on the shore, rolling back just before they touched my feet. A cold, salty breeze bit at my face as I looked around, trying to figure out why I was here.

I couldn't hear anything besides the constant lapping and crashing of the small waves, but that didn't mean I was alone out here; in the summer, the beach was a popular spot to camp out for our local homeless. I turned to my right and stared at the reaching expanse of the pier and contemplated going to it, knowing that some less desirable people may be hidden in its shadows. But as I looked left and saw nothing but a dark, deserted beach, I knew the pier was probably my best bet at figuring out what I was doing here.

I started forward, taking slow measured steps to make sure I wouldn't make any sounds as I walked, but I quickly realized I couldn't even hear myself moving. I looked down and saw that I wasn't making any footprints in the sand either, which was enough to stop me in my non-existent tracks. I tried to press my right toe into the soft sand and didn't even make a dimple. I looked around again and found that I was still alone, but suddenly had an irresistible urge to get to the pier and before I knew it, I was running full out towards it. I skidded to a halt just at the edge of the shadow the pier cast and, despite that momentary urge to get here, I just couldn't force myself to take that last step into the shadows.

I stood there, looking into the shadows, unable to see anything menacing, not so much as the form of a sleeping body hiding from the police as it took shelter, but nothing could make me summon up the courage to step forward. I looked up the beach and saw the distant form of two people running in sync with each other and I wondered vaguely what time it was, thinking it was too dark for a morning run. But as the two came closer and closer, I realized daylight started bleeding quickly over the mountains and down the beach, illuminating the water and coloring the damp sand from gray to a soft brown. I had never seen a sunrise come about so fast, but before I could think about it more, I heard a woman's blood-curdling scream.

"It's okay! It's okay!" a man said urgently and I turned to see the pair of early-morning joggers had reached the underside of the pier. The man was kneeling in the sand at the point where it met the water and the woman was standing back a few feet, peeking out behind her hands, not willing to see what the man was looking at. "He's not dead, honey, calm down and call 911."

I spun to face the man full on and realized he was rolling the body of a man over to drag him up out of the water, but as he slipped his hands under his arms, he moaned in pain and the man hissed, nearly dropping him in surprise. "His arm is broken," the jogger called back over his shoulder towards the woman. She had finally managed to get her cell phone out and called for an ambulance, having walked a few feet away from the water to speak to the operator.

"Okay, son, lets get you out of the water before you freeze your butt off," the jogger said, moving to the boy's other side and pulling him carefully to stand up and support most of his weight. They turned towards me and I held my breath trying to think of an explanation for standing there without helping, but they looked right past me, never noticing me. I looked from the man to the boy and felt my heart leap into my throat, nearly choking me. I was looking at Jimmy, beaten and bruised.

The world swam before my eyes. The water, sand, mountains, and people all ran together in a swirl of chaos and I thought I was going to faint. Just as I lost my balance, I woke in a tangle of sheets and limbs. I fought my way free of the mess I had made of my bed and crawled to the floor before I could stand up and grab my cell phone off of my desk. I dialed without thinking and only knew I had called Jodi first because I heard the feminine voice.

"He broke Jimmy's arm and tried to drown him!" I said in a rush, my voice still hoarse from sleep.

"What?" Jodi asked, her voice lost in her own fog of sleep. I coughed and cleared my throat before trying again.

"Jeremy!" I said urgently. "He broke Jimmy's arm and tried to drown him!" I was moving without thinking, grabbing clothes at random and fighting to get them on while cradling the phone between my cheek and shoulder.

"What? How do you know?" Jodi asked more clearly. Being shocked awake will speed up the recovery process every time.

"I just saw it in a dream. He was unconscious and washed up on shore under the pier. A couple of runners found him and called 911, he's probably at the hospital by now." I spoke a few of the words awkwardly as I pulled a shirt over my head while trying to keep the phone close enough to speak into. I never liked using the speakerphone option on my phone for fear one of my parents might be passing by.

"So then he's okay, I mean, technically anyway?" Jodi asked and I knew she wasn't moving to get ready yet.

"I guess so, why?"

"Well, I can tell you're trying to get ready and obviously planning to come get me and Steven and then what? Rush to the hospital?" Jodi said, using that tone of voice everyone uses when speaking to someone planning to do something completely stupid, like jump off the edge of a pier in a storm because it sounded cool at a party a few minutes ago.

"Well, yeah, of course," I said defensively, not knowing why I suddenly felt defensive.

"Shay, think about it, how do we know he's at the hospital? It is eight o'clock in the morning on a Sunday. We wouldn't even be up yet and somehow we already know Jimmy's in the hospital. What time was it in your dream?" I appreciated that Jodi didn't question the validity of my dream so I took the moment I needed to think back and get the answer to her question.

"Early, like sunrise, and since its summer, that's what? Six o'clock or something?" I said shrugging even though she couldn't see me.

"Okay, so he was found like two hours ago and we know about it even though we've been asleep? Do you want to explain that?" she asked and I knew she was snuggling back down into her pillows and covers.

"Yeah... okay, but we have to do something," I said and had to fight the urge to stamp my foot.

"I ah-ah-agree," Jodi said through a long yawn. "But we need to wait until it makes sense that we know about it. I'm sure my dad will be told and he'll mention it to me and then we can go to the hospital like good friends."

"Okay, but what if your dad doesn't say anything?" I asked.

"Then we'll think of something. You said his arm was broken, right?"

"Yeah."

"Okay, that's gonna take a long time to deal with. That buys us some time. Go back to bed, we've only had like three hours sleep. Take a few more hours and then we'll get together and try to figure out what to do," Jodi said, as rational as I usually was.

"How am I going to go back to sleep?" I asked, finally allowing myself to fall back to sit on my bed, feeling my body alive with unspent nerves.

"Because you have to. You know if you don't have enough rest, you won't be at your best and then how will you help anyone?" I agreed with her and let her off the phone without further argument. I didn't get undressed though, not wanting to admit that I had been hasty, but I did crawl backwards on my bed until I could lie back on my pillows. I had planned to stay awake and dwell on things, but sleep pulled me under before I could even start.

    Jodi's father didn't tell her about Jimmy in the hospital, not because he didn't know about it, but because he wasn't home when she finally decided it was time to get out of bed. It didn't really matter though; because the couple who found Jimmy didn't know any better and they had attracted quite a crowd by the time the ambulance arrived and Jimmy's blurred face was all over the morning news. We debated going to the hospital, not sure how it looked showing up, not really being friends of Jimmy. Luckily because Steven was on the Student Council and Jodi was in Band we could feign friendship by association.

    Steven had bought flowers in the gift shop so we wouldn't be showing up empty-handed. But when we got to the floor Jimmy was staying on, we realized we didn't have to worry about standing out. It looked as though half the school had shown up to see Jimmy and find out what happened. Jodi was carrying Steven's flowers for two reasons; one, so Jimmy wouldn't react poorly from getting flowers from a guy, let alone a gay guy, and two, so I could cling desperately to Steven's hand. I absolutely hate hospitals. There is so much pain and anxiety in them that the air, for me, was like trying to breathe through sand while tiny knives pricked my skin. I was holding onto Steven because he was so much a part of my life and we were so closely linked that I didn't have to shield against him, so I could use him as an anchor to help block out the masses.

    Sweetie, I don't mind being your rock, but seriously you're making my hand bleed, Steven thought at me. His thoughts, very calm, were a pale orange in my mind, rather than his usual deep red. He was trying very hard for me. I glanced down at our entwined fingers and realized my nails were digging into his skin, hard enough to cut half-moons into his hand. I gasped and let go quickly, watching as a couple of them welled with blood.

    "Oh my god, Steven, I'm so sorry!" I whispered, covering my mouth in surprise.

"Really, it's fine," Steven said, taking my arm and linking it through his, patting my hand as it rested on his forearm. "There, that should save me," he said with a smile. I couldn't smile; the momentary break from him had sent a flood of nausea over me, nearly making me faint. If Steven had taken a moment longer to take my arm, I would've ended up on the linoleum. We were waiting near the door for a shift in the crowd of people that had descended upon Jimmy's room. The nurses were having a fit over so many visitors, but Jimmy was one of the most popular kids at our school. Anything less would be unthinkable.

"How ya doin?" Jodi leaned towards me and whispered, touching my hand with hers, sending a gentle wave of cool air through my body. I realized her concern for my wellbeing was manifesting in her central power, a very interesting development.

"So long as I've got one of you, I'll be fine," I whispered back, returning her concern with my own surge of gratitude. I watched color fill her pale cheeks with the warmth of the emotion and she smiled at me again. I just couldn't smile yet.

"So, Jimmy, what the hell happened to you? We saw you being wheeled on a gurney on the beach." The three of us turned our attention back to the room when one of Jimmy's fellow baseball players asked the pertinent question we had come to ask.

"You know I really can't remember. I was at Cindy's house last night and then the next thing I remember, I'm waking up on the beach, half drowned," Jimmy finished with an awkward shrug. His arm was in a cast with a bar holding it up, straight out from the shoulder, the elbow at a right angle. The white plaster was already covered in a rainbow of signatures and messages from his many visitors.

"Oh come on, what are you saying? Cindy slipped you a roofie?" the same jock asked, laughing as he did.

"No, dumbass, I'm just saying I don't remember anything after that," Jimmy said, shooting the other guy a dirty look.

"Hey, where is Cindy?" some other random guy asked. I looked at Jodi then, asking with my eyes if she'd laid the calming spell too strongly, but she gave a quick shake of her head, telling me she didn't think so.

"Oh, she was here earlier, but she wasn't feeling great, so she took off. A headache or something," Jimmy explained. After that, the subject was changed to lamenting over the fact that Jimmy wouldn't be able to finish out the last big game with the team, but luckily for him, the college scouts had been around months ago and he had secured his scholarship to UCLA. Now he would just have to pray that they didn't find out about his arm before he had a chance to rehab it.

Okay babe, if we let this go on, we'll be here all day, Steven thought at me and with his direct thoughts, I could also read the underlying implication that he wanted me to use my empathetic abilities to clear the herd. I nodded, understanding, and took a deep breath as I closed my eyes to steady myself. I uncoiled my magic from my body, reaching out in a way that I could never quite explain and touched everyone in the room outside of the three of us. Suddenly everyone had the overwhelming urge to leave. Maybe they had plans they were late for or forgot something that suddenly had to be done right now. Those that couldn't be persuaded so easily were forced to feel suddenly uncomfortable and desperately needed some fresh air; they would never pick on anyone who suffered from claustrophobia again.

As everyone shuffled to say their goodbyes and file out of the room, we stayed to the side of the doorway, letting them all pass without really seeing us. Finally, we were alone with Jimmy. Jodi nonchalantly nudged the edge of the door with her foot, pushing it to fall closed before she stepped forward to talk to him. Steven slipped away from me to go with her, making sure to keep his attention on them while I turned to the door and traced my finger over it, murmuring a warding spell over it. That way any nurse or doctor who wanted to check on Mr. McCormack would just walk right by, missing the door until I broke the spell. I took an extra moment to speak a calming spell for my own sake, not wanting my empathetic abilities to interfere any more.

"Hey guys, I didn't really expect to see you here," Jimmy was saying as I turned and walked towards the bed to join Jodi and Steven.

"Well, we saw the news," Jodi said as casually as possible. Jimmy nodded as he looked at each of us in turn. Jodi set the flowers among all the other arrangements and cards.

"So you really don't remember anything?" Steven asked. We had decided I would do as little talking as possible, since of the three of us I knew Jimmy the least.

"No, man, it's really weird, right?" Jimmy asked and I realized I could feel tiny pricks of anxiety coming off of Jimmy every time someone pressed him for details about last night.

"I dunno, maybe you hit your head?" Steven offered and Jimmy nodded, his eyes going glassy, as if he wasn't really looking at Steven.

"Were you guys drinking?" Jodi asked.

"Actually, no, not last night," Jimmy said, as if he hadn't thought about that fact yet. "See, it doesn't really make sense. I mean, if we'd been doing something like that, I'd get why I couldn't remember, at least remember up until I wasn't at her house anymore, ya know?" Jimmy said, desperation dripping from his voice, the tiny pricks of anxiety becoming stronger, hotter against my skin. He wanted answers too and didn't have them. I felt for him, like a date rape drug victim waking up in the morning, not knowing who her rapist was or what exactly happened.

"Okay, guys, that's enough I think," I said, stepping closer to the bed and reaching a hand out to touch Jimmy's leg. Jodi and Steven stepped back, almost as if we had choreographed this. I started by opening a channel directly between Jimmy and me and began pushing calm and soothing warmth through him, letting him know he didn't need to worry. I watched as his face started to go slack as he gave over to the comfort I offered. It was so much easier than thinking about what happened last night, what almost happened. "Jimmy," I said softly, feeling the magic in my voice resonate like a bell through the room. He looked up at me, the trust of a small child naked on his face. "Jimmy, you have to remember," I said and he nodded slowly, never taking his eyes off of mine.

I moved up to the head of the bed, making sure to never let my hand leave his body, slipping up his calf, over his knee and thigh until I met his hand that was resting on his stomach, taking the route up his arm to his shoulder and stopping there. I leaned in closer to his face, keeping his gaze locked on mine and I knew he was in the trance I needed; not deep enough to be hypnotized, but just enough to be open to me and the memories he was suppressing.

"Remember, Jimmy, remember," I said, invoking a magic I rarely used. I didn't need to know who had done this to him, that we already knew, but we needed to know how and what had gone wrong. Someone doesn't wash up on the shore unconscious if you meant for them to live. His eyes clouded over and a spark of heat erupted between my hand and Jimmy's shoulder. In another moment Jimmy and I were standing inside Cindy's house. We could see the memory of Jimmy on the couch with Cindy, who was giggling, and the memory of me, Jodi, and Steven standing in the foyer of the house and hearing Cindy giggle. Now I knew why.

Jimmy was in a half pushup over Cindy who was laying on her back, smiling up at him. He was lowering his face towards her for a kiss when Jimmy, the one standing next to me, turned our attention to the window as it opened quietly and Jeremy came through with an agility he never exhibited before. Jimmy and Cindy on the couch hadn't noticed his arrival, which surprised me because I remember Cindy saying that Jeremy had come bursting in. I watched as Jeremy just stood there for a moment, watching his brother and Cindy, his face growing redder by the second until I almost expected to see steam burst out of his ears.

Suddenly Jeremy rushed towards the couch, his hands crooked into claws outstretched in front of him. Just then Cindy tilted her head up as Jimmy was working his way down her neck and she opened her eyes to see Jeremy closing in on them and she screamed as his fist came down and struck her face, explaining the bruise we saw when we rushed in. I could hear the three of us coming, but Jeremy only had eyes for Jimmy. He grabbed Jimmy and lifted him off of the couch with strength I knew he didn't really possess, knocking Cindy to the floor, and tore out of the room back through the window he came in.

Jimmy took me out of the house before Jodi, Steven, and I came to Cindy's rescue. We were standing in a fog, no road or sky to differentiate up and down. I reached out and touched Jimmy's arm, turning his attention to me. "Remember," I said, hearing my voice echo again, "even if you don't believe it happened. Jimmy, you have to remember."

The fog cleared, but it was still total darkness around us and I realized then we were hanging in the air above the ocean. I had to send more reassurance through Jimmy as I felt the first prickling of anxiety coming off of him. I had to be careful to keep him calm and in the trance, lest he break my spell.

"Shut up!" I heard Jeremy's scream rip through the odd calm of the ocean and turned to see him hovering in the air about fifteen feet away from us, holding Jimmy in the air in front of him by the front of his shirt. "Just shut the hell up!" Jeremy screamed again. "You have to listen to me now! You arrogant, spoiled brat!" He spit in Jimmy's face then and shook him violently. "Daddy's perfect little prince. Star athlete, handsome, chip off the fucking block, aren't you!" Jeremy screamed again and shook Jimmy roughly. "Let's see how well you throw a baseball without your pitching arm!"

I watched in horror as he tossed Jimmy into the air like a rag doll and caught him by his right hand. Jimmy screamed as I'm sure Jeremy nearly ripped his arm out of the socket. My stomach churned as he pulled at Jimmy's arm and grabbed it with his other hand just at the elbow, holding it at a right angle and brought all of his weight down on it with his knee and, even over the sound of the ocean, I heard it break in a sickening crack.

Jimmy screamed long and loud, drowning out Jeremy's laughter as he tossed Jimmy in the air again and caught him around both upper arms. A look came over Jeremy's face that contorted his features into something so ugly, so evil he didn't even look like himself anymore. He nodded, as if answering someone we couldn't hear, but I knew Jimmy was only crying in pain and not speaking. Jeremy's left hand convulsed around Jimmy's upper right arm and, with another loud crack, Jimmy screamed afresh in agony and Jeremy simply let him go, dropping him to the water below. "Can't be daddy's perfect little prince if you're dead," Jeremy said, softer than he had said anything else and was just suddenly gone.

I came back to myself in the hospital room, my hand still resting gently on Jimmy's shoulder. Jimmy's eyes were still unfocused and distant, not yet out of the trance. I leaned in close to his face and whispered, "You will forget this." Jimmy nodded slowly. "Sleep now, Jimmy, sleep and wake feeling calm and rested." I pushed calm, soothing emotions over him with my words, waiting until his slow blinks stopped and he drifted off to sleep before I broke contact with him and stepped away.

Once outside, I told Jodi and Steven what I had seen with Jimmy and, more importantly, that I didn't know where Jeremy had gone off to, but at least we knew why we couldn't find him again last night. We knew why he had gone after Jimmy and that he really was trying to kill him. Seventeen years of competition and jealously festering away at his self-esteem had borne a hatred that was nearly uncontrollable. Now we just had to get to Jeremy before he got to his father.

Chapter 13

In another ten minutes, I was pulling the car into a parking space outside of Nancy's shop and hurrying inside. Deb was manning the front counter as usual and the handful of customers that came and went throughout the day were milling around the newly installed shelves, browsing the merchandise. I was glad to see Nancy had gone with wood shelving, giving up the extra glitter of glass for safety's sake this time.

"Hey kids," Deb said brightly, smiling with her whole face when she saw us come through the door.

"Hey, Deb, you got a sec?" I asked, lowering my voice so the nearby customers wouldn't hear me. Deb furrowed her brow at me for a moment and then seemed to look past me, but not at anyone else and I felt a small pressure start just around my shoulders and I realized Deb was reading my aura, a trick she liked to use when assessing a situation. She nodded and beckoned over the part-time helper Tony to come around and take her place. She led us to the back room, closing the door behind us after turning the sign on the outside over to let people know a session was in progress and we were not to be disturbed.

"Okay, spill it," Deb said without preamble and I did. We each took turns detailing the events of the last few days of Jeremy's erratic behavior, trying to take extra time explaining the non-faerie creatures he had helping him and what I had seen in the memory Jimmy had shown me. Through it all Deb's face remained calm, concerned, definitely, but calm, as if she wasn't hearing the same bizarre story we were telling her. Once I finished my part of the tale, she stayed quiet for a few more moments, staring at me as if she expected me to continue.

"Well?" I finally said, breaking under the pressure of her stare and silence.

"Well what?" Deb asked and I nearly fell back with shock.

"'Well what?' Are you kidding, what do you mean, 'Well what'?" I asked, my voice rising and I didn't have the emotion to spare to care about it.

"What do you want me to do about this?" Deb asked and I realized I heard a tone in her voice I'd never heard before, impatience.

"Deb, you feeling okay?" Jodi asked, stepping forward to get a closer look at Deb's face.

"Of course I feel okay," she said a little waspishly. "You know, other than the fact that I have three teenagers coming to me for help after they've realized they've gotten too big for their britches and probably have accomplished nothing more than making the situation more difficult for those of us with real abilities!" Deb nearly screamed the last, her voice continuing to rise and become more and more angry. We three shrank back as one away from her anger and this strange display of emotion. Deb was always the kind of person to never show anger or impatience. If anything truly upset her to the point to make her angry, she usually just resorted to tears. She didn't cry because she was weak, she cried because she cared too much, and if something made her angry, you could almost hear her heart break.

"Whoa, what the hell is this?" Steven asked, his face was mask of confusion.

"Yeah, Deb, this isn't like you," Jodi said carefully.

"What's not like me? Telling you guys the truth about yourselves? Telling you that you take advantage of me?" Deb was taking steps towards us, trying to push us up against the wall. Jodi and Steven complied with her physical demands, but I stayed my ground. I remembered our last lesson before everything started going to hell and reached inside myself for that bit of magic, finding it folded neatly like a flower at dusk and pulled it out of me and into the palm of my hand. "You think you're the damn Three Musketeers and you can handle anything, so in you go, charging to the rescue only to screw things up!" I was unfolding the layers of magic, opening it and letting it uncurl from my hand, reaching out towards Deb. I saw it swirling through the air, reaching for her, sliding over her shields until I found a break in their usually impenetrable barrier and waited for the smell and taste of cloves to fill my mouth. It didn't. There was nothing alive and electric about her power today. She was a live wire that had been grounded to be controlled.

"It's not Deb," I said calmly and carefully, despite the icy lump I felt forming in the bottom of my stomach.

"What?" Steven and Jodi asked in unison, turning their attention from her to me.

"Something's wrong, like she's possessed or under a spell." As I said the last word, I felt the air in the room shift, just as it had when I had broken the glamour outside my tree house and I felt my lips curling into a smile. Deb's usually serene face was contorting into something made of rage and just before I knew she was going to lunge, I was pushing away from the floor and throwing my body on hers. I heard Jodi cry out in surprise and somehow knew that Steven was turning to lock the door behind him before anyone could investigate the commotion in the room.

"What do we do?" Jodi asked, a little frantic. She'd come down on all fours, putting her face next to mine as I braced myself to keep Deb on the ground. She was thrashing about and trying to claw at me. I had to straddle her stomach and pin her arms to the ground by her wrists.

"Steven! Get her legs!" I yelled over Deb's animalistic cries. She was bucking under me, trying to throw me off balance. I heard Steven grunt and lose his breath. Deb must have kicked him, but the bucking stopped and she was just squirming beneath me.

"Got 'em!" Steven said with a little more effort than should have been necessary.

"Okay, Jodi, you need to find what's wrong," I said through gritted teeth.

"What do you mean?" Jodi asked a little frantically.

"Find something! There's either a charm on her or a mark or something supernatural attached to her. Find it so we can get rid of it!" I was yelling again because Deb was yelling louder and Tony was banging on the door outside, yelling to be let in or told what was going on.

"Everything's fine!" Steven yelled over his shoulder at the door. "We're doing a reading!" But Tony continued to bang and try to jiggle the door handle. Luckily Deb had the key to the door in her pocket, so Tony couldn't let himself in. I was biting my lip to keep from clenching my jaw as I held Deb down. I felt like she was gaining strength, rather than losing it, as she continued to fight both me and Steven. Jodi was scrambling around, checking Deb's pockets, her necklace, her rings, bracelets.

"God, how much jewelry can one person wear!" Jodi's cried in frustration. "I'm not even sure if I'm missing something or not!"

"Here, switch with me," I said quickly, nodding my head towards Deb's wrists. Jodi grabbed them under my hands, pressing her arms to the ground by her forearms and I slid off of Deb. She immediately started bucking away from the ground before Jodi could throw her leg over Deb's torso. I didn't wait for Jodi to get into position before I started looking over Deb's trinkets and tattoos, recognizing them easier than Jodi or Steven ever would. Unfortunately, nothing as simple as a talisman or mark was out of place on her body. I even went so far as to tear off her shoes and check the bottoms of her feet, but there was nothing there to find. I swore under my breath and shook my head. "Okay, it's something magical. I'm gonna have to find it and cleanse her." I stood up and turned towards the door to open it.

"What are you doing?" Steven yelled, bracing his foot against the bottom of the door, holding it closed.

"I'm going to tell Tony to calm the hell down and get away from the damn door!" I yelled down at Steven, nudging his foot away as I turned the lock in the handle. Steven resisted moving his foot away for a moment, but finally let me open the door just a crack.

"What the hell is going on in there?" Tony asked, his voice quaking with fear, and he tried to look over my shoulder into the room, but I held the door pressed against me so he couldn't see in.

"We're doing a reading, it's a little intense, but nonetheless private like any other reading, okay?" I said calmly and forcefully as I immediately started projecting towards him. I sent waves of reassurance into him and throughout the rest of the room, urging everyone to trust me; the people behind Tony nodded and went about their business, browsing the shelves. Tony stayed where he was, one hand still gripping the door handle, staring at me like he knew I was trying to do something to him. "Tony," I said, pushing an extra wave of warmth over him and watched as his eyes closed for a moment against my reassurance. The smell of jasmine was suddenly strong and heady in the air between us.

"Everything is totally fine. Nothing is out of the ordinary in here," I said, one more caress of reassurance and he began to nod in agreement with me, his eyes glazing over for a moment. "Good. Please try to keep people away from the door, okay?" I asked with a smile.

"Yeah, no problem, of course," Tony said slowly, turning away from the door and telling the patrons who were no longer lingering by the door to please have some respect for other customers' privacy. I shut the door and locked it again and traced my finger over the wood in a complicated pattern as I whispered an incantation to help bar the door and muffle any more sound from within. It wasn't fool-proof, but, like the charm I put on the hospital room door, it should make people walk right by the door, forgetting their interest in it. I turned to find Jodi still straddling Deb's stomach, one hand pinning her wrists to the floor and one hand clamped over her mouth to keep her from yelling while I was talking to Tony. Steven was lying across Deb's legs, putting all of his weight on to them to keep her from bucking and kicking anymore.

"Okay, we need to bind her, I think," I said, surveying the trio on the floor. Deb's eyes went wide with shock for a brief moment before they narrowed, trying to pierce me with a glare I never wanted to see directed at me again.

"Is that necessary?" Steven asked, craning his neck to look at me.

"Yeah, I think so. We need to look for whatever is doing this to her and I don't think she's gonna sit still long enough for us to do it and I can't do it with you two sitting on her." I paused, thinking. "I mean, what if it's on her back?"

"You're probably right," Jodi said as she moved her hand away from Deb's mouth to get a better grip on her hands. Just as she uncovered Deb's mouth, Deb started speaking in a language we didn't recognize. I dropped to the floor and clamped my hand over Deb's mouth as fast as I could move. I felt her trying to speak against my hand and a burning sensation began to sear the palm of my hand. I steeled myself and used my other hand to hold her chin to keep her mouth closed.

"Great!" I said angrily and thought furiously through my cache of spells in my memory, trying to remember a silencing spell, but for the life of me, I couldn't remember one. The best I had was a sleep spell and I needed tea for that.

"What was that?" Steven asked, looking from Deb's face to mine.

"I don't know," I said and I could hear the anger in my voice. "Nothing I want her to be able to finish. We're just gonna have to do this a little more roughly than I would normally like."

"Do what you have to do, Terra," Jodi said and I could feel the fear intermingled with confidence radiating off of her and I took strength in that. I closed my eyes and concentrated on Deb's aura, realizing now how thick and cold it felt, so poisoned that I felt it coating my hands where I touched her face. I pushed past the taste of bile in my mouth and opened the channel between us. Deb began struggling again full force against the three of us, but we were already tensed for her reaction and she was unable to throw us off. I began pushing healing, warm light, and love into her, flooding the dark, stagnate pollution that was poisoning her spirit and mind.

"Maiden, Mother, Crone, all three, from abuse Deborah is now free," I whispered into the room, invoking The Fates to release Deb from the manipulation and back to her own course. "From pain and suffering Deborah is free, as I will it, so mote it be," I began chanting the spell over and over again, louder and louder as Deb fought against us. Jodi and Steven joined me in the chant on the second time through, our three voices finding that practiced rhythm easily, intertwining until we sounded as though we spoke with one voice. I felt the ground start to tremble under me and the coffee cups on the counter by the teapot clinked together as they shook, the door rattled against the frame and Deb let out a howl of pain, muffled against my hand. We all held on, riding the wave of the spell breaking under our command, both Jodi and Steven had their eyes shut tight, trying to keep their concentration.

"By the power of three times three set her free, set her free," I started the chant quickly, braced against Deb's mouth. "By the power of three times three set her free, set her free." Steven and Jodi started chanting with me again and the shaking grew in intensity, rocking the four of us on the ground and a small sprinkling of plaster broke from the ceiling, dusting us like powered sugar, but we never stopped the breaking spell. With one last violent shake, we were thrown forcefully away from Deb, knocking us into the walls and cabinets. Deb's body shot up from the ground by three feet before she fell back with a thud, her eyes closed and her body limp, knocked out by the force of the banishing.

I got to my feet slowly, a little dizzy from the force of the spell, and walked over to the cabinet over the teapot and found some peppermint leaves. I crushed them to release the oil on to my fingers. I turned and knelt by Deb's head and waved my fingers under her nose slowly, wafting the scent until she began to come to. Shaking her head slowly and her eyes fluttering open, she raised a hand to her head and moaned in pain. I nodded towards Jodi and she jumped up and began making a tea to ease pain and settle a stomach, something Deb had made for us more than once.

We took Deb home after that, Steven driving her in her car following behind me and Jodi in my car. I'd called Nancy to let her know Deb wasn't feeling well and had fainted during a reading so she couldn't quibble about wanting Deb to finish out the day. The tea Jodi had made her helped to ease the headache and back ache she'd given herself when she fell to the floor, but she was still feeling the side effects of being casted on. I always laugh when I see those televised exorcisms and, when the miracle happens, the person is totally fine and ready to conquer the world, when in reality you'd be more ready to take a twelve hour nap after a half hour with your head hanging in the toilet.

We were sitting in Deb's living room, giving her the time and space she needed to collect herself and change into pajamas. I don't know what it is about the right set of pajamas, but after a hellish day, they can do wonders to make you feel better. I loved Deb's living room; it was exactly what my living room would look like if I had access to the inventory at Nancy's store. The furniture was all dark, rich earth tones and so overstuffed you felt like you were sitting on clouds. The tables were laden with crystals of all shapes, sizes, and colors; trinkets and magical tools scattered around them.

I had picked up an obsidian globe about the size of a softball and was rolling it around in my hands while we waited. Deb always encouraged people to pick up anything that called to them, knowing it was probably because they needed the help it offered. Obsidian was good for banishing and protecting against negative energies and the moment I took it in my hands, I felt lighter than I had all weekend.

Steven was sitting in an armchair by the fireplace, a worry stone clutched in his left hand with his thumb rubbing circles over and over it. Jodi was pacing the floor, not having grabbed anything to help calm her nerves, just crossing her arms over her chest and keeping her eyes down as she walked.

"That's much better," Deb said as she came around the corner from the hall into the living room and gave us a tired smile. As beautiful as I always thought she was, I could never figure out her age, knowing she was much older than she looked, but it wasn't until today that I finally saw those years in her face.

"Feeling better?" I asked, setting the black crystal globe back on its stand beside the couch I was sitting on.

"Exhausted, but better," she said with a nod, walking over to the matching armchair across from Steven and slowly lowering herself into it. "I am so sorry about that," she said with a shake of her head, not meeting anyone's eye.

"Don't apologize," Jodi said quickly, walking over to her and resting her hand on Deb's shoulder. "It wasn't your fault."

"But it shouldn't have happened. I still don't understand how it did happen." I saw the confusion in her eyes, mingled with a little indignation. I understood how she felt; of everyone I knew, Deb would be the last person I would expect to be vulnerable to something like a possession spell.

"Have you done anything different lately?" I asked.

"No," she said a little too quickly, as if she had been trying to think of that very same thing. She stood up and started walking around the room, adjusting books and items here and there, an obvious nervous habit.

"Are you sure?" I pressed, getting up from the couch and walking towards her. I rested my hand on her shoulder, happy to feel her normal, warm pulsing aura back in place. "Think, Deb, have you done anything lately that would open you up to attack?"

"Maybe…" she said finally with a sad sigh. Her body seemed to shrink in on itself, her head falling and her shoulders rounding forward. I waited for her to tell us what she meant, not wanting to press her too much. I felt Jodi and Steven stirring behind me in the room, their anxiety pricking my skin like needles. I raised my free hand towards them, silently telling them to calm down and stay quiet. "I've been helping my niece," Deb finally said, her voice not much more than a whisper. I wasn't sure that Jodi and Steven could hear her.

"What do you mean?" I asked carefully, making sure my voice only carried curiosity and concern.

"She's coming into her powers, but my sister never had any, so she doesn't know what to do with her. They called me last month for help to keep her under control and start training her." Deb looked up, turning her face towards me and I realized her cheeks were wet with tears. Steven came over with a box of tissues in his hand. Deb took a tissue and wiped her face dry. I led her back to the chair and helped her ease into it.

"What's wrong with that, Deb?" Jodi asked.

"Well, they live in Maine and you can't do much more than counseling over the phone." I heard her voice start to shake, so I took her tissue-free hand in both of mine and re-opened the channel between us and started slowly feeding her a soothing comfort, much like a hot cup of tea on a cold and rainy night. Her cheeks flushed and the color came back to her face. "Well, I've taught her how to Astral Project so we can really work together, you know, the best we can without being in the flesh." Dawning comprehension flooded through me with her explanation and I mentally cursed myself for not thinking of it sooner. "I can talk to her all I want over the phone, but you can't get practical experience by talking and, since my sister didn't get any of the gifts, she can't practice with my niece and how is she going to learn without practice?" I could hear the desperation in Deb's voice, willing us to agree with her.

I could Astral Project with the best of them, but preferred not to do it because of the inherent risks it holds. When you Astral Project, you have a sort of out of body experience. You send your spirit, no, not your soul, out into the other planes and you can communicate with others who are also here on Earth with us and have projected their spirits into an Astral Plane. Some people believe you can also interact with those who have already passed away or angels and even some more sinister entities. It is that last that keeps me from practicing Astral Projection unless it is absolutely necessary and training a fledgling niece does not fall into that category for me.

The danger in Astral Projection that worries me the most is the fact that you have sent your spirit away from your body, along with your consciousness, leaving your body vulnerable back in the tangible world. More than that, as careful as you can be, you're still risking your spirit's safety as well. Oftentimes, all it takes is just a simple touch from an evil entity for them to taint you, which as I sat there watching Deb's face, I knew was what had happened to her.

"Deb, when was the last time you went to see your niece?" I asked, keeping the tone in my voice in check.

"Last night," she said with a shake of her head. I could taste the disappointment coming off of her like pennies on my tongue. Instinctively, I reached behind me to the bookshelf and blindly grabbed an Agate stone. As soon as I touched it, I knew I had grabbed the right one and I placed it in Deb's hands. She looked down and nodded, with a small smile, looking up into my eyes. "The student is quickly surpassing the teacher, young grasshopper." I smiled at her and closed her hands around the stone; Agate is said to protect against evil magic and psychic attack and I knew as soon as I put it in her hand she'd even sleep with it trapped inside her pillow case tonight.

"I think it's time you just go visit your niece in person, at least until we get Jeremy under control."

"I think you're right."

"We'll sweep the perimeter of the house and reinforce your shields with our own before we leave," I said, stepping away from her and drawing Steven and Jodi with me. She managed a nod and I knew she couldn't trust her voice just now. She rolled the stone over and over in her hands, but I could still feel her discontent and disappointment in herself. There wasn't much more we could do for her. We walked outside and Jodi set to working on each of the windows and doors while Steven found her inner shield that was wrapped tight over the house. I stepped father out to her property line and began working on the shield set there.

Chapter 14

My plan to go see Deb had been to have her help us try and locate Jeremy before he caused anymore destruction. We had figured out that he was staying off of our radar by flying, but just because that reached the limits of my abilities that didn't mean it would stop Deb. Deb was also a head member of the local Wiccan Coven and had access to resources that we didn't. If she couldn't find him, we'd hoped she would contact her coven for help, but after the trial she just suffered through, I couldn't bear to ask her for help. Jeremy knew we were looking for him and was trying to keep us away by hitting me hard, by hurting those I loved. I had wanted to tell Jodi and Steven to forget this and put them under lock and key with Jensen, but I knew not one of them would let me get away with that. So we drove over to Jeremy's house under the pretext of coming to see Jimmy and pretending not to know he was in the hospital just so we could make sure their father was still safe and sound.

After walking through Jimmy's memories of last night and listening to the angry things Jeremy said, I knew he was punishing people who had hurt him in the past. The next logical target would be his father, but I knew that was the most obvious choice so there was still the possibility that he'd strike somewhere else just to throw us off, like he did with Deb.

We walked up the front walk to the McCormack's door and waited after pressing the doorbell. Steven was trying very hard not to fidget, as he so often did when he had to lie. The butterflies in his stomach were making mine churn to the point that I had to grab Jodi's hand and feed off her self-confidence and cool exterior to calm down. Just as we were about to give up and turn away, the deadbolt lock turned and the door opened a crack.

"Yes?" Mrs. McCormack asked quietly.

"Hello, Mrs. McCormack, my name is Jodi, we've met before…" Jodi said, letting the sentence fade, waiting for her to make the mental connection for herself.

"Oh, hello, dear," Mrs. McCormack said a little more comfortably, opening the door enough so that we could see her clearly now.

"We just wanted to come by and see how Jimmy was doing," Jodi said with just enough of a smile.

"Oh, I'm sorry, but he's still in the hospital," she said with a shake of her head.

"He's still in the hospital?" I chimed in, concern dripping from my voice. "We didn't know he was hurt that bad." I tilted my head ever so slightly, keeping her eyes locked on mine as I very carefully *reached out* for her, making sure she wasn't tainted like Deb had been. As far as psychic abilities, she was practically a null, which surprised me a little considering Jeremy's obvious abilities; powers and abilities are often passed through the maternal side of the family. But other than the utter lack of psychic awareness, she was clean, save for the despair and self-loathing that coated her very being, classic signs of a woman trodden down by her overbearing husband, just one step up from being beaten.

"Oh yes, they're keeping him for a few days. Considering they had to resuscitate him on the beach, they want to make sure there isn't any permanent brain damage," she said that last in a whisper, her voice failing her.

"Oh, I'm so sorry we bothered you, Mrs. McCormack, we had no idea," Jodi said, laying it on thick and taking a step back, making like she would steer us to leave quickly.

"That's alright, dear, you didn't know," Mrs. McCormack managed a small smile.

"Is Jeremy at home?" I asked quickly, as if the thought had just occurred to me. Mrs. McCormack blinked at me, showing her surprise at the sudden question. "I just wanted to see how he's doing; I know this was probably a shock to him." I added a gentle wave of appreciation to wash over her, making her smile at me, appreciating my concern for the less popular of the two brothers.

"After what happened between you two and you're still worried about him?" she asked, leaning out of the door, closer to my face.

"Mrs. McCormack, I would never have pressed charges against him if it were up to me," I pushed another wave of appreciation towards her and watched as her face softened under my ministrations. "That was really all up to my parents, me being a minor and all," I said with a shrug and let her feel the regret I was showing in my face and voice. She reached out and touched my arm tentatively.

"We haven't seen him in a few days. After he broke out, he didn't come home. We…" she took a deep, shuddering breath, "we just don't know where he ran off to."

"Well, if he does come back, just so you know, I don't plan on testifying against him, so that should help get him out of jail sooner rather than later," I said, patting her hand that was still on my arm.

"I'm afraid that may not matter now, after the break out. He'll definitely get time for that," she said with a shake of her head before letting go of my arm. "It was sweet of you three to come check on my boys, but I need to get dinner started now." We said our goodbyes and walked back out to my car.

"Okay," I said, turning in my seat so I could look at both Jodi and Steven at the same time. "I think we have a lot of work to do. We need to figure out what the hell these things are and how to stop them and where Jeremy's hiding and we need to watch Mr. McCormack in case Jeremy strikes before we're ready."

"How are we going to do all that?" Steven asked.

"We have to spilt up," I said with a shrug.

"No!" they both shouted at me in unison, but it didn't startle me. I knew they would hate the idea of working separately, but it was the fastest, smartest thing we could do at this point.

"I know you don't like to do that, but at this point, I don't think we have a choice."

"Shay, we can't leave you alone. Jeremy's already tried to get to you more than once. Who's to say you're not his next victim instead of his father?" Jodi asked and I could feel her trying to impose her will on me. It's a strange sort of emotion to feel a mix of stubbornness and anger. When you feel intimidated by someone, that's when they're using that ability. I invoked my will and imposed it on her and watched as she shrank instinctively back from me, folding in on herself. I reached out and placed my hand over hers. *Don't do that again,* I thought at her very clearly and she nodded, but was still pulling away from me.

"I know I just missed something…" Steven said quietly from the backseat, having fallen back as well when I turned on Jodi, feeling the tension building in the car. I reigned in my power and pulled it back inside myself, letting go of Jodi's hand and watched as she took a steadying breath.

"Now, I think the best thing to do is have Steven stay here and watch the house. Keep your cell on and call us if anything, anything at all, seems out of the ordinary. Jodi, I think we each need to try to do some research on these things." I stopped to try and think of the best plan of attack. I sucked in my lower lip and started chewing absentmindedly.

"Shay," Jodi said tentatively.

"Yeah?"

"Maybe we need to try and contact the faeries. I mean, they did contact you first and warn you, maybe they can help?"

"Yeah, maybe…" I said, thinking over her suggestion. "But I got the impression they had no intentions of helping us."

"Maybe while you try that, I'll try and contact some other faeries and see if they can't give us some ideas about what these things are? If not, then I could try to invoke my Air Element and see if I can't find Jeremy." I could hear in her voice she wanted to help to make sure I wasn't still angry with her over the power play we just had.

"Okay, that's a good idea," I said with a nod and I felt the air in the car ease, as if it were holding on to the earlier tension, waiting for it to come again. "Steven, you gonna be okay on a stake out by yourself?" I asked, turning to look at him and feel what he was really feeling in case he tried to lie.

"Yeah, sure. I mean, so long as I don't look like some creepy stalker." He tried for a smile, but it looked more like a grimace. The important thing was I could feel the sincerity in his words.

"Don't worry, we'll shield you so you'll blend into the background. Even if someone looks right at you, their eyes should just pass right over you," I reached out and touched his hand, feeding him a little comfort and extra self-confidence to chase away his fear.

We all got out of the car and darted back across the street and into the bushes that separated the McCormicks' house from their neighbors. We made sure we were out of sight from anyone passing on the street or may be glancing out of their windows. Once I felt sure that we were safe, I nodded to Jodi to begin. I crouched in front of Steven and laid my hands on the very edges of his aura, feeling its heat pulse against my skin as I connected with his energy on a deeper level than our everyday connection. The air around us began to shift, coming alive with an electric energy as Jodi began working on building a special shield around Steven.

I began whispering the incantation as I plunged my fingers into the layers of his aura, feeling Jodi's magic prickle around us, and watched as Steven's shape began to blur right before my eyes. As it became harder and harder for me to keep my eyes on his face, I knew we had accomplished the spell; had we not known that Steven was crouched on the ground in front of us, we wouldn't have been able to see him at all, dismissing him as easily as any other shadow in the bushes.

Feeling confident that Steven was safe, Jodi and I got into my car and raced away, back towards our own neighborhood. I left Jodi at her house to work secretly in her room trying to use her own Air Elemental abilities to try and find out any clues she could to tell us what we were dealing with. I agreed with her that there was no reason to completely rule out the possibility that we may still be dealing with a type of faerie that until now we had never known existed. Jodi had pointed out the possibility that there were shape shifting faeries, so it could be something we were familiar with and they were just concealing their true form, or at least what we thought was their true form. So I left her to it while I was off, back to my house to try and contact the faeries that had made contact with me in the first place. They had warned me once; obviously they cared about our welfare, at least a little.

I slipped into the kitchen while my parents sat in the living room, my mother reading, my father watching the news and reading the newspaper simultaneously. I grabbed a small bowl, the milk from the fridge, and the honey from a cabinet. After mixing the milk and honey together, I quickly and quietly made my way back to my room just to climb out my window into the backyard, careful not to spill any of the milk as I raced to the fence and climbed over, dropping down into the orchard behind our house. I took a deep breath of air, thick with the scent of oranges, relieved I'd made it here without spilling the milk or drawing my parents' attention.

I walked between the orange trees, the waxy leaves brushing against my arms as I made my way through the rows until I had gone deep enough not to be seen by the houses that ringed around the edge of the orchard. I found the spot that I had been led to by Tegan and felt the slight difference in the energy here than anywhere else in the orchard. When magic has been performed in any way, it leaves a mark behind, whether in the air or ground or both. If you are in tune with nature and magic, you can feel it, taste it, almost see the difference when it is left behind.

 I sat on the ground, settling myself as comfortably as I could and set the bowl of honey milk on the ground in front of me. I closed my eyes and took a deep, grounding breath, finding my center and opening myself up to the earth below me and the air around me, surrounding myself in the energy. I *reached out* to the signature in the air, pulling it around me and calling out to the faeries that had left the signature behind. I could feel the answering pull of the faeries when I summoned them to me, acknowledging me, but they did not come.

 They knew who was calling to them, knew that I had brought a present as payment, and yet, they still did not want to come. I tried again, begging for their presence, hoping a little humility would speak to them, and yet, nothing. After what I thought must have been at least an hour had passed and not even an inkling of an answer, I let my shoulders fall and slumped forward, hanging my head, feeling the first pangs of a headache coming on.

 "Seriously?" I looked up, asking the emptiness around me, feeling my growing frustration, trying to keep it in check, knowing how fickle the fae folk were and would only delight in my baser human reaction. "Okay, fine," I said, rolling my shoulders to release the tension I was building there. "I'm good enough to warn, but not good enough to help? Is that it? Just not good enough, just too human."

 "Do you really think that'll help?" Tegan appeared before me, hovering in the air just in front of my face, so close I almost had to cross my eyes to see him.

 "Well, asking and begging didn't," I said, not bothering to hide my frustration.

 "The queens of the court deign themselves when they see fit. You can't expect Iris to come at your beck and call."

"Deign? So it is that I'm not good enough to help, very nice." I let Tegan feel my frustration, hoping it would bite along his skin as it would humans, and was satisfied to see him flinch a little under the weight of my power.

"Now, none of that, I did come to help you," Tegan said, fluttering a few feet farther away from me, his hands out as if trying to ward off my ability. I reigned in my emotions, pulling back my power.

"You did?" I asked, a little skeptically. "Can you help us?"

"Oh, very nice!" he said, letting me hear his offense, stamping a small foot in the air. "I answer your call and this is how you thank me? And you wonder why the greater powers are not answering you."

"I'm sorry, Tegan, I didn't mean it that way. I just…" I fumbled for the right explanation, coming up very short. I sighed and shook my head before saying again, "Tegan, I'm sorry."

"That's alright, luv," he said with a smile, drifting closer to me.

"I… Well, we do need help," I took a deep breath, feeling a tightness in my chest I hadn't realized was there. "We've been trying to stop Jeremy, but every time I think we gain a few feet of ground, something happens and we slide back even farther than where we started." I looked up to him and realized he was no longer floating in front of my face, but had drifted to the ground, near the bowl of milk, watching my face expectantly. I laughed a surprisingly loud and happy sound. "Oh, I am sorry. Please, help yourself," I said, waving my hand towards him and the bowl. He granted me a big, toothy smile and dunked his head over the edge of the bowl and took a long drink of the milk.

"Ah," Tegan sighed, still hanging over the edge of the bowl, his breath making ripples on the surface of the milk. "You added honey, quite a delicious surprise." He pulled himself back, tipping back over the edge of the bowl, his feet landing on the ground.

"I remembered when I was a child, the faeries always asked Jodi and me for milk and honey. It took a few tries to realize this is what they meant." I nodded towards the bowl with a smile. Tegan stepped away from the bowl, stumbling a little as if he'd imbibed in something stronger than just milk and honey. I reached out a hand to steady him, but he just fluttered the autumn leaf wings. "Next time I won't bring as large an offering."

"Well now, I wouldn't be jumping to any rash decisions," he said quickly, waving his hands in the air in front of him. I laughed, feeling a weight lift from my shoulders as I relaxed for the first time all weekend.

"Oh, wow," I said between breaths, wiping a tear away from my eye. "Thank you, Tegan, I needed that." I took in one more deep breath to fill my lungs.

"My pleasure," he said with a smile, dipping forward again in the air. "Now, on to business I'm afraid. How is it that I can help you?"

"We have no idea what we're doing any more," I said quickly, hearing my voice crack, catching myself before I burst into frustrated tears.

"I wouldn't agree with that."

"What are you talking about?" I stopped myself, hearing my voice raise almost of it own accord. I took a moment to reign in my emotions before continuing. "Jeremy is out there, wreaking havoc on my city, and I can't find him, can't stop him, have no idea what he's going to do next."

"Now, none of that is true and you know it," Tegan said, his voice more stern that I had ever heard it before. He fluttered over to me, hovering just a few inches in front of my face again. "You can find him, if you know how to look for him. You will stop him; you are much more powerful than he is with his borrowed powers. And you have already figured out what he's going to do next."

"What?" I blinked my confusion at him, at a complete loss for what else to say.

"Where are your counterparts right now?"

"Jodi's trying to contact her faeries from her childhood to see if they can't tell her what these things that are helping Jeremy are and Steven's watching Jeremy's house to make sure he doesn't come for his father."

"Exactly," he said calmly with a nod of his head. "You knew that he was going to go after his father, so you are doing something about that. And you knew that you were dealing with Miss Jodi's core power and have set her on course."

"Wait, what do you mean?" I asked, my eyebrows drawing together as I eyed him. "Jodi's core power? Faeries are just a familiar of the Air Element…"

"Ah, but you have said it yourself, these are not faeries that you are dealing with, are they?"

"Oh my god…" I whispered. A chill ran up my back, raising the skin on my arms and under my hair. "They're… Air Elementals?" Tegan only smiled at me. "But that would mean that Jeremy is an Air Elemental like Jodi. Are you telling me that Jeremy is an Elemental?"

"How else would he command these things?" he asked me, cocking his head to the side.

"But why didn't we *recognize* him?" When we were young, Jodi and I had always known we had some special connection to one another; feeling something stronger than friendship pulling us together, as if we saw a shadow of ourselves in the other. It wasn't until we found Steven and felt the same connection, the same pull that let us know we were kindred spirits, able to *recognize* each other on a much different level. Recognize was the word we had used and it had always seemed like the exact, perfect word. It was how I knew that Jensen, although gifted, was not one of us because none of us had *recognized* him.

"I do not know the answer to that. If I did, I would gladly give it to you." I could feel Tegan's sincerity, mixed with regret; he truly wished he had all the answers. I knew exactly how he felt.

"I just don't understand," I said, shaking my head. "I know that I am mostly an Earth Elemental, but I have strong enough powers in the other elements to recognize what I'm dealing with and these are not air elementals I've ever seen. And more than that, since this is Jodi's core power, as you said, she doesn't recognize them either."

"Again, that is an answer I do not have to give, luv," Tegan fluttered a few feet away from me and I could suddenly feel a change in the air and I knew he was preparing to leave again. "But you know the answers to all of these things, Terra, Earth Mother. You just haven't understood them yet." And with that, he was gone.

I sat there in the thick quiet of the orchard, breathing in the citrus and waxy sap of the trees around me. I needed to go see Jodi, check on her and see if she'd found out anything. Although Tegan had been vague, I knew he was right, that the answers had been in front of us this entire time. I knew quite a bit about the different familiars of the four elements, but Jodi had always connected the most with faeries as a child so we didn't pay much attention to the alternative creatures that were air elementals. That had been our undoing with dealing with Jeremy. Jodi had been right about faeries; they were fickle, they only helped when they wanted to, and if it benefited them more to be disruptive or chaotic, then that's the way they behaved. It was that reasoning that had made Jodi and Steven insist that we consider that these things were still faeries, but something in my gut had told me they just weren't. Now I knew I had been right.

    I picked up the half empty bowl and laughed quietly, "Wow, have a drink, Tegan," I whispered to the air with a shake of my head. I could have sworn I heard the answer of tinkling bells echoing in the distance. I walked over to one of the trees and poured out the rest of the milk and honey at its roots and whispered a blessing before making my way back out of the orchard towards my backyard fence. I was up and over the fence and in my backyard, making my way back to my window, when I saw movement on the other side of the back door and realized my parents were moving around. I ran the last few feet to my window before jumping up on the sill and tumbling over into my room. I scrambled up and rearranged the curtains back over the window to cover the fact that the screen was missing and stashed the bowl in a drawer in my desk before I heard my mom knock lightly on my door.

    "Honey?" she asked through the door.

    "Come in, mom," I said back, falling into my desk chair, feigning a relaxing atmosphere.

    "Hey, sweetie, how are you feeling?" my mom asked, leaning into my room, holding on to the doorknob for balance.

    "Oh, better than yesterday," I said with a small smile.

    "Good, you hungry? Your dad and I are thinking of going out for dinner."

    "Oh, I'm good. Actually Jodi called a little while ago, I was thinking of heading over there?" I made sure to sound like I was asking so it didn't sound like I was just telling my mom what I was doing.

"On a school night? It's getting a little late to be going out," she said.

"But mom, it's the last week of school. We aren't doing anything in any of our classes besides talking or pretending to watch movies." I watched as she searched for a better argument in her mind. "I don't even have any homework anymore. Besides, I'm just going to her house, we're not going out out."

"Well, alright, I guess, but not too late, okay?" I agreed and we said our good byes. I waited until I heard them drive away before I left so that I could always claim that I had waited a while until I had left if they tried to say I was staying out too long. Once I was sure they were well away from the house, I grabbed my purse and a sweatshirt and was out the door and on my way to Jodi's.

Chapter 15

"They're air elementals?" Jodi asked skeptically as we sat in her bedroom, playing the stereo loud enough to make sure her nosy sisters didn't try to eavesdrop on our conversation.

"That's what Tegan said," I said with a nod.

"But I thought he didn't know what they were when he first came to you? Neither did the faerie queen," Jodi asked.

"I guess things changed." I pushed myself up from her bed and sat up straight, turning to look at Jodi. "Okay, however they knew and however long they may have taken to tell us, we know now. Now we need to figure out what kind of creature they are so we know what we're dealing with."

"Right," Jodi said, sitting up straighter too. "So they've been making us think they're faeries, even though we didn't fully believe that in the first place, they can fly, which confirms they really are some sort of air elemental…" I chose not to point out that she was the one pushing to get us to just call them faeries this whole time. Jodi was bright and had a lot of potential, but in many ways she was very young. I may be stubborn a lot of the time, but Jodi had a habit of jumping to a conclusion and wanting to stick to it, not willing to say she could be wrong. Then when proved wrong, she just ignored her previous errors as if she hadn't made them.

I lifted my face towards the ceiling, tracing patterns in the glow-in-the-dark sticky stars her father had put up there so many years ago, trying to rack my brain for any ideas. I let my gaze drift down from the ceiling to the tiny figurines suspended by nearly invisible wires. The porcelain faeries looked less like real faeries and more like tiny women with beautiful, iridescent wings sprouting out of their backs, dressed in angelic, gauzy gowns, and barefoot with five perfect little toes. Suddenly I felt a cold lump form in my stomach and my mouth fell open while I blinked stupidly at the little figurines.

"Terra?" I both heard and felt Jodi speak my elemental name as I always did when she chose to use it, but I didn't turn to look at her. She followed my gaze up to the ceiling and to the little dolls hanging from the ceiling and I knew she realized the same thing I did. We turned and looked at each other and after another moment of stunned silence, we whispered together, "Sylphs."

One of the most difficult things about magical and mythological creatures is finding hard core facts about them. Go to any major book store and you'll find a whole section devoted to the Occult with a dozen books on all the different magical things therein, but the trouble is we have to rely mostly on people's interpretations of things. It's not like history books or scientific books where you can fact check one author against ten others; in the magical world there is a lot more leeway on being allowed to just write whatever you want, whether or not you're making it up. So it goes with the different elemental creatures.

Sylphs have been commonly mistaken for faeries for a very long time. It wasn't until Paracelsus, a German alchemist, back in the 1500s first classified four different creatures for the four different elements that anyone knew what a Sylph was. Sylphs are creatures of pure air, which is why people think they can fly and therefore oftentimes confuse them with faeries. It is believed the Sylphs can shape change if they wish, but most who have documented seeing a Sylph generally describe them the same way; tiny, beautiful women, when they aren't choosing to be invisible. Personally, I have no idea if we've ever encountered a Sylph, mainly because of their ability to shape change. Like so many of the other air creatures, they enjoy a little chaos and would find it funny not to reveal their true self to us. I explained all of this to Steven as we hid in the darkened interior of my car across the street from the McCormacks' house.

"Why didn't you think of that before?" Steven asked.

"Honestly," I said glancing to look at Jodi, who nodded at me to continue. "We just forgot about them," I said with a shrug. "The problem with Air Elementals is that so many of them can change shape to hide their true identity and really we never had much luck with Sylphs when we were kids so we gave up on them. Jodi works well with faeries so that's her creature to call."

"So then how do you know we're dealing with Sylphs now?" Steven asked.

"Because," Jodi jumped in before I could. "Jeremy said whatever these things are told him they were faeries, but none of us can see them and Shay and I have second sight, so we know that's a lie and they work with air currents, lifting Shay and Jeremy those times. It just fits."

"Is it okay that I'm a little skeptical?" Steven asked as he looked from me to Jodi and back again.

"Of course it is," I said. "Like I said, no one knows enough about Sylphs to be an expert on them."

"But the same could be said about all the other elemental creatures. Most of what we work with comes from pure belief in them."

"That's true. You tell the average person that faeries and gnomes and salamanders are real and they'll think you're crazy," I said with a smile. "But we know different. I've explained this to you before: if it's real for you, then it's real and that's all that matters. Trying to convince the world that magic is real will drive yourself crazy. And the same goes for this situation right now." I glanced over to Jodi and she nodded again, encouraging me. "I'll grant you that we can't be totally sure these are Sylphs, but it's the first real lead we've had, so we're going to follow it."

"Yeah, okay, I guess you've got a point there," Steven said with a nod of his head. He turned and looked out the window towards Jeremy's house. "So what do we do now?"

What do we do now, that was the question I had been asking myself all weekend. Magical creatures are not immune to attack, but it is incredibly difficult to harm them and, with little to no real documentation on Sylph lore, it was going to be even more difficult for us. With Earth or Fire elements, you can usually combat them with Water, but with Air, the only real way you can combat them is with fire and that didn't always work out the way you wanted it to. Fire was one of the most dangerous elements to control. That was why Steven's abilities were not as strong as Jodi's and mine. I could spend days working with him on a new skill, but because Fire was so volatile, we might not even make a dent by the end of the week.

Last fall we had learned that Steven could raise the core temperature of a person, which led me to believe that he would eventually be able to call fire into his hands one day. Steven could also anchor into Jodi's Air Element and use her as fuel when dealing with fire. I was able to anchor into both of them and use them as ammunition, but that little trick took a lot out of me and could be detrimental to the environment around us if it got out of control. But I believed that Fire and Air were going to be the keys to combating the Sylphs, if we could catch them.

I'd called Jensen and asked him to play lookout at the McCormacks house so that the three of us could try to get some research done and work on locating Jeremy.

"Are you sure this is safe?" Jensen asked after I brought him up to speed on our theories.

"No," I said with a smile.

"No, I mean, look at what he's be able to do. He's getting stronger or those things are. First he's able to nearly throw you off that balcony and then he's able to break that window in the police station and those are supposed to be bullet proof and then he blew out a goddamn wall in the station." He took a deep breath. "If he tries to hurt you again…"

"Listen, I promise, if he does, I won't try reasoning with him this time, okay?" I said, dipping my head so I could look up into his eyes. "If he tries to hurt me again, I'll fight back, with all that I've got. You know I can take care of myself, you were there last fall."

"Yeah, I was," he granted me a sad smile and nodded his head. "You were pretty amazing." He pulled me into him, wrapping his arms around my shoulders and squeezing almost too tightly. "It just seems every time you have to deal with something like this, I'm sitting on the sidelines watching. I hate that."

"Last time you were bound and stuffed inside a duffle bag," I said, wrapping my arms around his waist.

"And this time I'm watching over some jerk's house."

"Not necessarily, you're just doing this for me right now in case Jeremy shows up and if he does, then you'll be here and you can help if I need it."

"That's true," he said reluctantly. "But if you find him somewhere else, then here I am sitting on my ass, twiddling my thumbs."

"Jensen…" I started to say something to comfort him, but the words died on my lips.

"God, listen to me," he said suddenly, letting go of me and pushing me back gently. "Whining like a child, expecting you to stroke my ego when you're trying to save the world again."

"I'm not trying to save the world," I said a little confused.

"You know what I mean," he shook his head sharply and rolled his shoulders. He gripped me by the shoulders and leaned down a little to look me in the eye. "I'm holding you to your word. If you need to, you fight, fight as hard as you can."

"I will," I said, feeling my throat tighten.

It was time to cast again. Because I had promised my mom that I wasn't going anywhere but to Jodi's house, I couldn't go back to my place for supplies, so we'd have to do with the back up supplies I always kept in the trunk of my car. We debated where to go, but ultimately decided that, since we were dealing with Air Elementals, our favorite spot, being the beach, just wouldn't be conducive to our efforts. So we were headed to a forest. Although, it really wasn't as much of a forest as a wooded area of a park we used to play in as children. This was the same park we first discovered faeries were real and had laid magic into the ground without ever knowing what we were doing.

"So what's the plan?" Steven asked from his usual spot in the backseat. "We still don't know where Jeremy is or how to get rid of these things."

"That is the plan: trying to locate Jeremy, maybe bind him, or unbind him," I said, turning onto the darkened street leading towards the park.

"What do you mean unbind him?" Steven asked.

"Well, it's just a thought, but these things seem to have some control over Jeremy, so he might be bound to them. If so, we'll have to try to break that bond before we can attack the Sylphs," I explained. "If we try to attack those things while they're still connected to Jeremy, we may hurt him."

"So?" Steven said with a little extra venom in his voice.

"He doesn't mean any harm, Steven," Jodi chimed in for me. "He's just in over his head. Poor kid's been beaten down his whole life and now finally has some power over people. We agreed that if he was in his right mind when the Sylphs showed up, he wouldn't have let them override him."

"You agreed. I still have my doubts."

"Good, then you can be the resident cynic this time around," I said as I pulled the car up against a curb and cut the engine. "It'll be a nice change in the line up." I smiled at Jodi who punched me lightly in the shoulder before we climbed out of the car. I popped the latch on the trunk and pulled out the backpack that held our back-up supplies and pushed the trunk lid closed before leading the way into the park, towards the thick shadows that the tree line cast, cutting out all moon and star light.

"Well this doesn't have horror movie written all over it," Steven said as we stepped into the wooded area. All city sounds had faded away as if we had walked into a room with no windows and shut the door behind us. I hesitated a few moments, letting my night vision kick in before I continued walking. I felt my magic inside me shift automatically, swirling in my core before plummeting down into the ground only to soar back up through me in a constant revolution. My body was alive with the new energy; this place knew me, recognized me, and welcomed me back. A sudden, but gentle breeze kicked up around us, rushing through our hair and over our skin.

"Good to be home, isn't it?" I said over my shoulder to Jodi and she smiled brightly at me with a quick nod. In that moment, she looked five-years-old again.

We walked through the trees, carefully picking our way over upraised roots and bushes, until we were so deep we couldn't pick out a street lamp or house no matter which direction we looked. I led us a few more yards in until I found a clearing wide enough to cast our circle, finally setting my backpack on the ground and motioning to Jodi and Steven to get to work.

Usually when we drew our circles we did so with our athames, but we each only owned one sacrificial knife and therefore had no back up stashed in the backpack. An athame is almost purely symbolic; it is used to direct magical energies, cut herbs for potions, and cut open circles when we needed to pass in and out of them without breaking the circle. We never actually sacrificed anything. So tonight I fished out the container of salt from my back pack and handed it to Jodi to draw the first circle.

As a safety precaution, I preferred to work within two circles, one inside the other. It makes it that much harder for outside energies and creatures to break through. Once, when we were casting at the beach a few years ago, we had cast a double circle so we could practice wind spells with Jodi and an Undine – a water elemental – tried to shimmy up the beach and into our circle. She made it within the first circle, but not past the second one, becoming trapped between the two circles. Since that night, I always insisted on double circles.

Jodi stretched out both arms, her far one holding out the salt and Steven holding her free hand with his outstretched arm, ensuring they were far enough away from the center where I was crouched pulling out supplies so that we would have enough room to work. Once Jodi had sealed her circle, Steven took the salt from her and began walking his circle, murmuring the incantation for protection as he walked, letting the salt fall from his hand in a shower of white onto the ground.

I was pulling out the candles, silver bowl, water bottle, pouch full of blessed dirt, a red candle, and a feather, each representing one of the four elements, when I felt the air shift around me and a jolt of energy race up my spine and I knew Steven had sealed his circle. I pulled out some black chalk and parchment paper, setting them in front of me, and folded up the now empty backpack and tucked it under me to keep it out of the way. I settled myself on the ground as comfortably as I could and motioned for Jodi and Steven to do the same. We clasped hands to form a circle out of our arms and closed our eyes, Jodi and Steven bowing their heads as I lifted mine to the sky.

"In this our hour of need we call upon the Four Corners, help us this night to set things right. I invoke our magical abilities, summoning Terra, Earth Element of the North, Fae, Air Element of the East, Drake, Fire Element of the South." I said the words loud clear into the woods and felt the energy inside our circles rise around us, swirling with power. It cut through our bodies as it danced around us, leaving more and more power behind inside us each time it passed until I could feel my fingers tingling with the magic waiting to be used. I lowered my face slowly, easing my eyes open and looked upon Jodi and Steven and saw them as their true selves, as Fae and Drake. Fae glowed with a white electric light while Drake seemed to burn with warmth and molten red light.

"I call upon the Faerie Folk," Jodi began, keeping her eyes closed, but turned her head up to the sky just as I had done. "Join us, help us, we are familiars and beg for guidance." I could hear a rustling in the trees around us, but not so much as a whisper inside the circle.

"We call for ability by the power of Mother and Earth," I said as I let go of Jodi and Steven and reached out for the pouch of dirt and poured it on the ground in front of us.

"We call for guidance by the power of Intuition and Air," Jodi said as she laid the feather in its appropriate spot on our makeshift altar.

"We call for aid by the power of Summer and Fire," Steven said as he reached for the red candle and brought it to his lips, blowing gently on the wick, causing it to ignite. He set it carefully into the center of the pile of dirt I had poured.

"We call for insight by the power of Invention and Water," we said in unison as I opened the bottle of water and Jodi and Steven held the silver bowl in their hands. I poured the water into the bowl and let them set it in its place. As it touched the ground, the flame on the candle flickered wildly and the feather lifted into the air a few inches as the water in the bowl began to swirl in a tiny funnel and the dirt began to swirl up around the candle it held in place.

We watched in silence as the four items reacted to our spell, growing more and more volatile until the water was swirling above the edge of the bowl and the dirt encased the candle, leaving only the now five inch tall flame visible. The feather floated higher into the air until it was hovering above our heads on a breeze none of us could feel. Suddenly a crack of thunder sounded overhead making all three of us flinch and duck our heads as a small bolt of lightening hit the feather, but when it fell back to the ground, it landed with a hard thud.

We opened our eyes to see a crude knife sticking out of the ground where the feather should have fallen. The water and dirt were settled in the bowl and on the ground and the flame on the candle flickered gently, as if nothing happened. We sat there in silence for a few more moments to be sure nothing else happened before both Jodi and I reached for the hilt of the knife simultaneously. Our fingers touched the metal at the same time, jolting us both so hard we cried out in shock as we snatched our hands away. But when we looked back, the knife was gone again, not even leaving the feather in its place. My fingers tingled where they had touched the knife and when I looked down at them, I saw a residue on the tips of my fingers.

"I think that was iron," Steven whispered as he leaned over and looked at my hand.

"Of course," Jodi said, looking at her own fingers and the metallic residue on them.

"Why of course?" Steven asked.

"Because iron works against Faeries," I said, looking up from my hand to Jodi, who was nodding her agreement.

"But you said these weren't Faeries," Steven turned his confused face to me.

"They aren't, but they have so many qualities that are similar to Faeries that they are often confused with Faeries. It stands to reason…" I looked back down at my hand.

"That iron will work against them," Jodi finished for me.

"Then why did they take the knife back?" Steven asked.

"They didn't. Fae and I have the iron in us now." I looked up to Jodi to see if she agreed with me.

"To use with our magics to fight against the Sylphs," Jodi said with another nod.

"I think so too," I said, calling up a tendril of energy and pushing it into my hand, directing it out towards the silver bowl in front of me and watched as the side began to melt against the shot of power.

It took us a few minutes to regain our composure after that. It is a rare and special thing when you can actually conjure a tangible object, even if it did disappear just moments later. I reached out for Jodi and Steven's hands before saying, "Okay, now we need to try and find Jeremy."

"How are we going to do that?" Steven asked, keeping his voice at a whisper, as if afraid his doubt would scare off whatever was helping us.

"Using Fae's power," I said, using Jodi's elemental name.

"My power, what do you mean? How?" Fae turned terrified eyes to me.

"Drake will act as an anchor and you and I will summon up a searching wind and try to hunt him out, like a bloodhound," I explained.

"Whoa, why am I the anchor?" Steven asked quickly, sounding more than a little afraid.

"What's wrong? You've anchored before for both of us." I furrowed my brow at Steven, feeling the tension in his hand.

"Yeah, but these things…"

"Honey, we're in the circle, remember?"

"Oh yeah, good point," Steven said with a nod and I was glad to see and feel him relax. "Okay, go."

"Wait!" Jodi said quickly as if on that simple command I would spring us into the air without preparing her. "What makes you think my power will work? You didn't say anything about this before."

"I know, but inspiration just hit, probably the magic we raised in the circle," I said, but saw that my explanation wasn't enough for Jodi. "I just had a thought that if these things really are Air elementals, then we should be able to track them with Air. What faster way to do that than with wind? Especially if they're hiding him with air."

"Yeah…okay," Jodi said reluctantly.

"Don't worry, I'm going to be guiding you and Drake is going to be our anchor. It'll be safe, I promise." I gave her hand a squeeze.

"And why is it such a good idea that I anchor?" Drake asked, drawing my attention back to him. "I mean, you're the stronger anchor."

"That may be, but Fire feeds off Air. If things get out of control, you can invoke your power, guided by me to Fae, and we can pull her back." I waited until Steven nodded his agreement before turning my attention back to the center of the circle.

We worked quickly to clean up the altar and banish the circles when we were done. Jodi and Steven each banished their own circles, walking in the opposite directions they had gone to cast the circle, muttering the incantation and thanks needed to properly erase the magical barriers the circles created. I said a blessing for the ground where we had worked and specifically on the point where the iron blade had struck, hoping to heal any damage it may have caused. But, as I laid my hand on the ground, there was no answer of burning pain, only the rich healthy soil beneath my palm. I breathed a sigh of relief and swung the backpack over my shoulder and led us out of the wooded glen.

I had guided Jodi into a trancelike state, Steven and I still holding each of her hands as I did so. I closed my eyes and summoned my Second Sight and saw Jodi's form alive with an electric white light and Steven's warm, red fire off in the corner of my eye. Vaguely I was aware of a phantom weight on my back, but I tried not to pay it any attention, as whatever my higher self was wouldn't help us right now. Carefully we focused Jodi's energy to a point in the center of the three of us, building on it until we felt a breeze course around us, fluttering through our hair, skimming over our bare arms, looking for a way out of the circle. That was the tricky part; letting the energy out of the circle while simultaneously keeping any unwanted things out. I peeled back the layers of our circle until a small opening appeared and the breeze flew out immediately, as if sucked out. I built back the layers as quickly as I could while Jodi and Steven focused their energies on keeping the seeking wind nearby.

When I was ready, I opened the channel between Jodi and me and we sent our energies into the wind, allowing it to grow until we neared the point where we wouldn't be able to control it anymore and then sent it out, whipping through the city, searching for Jeremy's signature. It took over an hour for us to find any hint of Jeremy's whereabouts, more than once finding a signature and only coming to realize that it was a place Jeremy had been, not currently was. More than once I had to summon more power from my link to the ground we were sitting on and feed it to Jodi to keep her nerves calm and give her patience. Finally, when Steven was just about to pull us back, we felt the unmistakable pull that told us we had found Jeremy. He was at Jensen's house.

Once we were out of the woods and back inside the car, I threw the gear into drive and was tearing down the street, steering with one hand and dialing Jensen's cell phone number with the other. He answered on the first ring. After I told him what we knew, he was off the phone and running before I could tell him we were on our way. Jensen didn't have a car with him and I debated going to get him first or just driving to his house, where his mother was alone. Jeremy didn't live far from Jensen and I knew he'd want us to get to his mother as fast as possible and, with that thought, I slammed the gas pedal to the floor and raced to his house.

Chapter 16

As I drove, I said an incantation under my breath, hearing Jodi and Steven catch on and repeating it each once, binding the spell three times. It was more of a charm than a spell, but it made the caster harder to see and therefore my car less noticeable. Not so much that other cars would hit me, but enough that my speeding and weaving through traffic could go unnoticed by a hidden cop. It was a nifty little tool I liked to use when I was running late or at the end of the month when I knew there were likely more cops on the road than at any other time.

Out of the corner of my eye, I could see that the sleek, dark lines of my car were blurred and gave me a small pain in my head if I tried to look at them too hard. Satisfied that the tripled casting had worked, I focused my attention forward and getting to Jensen's house in one piece. I knew Jensen's mom was home alone; Jensen being on a stake out for us, his brother Ian being in prison, and their father out of town at a convention in San Francisco. My gut twisted against my spine at the thought of that sweet, tiny woman at the hands of Jeremy in his tortured state of mind.

I heard Steven saying a little prayer in the backseat as I took another corner at breakneck speed, but not once did I slow down. Jensen's driveway was wide enough for two cars and luckily he was parked on the street, leaving his mother's car standing alone in the driveway. I tore into the vacant spot, coming within a hairsbreadth of the garage door and slammed the emergency brake as I threw open my door and nearly fell face forward onto the cement in my rush to get to the front door. Jensen wasn't here yet. I ran up the front walk, Jodi and Steven so close behind we nearly stepped on each other. I had a second to debate whether or not to knock on the door or just bust in. I didn't hear anything inside to indicate anything was wrong, so, with more control than should have been necessary, I balled up my fist and rapped hard and fast on the door, bouncing on the balls of my feet as we waited.

Just as I was reaching for the doorknob, my patience nearing the end of its tether, I heard the footsteps on the other side of the door.

"Shayna, sweetie," Jensen's mom said with a quick smile, showing her surprise. "What are you doing here so late? I thought you and Jensen were out…"

"Hi, Mrs. Cavanaugh," I said, plastering on the smile all boy's mothers love. "Yeah, we were, but I had to go pick up Jodi and Steven, their ride abandoned them," I gestured over my shoulder to them behind me, "so Jensen and I said we'd just meet back here. He's not here yet, is he?" As I said the lie, I remembered Jensen's car sitting right out front against the curb and mentally kicked myself, but I felt more than saw both Steven and Jodi moving behind me to block her view of the street. Luckily she wasn't a tall woman by anyone's standards, being even shorter than my five foot four.

"No, no, he's not, but you're welcome to come inside," she said with a smile as she stepped back, holding the door open for us.

"Thanks," I smiled at her again and led Jodi inside.

"Oh, please, let me," Steven said, putting on his most charming attitude as he took the door from her, still blocking her view of the street and closing the door behind him before she could see Jensen's car. I mouthed "Thank you" to Steven and he gave me a wink in return.

"Um, Mrs. Cavanaugh," Jodi said, turning before she walked too far into the house. "We heard sirens just a little bit ago, is everything okay? I mean, did you hear or see anything around here?" I mentally thanked Jodi, laying a hand on her arm to convey the message. I needed to get control of my nerves and stop trying to zone in on Jeremy so I could assess the entire situation.

"No, I don't think so," Mrs. Cavanaugh said, her brow knitting together as she cocked her head to the side, trying to remember something that didn't happen. "You heard sirens in this neighborhood?"

"Well, we had to pull over for some cop cars and an ambulance and they looked like they were coming this way," I said with a shrug, taking up the story.

"Hmm, well, I was in the shower, maybe I missed something. Let's go turn on the news," she said, walking forward towards the living room. We followed, but I stopped hearing footsteps running up the walk outside the front door and turned to see Jensen's red face as he nearly burst through the door.

"Hey," I said brightly and quickly, rushing over to him and grabbing him by the shoulders and spinning him around so his back was to the rest of the house. I gave him a kiss, willing him to catch his breath and let the blood drain from his face. "It's okay," I whispered as I rose up on my toes to wrap my arms around his neck in a hug. "Nothing's happened yet."

I felt Jensen relax beneath my embrace and slide his arms around my waist, almost crushing me in a hug. "Thank you for getting here so fast," he whispered into my neck, hiding his face in my hair.

"Honey, were you running just now?" his mom asked, walking back a few steps towards us. I let go of Jensen and took a quick look at his face, satisfied he was close to his normal color before I nodded and stepped back.

"Oh, I uh…" he struggled for a moment.

"Did you hear the sirens too?" Steven asked quickly, nodding his head vigorously over Mrs. Cavanaugh's head.

"Sirens? Yeah, you heard them too?" Jensen asked, taking up on the excuse.

"Well, I didn't, but your friends say they did," Mrs. Cavanaugh said, gesturing to us with her hand. "We were just going to the living room to check the news."

We each took a spot on the large, overstuffed L-shaped couch in the sunken living room. Jensen strategically placing himself next to me, but still close enough to his mother, should he need to throw his own body over hers to protect her. We flipped on the television and Jensen surfed through the local cable channels looking for news reports.

There was in fact some sad accident on one of the channels, with police cruisers and ambulances on scene, but it was in L.A. unsurprisingly. It took a lot for any story out of our small county to make it on television. We knew there'd be no story, since there were no emergency vehicles in the neighborhood, but it gave us all time to think. Jeremy was here somewhere or at least had been in the last hour, but something inside me told me he was still here.

"Oh well, guess it wasn't anything too terrible," Jensen's mom said, startling me from my thoughts. "So, you kids planning on staying here tonight?"

"If that's okay with you, mom," Jensen said, keeping his voice impressively calm and even.

"Oh, that's fine, honey. Why don't I fix you guys some snacks then?" She said with a smile and stood up, starting to walk from the room. Jensen's mom always struck me as a strange combination of modern woman and 1950's housewife. She was going to fix us snacks and drinks no doubt, whereas the rest of our mothers would have just told us to help ourselves to the fridge, reminding us we all had two legs that worked just fine.

"I'll help you, mom," Jensen said quickly, nearly jumping up from the couch in his rush to get to her.

"That's okay, sweetie," she said, putting up a hand to stop him. "I can manage by myself. Don't be rude and leave your friends alone."

"No, mom, really, I want to help," Jensen said, pressing forward against her hand, trying to usher her forward. I knew there was no way he was going to let his mom out of his sight tonight until we caught Jeremy.

"We'll be fine, Mrs. Cavanaugh," I said, standing up so I could face her since Jensen had managed to get her around the couch and almost out of the room.

"I don't know what's gotten into you tonight, Jensen," she said with a shake of her head, but she gave up and walked out of the room. Jensen threw me a look that said he was grateful for my help. I waited until they were down the hall into the kitchen before I turned around to assess the room.

"First things first," I said, stepping around the coffee table and walking over to the large sliding glass doors that took up most of the back wall that lead to the backyard and began quickly pulling the curtains closed against the black night. The lights in the house would keep us from seeing out but we'd be completely laminated to anyone outside.

"Now what?" Steven asked, looking around to make sure there wasn't another way for Jeremy to get the jump on us.

"We need to find him," I said matter-of-factly.

"Great, how?" Steven asked.

"Um, Steven, come here," I said, reaching towards him and waving my hands at him urgently. He hurried over to me and we clasped hands. I closed my eyes and centered myself, opening a channel inside of me and pushing it down past the floorboards, the foundation, and into the earth below. I drew up the energy and power into me and began to feed it into Steven. He caught on quickly and drank in the power I offered him. I felt him directing the power just as we had practiced so often. Knowing his best offensive abilities lay in his hands, he let the power build up in his palms and fingers until it spilled into his arms and overflowed into the rest of him so he could draw on that reserve when his hands ran out.

When I sealed the channel between us, there were a flush to Steven's cheeks and a light sheen of sweat on his forehead. His hands felt like they had been thrust into a fire and were nearly unbearable to hold. When I let got of his hands, I saw that my own usually pale hands were red with his heat.

"Now go into the kitchen and don't let Jensen's mom out of your sight," I said.

"What about you two?"

"Don't worry about us. If Jeremy shows up, I trust you to know what to do. Now go," I said as I spun him by the shoulders and gave him a push towards the hall.

"Now what?" Jodi asked, drawing my attention back to her.

"How do your hands feel?"

"Still tingly from earlier."

"Good, me too," I said with a nod and reached a hand towards her. Jodi came to me quickly, taking my left hand in hers. I was still drawing up power and energy from the ground below and began feeding it to Jodi just as I had done with Steven. After a few moments I felt the power begin to rebound back on me, as if she had taken all of the power her body could hold. I broke the channel carefully, but motioned her to remain next to me while I separated myself from the channel I had opened below me. When I was free, I felt a burning sensation in my right hand and looked down to see the metallic liquid pushing against the skin of my fingers and palms, coloring the skin in an odd, almost reptilian way.

"Does it burn you too?" Jodi asked and I saw that she was examining her right hand as well.

"A bit, but not enough to hurt."

"Yeah, yeah, me too," she nodded, taking a moment to break her gaze away from her hand and look back up at me. "What now?"

"We find the son of a bitch."

I debated searching for Jeremy outside, but decided the risk of being outside, away from help and in the dark, just wasn't wise now that I knew we were dealing with Air Elementals. Jodi had tried locating them with her inner abilities, but either their signature was still too foreign to her to recognize or they had learned to block against her. We decided it was safer to stick together so we headed up the stairs together, fighting the urge to hold hands like two children braving the long dark hallway.

I kept my back against the wall as we walked up and Jodi walked backwards, watching for an ambush and trusting me not to let her walk into anything behind her. When we reached the top of the stairs, I put my hand out, waiting for Jodi to walk into it. *Okay, wait, we're at the top,* I thought at her, grateful we could communicate like this. To my left was a guest bathroom and all the other rooms were along a walkway to the right. *I'm going to check this bathroom. You watch the hall and the stairs and then we'll work our way down, room by room.*

Okay, Jodi thought at me with a nod. Her yellow thoughts were so bright I instinctively squinted my eyes against them. Her anxiety was running as high as mine. As I took a step towards the bathroom door, Jodi took the final step up onto the hallway floor and off of the stairs, keeping her back to the bathroom in order to watch both ways. I started to reach for the doorknob and had a flash of every horror movie I'd ever seen where someone stands in front of a closed door and makes a perfect target of themselves. I reached back and pushed Jodi gently to the side. *What?* she asked.

Don't stand right in front of the door, I answered and she nodded, understanding, and took a step back towards the stairs, putting the corner of the wall in her back. I turned and pressed my body against the wall and reached to turn the doorknob. I heard it click and let go to nudge the door open with my foot. I pushed hard enough so the door would open all the way until it made contact with the wall, ensuring Jeremy wasn't hiding behind it. I slid down the wall silently until I was on my knees so that I wouldn't be in

Jeremy's line of sight before I leaned forward to look inside. It was empty. I took a deep breath and blew it out quietly. I double checked the tub and even the cabinet under the sink, just to be sure, before turning back to the door and nodding Jodi forward.

We checked every room, Jensen's, Ian's, and their parents, not finding Jeremy in any. That only left the master bathroom. Jodi reached out and touched my arm. *Do you think he's in there? She said she was in the shower, she would've seen him*, she thought at me.

Not if he waited outside the window or something until she was done, I answered.

But he didn't. I mean, she was fine when we got here, Jodi furrowed her brow at me.

Better safe than sorry, I urged and Jodi agreed and we checked the bathroom, Jodi staying in the doorway to make sure we weren't taken by surprise. But like all the other rooms, this one was empty as well. *Damnit!* I thought angrily, nudging Jodi forward by the shoulder.

Is there a basement or something? Jodi asked as we walked through the hall and back to the stairs.

No, just the guest bath downstairs and the kitchen and garage. I guess he could be in the garage. If he'd been in the kitchen, we'd know by now. Jodi nodded her agreement and we trudged down the stairs.

"He must still be outside or in the garage then," Jodi said over her shoulder as we walked back into the living room. "What now?" That was a question I was seriously getting tired of hearing, but I took a deep breath and blew it out audibly, keeping my frustration under control.

"We wait, I guess," I said, starting to pace the living room as Jodi took a seat on the couch.

"Here we are," Jensen's mom said brightly, carrying a tray of quartered sandwiches with a bowl of chips. Jensen and Steven followed her with drinks, setting everything on the coffee table.

"Thanks, Mrs. Cavanaugh," Jodi and I said together, but only Jodi reached for a sandwich and I continued to pace.

"Everything okay, dear?" Mrs. Cavanaugh asked me.

"Oh, yeah, fine," I said with a forced smile and made myself stop pacing, taking a seat on the arm of the couch, knowing I couldn't take a seat on the overstuffed couch and be comfortable.

"If you're sure," she said, watching me with concern plain on her face. "Well, I think I'll head upstairs, leave you kids alone."

"No!" we all four yelled so suddenly she jumped back a step, her hand flying to her chest as if to keep her heart from bursting out.

"Well!" she said, her voice breathy as she looked around at the four of us.

"Sorry, mom. We just meant there's no reason to leave just because we're here," Jensen said, reaching out to touch her arm.

"Now since when have four teenagers ever wanted to hang out with someone's mom?" she furrowed her brow at her son, but didn't pause to let him answer. "Something's wrong and I want to know what, right now, Jensen Michael Cavanaugh." We were caught. Whenever a parent middle names you, you know you've pushed your luck.

"Sorry, Mrs. Cavanaugh," I said, taking a step towards her to draw her attention away from Jensen. "It's my fault, this whole thing with Jeremy, we're all pretty spooked."

"Oh, of course," she said, tilting her head to the side and fixing me with a concerned mother's stare. "They haven't found him yet, have they?"

"No, he's still out there and we think he's trying to hurt people that are important to me, so we got worried about you because we realized you were home alone." Sometimes the truth is the best way to lie.

"Well, isn't that sweet," she said with a smile, walking over to me and taking me into a hug. "But as you can see, I'm fine now and, with you four here, I can't imagine him being able to do anything." She patted my shoulder and turned towards Jensen. "I'm going to go ahead and go upstairs, but" she raised her hand to forestall our arguments, "I'll keep my door open so if anything happens I can call for help, alright?"

"Mom," Jensen said. "I just don't feel like that's gonna be enough."

"Don't be silly," she said with a shake of her head and started walking towards the stairs. "There are locks on all of the windows and the only doors in and out are right here and with two strapping young men here, what could happen?"

"Famous last words," Steven mumbled as Jensen's mom started up the stairs. We waited to do anything until we heard her walking above us, in her room and not calling out for help.

"Now what?" Jensen turned to ask.

"I am really getting tired of hearing that question," I said, rubbing my temples with my fingertips. "Jensen, go up real quick and make sure she left her door open and double check all her windows. We already cleared the upstairs, but who's to say he didn't come in after we left." Without a word, he turned and hurried up to do as I said.

"And we need to check the garage," I said to the other two, who nodded in agreement. We walked into the kitchen as quietly as possible, checking the downstairs bath on our way. I motioned for Jodi to stand to one side of the door and me to the other with Steven standing back and off to the side, out of the line of fire, before I opened the door in the same way I had all the other doors upstairs. When nothing leapt out at us, we inched through the door, keeping our backs against the walls as best we could.

Jensen's father had turned the garage into a work room much like my dad had done to ours. There was one wall covered in a wide work bench with all kinds of hand tools on it. Another wall was cabinets and the third wall was lined with a table saw, a wood lathe, and a couple of other cumbersome tools I couldn't make out in the dark. Luckily the center was bare, where he usually had a collapsible table, but it was broken down and hanging on one of the walls. Not many places to hide. I reached over my shoulder awkwardly and flipped on the light switch, never turning my attention away from the room.

When the garage flooded with light, I held my breath. I was sure both Jodi and Steven were doing the same, but nothing happened. My sense of Jeremy hadn't grown or weakened at all, which meant he probably wasn't there, but I made sure we checked everywhere before we called it safe. We checked all of the cupboards, even the ones too small for him to hide in and behind and around all of the large tools and under the work bench before we walked back out, locking the door from the inside just in case.

"Well, he's not in the house then," Jodi said as we walked back into the living room.

"Is it weird that I'm a little disappointed?" Steven asked as he fell onto the couch.

"A little, but I understand," I said as I resumed my pacing. Jensen came back down just a few moments later, standing at the foot of the stairs, as if afraid to get too far from his mother.

"All the windows are locked and I checked the other rooms up there too before I came back down and locked all those windows too," Jensen said. He crossed his arms over his chest, looking very much like a junior body guard, his feet hip-width apart and his knees loose, ready to pounce. I wanted to smile at the pose, but just didn't have it in me right then.

"So now we wait?" Jodi asked, looking to me for the answer.

"Now we wait," I said, grateful she hadn't asked me "what next?" I started pacing again, feeling the energy coursing through my body just waiting.

It wasn't until an hour later when Jodi finally broke the silence, unable to stare at a muted television set any more. "Dude! I'm going to go insane. We need to do something while we wait."

"I don't want to be distracted," Jensen said from his post by the foot of the stairs. Over the last hour he had gone to check on his mother four times.

"Fine, you stay there, but Jodi's right, we'll go stir crazy," I said, stopping my worried pacing. "I'm gonna burn a hole in your mother's carpet if I don't stop. Jodi, Steven, follow me," I said, waving them up from the couch and turning to the sliding glass door I had been pacing in front of.

"Whoa! Where are you going?" Jensen said suddenly, almost taking a step away from the stairs.

"Outside. We'll start working on the external shields to reinforce them, like I did in the tree house."

"Can't you do that from in here?"

"Yes, I suppose so, but I don't want your mother to come down stairs and see us in a circle doing our thing."

"I can warn you if she comes down."

"No, Jensen. If we do it in here, we'll have to be in more of a trance than outside and warning us won't help us come out of it in time. It's not something we can just stop doing, we'll cause a rip in the shields," I tried to explain calmly while Jodi and Steven looked from me to Jensen like they were watching a tennis match.

"I don't like the idea of you going out there," Jensen said.

"I'm not going alone," I said, trying to keep my voice even and not be offended by his lack of trust in my abilities to fight Jeremy.

"Not just you, Shayna," Jensen said a little defensively. "I don't like the idea of any of us going outside."

"We'll be within yelling distance and you have neighbors," I said, reaching a hand to draw one of the curtains back. "If Jeremy is stupid enough to try something outside, again, there are people around."

"Wait-" Jensen started to protest again, but was cut short by the sound of a dull thud on the ceiling overhead.

"Your mom!" I whispered urgently to Jensen, but he was already spinning around and running up the stairs. Steven looked at me, I nodded quickly, and he turned to follow in case Jensen needed back up. I kept staring at the ceiling and reached out a hand towards the direction Jodi had been standing. When I felt her fingers entwine with mine, I thought at her, *He's still flying...*

What do you want to do? Jodi asked.

Honestly, I'm not sure yet. I know the shields on the house are fine, I check everyone's every couple of months... As a group, we each built shields on all of our houses and any houses of nearby family and significant others. Every other month on the first Saturday of the month, I *go out* and check all of the shields to see if anyone needs repairs or not.

Then how is he on the roof?

It's to help keep magical attacks away; it doesn't do much for physical. I ended the thought with a mental sigh. Jodi squeezed my hand as if to reassure me, but jumped suddenly when we heard a crash just outside the sliding glass door.

Do we dare? Jodi's nervous thoughts floated to me, but I had a hard time hearing her, all of my attention on the curtained door beside me.

"What is going on, Jensen?" Mrs. Cavanaugh said, sounding torn between annoyance and fear as they came down the steps, Steven walking very carefully backwards to watch behind them.

"We heard something outside, mom. We got worried. If there is something or someone outside, I'd feel better if I knew you were okay," Jensen said, steering her towards the couch and urging her to sit.

"Well, if you think there's a prowler outside, we should call the police," she said calmly, reaching for the phone on the side table. None of us stopped her, hearing a new noise coming from the kitchen, but faint, like a scratching at the window. "Is that what you heard?" she asked.

"No, that's new," Steven said, looking to me for confirmation. Then another creaking noise came from just outside the front door and we turned as one towards it, but were quickly distracted by the sound of something breaking in the back yard.

"Oh my God, that sounded like my pots shattering," Jensen's mom said, starting to rise from her seat on the couch.

"No, mom," Jensen said quickly, pushing her back down. "You don't know what's out there. Just go ahead and call the police."

"I don't understand what's going-" another loud crash from the backyard cut her off.

"Mrs. Cavanaugh," I said very calmly, not taking my eyes off of the curtains. "Call the police. Tell them I'm here and we think Jeremy McCormack is trying to break in." I felt her staring at the back of my head and knew she wasn't moving, so I concentrated on that spot she was looking at until I could feel her emotions and sent a jolt of power down the line to her and gave her emotions a push. I was rewarded to hear the beeps of the phone as she punched in 911.

"Shay, what are you doing?" Steven asked from somewhere behind me as I reached forward, grabbing the edge of the curtain.

"We're going outside," I said calmly.

"What are you talking about?" Steven asked again.

"Steven," I said, turning my attention from the door finally. "He is trying to distract us, make us think he's in all these different places, but I know he's out here, isn't he, Jodi?" I turned and looked at Jodi. She looked at me confused for a moment and then I saw the mental click behind her eyes. When we had sent the searching wind for Jeremy earlier, it had created a link between us and now Jodi and I could feel Jeremy and knew he was hiding in the shadows in the backyard, shrouded by his elemental creatures. Jodi locked eyes with me and then nodded slowly.

"Shay, are you sure this is a good idea?" Jensen asked from beside his mother as she spoke to the 911 operator.

"It's the only idea right now. I don't want your mom hurt like Deb was just because he's trying to get to me through everyone else. That isn't fair," I said.

"Then I'm coming too," Jensen said, taking a step away from his mom.

"No," I said quickly. "You stay with her. If you pick anything up about us, you can warn me, but if you pick up something about your mom, you may be too far away to protect her." We looked at each other for a few moments and I felt his emotions warring inside him, his instincts telling him to find a way to protect both his mother and me, but we both knew, of the two of us, she needed his protection more.

"Be careful," he said softly and I felt his affection travel across the room and into me. I had a moment of selfish guilt that I couldn't be the girlfriend he deserved. I steeled myself as I gripped the edge of the curtain again and tore it back, reaching for the door and sliding it open to step outside.

Chapter 17

It was full dark outside; if there was moonlight, it didn't penetrate the backyard. I had decided not to turn on the back porch light, not wanting to give Jeremy the upper hand by being able to see me clearly and ruining my night vision. Once Jodi and Steven were outside with me, we let the curtains to the living room fall closed, blocking out all of the light from inside. I allowed us the few moments needed to let our eyes adjust to the sudden darkness, feeling them go wide, as if trying to take in any light possible.

In the last couple of days, my empathetic abilities had been running so high because of Jeremy's volatile emotions, I had started putting up stronger and stronger shields against everyone. Now, as I stood there, I felt the inexplicable pull from the core of my body straight out to the back fence. That was Jeremy, seething in a fury that was only partly his. I began stripping down the shields I had built these last few days, exposing myself, not only to Jeremy, but to everyone. I brought my shields against other peoples' emotions down to the every day level I usually carried them at and was suddenly so aware of Jodi to my right and Steven to my left that it felt like they were extensions of my body. A heat so strong I thought surely my face must be burning red was just a few dozen feet in front of me. Jeremy.

I focused on the channels between Jodi and Steven, giving them some of the pent up energy that had kept me pacing earlier until I could see the faint hue of red and yellow out of the corners of my eyes.

Fae? I thought at Jodi without making any physical connection with her.

I hear you, Terra, Jodi answered me; I could hear the thrumming of surprise laid under her careful thoughts, keeping herself in control. There had been only one other time in our lives that we could hear each other's thoughts without touching, when we were about to take on Ian and the demon he had summoned. We had built up so much power, so much magic between us, it had burst out of us in new abilities we hadn't kept once the night was over.

Drake? I thought at Steven in the same way.

I can hear you both, Steven answered and I could feel a small tug from Jodi's direction, as if hearing Steven as clearly as I could had startled her.

We need to surround him, I started planning immediately. *I am going straight for him, keeping his attention on me. Drake, I want you to circle around that way.* I made no physical move to direct him, not wanting to alert Jeremy to my plan, but what I wanted Steven to do had come with my thoughts and I knew he understood. *Fae, I want you to circle around in the opposite direction, but I need you to summon an Air Elemental so that we can cover him from above.*

Okay... she thought, but I could hear and feel her trepidation, scared that she couldn't do it as quickly as we would need her to. I took some of the power I was getting from Steven and redirected it to Jodi and began mentally guiding her to call up her power and send it out, searching for help. Almost immediately sounds came, but I knew they were from Jeremy's Elementals and not ours. The same, bone jarring creeks and squeaks we had heard inside began to sound all around us. I fed them both calm reassurance; it was just a glamour.

Soon I heard the rustling of the leaves in the trees in the backyard and felt a wave of relief rush out of Jodi. She had managed to call to the air spirits in answer to her call for help. The wind swirled overhead, whipping my hair around my head and rushing over my shoulders towards Jeremy. I balanced out the transfer of energy again and took a step forward; Steven and Jodi turned in opposite directions and began to circle to the sides.

"Jeremy," I called out loud and clearly. "I know you're there, I can see you," I could feel his doubt. He didn't believe I could see him in this darkness, hidden by his Air Elementals. I reached inside of myself and called up more power, feeding it into my Empathetic ability before I spoke again. "I can feel you," I said, feeling the power resonate in my voice, carried on the rushing wind and striking Jeremy. I heard as the breath was knocked out of him and he struck the fence he was standing in front of. I kept my adrenaline in check as both my power and Jodi's elemental charge blended so well together to combat the same target. I continued forward, taking slow, sure steps, not wanting to come too close to him.

I opened my hands, palms forward and fingers splayed, tips pointing to the earth. I felt the coursing heat of the metal hidden under the skin, but it wasn't enough. I sent the mental picture of my pose to Jodi. She mimicked me. Then I turned my attention to Steven, calling on his aid to send us the heat of his power and almost immediately I felt the burn in my hands. I smiled in spite of the pain.

"Jeremy, I don't want to hurt you," I said, letting my power continue to reverberate in the tones of my voice, becoming a pressure on his body thanks to the link we had developed over the last few days. "We wanted to help you, but now we have to stop you." I called upon my Elemental magic then, feeling the power directed through my fingers and into the ground, racing towards Jeremy. The roots of the plants sprang up around him, breaking through the ground and shackling his ankles, holding him fast to the spot he was standing on. I heard him yell a curse, nearly falling over.

We stopped, only a few feet away from him now. Jodi's energy was reaching a fevered pitch, both excited to be helping so much more than she ever had before and terrified to lose control of her concentration. The wind whipped around us in answer to her spiking emotions. I took some of the control that comes with Earth magic and sent it to her, trying to balance the veracity of Air magic.

"Jeremy," I called to him again, but this time my voice was soft, letting the magic and power call to him.

"No," he said angrily, almost waspishly.

"Jeremy, we have power," I said, letting the roots that held him tighten around him to emphasize my words. "We have magic." Jodi's wind lashed at his face, careful to stay above him. "We can teach you," I said, letting another bolt of power race down my voice and strike him again, knowing it was only pushing him against the fence, not really hurting him.

"Lies, pretty, pretty lies," I heard the whisper under the sound of the wind and the racing blood in my ears, but it wasn't Jeremy's voice. This voice was vaguely feminine and definitely not human. "They would hurt you, yes," it hissed and I knew it was whispering in Jeremy's ear. "Yes, pretty, pretty lies to hurt you."

"Jeremy, if it were lies," I started to say and I felt him jerk his head up and knew he was looking at me, amazed I had heard the voice. "If it were lies," I continued, "why would we have tried so hard and so many times to reach you?" I fed just an ounce of trust and compassion down the line we had drawn between us, not wanting him to feel pushed into believing me.

"Because she would have your power for herself," the voice whispered around us, but quieter this time, as if trying to keep me from hearing it.

Are you two hearing this? I thought at Jodi and Steven.

Hearing what? Steven asked and answered my question all at once.

I hear it, Terra, I hear it, Jodi's yellow thoughts came to me, cool and a little afraid.

"We have our own power, and the ability to share it, we don't need to take yours," I said, willing the roots around his ankles to loosen just a little, urging Jodi to calm the wind just a bit. "Come to me, Jeremy, come to us and away from these things and we will help you."

"Come to us, Jeremy," Jodi repeated and I felt the stirrings of a spell in her words.

"Come to us, and away from these things," Steven took up the line and I felt the power building; they were speaking on instinct.

"We will help you, Jeremy," I said, now feeling the true ringing of the power through our tripled connection.

"Come to us, Jeremy," Jodi repeated, followed by Steven.

"Come to us, and away from these things," Steven said. I felt Jeremy straining against us, letting his warring emotions have their way with him and in that he was giving these Elementals more power, more control over him.

"Jeremy," I called to him again, pulling on the power from the ground and he struggled against me, but I could feel that part of him wanted to come to us.

"Come to us, Jeremy," Jodi repeated again, building on the spell.

"Come to us, and away from these things," Steven said, pushing his power into his words and I saw the mental image of Jeremy being bound by these things, and just then a rush of wind struck against my shields and I knew his Elementals were striking out against us to stop the casting.

"Shayna!" Jensen's voice called out from behind me, distracting me momentarily. I was careful not to turn my back on Jeremy, despite the strong urge to look at Jensen, but even still it broke just enough of my concentration that Jeremy's creatures took advantage and tried to rush me.

I felt the energy in the air shift and their anger bit along my skin like scorpion stings and, for just a moment, I couldn't breathe. I stole back the power I was feeding the ground to bind Jeremy's legs and transferred it all into my shields, bracing behind them as the impact hit, just inches away from my face. They swirled like angry bees, but couldn't reach me behind my shields. Jeremy took the chance to dance away from the upraised roots that were now loose around his feet.

"See the pretty lies, she is afraid of you, afraid of your power." I saw the light glint in Jeremy's eye at the thought they were trying to force-feed him.

"Jeremy, don't listen to them! They're lying!" I yelled over the buzz of their voices, not sure if I was the only one having trouble hearing over them. "It's not your power, it's theirs! They're trying to make you think you're controlling them, but you aren't," I said, watching the confusion plain on Jeremy's face and felt it churn his stomach. I had voiced the very same doubts he had been thinking lately, but possibly was too scared to say them out loud.

"She would make you weak, but we know you are not weak," they whispered sweetly in his ear and I had a vision of a lovely, lithe figure standing by Jeremy's shoulder. Spun gold hair tickling his cheek while she nuzzled his throat. I watched this vision, trying to keep my attention on Jeremy's face, but knew he wasn't seeing the hundreds of tiny creatures we always thought were surrounding him.

You see her too, don't you? Jodi's thoughts came to me and I knew I didn't even have to ask Steven if he could, knowing he couldn't.

Yeah, yeah, I see her, Fae, I answered her.

But is it like you really see her or more that you just know she's there? I felt Jodi's confusion more than heard it in her words.

You're sharing my vision. I'm getting it from his emotions and, since the link is so strong right now... I felt the understanding echo back from her without her saying anything. I turned my full attention back on Jeremy. I summoned up more power from the ground and gave a little mental warning to Jodi and Steven to keep their heads in the game before I spoke, pouring the power into my words.

"Jeremy, I know you're not weak," I coated my words with the power and my Empathy, willing him to trust me. "That's why I wanted to help you. I've never lied or *tricked* you…" I pushed a little harder with the last part and was rewarded by the change in his eye; I struck something inside him. "She's tricked you, hasn't she?"

He hesitated and I knew he wanted to answer me, but there was something stopping him. He was afraid of the Sylph that was nuzzling him. I drew on my lines between Jodi and Steven for strength and then sent the impulse of mistrust through my connection with Jeremy, pushing at his doubts that the Sylph only had her own interests at heart, not his.

Jeremy looked at me then and, for the first time since before all hell broke loose in the jail, he looked at me clearly; no magic, no tricks. I nodded at him, let him feel my sincerity, let him feel all of our concern for him. He took one slow step towards me before I heard a disembodied scream rend the eerie calm we had created. I had one second to decide who to protect, but there really wasn't a choice. I cut my ties from Jeremy in a skin burning jolt and flung my powers out behind me to Jodi, Steven, and finally Jensen, leaving myself more exposed than I normally would.

I watched the fear and confusion on Jeremy's face as tears sprung in his eyes and a shadow reared up in front of him, distorting his figure and finally hiding him from our sight. In the next second, he was gone. The screams continued, turning towards us. I heard Jensen behind me, yelling my name, running towards me. I braced for the impact again and was vaguely aware that this time, it wasn't going to work; I had left myself too exposed. The wind ripped at my face and battered my body. A jagged cut opened over my cheek and a burning sensation was clawing at my arms, but I stood my ground, pouring my powers into the shields of my friends.

I fought the urge to close my eyes in the last seconds when I knew the major impact was coming and knew it would all be black in a moment anyway when I saw Steven racing to my side. His arms circled my waist and hefted me into the air. He threw me back behind him into Jensen's arms, who caught me and spun us around, bringing us to the ground and shielding my body. I screamed my protest, trying to fight him every inch of the way. In the last few seconds before Jensen's torso covered my face as I made contact with the ground, I saw Steven standing in the exact spot that I had been in, his arms spread wide, making a target of himself as the shadow arced above him. When my sight was lost, I had a vision in my mind of Steven standing there, body engulfed in flame, an inferno against the night. Another few moments and the screams had stopped, replaced by Jodi's cries as she wailed Steven's name.

I pushed at Jensen trying to get him off of me, but he was too heavy for me. I felt my anger pitch and my skin burn with it when he refused to let me up. I clawed at him, my nails finding purchase on the skin of neck and arms. He swore above me. When he flinched, he gave me just enough momentum to get my torso out from under him. I knew I was screaming at him to let me up, but he wasn't listening. Finally, when I knew I would explode from anxiety as I listened to Jodi sobbing over Steven, I pulled my hand back and reached out to slap Jensen. Cupping my hand, I popped him over his ear, hearing the echo as I disturbed his equilibrium. He swore again and finally let me up as he covered his ear with his hand and tears sprung to his eyes in reaction to the pain. I crawled away from him and scrambled to stand, racing over to Steven.

Jodi was already kneeling on the ground at his shoulder, trying to shake him awake, but looked as though she was afraid to touch him. I understood why when I fell to the ground at his other shoulder. There were burn marks on his face and his clothing was singed and frayed, holes showing red angry welts on his arms and chest. Thin lines of smoke drifted up from his body into the air.

"Oh god, I didn't imagine it," I said, my voice barely above a whisper.

"I don't know how he did it," Jodi said between sobs, covering her face that was quickly becoming streaked with makeup.

"The extra power I was feeding you, he..." I stopped, swallowing past a lump in my throat. "He must've redirected it." I shook my head and laid my hands carefully on his chest, feeling his heart beat strong and steady under them and took a moment to send up a silent prayer of thanks for that. I started pulling cool, healing energy up through the earth beneath him just as we heard sirens racing down the block and closing in on the house fast. Water bubbled up from the ground, rising around his body, causing steam to billow from his skin.

"Oh god, how do we explain this?" Jodi said quickly, her head whipping up from her hands towards the house.

"We'll say he went out to check and see if Jeremy was still here. He must've lit a cigarette while out here and some accident happened, we won't be clear on exactly what," I said, the story coming almost too easily to my lips.

"I'll run and tell my mom so she doesn't blow it for us," Jensen said and before I could say anything, he was already half way across the yard. He was still holding his ear and I saw him stumble as his feet hit the back patio. Guilt stung through me for hitting him so hard, but I knew in my heart I could've done much worse to him if I hadn't used physical force.

"Steven doesn't smoke," Jodi said, bringing my attention back to her, her blue eyes wide with anguish and fear.

"They don't know that," I said, my voice a little clipped. "We can't tell them he set himself on fire to save me. They'll lock him and us up in a sanitarium, Jodi."

"Of course," Jodi said, shaking her head as if trying to clear her muddled thoughts. I felt a sweat breaking out over my forehead. I was having a very difficult time blocking out the waves of terror coming off of Jodi in such close proximity while I worked on Steven, but I knew I only had moments left before the cops and paramedics came through the back door. Steven moaned quietly, his head moving just an inch and Jodi gasped, her hand flying to cover her mouth in surprise. "Oh my god, Terra, you're doing it!"

"Terra?" Steven asked, his brow wrinkling and I could feel it was half in confusion and half in pain.

Don't talk, I thought at Steven calmly. *Help is here, just stay still,* I mentally relayed our alibi for his injuries as the cops came rushing through the back door. Just before I broke contact with Steven, I realized he had no memory of what he'd actually done to hurt himself in the first place. I wasn't looking forward to explaining it to him when he woke up later.

Steven was in the hospital, his wailing mother crying over his body, and we were in the hallway, the heady mixture of antiseptic, bleach, and death filling our nostrils. Jodi was sitting on a hard plastic chair, her head back against the wall behind her, and I was pacing in front of her, every nerve on edge as I held out the sheer weight of the building around me. I hate hospitals. I always have, ever since I was a child and had to come in for the first time since I was born to have stitches in my chin when I split it open in a car accident. My mom rushed me inside, blood running down both our shirt fronts, a little frantic and wide-eyed. All the while, I wasn't making a sound.

The doctors told my mom that I was in shock so I didn't realize it hurt, but I knew better; it was the screaming and the wailing all around me that kept me silent. I was having a very hard time breathing for all the weight that pressed down on me anytime my mom let go of my hand. Luckily, when they finally took us in, they took us right to pediatrics, which was on the same floor as obstetrics and suddenly the weight became lighter, bearable. I learned later that I had finally found the balance in the hospital when I found where new life was coming into the building and joy and happiness intermingled with pain and anxiety.

But tonight I was stuck in the intensive care unit with Jodi and toeing the line of my sanity as the pain coursed over and through my body of so many people in pain and torment. I wasn't going to last much longer, but the cops had asked us to stay for questioning, me especially. I had tried to leave the wing on the pretense of finding a vending machine, but an armed officer stopped me at the end of the hall and sent someone to get us some cold sodas for us.

"You doin' alright, babe?" Jodi asked after I passed her for what must have been the hundredth time.

"Not really, no," I said honestly as I spun on my heel and began the trek back.

"We need to get you out of here," she said, pushing herself up as I neared her. "You've lost all the color in your face and I think you're sweating." I instinctively slapped her hand away when she reached up to check my temperature on my forehead.

"Sorry, I just can't." I shook my head and kept walking. "Just try not to touch me right now."

"Some contact might help, you know," she said, but I couldn't hear her clearly; I was still catching snatches of long ago screams that still echoed in the halls despite how much of my energy went into blocking them. "Shay!" Jodi said sharply, grabbing my arm and spinning me to face her.

I felt my eyes go wide and a snarl bubbling up my throat. I saw the momentary fear flicker through her face, but she held onto me anyway, trusting I wouldn't lash out at her. Her fingers dug into my skin, her nails biting into me, just sharp enough to pull me back from the edge and clear the fog in my head.

"I'm sorry," I said, shaking my head.

"Don't be, just anchor to me," Jodi said as she guided me to the row of chairs she had been sitting on. It took me longer than it should have to open the natural channel between us because I was afraid to take any energy away from keeping out the hospital, but eventually I felt a cool air caressing my face, drying the beads of sweat on my forehead. I closed my eyes and concentrated on the Air and felt it swirling and building inside of me like a soothing breeze on a hot summer day and gave myself the moment I needed to bask in it.

"Better and better," I whispered, feeling some of the tension seeping away from me. "If only they'd let me leave! Even with you helping, I can't stay here too long; it'll kill me."

"I know. I don't know why they're keeping us here," Jodi said and finally I heard the anger in her voice.

"It's probably because they know Jeremy was involved," I said with a sigh, slumping forward over my knees, keeping my hand clasped around Jodi's, looking for all the world just like two friends comforting each other over the horror of their friend's terrible accident.

"What I don't get though is where my dad is," Jodi said and when I turned my face to look at her, I saw her staring at the rookie cop at the end of the hall that had stopped me earlier.

"Probably investigating at Jensen's house," I said, but now it was her turn not to really hear me. "Hey," I said, shaking her arm to draw her attention back to me. "Call your dad. Get him down here to get us out of here. We'll go back to my place or yours and then we'll go after Jeremy."

"I don't have my phone. We left everything at Jensen's house when the ambulance came, remember?" Jodi said.

"Go over to the nurses' station. I'm sure they'll let you use their phone," I said, nodding towards the counter just a few feet away from us. Jodi nodded and, as one, we stood and walked over, hand in hand so I wouldn't lose it again, and Jodi called her father. It wasn't long before we had our own police escort out of the building, much to the dismay of the rookie who would've stopped us until he saw Jodi's father and paled at the sight of his grim face.

I fought the urge to stick my tongue out at him as we passed, noticing that one hand rested on the butt of his gun and the other on his radio, as if wondering how to best stop us from leaving. I felt my anger color my cheeks as I glared at him. How dare he threaten me like that? Jodi realized I wasn't right next to her and turned to see me giving the rookie a death stare. I felt her hand on my arm, urging me to let the insult go. I took one last breath before I turned to leave with her.

Jodi's father drove us to my house, planning to just drop me off and take Jodi home, but after much cajoling from his baby girl and the terrified look on my face, he consented to let Jodi spend the night on the promise that in the morning we really would be on our way to school. The thought of such normalcy startled me. I was losing track of time and days.

Not surprisingly, my parents were waiting for me at the door when we walked up, Jodi's father having called them to tell them what had happened. We gave them the story of hearing a prowler outside, thinking it was Jeremy and Steven going out to check, saying that he had some strange accident near some yard tools where gasoline must've been, but we didn't really know all the details since he was outside alone. It didn't take near as much convincing for my parents to agree to let Jodi stay over on a school night after seeing how shaken I appeared to be. I think it was that fact alone that let me off the hook of being in trouble for leaving Jodi's house when I promised not to. We just had to promise to get to bed early before they let us pass into the hall and head to my room.

"What are we doing?" Jodi asked as soon as we were inside my room and my door was shut.

"We need to get out to the tree and get some supplies and then we'll try to link into Jeremy again and go-" I stopped short and swore an oath.

"What?" Jodi asked quickly.

"My goddamn car is parked in front of Jensen's house," I said, my fists clenching hard enough to let my nails dig into the palms.

"Oh shit," Jodi muttered.

"Yeah, 'oh shit' is right." I took a deep breath in and motioned with my hands for us to calm down. "We'll just have to work from here, wait for my parents to go to bed, and then we'll take one of their cars." Jodi cocked an eyebrow at me as if she could see a thousand holes in my plan. "They go to bed early and my dad snores really loudly, we'll be fine. Besides, what other choice do we have right now?"

We had to wait over an hour before I heard both my parents finally go to bed and shut the bedroom door behind them and then another fifteen minutes to make sure they weren't coming back out again. I decided the best thing to do was not to go through the house at all, so I popped the screen off of my window and we climbed out into the backyard, racing to the ladder leading up to my tree house. Once inside, I decided to open both the windows and let the night air in since we were, after all, working with Air magic.

I could feel the tension and excitement thrumming along Jodi's body as we pulled out the supplies we needed and began casting a protective circle around the tree house. "I know our nerves are going, but why do you almost seem happy about this?" I asked Jodi as we laid out the supplies between us.

"Because we're stopping this now, tonight, before that Sylph can hurt the rest of us," she said, the determination in her voice matching the energy pulsing off of her.

"We don't have Steven here now for our anchor or for his Fire," I pointed out.

"Yes, we do," Jodi said, setting an obsidian crystal down in the middle between us. "We have you, that's all we need."

"What?"

"You can link to Steven and draw on his power," she said matter-of-factly.

"He so far away though. I've never tried that so far apart"

"We could hear each other's thoughts again tonight," she said, finally resting her hands on her thighs and looking up at me. "You have that power, Shayna, I know you do. You're Terra, Earth Mother, remember?" It was a humbling moment for me, looking into the blue eyes of my sister, so much trust and faith in them, no trace of the small amount of jealousy she always seemed to carry with her. She knew I could do this with her and right now all the petty teenage rivalry was gone. I felt my eyes well with the emotion and a tear escape, rolling down my cheek and falling onto the sacred cloth we had laid down for our tools.

"We join hands this night, Earth Mother and Air Spirit, calling upon the elements to guide us in our magical workings," I intoned, reaching out to take Jodi's hand and felt the warmth in our hands and thought of Steven, the missing link between us. A vision of a hospital room flooded before my eyes, my legs itched under the over-starched sheets and needles pricked my arms, arms that were too long and muscled to be mine. "We join hands this night, Earth Mother, Air Spirit, and Fire Child," I whispered and felt the air stir around us, answering our call, ready to finish this.

Chapter 18

The temperature outside was in the mid-fifties, crisp and refreshing, but inside the tree house I would've guessed it was well over a hundred degrees as the sweat rolled down our foreheads into our eyes, tickling the backs of our necks, plastering our hair to our foreheads. I thought the rise in temperature was Steven's fault once I had linked to him and thought maybe his powers were manifesting out of his control considering his injuries, but somehow I knew that wasn't right. Jodi and I both felt the burning sensation of the metal trapped in our fingers swirling under the surface of our skin. That metal was the answer to taking down the Sylph that was controlling Jeremy, but how to use it was another question all together.

I could hear Jodi's ragged breathing and opened my eyes to see the bright patches coming to life on her cheeks, washing out any other color she had, and I felt a pang of worry that she might faint from heatstroke if we kept this up. My mouth had gone dry in the heat from speaking the incantations to raise our power and the magic needed to take on the Sylph and never before had I missed the fourth element of Water from our circle more than I did right then.

"You have your answers, why do you continue to seek?" the familiar, bell-like voice sounded in the room, echoing off of the wooden walls and inside my mind. I opened my eyes to see Tegan standing between us, in the middle of our tools on the sacred cloth.

"We don't have our answers," I said, not surprised to hear my voice was a little breathy as if I had just run sprints in P.E. class.

"You have your answers and you have your tools, go find the Sylph, do what must be done, what only you two can do," he said again, his hands on his hips. The fall leaves that were his wings opened and closed so slowly they didn't even make the flame on the candle waver.

"We don't know how to use our tools," Jodi said, trying to cut through the faerie logic, looking for more help than I knew we were going to get out of him.

"You know without knowing how you know, Air Spirit. Go and do what you must do," he said and I bit the inside of my cheek to keep from asking him just what the hell he was talking about. I felt a surge of impatience from Jodi that set my teeth on edge and knew that she too was trying to keep her temper under control.

"Fine," I said, cutting off Jodi before she could get the words out to argue with him. "We know without knowing, but we don't know where we're going and we've wasted enough time these last two days racing around trying to find them, so we're trying to find him now."

"You know where he is, or where he will be. Stop questioning yourselves and go," Tegan said calmly, pushing off of the floor lightly and hovering in the air between our faces. I noticed that there was a fine line of worry creasing the usually smooth skin between his eyes, the only hint that he too was scared of what the Sylph was planning. Even the light he always seemed to emanate was dull.

"Why must it always be riddles?" Jodi asked, her frustration coming through clearly.

"Because you humans are stubborn. If it is too easy, you question it," he said, turning to give Jodi his full attention.

"We are too stubborn!" Jodi cried with a sputtered laugh.

"Okay, fine," I said, giving Jodi's hand a squeeze as I cut her off again and drew Tegan's face back to mine. "So if it's too easy, then the obvious answer is probably the right one." Tegan didn't say anything to confirm or dispute that, so I continued, "I think he's going after his father after what I heard him saying to his brother." Tegan gave the faintest of nods. "But, I've thought that since he went after his brother and he didn't go right after his father. First he went after Deb and then after Jensen's mom trying to punish me, so to think he's finally stopped me and gone on to his Dad isn't necessarily the obvious choice yet."

"Does he know you've left the Fire Child's side?" Tegan asked and I thought of the cops keeping Jodi and me in the hospital when we tried to leave and the knot in my stomach went cold.

"What if I'm wrong? What if he tries to hurt someone else while we're at his house?" I asked, tasting my fear like copper pennies on my tongue.

"There are always casualties in a war, Terra, you know this," Tegan said, floating a few inches closer to my face.

"But I can't let innocent people fall because of me," I whispered.

"Terra," Jodi said softly, pulling my attention back from Tegan. "Who else can he go after? Everyone who he could go after is at home, under the shields, and we'll be together, so he can only get to me once we find him and that's a risk we're already preparing for." We held each other's gaze for a few quiet, tense moments before I gave the briefest of nods and we began uncasting the barrier spells we'd formed to work in the tree and by the time I had opened my eyes again, Tegan was gone, presumably still within yelling distance, but with faeries, one can never really be sure.

I ran my thumb over the tips of my fingers where the iron swirled under the skin and tried not to think of what we would have to do to get it out and use it against the Sylph. Molten metal was definitely on my list of things to avoid and now, like some damn masochist, I was going to try to draw this out of my skin as a weapon. Just another day in the life of me.

We crept down the ladder braced against the tree, each of us with a bag slung over our shoulders, containing a few tools we didn't know whether or not we'd need and decided we'd rather have them and not need them than need them and have left them behind. We brought ceremonial knives we'd charged with power but had yet to have a chance to use. They weren't iron, but the blades were live and any metal would help right now. We both had a full container of salt, one of the most convenient and simple tools in magic and still one of the most effective. You could draw a circle of protection with it in a second and you could banish evil spirits with it like a bullet shot from a gun.

Other than that, we had haphazardly thrown in amulets and binding cords of various colors, not really sure what would work against the Sylph. I had a feeling though that, with all these tools, we were really just hoping to find the weapon that would work and keep us from using the metal that still burned in our fingers. I took both bags and dropped them into my room from my still open window before giving Jodi a leg up onto the sill. She helped me slide in without making much noise before checking the hallway for sounds from my parents, but she withdrew her head and gave me a thumbs up that all was clear.

I dug in my closet for two hooded black sweatshirts and tossed one behind me to Jodi, who slipped it on as I pulled mine over my head, quickly grabbing my hair and twisting it into a ponytail. We were both already wearing dark jeans and I didn't want to take the time to quibble over our tennis shoes being too light in color and change them. We grabbed our bags and crept out of my room, leaving the T.V. on with the volume turned down low to cover the lack of any sound from within. Luckily, I always slept with the T.V. on so my parents wouldn't find this strange. Jodi waited for me by the front door while I dug in my mom's purse for her keys. When I found them, I kept my hand cupped around them to keep them from jiggling and announcing our escape. We ran to the driveway and slid into my mom's sedan, pulling our doors shut carefully to make as little noise as possible.

 I put the gear into neutral and released the emergency brake to coast backwards down the driveway, turning the wheel sharply at the bottom of the slope so we'd back away from the house and drift in front of the neighbor's before I turned the key in the ignition and started the engine. We were turning around the second corner before I heard Jodi's exhale loudly and felt the razor sharp edge of her anxiety easy up just a little.

 "God, you would think we were sneaking out after curfew to see boys or go to a party or something," Jodi said with a shaky laugh, but I knew she was only trying to cover her growing agitation.

 "Let's promise, when this is over, we do something stupid and normal like that," I said, watching the traffic light in front of me phase to green. Jodi laughed again and this time it sounded closer to normal.

 We were pulling up in front of Jeremy's house again, but this time made no pretense of parking across the street or hiding my mother's car, which was a standard four-door mom-mobile; the best way to keep it inconspicuous was to have it right out in the open. We watched the house for a few moments. All of the windows were dark, but the front porch light was still on, as if they expected someone to come home late, but all three cars were accounted for.

 "So what's the plan?" Jodi asked, still looking out her window. "Are we waiting until we see Jeremy make a move or do we go in guns blazing and warn his parents or what?"

 "Guns blazing?" I said, smirking and letting the joke ease the tension in my shoulders. "Easy there, cowboy."

"You know what I mean," she said over her shoulder and I felt her own tension give way just a bit.

"Actually I *was* thinking of going in and waiting for Jeremy," I said gauging the distance from the car to the front door. "But not going to warn his parents."

"What?" Jodi asked, turning her startled face to me.

"What? How do you think that'll go over?" I asked, tilting my head to the side and looking her in the eye. "Hi, Mr. and Mrs. McCormack, I know this sounds crazy, but your son, Jeremy? Well, he has supernatural abilities and can communicate with faeries and seems to have gotten himself mixed up with an evil faerie; a Sylph to be exact. We have reason to believe that he's on his way here to try to hurt you or, worse, kill you. But never fear! We, two teenage girls, are here to save the day!"

"Yeah, okay," Jodi said reluctantly with a nod. "When you say it like that, it does sound kinda crazy."

"No, what's really crazy is that's really what's going on here," I said, trying very hard not to laugh.

"No kidding," she said with a shake of her head. Jodi reached down to the floor by her feet and grabbed the bags we'd brought with us, handing me one and slinging the other over her shoulder. "So, through the front door?

"No, the light's on, I don't want to be seen trying to break in," I said, putting the car keys into an inside pocket of my bag. "Let's circle around back. All the houses in this neighborhood are the same; they should have a sliding glass door for their back door."

"Can you see which side the side gate is on?"

"To your right," I said, squinting through the dark over her shoulder.

"Let's go," Jodi said and my stomach did a flip and I knew that it was her butterflies I was feeling this time. I took a deep breath with my hand on the door handle and sent up a silent prayer for help before stepping out and following Jodi at a dash, bent over, trying to stay below a normal eye line. Luckily they didn't have a lock on the side gate and, with a simple tug of the nylon cord sticking through the wood, we were able to open the gate and slip into the backyard unseen.

Our luck didn't hold out for the back door though. They did, in fact, have a sliding glass door, but they had remembered to lock it before going to bed.

Hey look, Jodi thought at me, nodding towards our feet and I saw the doggie-door they had installed into a panel, taking up a foot of the door's width.

Oh crap, do you think there's a dog? I thought frantically.

If there is, it's locked up somewhere. Otherwise it'd be out here already, Jodi reassured me and I realized she was right and clung to that logic for all it was worth. I crouched down and got on my hands and knees and reached out to test the doggie door. The flap gave easily under my fingers; they had forgotten to put up the plastic guard that would keep the dog in or out of the house depending on when it was slid into place. I reached up for Jodi's bag and pushed it through with mine and started to wriggle my way through. I had to put one arm and shoulder through at a time, nearly giving myself a cramp in my left shoulder. I turned on my side to get my hips through, but after that I was scrambling quickly to my feet, listening for any signs of life before I turned and unlocked the sliding door and let Jodi in the easy way.

"Wow, glad you did that and not me," Jodi whispered as quietly as possible as she slid the door shut behind her, remembering to lock it again. "I don't think I would've gotten my hips through that."

"Oh shut up," I said automatically, squashing any discussion on the trivialities of body image. I was giving myself a few moments to let my night vision kick in as I scanned the dark room we were standing in. As the shadows in the room finally started to take shape, I realized we were standing in the living room.

"Now what?" Jodi asked and I tensed.

"Dude, I swear," I whispered, rolling my shoulders, "if I never hear that question again, it'll be too soon."

"Well, what do you want me to say?" Jodi asked and I could hear the edge of annoyance in her voice and the pinprick of anger flare from her as she took my comment as an insult.

"Sorry, I just…" I shook my head trying to clear it to explain.

"No, no, don't," she said, raising a hand to stall me. "I understand, but seriously, now what?"

"Yeah, now what?" I repeated, keeping my attention divided between the hallways that led off of the living room. "Guess we should find out if he's here yet. Keep watch."

"Okay," Jodi said and I was already closing my eyes, holding up my right hand and concentrating on the power just days ago Deb and I had been practicing with. It didn't take too long to search the house, only registering three signatures, all in the same room and I knew it was Jeremy's parents and the weaker point most likely the dog the door had been installed for.

"He's not here yet," I whispered to Jodi once I came back to myself, feeling the tingle of power dancing over my skin.

"Now wha-" Jodi stopped herself as I threw a look over my shoulder at her. "Do you want to go into his parents' room and wait there or do you think he'll try another way in?"

I gave her a smile of thanks for making a suggestion rather than just leaving it all up to me. "I really don't know. I mean, yeah, we can go check on them, but I don't know if he'll come climbing through their window."

"He did at Cindy's house," Jodi prompted and I nodded, remembering the scene.

"You're right, let's go," I said, reaching for the bags and tossing one to her before heading down the hall to our left that led to the bedrooms.

Hey, Jodi's thoughts stopped me as we creeped down the hall, touching my arm. I turned to look at her, my heart pounding in my throat as we stood there, knowing the McCormack's could open their bedroom door any second and we were lingering in the hall. *Look,* she thought, nodding towards the door we'd stopped in front of. I turned and saw the closed door that was covered in warning signs and fake crime scene tape telling people not to enter.

I reached for the door knob and, as my fingers touched the metal, a shock ran through me, nearly making me stumble back, but I held on, letting the electricity bite my skin as I turned the knob. As soon as the door was open, the current died and the knob was lifeless in my palm.

What was that? Jodi asked, touching my shoulder tentatively.

It looks like, I started to explain but stopped myself to check the other side of the door and found nothing hanging on the knob on the other side to explain the electricity. *Seems Jeremy wasn't entirely unschooled. Some sort of barrier spell.*

Seriously? Jodi asked and I could see the dull yellow of her thoughts in my mind, coloring her words with disbelief.

Weak, but impressive anyway. Now, let's see what we've got here, I motioned her further into the room so I could shut the door behind us.

"Do we chance a light?" Jodi whispered and I shook my head, not seeing a dimmer on the light switch. I walked over to the curtained windows and pulled them open slightly to let in the moonlight only to find Jeremy had put black paper over the glass. "Oh come on," Jodi whispered with disgust. "How cliché goth can you get?"

I ignored her, silently agreeing with her, and walked over to the closet, opening it to see a string hanging down above my head and reached up and pulled on it. The light clicked on inside the closet. I turned to see that its illumination didn't reach within a few feet of the door, so if his parents did pass by they wouldn't see the line of light under the door.

"Nice," Jodi nodded and turned her attention back to the room. "Is it weird how neat everything is?"

"Yeah, I kinda expected it to be a cluttered mess too," I said, looking at the spotless floor and desk that was so organized it hinted of obsessive compulsive disorder.

"You'd think he was an Earth Element, not Air, looking at this," Jodi said, sweeping her hands out.

"Hey, my room doesn't look like this," I said a little defensively, walking over to a small bookshelf in the corner.

"No, yours is much warmer and more welcoming, but remember, Earths can be stubborn and set in their ways with their rules and everything. Looks like he's taken that to an extreme." I had to agree with her on that. I scanned the bookshelf, but saw only fiction titles of books with creased spines and ragged edges like he had reread the same collection a hundred times.

I stepped back and looked around again trying to notice anything out of place, but that seemed to be the plan; if nothing was out of place, then his parents wouldn't go snooping around for anything because they could see everything. "Or can they?" I asked out loud.

"What?" Jodi asked, turning her attention from Jeremy's desk drawers.

"I was just thinking, since it's like everything is out in the open, not hidden under clutter, his parents wouldn't go snooping," I explained, walking towards Jeremy's bed, which was made, complete with hospital corners. "Because they can see everything," I said, dropping to my knees in front of the bed and lowering myself to the floor. "Or can they?" I repeated as I shimmied under the bed.

Unsurprisingly, there wasn't so much as a wayward sock or shoe under there. I spread my hands out and slid them over the floor, searching for something out of place. I shifted towards the head of the bed and continued sweeping my hands over the floor until the tip of my finger caught on a groove.

"That's what I thought," I said to myself and clawed at the loose floorboard, prying it up to reveal a gap under it. I slid my hand in slowly, trying to keep all thoughts of bugs and vermin from my mind, reaching until I felt the cool firmness of what I was expecting, a book. I grabbed it and shimmied backwards out from under the bed and sat up on my heels and set the book on the bed.

"Sneaky, sneaky, sneaky," Jodi whispered as she came over to look at the journal. I dusted myself off and grabbed the book and headed over to the closet to use the light.

"I'd feel really bad about this if he hadn't been acting like a rampaging psychopath these last few days," I said as I opened the front cover.

"Is it his grimoire?" Jodi asked in a whisper as she crouched down next to me to get a better look at the book as I turned the pages.

"Yeah, I think so," I answered and began trying to read what he'd written, but his handwriting was worse than mine and it seemed that half of it was written in some sort of code. Paranoia at it's best. I managed to make out some symbols I recognized, but nothing that wasn't mainstream, that he couldn't have picked up just watching television. I was glad to see there wasn't anything overtly evil written anywhere, at least not in anything I could make out. Only Jeremy knew what the coded text said.

"Is that gibberish or a code?" Jodi asked, pointing to a line of text.

"It's a code," I said, shaking my head. I closed the book and opened it from the back, finding long entries in the pages there, but again, written in a way that I couldn't read.

"Dude, he needs some serious help." Jodi said, standing up and walking back over to a dresser.

"No, wait," I said, a spark of a distant memory from history class came to mind and I stood and walked over to the dresser Jodi was standing at where a large mirror was affixed to the wall above it. I opened the book wide and held it open towards the mirror and I was finally able to read what Jeremy had written.

"What the hell?" Jodi asked, furrowing her brow as she leaned closer to the mirror to read.

"Remember History last year? That thing about Da Vinci? He wrote backwards to keep people from stealing his ideas..." I explained quickly as I continued to read through the mirror. Again, it wasn't anything terribly bad, mostly just the ranting of an angst ridden teen, but on the next entry I found what I had been looking for; Jeremy started talking about his encounters with a beautiful girl in the woods. Eventually he figured out that she was a magical creature, thinking she must be one of the mythical nymphs everyone thought had become extinct.

Jeremy went on for pages about her beauty and how much she cared about him and the promises she made to help him right the wrongs in his life because, as she explained to him, he was an amazing sorcerer who deserved to be worshiped. It took a lot of my self-control to keep reading and not throw up what little I had eaten that day.

"Wow, talk about stroking a guy's ego," Jodi said as she leaned back, clearly having read enough.

"Well that explains the mood swings," I said, pulling the book away from the mirror and closing it. "She's brainwashing him and coaxing him into these violent reactions, probably just to entertain herself. I hope when we get her the Faerie Court punishes her to the extreme."

"Faerie Court?" Jodi cocked an eyebrow at me like I was the crazy person in the room.

"Dude, you think they have Fae Queens and Kings, but no actual courts?" I waited, but her expression didn't change. "Don't you remember the stories about the Seelie and Unseelie courts?"

"Yeah, of course, but those are just stories."

"Why?" I asked, turning to face her. "Why are they just stories? I mean, is it so hard to believe? We've known about faeries all our lives. We know there are royals in that world. Why would you think all of the stories are just stories?"

"I guess, but," I stepped forward and shot my hand out to cover her mouth just as I heard the sigh of a door opening. *Oh my god!* Jodi thought at me, her thoughts so bright I almost squinted instinctively. I held my breath as I listened and heard slow footsteps, as if someone was sneaking down the hallway.

Get under the bed! I thought at Jodi before ripping my hand away and spun, creeping over to the closet and grabbing hold of the light string and pulling on it so slowly that when the light went out there wasn't the sound of a click to accompany it. I heard the steps stop just outside the bedroom door and grabbed the closet door, pulling it almost shut to hide behind.

The light from the hallway pooled around the threshold of the bedroom door as Jeremy's father peered in, confusion plain on his face. He reached over with his free hand and turned on the bedroom light.

"Honey? What are you doing?" I heard Mrs. McCormack's sleep logged voice from behind her husband who was still scanning the room.

"I thought I heard something… or saw something," he said.

"Well, which was is?" she asked.

"I don't know, I guess it was just the wind or something," he said finally, shaking his head and reaching to turn off the light. He stopped just inches from it and looked at the open closet door again.

"What is it?" Mrs. McCormack asked again.

"I don't remember that being open," he said, nodding towards the door.

"Well, maybe it wasn't shut all the way and it just opened on it's own," Mrs. McCormick said easily, but I was acutely aware of her anxiety and, although I was no mind reader, her emotions were screaming at me that she was afraid Jeremy had come back for refuge or shelter and didn't want her husband to find him here. "Come on, honey, let's go back to bed," she said, pulling gently on his shoulder from behind. It took him another moment of staring at the opened closet before he finally nodded and turned out the light and left, shutting the door behind him.

We waited until the hallway light was turned out and could hear them close their bedroom door before either of us crawled out of our hiding places. I started to dust myself off out of habit, but realized there wasn't so much as a speck of dust on my jeans. "Wow, we really need to get this poor guy a hobby once this is all over," I said as I laid the grimoire on his desk.

Before Jodi could respond, we heard a loud crash and the raised voices of Jeremy's parents from their room. Scenarios of Jeremy bursting through the window and attacking his parents ran through my mind with the possibility that the two adults had gotten into a heated argument over something. No matter what, something was wrong and we were here – we had to do something. Jodi was at the door before me, flinging it open. We ran down the hall to their bedroom at the end.

We nearly tumbled over each other in our haste to get inside, righting ourselves just in time for me to see a wooden jewelry box flying through the air right for us. I grabbed Jodi by the shoulders and pulled her roughly to the floor with me, letting the jewelry box shatter against the wall above us. There was such a cacophony of sounds I couldn't make out the screams from the crashes.

I looked up and saw Jeremy's mother cowering at the head of their bed, clutching a pillow for protection while Jeremy and his father were caught in each other's grip, wrestling. I vaguely noticed the fact that Jeremy held a knife in one hand and that was why his father was trying to wrestle him, to get it away from him. For some reason, he couldn't over power his much smaller son.

I clawed at the bag on Jodi's back and found the container of salt inside. I opened it quickly and poured a palmful into my hand and flung it out, aiming for the air just past Jeremy's shoulder, towards the window, and heard a spine-chilling scream. The room seemed to freeze in time when the scream sounded. Jeremy finally noticed us on the floor in front of the door. His face contorted into a snarl, but I was watching as the Sylph materialized where I had thrown the salt. She was beautiful and terrible all at once, the anger at being caught ruining her lovely face. I only had a moment for that to register before she was flying at me, fingers crooked into claws, aiming for my face.

    Jodi tried to keep herself in between the Sylph and me, using herself as a target much like Steven had done in the backyard, but the faerie merely threw Jodi out of the way like a child with a ragdoll. I was speaking a binding incantation before I even realized the spell was flying from my lips. She hesitated, inches from me and I felt her fury like fire on my skin, churning my stomach. I stumbled on the words in my haste and she took the momentary falter and closed the distance between us, grabbing me by the front of my sweatshirt and lifting me off of the ground.

    I heard Jodi's voice over her snarls, trying for a banishing spell and I knew it was starting to work because the complete rage in her face gave way to a flicker of frustration. The Sylph roared suddenly and pitched me sideways into the wall. As I crashed, my head bashed into the corner of a dresser and everything went black.

Chapter 19

I was dreaming again. Five years old and in a field of clover with Jodi sitting a few feet away while we plucked the tiny white flowers out of the clovers and made chains out of them. We were each already wearing a crown made out of the chains and were working on matching jewelry. I saw a ladybug crawling on my bare knee as I reached for another flower, making me hesitate, afraid I'd scare it off. I blinked at the size of my legs, realizing I wasn't just remembering something from so many years ago; I was reliving it.

"Make a wish," Jodi said, having looked up to see what had caught my attention.

"What?" I asked and was confused to hear a child's voice come from my mouth.

"Remember? Make a wish," she prompted again, nodding her head forward for emphasis. In the back of my mind I knew there were more important things that I should be doing or worrying about than watching this ladybug crawl in circles on my knee while I thought of a wish.

"Hurry or she's gonna fly off to get someone else's wish," Jodi said, turning her attention back to her growing chain. I breathed in deep through my nose and closed my eyes, holding in the breath.

I wish I knew what to do, I thought automatically and opened my eyes and blew out the breath. The ladybug immediately opened her wings and flew off, bobbing up and down on the air currents until I couldn't see her anymore.

"Good job. Now she'll take your wish to the faeries and maybe it'll come true," Jodi said as she plucked another flower from the ground.

"What?" I asked, having forgotten my own chain now lying tangled in my lap.

"What?" Jodi repeated back to me with a furrowed brow.

"What are you talking about?" I asked, trying not to become lost in the fact that Jodi was sitting there, so tiny and making her blue eyes seem big enough to take up most of her face. It was bizarre to think I was on eye level with her and not looking down at her from an adult frame.

"What's the matter with you?" Jodi asked, dropping her hands into her lap. "Are you forgetting everything the faeries told us?" She waited for me to respond, studying my face like she was looking at a stranger. "Fine," she said with an exasperated sigh. "The faeries told us that ladybugs are the barer of children's wishes and to be careful not to step in toadstool rings in case the faeries are dancing there and to never bring iron with you if you want the faeries to see you as a friend."

"Iron?" I asked, hearing how lame I sounded even to me, knowing that I'd get another sigh and eye-roll from my tiny friend.

"Oh my god!" Jodi said, granting me that eye-roll I expected. "Iron can kill a faerie, remember? And since you're a…" she hesitated, looking up and off to the right as if trying to remember something and it would be written on the sky above her. "Oh right, you're an Earth Child and can call iron from the dirt in the Earth and the blood in your veins, so you must be that much more careful than the rest of us." Jodi said in a voice that made me think she'd memorized that speech so she could repeat it back at a moment's notice.

"I can call the iron from the ground and in my blood?" I blinked my surprise at her, but her attention was back on her ever-growing flower chain.

"Yep," she said casually, "and they say that someday you might be able to teach me how to do the blood one because there's some oxygen in blood."

"Because you're Air," I said carefully, not wanting to tell her something she didn't yet know, but thankfully she nodded without looking up. "And that's why she's been keeping him off of the ground and out of my reach," I said, hearing my own disbelief, the memories suddenly flooding to the front of my mind.

"Who?" the tiny Jodi asked me, looking up from her chain again, but before I could think of an answer, the world around me was becoming dark, stealing away the foliage around me. The flowers and clovers were harder to see and when I looked back up to Jodi, she was gone. Vaguely I could hear voices raised in anger and confusion swirling around me like water rushing down a drain. Bursts of lights were erupting behind my eyelids, making me cringe.

I willed myself to swim up through the blackness and break the surface.

Sounds came back first. Still in a strange echo, it wasn't until I was finally able to pry open my eyes that I saw Jodi and Jeremy's father screaming at each other over me. It took me longer than it should have to realize I was lying on my back on the floor, probably where I fell after hitting my head as I was awkwardly wedged between a wide dresser and the wall.

"I've had enough of this crazy bullshit!" Mr. McCormack yelled, spittle flying from his lips. "I'm calling the cops and reporting your break-in!"

"I told you we were here to help, you jackass!" Jodi yelled back and even from the strange angle I could see her usual deep blue eyes had faded with an icy edge to them.

"Help?" he scoffed. "How? By telling me that my son was here to kill me?"

"Well, he wasn't here to bake cookies," I said roughly, feeling the dryness in my throat as I pushed myself up on my elbows.

"Oh thank God!" Jodi said, dropping down quickly to take my hands and help extract me from the corner.

"I don't care what you accused my son of doing to you. That doesn't give you the right to break into my house," he yelled down at both of us, trying to loom over us and I finally felt the heat of his anger radiating off of him and into my skin, down to my veins. I closed my eyes against it as Jodi helped me to my feet and I took the moment I needed to reinforce my shields against him just as my skin started to run red with his heat.

"You're right, but you are grateful that we were here to stop Jeremy," I said pushing my empathetic magic into my voice, feeling the air around us sing with power. My magic was so close to the surface it felt as if it was bubbling out of me. Light glinted between my fingers and from the corner of my eyes, I could see the burgundy glow of my hair as it floated gently on a wind that shouldn't have been in the room. I took a deep breath, drawing the magic further into me, and I realized I could still smell the field of clover around me.

Mr. McCormack blinked at me, his mouth open, but words caught in his throat. Jodi squeezed my hand in hers, offering her added power. "You are not angry in the least," I said, my voice echoing around us with its weight, and he nodded slowly at me. "You are thankful that we took the attack and saved you and especially your wife, whom you love." I forced my will on him and watched as he shrank back from me under the weight of my power and he nodded again.

"Thank you so much," he stammered, blinking rapidly to clear his vision. He reached out a hand to me and I took it, despite the anxiety I felt from Jodi, wanting to pull me back from him. "Thank you so much," he said again, shaking my hand. I think he would've kissed it if I would've let him.

"You're welcome," I said, pushing one last wave of emotion into him, reinforcing these newfound feelings and erasing any lingering doubt he may have had about us. All thoughts of calling the police were completely forgotten.

"What," he started to say, but his voice failed him and he had to take a moment to think, remembering how to talk through my magic. "What are you going to do now?" he finally managed.

"You aren't going to hurt my son, are you?" Mrs. McCormack asked, drawing our attention to her on the bed where she was huddled, still clutching a pillow to her chest. I saw the worry in her wide eyes. The strain this week had put on her heart had aged her several years and I hoped, when this was all done, I could help ease some of that strain.

"No, Mrs. McCormack, we are not going to hurt Jeremy," I said carefully, redirecting some of my powers to her, envisioning soothing caresses over her cheeks and forehead, comforting her like a mother would a child. "We only want to help him before he hurts himself," I explained and watched as the magic worked on her, easing some of the creases in her brow, slowing her heart rate back to a normal pulse before I eased Jodi and me towards the door.

"Shayna," Mr. McCormack said, reaching out and touching my shoulder to stop me just at the door. "I am sorry for what he's done. I think maybe I have a lot of apologizing to do where my son is concerned." I caught his gaze with mine and pushed into his mind, searching for the meaning of his words, happy to realize he meant that he was probably mostly to blame for Jeremy's behavior, rather than, for once in his son's life, blaming Jeremy for everything.

I pulled the door closed behind us and drew a protective charm over the door with my fingers, feeling the tingle and burn of magic on the tips. I looked at my hand once I finished and saw the swirling iron just below the surface of the skin, closer than it ever had been.

"Shay?" Jodi's faint whisper brought my gaze up and I saw her staring at the door. Turning to look at it, I saw the shimmer of silver fading into the wood in the pattern I had drawn with my fingers.

"I guess we don't have to do anything special to get it out of us," I said, my voice not much more than a whisper. The iron shimmered in the faint light in the hallway until it was totally absorbed into the wood and no traces were left behind.

"Did it hurt?" Jodi asked and I was surprised not to hear any hint of fear in her question.

"It burns a little," I said honestly, not wanting to lie to her for fear the burn would hurt her more than me and break whatever concentration she would be using when trying to use the metal in her hand. We stared at each other for a moment before she nodded briefly, accepting the warning without comment.

"What did you say to them?" I motioned to the door and Jeremy's parents beyond with a nod of my head.

"The truth," she said in a whisper as we took a few steps away from the bedroom door. "Well, some truth anyway."

"What do you mean?"

"Basically that we thought Jeremy had been tricked into using some black magic and the cops wouldn't believe us, so we wanted to try to help him ourselves." I stared at Jodi for a few moments letting the half lie sink into my mind.

"And what did they say?" I asked calmly.

"Well, the mom didn't say anything, just sat there crying like she was. But the dad, well, he just started yelling about us breaking in and basically just ignored what I said," she finished with a shrug.

"Okay," I said, blowing out a breath and shaking my head.

"How did you have so much magic to spend so easily?" Jodi asked, bringing me back to the matter at hand. I glanced at the bedroom door and saw that there were no traces of my protective glyph on the wood.

"I know how to stop the Sylph," I said and I explained what happened while I was unconscious on the floor and the memory I had relived.

"Oh my god," Jodi whispered behind her hand. "I totally forgot about that." Her blue, blue eyes were wide and she shook her head slowly and I knew she was remembering all the details of that afternoon so many years ago.

"So did I, but that's obviously what Tegan was talking about when he said we know without knowing how to stop this."

"But you never did show me how to pull iron from blood and I don't think I've ever seen you try to pull it from the earth either," Jodi said, dropping her hand from her mouth.

"I know, but, I mean, I know how to make the plants grow and how to draw water up from the hidden streams and wells far below the surface; it cant be that much harder, can it?" Even I could hear the uncertainty in my voice.

"Shay, we're talking about splitting particles here. There is iron in the dirt, but it's all mixed together; not seeds in the earth or water laying in wait, separate from the dirt."

"Well, we've done more spectacular things in times of crisis," I said, tearing my gaze away from her and looking down the hallway. "We'll just have to have faith we can do this too." With that, I reached for her hand and intertwined our fingers and started walking down the hall and out into the main room.

"Any idea where you're going?" Jodi whispered to me as we crossed the room, heading for the front door.

"No idea, I just know they aren't in the house anymore," I answered as I came to a stop a few feet from the front door. I turned and grabbed Jodi's other hand in mine and closed my eyes, concentrating on my breathing and centered myself. Reaching down, I pushed through the floor and the foundation of the house until I could feel the steady, low pulse of the Earth below us and grounded into it. I felt Jodi's pulse quicken with the automatic surge of power as the Earth's magic responded to my touch and surged up into me and through our joined hands and into her. Carefully, I fed the magic and extra power into our defensive shields and our magical reserves, recharging our depleted bodies, much like soldiers stashing extra bullets in any pocket they could find before leaving the safety of their foxhole.

I carefully pulled my energy out of the Earth, stopping the flow of power without causing a backlash, and let got of one of Jodi's hands. We turned to the front door and closed the distance of those last few steps before I reached for the handle and pulled the door open. The cool, crisp night air rushed around us, sending chills up my arm, but I felt a tingle of power rush through Jodi's hand and into mine as her element swirled around her and caressed her skin like a lover. I smiled, glad to feel some confidence coming from her, and took a step over the threshold. I let go of Jodi's hand and turned to pull the front door shut behind us and to draw another protective symbol over the wood when I felt the tingle of power run up the back of my neck.

I shoved the door open and spun around, catching Jodi's arm and hurling her back through the door as I heard the night air scream in warning that the Sylph was flying from the shadows towards us. Her beautiful face was rent with fury and her slender fingers were crooked into claws as she rushed towards me. I spun and dove through the door, catching the edge and slamming it shut as I tumbled to the floor. Jodi was right behind me, darting to the door and quickly drawing a banishing symbol over the wood. The door shuttered against the force of her impact as the Sylph struck it, but the door held. Jodi threw all the locks once she finished with the spell and turned a pained face to me, holding up her scorched hand for me to see.

"It burns a *little*?" she demanded angrily. "A little, my ass!" I shrugged awkwardly from my position on the ground before pushing myself up and running to the back door, throwing the locks into place and drawing the same symbols there.

"What do we do?" Jodi asked, after returning from drawing the symbol on the door leading to the attached garage.

"We can't stop her from coming in forever," I said as I looked around at all the windows surrounding us in just this room.

"It's worth a shot," Jodi said, a hint of sarcasm in her voice.

"She'll just go after someone else to hurt us. I don't need that guilt," I said, rubbing a hand over my eyes, suddenly feeling a little bone-weary.

"I know, I know," Jodi said, looking around. "Then what do you want to do?"

"We'll have to let her in, but draw her to a place that'll work in our favor, not hers," I said. Something inside me told me to go to the garage. It was the farthest away from Jeremy's parents we could get while still being inside and, if it was anything like all the other ranch style houses in the neighborhood, there would be open rafters in the ceiling. I told Jodi my idea and, having nothing else to suggest, she agreed and we made the mad dash past what felt like a hundred windows into the garage.

I had to stop myself from slamming the door shut behind us, fearing the noise would draw the Sylph's attention before we were ready for her. Jeremy's parents had washer and dryer hook ups in the garage, just like I had expected based on the layout of the house, and they were just inside the door. I grabbed Jodi's hand and pulled her back towards me. I gave her a push towards the washer and pointed up to the rafters above us. She nodded her understanding and pulled herself up on the washer while I watched the side door that led out of the garage into the side yard.

Jodi tapped my shoulder to get my attention and motioned that she needed help reaching the rafters, which did not bode well for me since we were the same height. I pulled myself up onto the washer next to her and interlaced my fingers to give her a leg up. Butterflies swirled in my stomach as I watched her scramble to pull her legs up and get her body over the rafter safely. Once she was up, she lay down on her stomach and reached out a hand to me, but I only shook my head at her, knowing neither of us was physically strong enough to pull the other up. I turned and looked at the shelves installed on the wall above the washer for cleaning supplies and considered how strong they might be. They only needed to be strong enough to hold my weight for a few seconds so I could get my hands on the rafters above.

I glanced up at Jodi and she nodded again, letting me know she agreed with what I was thinking, and pushed herself up to crawl closer to the wall and get into position to help me up once I was higher. I closed my eyes in spite of the warring butterflies in my stomach and pressed a hand to the exposed beam in the wall near the shelves. Feeling the wood hidden there, I tried to seek for an answer to how strong the shelves were, but before I could fully reassure myself, I heard a rustling in the side yard and knew if I didn't move now, Jeremy and the Sylph would be on me before we were ready. With one more gulp of air, I grabbed the shelves and started to climb them like a ladder.

The thin wood bowed under my weight, but the braces held while I made my way up. Almost frantically, Jodi and I grasped hands once I was as high up as the shelves would get me and she pulled hard enough to burn my skin while I reached with my free hand for the nearest rafter. I managed to hook my right leg over the rafter and get myself up with as little grace as possible as I heard the wood begin to splinter under my left foot as it slipped off of the shelf. We both took a moment to catch our breath and slow our racing hearts while I rubbed my wrist where Jodi's grasp had burned the skin.

Now what? Jodi's yellow thoughts whispered in my mind as she pressed her fingertips to my knee.

We get a little farther away from that door, I answered, nodding towards the side door where I had heard noises coming from. As quickly as possible, we scrambled over the beams, trying to ignore the mossy spider webs that caught on our fingers and our hair. It took more than a fair bit of self-control on my part not to have a panic attack right there while I frantically batted the webs away.

"That's far enough," I whispered as softly as I could as Jodi crawled just out of my reach, making it dangerous to reach out to her to create the physical link we needed to speak mind to mind. Jodi opened her mouth to speak, but I quickly waved her into silence and pointed down at the side door, hearing the wood creak under the strain of being pulled open. Clearly it wasn't a door often used, but then, from the looks of the garage, it didn't seem like Jeremy's dad used the garage for much more than storage space.

The door stopped moving after it was opened just a crack and I couldn't see any shadows at the bottom of the door to let me know someone was waiting there. Energy swirled around me, the very air in the garage coming alive with magic and power, but instead of singing through my body, it felt like a thousand fire ants biting along my skin; this wasn't our power, it was the Sylph's. I was desperate to speak to Jodi, but I didn't dare move or tear my gaze away from the door, knowing they would be waiting for just the right moment when our attention was distracted.

Shay? Jodi's yellow thoughts whispered in my mind and I couldn't help but look up sharply at her, my eyes wide in shock, realizing I assumed all three of us needed to be together to have enough power for us to speak mind to mind without physical contact. *Yeah I know,* she thought at me. *I could hear you too.*

But I wasn't thinking at you, I responded, turning my eyes back to the door that still hadn't moved.

No, I know, but I started hearing you. You were thinking about not looking away from the door in case the Sylph was waiting for that, her yellow thoughts were an almost perfect echo of mine that sent chills down my back.

This is pure Air magic, isn't it? I asked, shifting my weight slightly, trying to ease the ache forming in my thighs.

I think so, but how can I tell for sure?

How does it make you feel? I asked.

Like we just drew a circle of power and poured all of its energy into me, Jodi said and I could feel her excitement barely contained as her thoughts became brighter, making me want to squint against them again.

It feels a little foreign to me, like being shocked with low level electricity, which is how Air magic always feels to me, but this almost freaking hurts. I shifted again, putting more of my weight on the balls of my feet. *It must be boosting your abilities so you're able to open the channel between us.*

Like you did last year when we were on the mountain, Jodi offered and I just nodded in response. *Okay, what do you want to do then?*

Well, I think, since you're responding so well to the Sylph's magic, you need to concentrate on her while I go after Jeremy to contain him and try to break the link between them.

But... Jodi's thoughts faded a little as she hesitated and I could feel her anxiety laced with fear travel across the short distance between us and stir my stomach. *I don't know how to stop her.*

You will, I'll help you, don't worry, I said, grabbing a hold of the connection that was making me feel her fear and pushing confidence into her. I felt the nerves churning my stomach ease and

Jodi's mental sigh of relief. I kept the connection between us open, not wanting to have to spare the precious few moments it would take to open it back up once the mêlée was underway.

Jeremy's going to come in first, I thought at Jodi as I felt the energy in the air spike.

How do you know that? Jodi's thoughts were near erratic now with all the pent up energy she was taking into herself.

No idea, I thought back with a shake of my head.

Awesome, I feel so confident now. I smiled at the casual sarcasm and braced myself, placing both hands on the beam outside of my feet, centering my body weight for the drop.

Don't focus on me, do you understand? I pushed the weight of my will into the connection between us, not wanting her to argue with me.

How can I not?

Because if you do, then the Sylph will get to you or me before you realize it. I need you to watch the door and wait for her to come in. Do not focus on me, do you understand? I asked again.

Yes, she replied reluctantly and the power in the channel between us was so great I could almost hear the unspoken thought that she didn't like it.

The door creaked again and I watched as the opening grew wider and a shadow crossed behind it, hiding the person approaching. I concentrated on the energy Jodi was emitting and pulled an extra bit into me, letting the power feed my reserves. Jeremy stepped around the door, stopping at the threshold, and scanned the darkness, letting his eyes adjust to the lack of light before he took a half step inside and stopped again. I could feel the pulse of my heart in my throat and the heat of the built up magic and nerves in my cheeks; tiny beads of sweat broke out over my forehead and my hand itched to wipe them away.

Jeremy tilted his face up, but kept his eyes from the rafters and I heard him sniff a couple of times. He was actually testing the air like an animal would. I watched as he turned his head back and forth, sniffing in each direction, which just sent my nerves dancing in a whole new way. Had he learned a new spell that would develop his senses so much that he could draw out scents in the air like a wolf or a dog could? Finally he took another step inside, in the direction I was hiding above.

What the hell was that about? Jodi's nervous thoughts nearly made me jump after all the silence, but I just shook my head ever so slightly, willing her into silence rather than wasting the attention it would take to form the thought. Jeremy was walking towards me now. His steps were slow enough to make me want to scream at him to hurry up, but all too soon he was directly under me and the time to act was upon me.

Brace yourself, I thought at Jodi as Jeremy took one more step forward so he wasn't directly under me anymore and I pushed away from the beam and dropped down like a rock on his back, slamming him into the concrete on the floor. He landed in a heap and I heard all the air rush from his lungs. I buried my knees into his back, grinding against his ribs and making him cry out in pain, which almost made me smile in satisfaction. I twined the fingers of my left hand into his hair, twisting it against his skull to hold his head down. I brought the image of the iron knife from the forest into my mind and focused on it. I crooked the fingers of my free hand into a claw and felt the now familiar burn of the iron sear my skin. I suddenly had an image of drawing iron from blood.

I pulled back on his head, using his hair as a handle, stretching out his neck, and brought my burning hand down on it, clutching his windpipe. He made a gurgling sound that mingled with the sizzle of burning skin. I crinkled my nose at the smell and adjusted my grip so I wouldn't strangle him to death, but held on tight with my other hand and bounced on my thighs to drive my knees into him harder when he struggled beneath me.

"Stay still, Jeremy, and you don't have to get hurt," I whispered to him through clenched teeth, but to my disbelief, he was actually smiling. Although I wouldn't call it his natural smile; more the grin of a crazy man who has no idea that a room with padded walls was waiting for him. Just then I felt the air in the garage come alive with energy, like a live wire dancing dangerously close to a pool of water. I didn't have to look around to know the Sylph was there and the frenetic energy searing my exposed skin was just a measure of her anger.

Now! I thought at Jodi in a mental scream that was so bright green the shadows in the garage took on a hint of color, sending the image of pulling iron from blood to her. I felt more than saw Jodi jump from her hiding place and collide with the Air spirit. Jeremy screamed under me and started to buck under my weight. I instinctively gripped harder with both hands, feeling the heat of the iron in my hand sear the soft skin of his neck, but he didn't seem to notice. We were rolling on the ground now, him on top of me and me on my back, trying to remember how to breathe. Jeremy was flailing so wildly on top of me I couldn't get a full breath and finally just let go of him.

I braced myself as I sucked in great lungfuls of air, expecting him to turn back on me, but he just scrambled to his feet and started to make his way towards Jodi, who I now saw was in a physical fight with the Sylph. I could hear the slap of flesh on flesh as Jodi's fists connected with the Sylph in a very human way and in between the blows, ever growing sparks of electricity were flying between them.

"Iron, Fae! Iron!" I screamed at Jodi as I rushed to my feet and started after Jeremy. I grabbed a screwdriver as we passed a workbench and spun it in my hand so I was holding the skinny metal end. I brought my hand up and slammed the blunt handle just above the soft spot on his shoulder aiming for his mandible angular at the point of his jaw below his ear. Jeremy folded to his knees in the shock of pain and I kicked him square in the back between his shoulder blades, throwing the screwdriver away into the mess of boxes on the other side of the garage before mounting him and twisting his right arm behind him and grabbing his hair at the crown of his head to stretch his neck backwards again. I brought the heat of the iron again into my hand and seared his wrist with it, projecting that image to Jodi with all the power that I had.

Jodi hesitated for just one moment, drawing the iron into her hands for the attack, but that moment was enough for the Sylph to take advantage . She screamed in an ungodly voice and I thought my ears would surely bleed from it before she launched herself at Jodi, sending them reeling into the boxes where I had thrown the screwdriver. I screamed for Jodi as Jeremy began to struggle under me again. With little choice left to me, I gripped his hair tighter, drew his head back again, and slammed his head into the concrete floor with a smack that had my stomach roiling. He went limp under me instantly. I took just a moment to find his pulse in his neck; it was slow and steady as if he were only sleeping. Satisfied, I scrambled to my feet again and tore my way through the boxes until I found them.

The Sylph was encased in the brightest white light I had ever dared lay my eyes on. Tears sprung from my eyes and rolled down my cheeks before I could wipe them away. I squinted against the light, desperate to see Jodi, and realized she too was adding to the brilliant glow. Although nowhere near as bright as the Sylph, Jodi's body shone with the pure Air magic that was her higher self.

They were trapped in a battle of wills, each just barely holding the other off and no doubt inflicting enormous amounts of pain, if the searing of my skin was anything to go by. My empathy for Jodi nearly had me doubled over , but I pushed the pain back, not willing to give into it. I tried to split my concentration between Jodi and my shields, willing more strength into them when I saw the small flames licking the edge of my aura. I remembered Steven forming a shield around me on the balcony of the bookstore made of his power. The heat of it hit me and I struggled to find a breath. I closed my eyes against the light and heat and pulled it into me and funneled it with a thought to Jodi, letting the heat from Steven fill her and bring the molten iron in her hands to life. I felt the momentary burn of it hurt her and, in turn, backlash to me, but we concentrated and she directed the magic through her hands to attack the Slyph.

Terra, Jodi's thoughts were whisper soft in my mind, *to your left, there are splintered boards. Some have iron nails in them.* She didn't even have to finish the thought; I simply lunged for a board, grabbing it like a baseball bat, and swung with all my strength at the back of the Sylph, the nail embedding into her shoulder blade. She screamed again and I was forced to let go of the board and cover my ears as the pain of her scream lanced through me.

We have to do it together! Jodi thought at me suddenly, her hands grabbing at mine and pulling me up from my knees. I hadn't even realized I had fallen until that moment. The Sylph was on the ground, writhing in pain and trying desperately to reach behind her and grab the board now stuck in her back, but it was in too awkward a position for her to reach. Jodi pulled me over to her and clasped both our hands together once we were standing over her, creating a circle with our bodies.

"With the power of Earth and Air we banish you," Jodi and I said in unison and I could feel the magic between us grow instantly, swirling around us in a vortex, the swirl of air and magic drowning out the screams of the Sylph. "With the power of Earth and Air we will this area clear." We raised our voices with the power growing stronger. I felt the burn in our hands as the iron beneath our skin grew hot, but this time the burn didn't hurt. I took strength in that and directed the power of the iron to the writhing form of the Sylph on the ground and felt rather than heard her scream as the light of her magic began to fade rapidly. "With the power of Earth and Air we banish all spirits that don't belong here!" We all but yelled the final line of the incantation and felt the ground beneath us rock and the walls around us shook with one final scream of the Sylph.

A bolt of electricity shot between us, blowing us apart, and we were flying back into the boxes. The air rushed out of us as we hit the ground and, before I could blink, the world went dark and the garage around us disappeared.

Chapter 20

Before I opened my eyes, I was acutely aware of the taste of moist earth in my mouth and my entire body hummed with more power than I had ever felt when not sunk into the ground. That was how I knew we were underground before I opened my eyes. When I finally did open my eyes, confusion hit me hard. I could feel the presence of a hundred energies around me, but I was looking up at an earthen ceiling. I pushed up on my elbows to sit up, the room shifting as I did, making me dizzy. I closed my eyes again until I was confident that the world had righted itself.

I could feel Jodi's presence behind me, her signature my only comfort. I got to my hands and knees and crawled over to her, shaking her gently to get her to come round before I really assessed where we were and what was going on. Though, in the pit of my stomach, I was pretty sure where we were. Jodi blinked slowly, her wide blue eyes focusing on my face as consciousness and awareness came back to her. I helped her sit up and wrapped an arm around her shoulders, holding her hand with my free one.

"Welcome, Terra, Earth Mother." A vaguely familiar voice resounded within the cave-like room, drawing my attention off to the left. We shifted together to face that way and, once again, I saw I was in the presence of Iris of the Shattered Light.

I inclined my head towards her in a makeshift bow. I knew that protocol said we should stand up and bow to her, but after the fight in the garage with the Sylph, I just couldn't put myself, let alone Jodi, through the hell of trying to get to our feet just then.

"Welcome, Fae, Air Spirit." Iris nodded ever so slightly to Jodi, who was trembling in my arms now. I had tried to convey the terrible beauty and power of the higher faeries, but nothing quite compares to being in their presence.

"Shay," Jodi whispered to me, her voice trembling, "where are we?"

"I think we're in the Sidhe," I whispered back, letting my gaze drift away from Iris and her almost unbearable beauty to take in the room around me. We were definitely in some sort of official room; Iris was sitting on a raised throne and the same motley crew of faeries from the orchard surrounded her on all four sides. Large oppressive figures stood behind her, looking almost treelike in appearance while smaller, more elegantly decorated beings were on either side of her. These were handsome and beautiful, naked and enticing, as only nymphs could be. Still farther below them and tumbling from Iris' feet were tiny creatures resembling frogs, birds, and flowers. floating in the room were beings much like Tegan.

More and more faeries of varying degrees of magical appearance ringed the room around us. A strong part of me wanted to stay here and find out everything I could about all the different kinds of Fae Folk, but that was part of the draw of this place. Once the Children of Danu retreated into the mounds of the Sidhe, their magic called to the rest of earth's magical creatures, drawing them home. If you went into the Sidhe willingly, you risked your life. Time for mortals stops within the Sidhe and what feels like hours to you really translates into days and months and, before you know it, a lifetime has gone by and you haven't aged a day. The terrible truth was, though, once you left the Sidhe, your years would come rushing back to you all at once and the stories say many a human was found dead at the gates of the Sidhe.

My mother told me the stories her grandmother had told her and I knew that it was also possible, if the Sidhe wanted to it could simply alter time backwards and you could spends days and weeks here and when you left only minutes may have passed in the human realm. I prayed that was the case for Jodi and me right now. I swallowed audibly and turned my attention back to the patient Iris, who was watching me closely, gauging my reaction. I tried to look both humbled and confident under her stare. I hadn't been afraid of her in my own world, in my backyard, but here in her kingdom in this magical place, I was at her mercy.

"We are grateful to you," her voice echoed through the room, the power of it singing through my body. "You have brought the traitor to justice."

An earsplitting wail cut through the silence. Jodi jumped under my grasp and we flinched together, looking for the source of the noise. We watched as a creature that could only be described as a Minotaur entered the room. I had always wanted to see the woodland creatures of the stories I'd heard as a child, but in that moment I realized how dangerous our childhood dreams could be.

Here I was, within killing distance of a true monster. He was massive, at least nine feet tall and three feet wide in the shoulder. The horns that burst out of his head were as big around as my arms and sharper than any spear. Soft brown fur curled down his torso, disappearing into the cloth pants I was relieved to see covering his bottom half. The only other clothing he had on was a crossing of thick leather straps over his massive chest. I dragged my eyes back up the long length of his body, meeting his eyes finally. I saw a human intelligence there, which just made him even scarier.

He had an iron chain grasped in his hands and was dragging something in behind him. He snorted loudly, a white puff of hot air bursting from his bull nose, before hauling the chain bound form into the center of the room. This was the source of all the noise. It was the Sylph. I felt Jodi tense under me while I fought to keep my face calm, but we were entirely too close to her for comfort. He let the chain fall to the stone floor. I realized then that faint wisps of smoke were rising from the Sylph's body where the chain touched bare skin, telling me it was made of iron. With it wrapped around her, there was no fear that she'd be able to stand up and attempt escape. With one more loud breath, the Minotaur turned and stalked out of the room, taking some of my tension with him.

I watched the Sylph writhe on the floor, my stomach churning with her cries, but I couldn't find any pity inside me for her. After what she'd put us all through, I almost enjoyed her pain. That was a difficult realization for me, but at the end of the day, no matter what magic I have, I am still human. I still have baser emotions.

I swallowed hard and tightened my grip around Jodi's shoulders and started to maneuver us off of the floor. Once we were on our feet, we continued to cling to each other, all the while trying to keep our heads held high in front of our audience. I turned my attention to the still silent Iris, almost afraid of what I knew was coming.

"Sylph," Iris finally spoke, "you have been brought here on charges of malicious intent to harm humans. More importantly, you risked the exposure of our world." I closed my eyes against her echoing voice. We were here to witness her trial or execution possibly. I wanted to get out of here right now.

"Do you deny these charges?" Iris asked. Everyone turned their attention to the pitiful mass on the floor. She'd gone still in the past few moments and I wondered if she'd finally passed out from the pain of the iron on her skin, but when I heard the weak laugh bubble out of her, I knew she was still awake. The laughter grew as the moments stretched until it was bouncing off of the earthen walls, maniacal and eerie.

"Sylph!" Iris commanded, her voice reverberating and hurting our weak human ears. Jodi clung to me a little tighter, trying not to whimper in pain or fear. I stroked her hair slowly. I had to believe we were safe here and I wanted her to believe that too.

"Do you deny these charges?" Iris asked again, but I could hear the patience slipping out of her voice. This was not the same calm, regal entity that I had met only days ago. Her anger was something terrible to behold. My animalistic sense of survival was telling me to run, get away, but I had no idea how to get out. If only I had a pair of ruby slippers right about now.

When the Sylph continued to laugh without answer, the Minotaur stepped back into the room, his bare feet making no noise on the stone floor, but pooled at his feet was a length of whip, the braided thick end gripped in his hand. I heard a soft scrape against the stone and caught a glimpse of an iron barb tied to the end of the whip. I started to shake my head back and forth as I watched the Minotaur's whole body shift, his arm arcing behind him, his back curving. Just as his stomach muscles began to contract and he threw his arm forward, whipping the leather, I covered Jodi's eyes with my hand and spun away from the Sylph, focusing on the wall past Jodi's shoulder.

I heard the crack of the whip when it snapped at the Sylph's body. Her scream tore through the air as her body took the beating. My stomach roiled even though I refused to look. Usually I won't look away from another's pain and torment, but this wasn't needless suffering, even I couldn't argue that, so I wouldn't watch this. I wouldn't be strong with her. After an eternity, the snapping and swishing wind stopped. So had the laughter.

"I will only ask you this once more," Iris said, her voice drawing our attention again. It was softer now, closer to the voice I had enjoyed from the orchard. "Do you deny these charges brought against you?"

"No," the Sylph whispered. When I finally looked at her, I saw the gauzy dress she had been wearing was reduced to strips and her skin was a mess of welts and bloody ribbons. Blood eked out of the corner of her mouth as she spoke. Her beautiful blond hair was stained and matted with skin and blood. She began to tremble in pain and cold from the stone she was lying on. I knew I would have nightmares of this moment for the rest of my life.

"Very well," Iris said matter-of-factly. Jodi began to tremble in my arms. She didn't want to witness this, but I had a feeling, because we were intended victims of the Sylph's crimes, we would have to bear it. Swallowing against the gore in my stomach, I tried to focus on the wall past Iris' throne. I wasn't sure how you killed a faerie, but I knew I didn't want to watch it. As I was blinking back the sting of tears, I became aware of a presence standing beside us. Turning slowly to look, I found the monstrous Minotaur looming over me. He no longer held the bloody whip, which I was grateful for, but he now held a wooden bowl full of salt.

"What?" I asked lamely. He seemed to be waiting for me to do something with the salt.

"As a victim of the traitor, you have the right to take vengeance on her," Iris said. I turned my face to look at her, unnerved at how calm she was at all of this.

"I don't understand," I said, nodding towards the bowl of salt.

"You may bind her for the execution."

My stomach lurched then, unable to handle the concept of rendering another being helpless to wait for their death. I felt myself shaking my head again before I was aware of making the movement. Jodi was trembling again and I gripped her a little closer to my side for my comfort as much as hers.

Iris regarded me carefully, one fine brow arching as we held each other's gaze. The minute stretched in the silence. Finally, just as my knees began to weaken, Iris nodded. Even though he wasn't looking at her, at her nod, the Minotaur turned and walked away from me. I really didn't want to watch. Everything inside of me screamed to look away, but I tracked every movement as the

Minotaur gathered handfuls of the coarse salt and flung it at the still bleeding Sylph.

She started out screaming as the crystals settled into her open wounds, but by the time the Minotaur was scraping the bottom the bowl she was hardly whimpering. She was giving into the pain, her mind slipping away from reality and shutting down so she didn't have to deal with it anymore. I should be delirious with her pain as well, but here in this alternate world I couldn't feel anyone's emotions. Not even Jodi, who was closer to me than anyone else, was affecting me. I knew she was fighting off a panic attack and tears just from the tremble of her body, but if it weren't for that, I'd have no idea what she was going through.

Once the salt binding was finished, the Sylph was staring glassy eyed at the ceiling, the muscles in her body were loose, and all the tension had seeped out of her. If she had been human, she would have bled to death by now. The bowl was gone and I had no idea when it had disappeared. I was losing moments in this nightmare. The Minotaur clapped his hands together to dust them off and reached behind him, pulling a wicked blade from the sheath on his back, finally telling me what the leather straps were for. I could see that the blade was iron from where I was. This was it. The sylph that had plagued me was going to die.

Jodi shifted her weight and turned in my arms to bury her face in my shoulder. I couldn't blame her for it. I began to stroke her hair again, watching the blade rise into the air before it began the decent to the floor, finding a home in the sylph's chest. It struck deep into her heart and with one final, pitiful whimper, the sylph's eyes went dark as the life went out of her.

I'm not sure what I expected, maybe for her body to burst into a shattering of light or pixie dust, but I didn't expect for her body to just lie there on the cold stone floor. The Minotaur pulled the blade free of the body and slipped it back into the sheath. I noticed he didn't bother to clean the blood off of it. He looked at me and gave me a nod that I couldn't bring myself to return before he turned and walked out of the chamber. Two other creatures came forward to gather up the body, that's all I could refer to it as now, and carried it silently out of the room.

"Are you satisfied?" It was Iris speaking and, when I turned to look at her again, I realized the question was directed at me alone.

"I didn't ask for that!" I gaped at her, revolted at the idea that I had asked for this.

"No, but as the victim, are you satisfied?" Her voice as so level, so damn calm I felt my temper rising inside of me like something alive. In that moment, I wanted nothing more than to lash out at her violently.

"I didn't ask for that," I said again, gritting my teeth against everything else I wanted to scream at all the calm faces around me.

"These are our laws," Iris said. "Whether you were the victim or not, it was how it would always have been. Are you satisfied?" No, I was not satisfied. Death would never satisfy me. Yes, I had always known somewhere deep inside of me that the sylph would have to be killed to stop her, but I had held on to a tiny bit of human hope that she could have been reached before it came to that. But when I saw her locked in battle with Jodi, I knew that if Jodi was in mortal danger, I would have driven any and all iron I could lay my hands on into the sylph's heart until she went still under my hands.

"What about Jeremy?" I asked.

"What about him?"

"He was a victim too."

"So he was." Iris waved her hand and Jeremy materialized where Jodi and I had come to on the floor. His body was still limp and his eyes were closed. Two of the guards that stood at Iris' side moved forward and gathered Jeremy up, carefully, and walked out of the chamber.

"What are you doing with him?" I demanded.

"I promise, he will be taken care of. He can stay here with us as long as he desires." I considered what she said and then nodded. "Now, what say you?"

"We just want to go home," I finally said.

"Very well," Iris inclined her head towards us.

When I opened my eyes again, I was standing inside Jeremy's garage, Jodi still trembling in my arms. Everything was exactly as we had left it, except the sylph and Jeremy were gone now. If even five minutes had passed, I would have been surprised.

I hugged Jodi a little tighter to my body, suddenly feeling all of the terror and relief flooding through her now that we were back in our own world. I had always wanted to visit the Sidhe, it was one of my greatest wishes as a little girl, but now that I had been there for an execution, I felt different. With the death of the sylph, of a fae creature, something had died inside of me as well.

Chapter 21

I had a lot of explaining to do when the cops got to Jeremy's house. A nosey neighbor called to complain about the noise we were making. Officer Adams wasn't too happy to find out that I was at Jeremy's house in the first place and was even more put out when he found out that Jeremy was gone again.

When I saw the look in the officers' faces, I was grateful to Iris. The thought of Jeremy safe in the Sidhe pushed the image of the dead sylph out of my mind just for a moment. Really, the poor kid just needed some friends and none of this would've happened.

I can't even tell you how angry Deb was with us when she saw us on the late night news as a camera spied Jodi and me being walked out to a police cruiser. I've never heard her use that kind of language; just more things for me to explain once the feathers finally settled. Our parents weren't too happy with us either once we were dropped off at our homes that night.

I insisted that I be allowed to walk Jodi to her door when we pulled up to the curb in front of her house and had my empathetic powers turned up full charge when her mother opened the door. Before she could even change her facial expression, I unleashed my power on her, making her forget her anger and simply be happy to see her daughter safely home. Jodi's father was a harder nut to crack at first and he was halfway down his front walk, barreling towards the waiting officers, before I had my hooks in him and changed the direction of his energy into the intense desire to shake the hands of the officers that delivered his daughter home in one piece.

I was more than a little drained by the time we got to my place and it took the last of my reserves to keep my parents' anger at bay when I came through my front door. I focused most of the little energy I had left on my dad, figuring I could just tell my mom most of the truth in order to calm her down, which, to my great relief, worked. I reminded her it was her fault I was what I was because it was her genes that had passed down the family "gifts" as she liked to call them. I had to promise not to go off trying to reason with a manic depressive bent on killing me ever again though, but that was an easy promise to make, even if I did secretly know there was always the possibility of breaking that promise in the future.

I all but collapsed on my bed, fully dressed, once I got inside my bedroom. My cell was resting on my bedside table and vibrated briefly against the wood, telling me that I had a message. I groaned as I rolled over to reach for it, knowing it would just go off every ten seconds if I tried to ignore it. I saw on the front display screen that I had missed over twenty calls in the last couple of hours. Had it only been a couple of hours? I flipped it open and saw that it was an almost even split between Jensen's and Steven's calls. Before I could decide who warranted the first call back, the phone shook in my hand and Jensen's picture flashed on the screen.

"Hey," I said, hearing the gravel tone of my voice and became very aware of how dry my throat was.

"She lives! Amazing!" Jensen replied with a little more sarcasm than I wanted to hear just then.

"I just got back. I was dialing your number just as you called me," I half lied.

"Well, at least I beat out Steven," he said grumpily.

"Keep it up and I'll hang up and call him instead," I warned as I fell back on my pillows, closing my eyes and rubbing them with my free hand.

"I'm sorry, you'll have to speak up, it's kinda hard to hear you," he said, reminding me of our earlier altercation.

"Maybe next time when my best friend is dying feet away from me, you'll get your ass off of me and let me get to him," I snapped at him, all my earlier guilt very suddenly gone. I hear the crackle of static as my anger tried to slip through the electrical lines and bite at him. We were silent for a few tense moments before I heard him sigh.

"I'm sorry, it's just I've been freaking out over here knowing something was happening, something bad, and couldn't get to you to help," he said and I could hear the hours of worry in his voice.

"I know and I am sorry. I really did just get home, I wasn't going to wait until morning to let you know everything was okay," I managed to say before a huge yawn escaped me, not really sure if I was still half lying, but was too tired to care at that point.

"No apology for nearly busting one of my ear drums?" I heard the slight annoyance in his voice, but I realized I really wasn't sorry.

"No, I'm not sorry for that," I said bluntly and when he didn't automatically respond, I continued. "You shouldn't have tried to keep me down when Steven was so badly injured; I don't care what your reasons were. I could've done so much worse, so you should be grateful I controlled myself as much as I did." I heard him huff over the phone and right then, I knew there would never be anything more serious between us than a casual thing. He still didn't understand me.

Jensen sighed lightly before saying, "I guess I'll let you get some sleep. I'll pick you up in the morning and we'll grab Jodi and Steven for breakfast before rehearsal."

"Oh shit, that starts tomorrow, I totally forgot," I said. It's funny how the mundane things don't stop when the extraordinary take over your life.

"I thought you might've, that's why I said something." He was trying to be casual, but the damage was done; now it was just a matter of time. "Just think of it this way, at least classes aren't until after lunch." Since graduation practice was in the morning, they'd granted the rest of the school a half day schedule all week until Thursday when graduation happened for real; then the school year would finally be over. Jensen offered to text both Steven and Jodi the invites to breakfast in the morning so I could just pass out without bothering. After we said our goodbyes I thought seriously about going to sleep, but Steven had been calling, I couldn't ignore that.

"Terra," Steven's voice was rough and tired through the phone, but just hearing him speak was a salve on my emotional wounds.

"Drake," my voice caught in my throat as tears sprung to my eyes. I had to swallow before I could speak again. "Thank goodness you're okay."

"Thanks to you," he rasped. "The doctors don't understand why I healed so quickly but mostly I just look like I had a really bad sunburn and my skin peeled."

"So it worked then, the water?"

"Yeah, it worked," his voice was softer now and even across this distance I could feel his relief giving way to the fear he'd been afraid to feel. He'd come incredibly close to killing himself.

"Drake, listen," I started to say, but he stopped me.

"Terra, I don't really remember what happened, but I know you saved me, please don't feel bad, okay?"

I nodded, tears spilling down my cheeks, before I remembered he couldn't see me, so I said, "Okay."

"I know you're half-lying, but I'll take it."

"Drake," I whispered, my voice breaking, "thank you."

"Thank you, Terra."

"I love you."

"I love you, too."

I woke up the next morning still exhausted and feeling very grungy in my clothes from last night.

I barely had my hair combed out and caught in a ponytail before I heard the knock at the front door. I grabbed my bag, blew a kiss to my mom, and hurried out the door. Jensen was standing on the front step with a Starbucks coffee cup in his hand and smile on his face.

"Thought you'd like this a bit better than flowers," he said, with that grin that had won my heart last fall, and handed me the warm cup of coffee.

"Thanks," I said as I took a deep breath of the intoxicating aroma.

I started walking towards his car. Usually I liked to drive my car, maybe it was a control issue with me, but I felt like death warmed over and didn't even think twice as Jensen held open the passenger side door for me and I fell inside. The day was little more than a blur to me. I felt like I was on auto pilot and just going through the motions until I found myself saying goodbye to Jensen, taking my car home from his house.

When I got home, I went to my room and tore off most of my clothes just to collapse in my bed again for an afternoon nap. The light from my window was fading when I finally began to stir and wake from my near coma. As I swam up into consciousness, I heard a familiar tinkling of bells just outside my window. I smiled and crawled out of bed, grabbed my discarded jeans and pulled them on and slipped on a pair of tennis shoes, not even bothering with socks, and walked over to the window.

I popped the screen off and climbed over the sill a little clumsily and made my way through the backyard and up and over the back fence, dropping down into the orchard behind the house. Inspiration hit and I slipped off my shoes, letting my feet sink into the moist earth before taking off at a jog through the trees, reveling in the feel of the waxy leaves that brushed my arms as I passed. I followed the sound of the bells without paying attention to where I was going and yet somehow knowing the way.

Finally, the urge to run fell away and I felt an odd tingling shoot up through my bare feet as I took one more step forward. I stopped and looked around, still hearing the soft chime of bells and yet not seeing anything. Confused, I took a deep breath and closed my eyes before whispering, "In this the early evening light, I open my eyes with second sight." Slowly, I opened my eyes, almost reluctant with the fear the incantation wouldn't work, but when I blinked my vision clear, I saw Tegan's smiling face floating just inches away from mine.

"There's the lass," he said, his fall leaf wings beating as furiously as a hummingbird's.

"Why did I have to re-do the spell?" I asked.

"Most likely because you drained your powers last night, love," he said, beginning to drift slowly backwards, away from me. "Let's be off now, she's waiting." And before I could ask who was waiting, he was off like a fallen leaf caught on the wind. I followed quickly after him and was suddenly very aware of all of the life in the trees and air around me. When I took a moment to look as we hurried through the trees, I could see the hidden faces of other faeries watching us as we rushed by.

"Well met, sister." I nearly fell in my haste to stop short when the honey sweet tones of the Faerie Queen, Iris of the Shattered Light, shocked me as we came around one last bend of trees. I heard the answering laugh of dozens of faeries, gnomes, and all other manner of magical creatures. I just stood there, staring stupidly at the beautiful creature in front of me, surrounded again by her entourage of fae creatures, taking comfort in the presence of my familiars, the frog faeries and gnomes.

It was surreal to see her there, calm and beatific as if last night had never happened. The Iris from last night was cold and ruthless, dealing out a death easily. It made it hard for me to like her as much as I thought I had originally, but somehow I was still glad to see her.

It was the power of the Fae. I knew faeries could be malicious, but when you think of the diminutive faeries, it's not that big of a deal. When they were as large as humans, their malicious sides were bigger as well. I shook my head, wanting out of that train of thought.

"Did you call me sister?" I asked when I finally managed to find my voice again.

"Yes, we did," she answered and her voice was that of a large, deep bell that reverberated somewhere deep inside of me. I had to concentrate so much harder this time not to become lost in her light and dark beauty; I must really have depleted my stores of magic and power. "You and your sister Fae have proven yourselves worthy of your gifts and the favor of the Faeries and their Courts."

"Thank you," I said and heard how the words sounded more like a question. The memory of last night kept flashing behind my eyes, confusing me.

"Do not be nervous," Iris said, stepping forward and reaching out to take my hand in both of hers. Her skin was smoother than silk and warm, hinting at the magic contained therein. "We wished to extend our thanks for ridding our two worlds of the Sylph you banished last night and wanted to grant you the debt of our court."

"What does that mean?" I cringed internally at the stupidity of my question, wishing for once in my life I could just be smooth and catch on a little quicker.

"Should you ever find yourself in need of help, we are in your debt and will answer a favor if you should ask it," she said and I heard no note of condescension for having to explain herself to me. My mouth was suddenly dry and I could only blink stupidly at her for a few moments before I could remember to say thank you.

I was having a very human moment, trying to reconcile the two versions of Iris in my mind. It was so easy to just bask in her beauty, but I was still terrified of her. She gave me one of the most beautiful smiles I had ever seen in my life, that made my heart ache at the sight of it, before she gave my hand a final squeeze and began to fade away, taking all of the little faeries with her.

"Well done, lass, I had all the faith in the world in you," Tegan said from behind me. I turned to see him floating nearby again. I held out a hand for him. He alighted on my palm and I was again surprised to feel the weight of him before moving him to my shoulder and started walking back towards my backyard. I felt the familiar power thrumming through my body again, as if I had been recharged, and glanced down at the ground to see a ring of the darkest purple irises had sprung up around me.

"She grants you her favor," Tegan said appreciatively.

"It's like she recharged all my power."

"Yes, it is very much like that," he said with a knowing smile.

"What about Jodi?"

"Who?" he asked in a teasing voice.

"Fae, the Child of Air," I said a little exasperatedly. "She showed a great amount of power last night that I've never seen her show before. Is that going to stick around?"

"Oh, I believe you and your small coven will surprise us all in the very near future," he said mysteriously, both annoying me a little and sending chills up my arms at the same time. It looked like Jodi was going to get her wish after all and was going to be catching up to my powers faster than we ever expected.

Tegan stayed with me for the rest of the week and I came to realize his presence was mostly due to the fact that the Faerie Queen wanted to make sure Jodi and I had control over the quickly developing powers we had kept after the banishing of the Sylph. Once satisfied, he faded away, promising to always just be a simple call away. I was sad to see him go, having become accustomed to his presence, but grateful to know the Faeries themselves had faith in us. Jodi joined me in weekend lessons with Deb that summer, needing to control the electric ability her enhanced powers brought with them and I was happy to see she took the responsibility of new powers with great seriousness and didn't take to showing off.

Graduation and Daisy Chain went off without a hitch, all the girls dressed in pretty white dresses and Steven looking very dapper in his chinos and crisp white shirt. By Friday you couldn't even seen a hint of red on his cheeks from his burns. The only interesting point of the afternoon was when Jodi and I gathered up the swag to spread out between the two lines and the plastic leaves shuttered and fell away to reveal a real chain of ivy and beautiful white flowers sprung up along the vine. We laughed it off and didn't draw attention to it, remembering to try out this new trick in the safety of our favorite forest glen this summer.

Acknowledgements

Thanks to my mom, my first and most dedicated fan. Thank you for encouraging me to read anything and everything I ever wanted. Because of your love of books, I grew up loving books and because of that I became a writer. Without your encouragement these books would never have been.

Thanks to my husband. My best friend and the love of my life, you live with my crazy every day and still stick around. Thank you for your unwavering support and encouragement to sit down and make up stories every day.

Thanks to my editor, Cassie Robertson. You have helped me make my stories so much stronger and I cannot thank you enough for that.

Thanks to Juanita, my new favorite. Thank you for reading and for your insight. Because of your keen eye and suggestions I found new layers of love between my characters, I am so grateful for that.

Thanks to the amazing book bloggers who have helped me along the way. To Cade, Trish, Julie, Deb and Savannah, you ladies were the first to help me support my first book. Your kind words gave me the confidence to keep going and to publish Air. Thank you all so much.

Thanks to my friend Deputy Adam Garnier. Thank you for answering my endless questions about procedures and protocol. And thanks for the tour of the jail, that wasn't creepy at all.

And to everyone else, who has offered their love and support, or even just your time by reading my books, you mean so much to me and I hope you keep going with me on this journey with Shay and her friends.

Awesome blogs: Braintasia Books, YA Bound, A Tale of Many Reviews, I Heart YA Books and Books with Bite.

About the Author

Shauna Granger lives in Southern California with her husband and still goofy dog. When she isn't writing Shauna enjoys reading, shocking we know. She is nerdly excited to start her own book club.

She is hard at work on the third installment of the Elemental Series: Water.